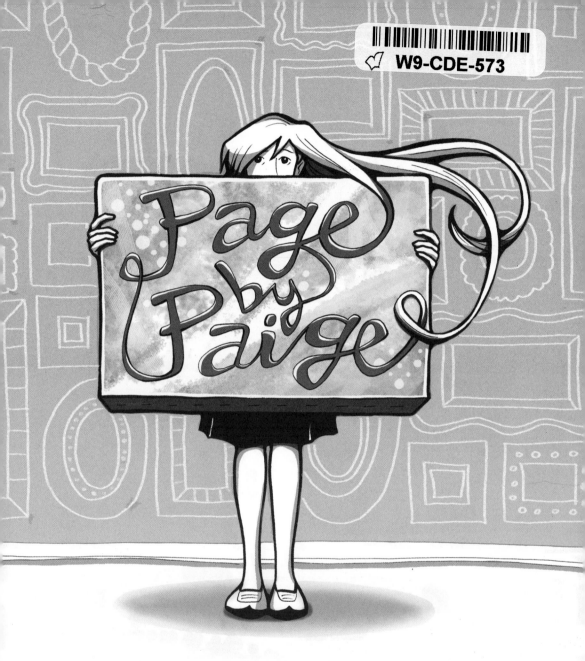

Laura Lee Gulledge

AMULET BOOKS
NEW YORK

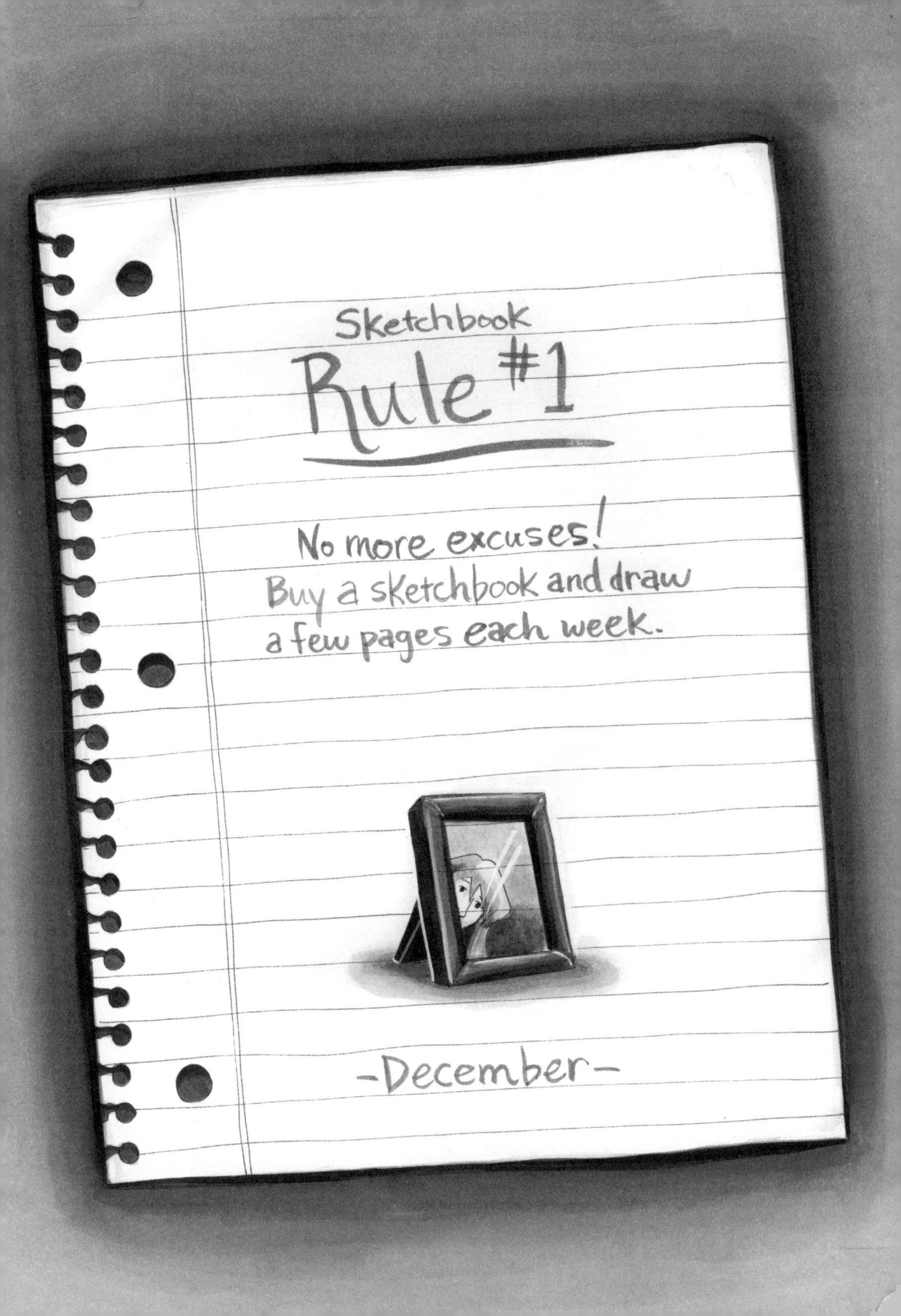
Sketchbook
Rule #1
No more excuses!
Buy a sketchbook and draw
a few pages each week.
-December-

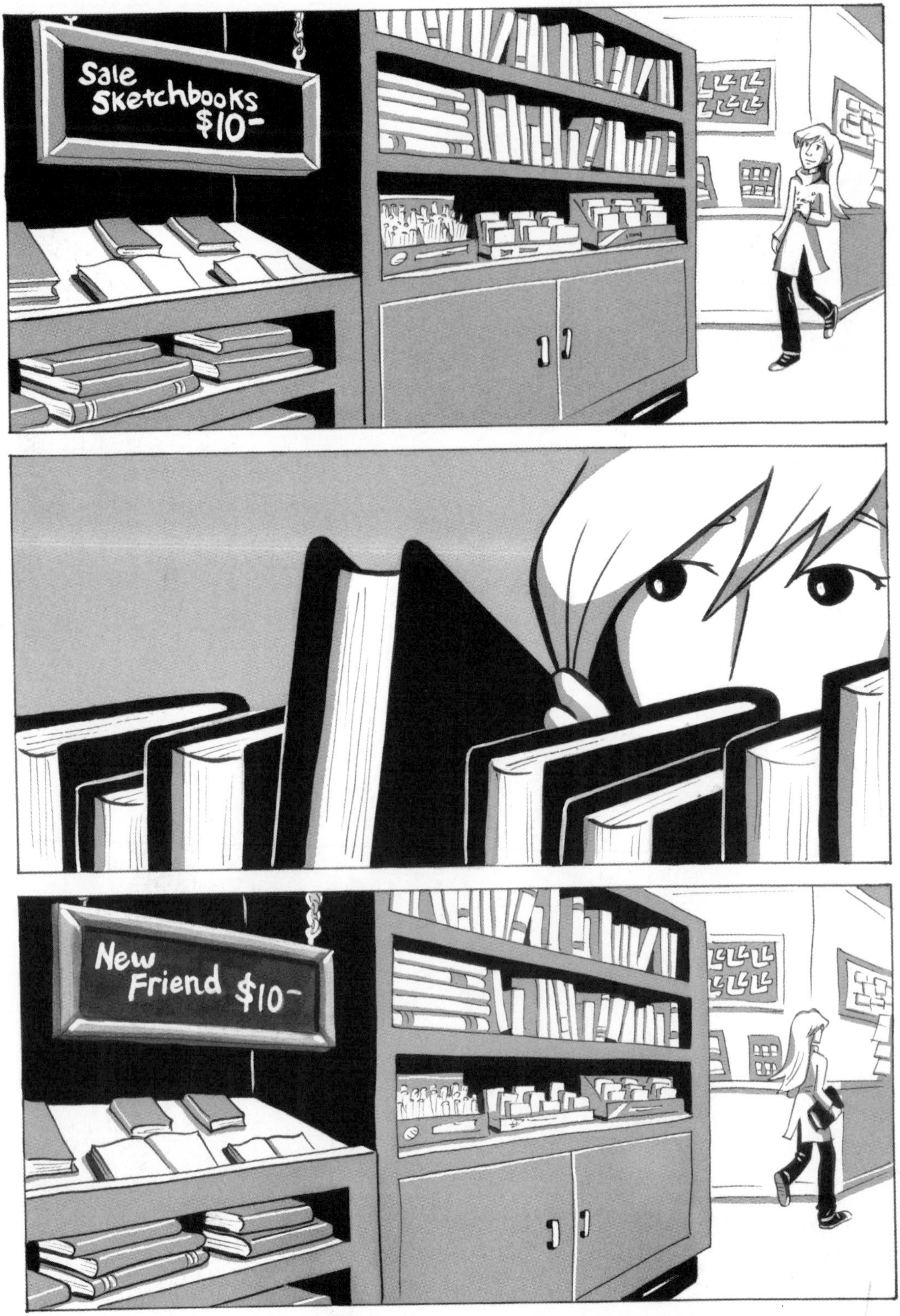
Sale Sketchbooks $10-
New Friend $10-

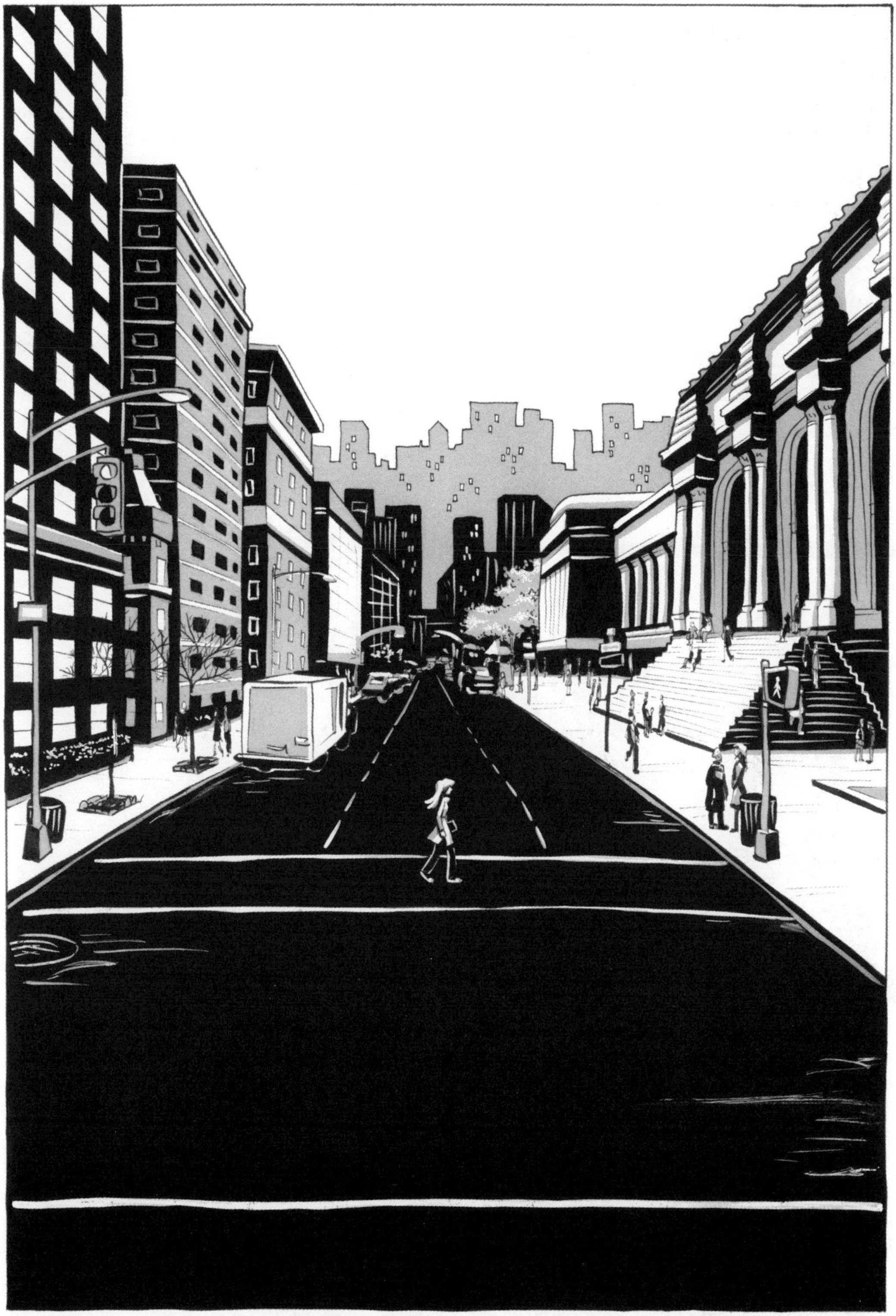

Today is my third day living in *New York*.

And I feel really...alone.

So I decided to hunt down some familiar faces.

This one was painted 200 years ago. She's French.

I don't speak French, but she still speaks to me.

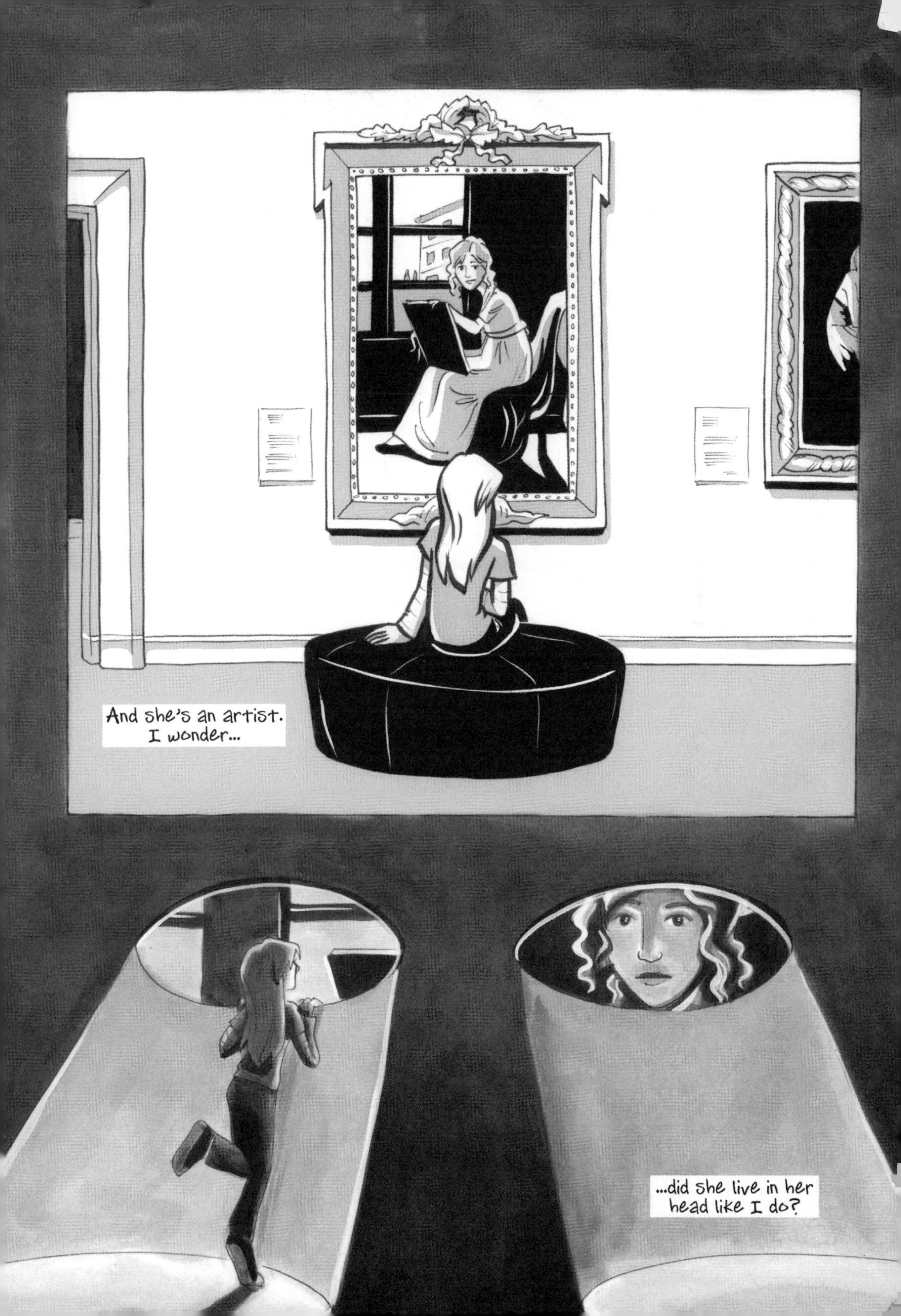
And she's an artist.
I wonder...
...did she live in her head like I do?

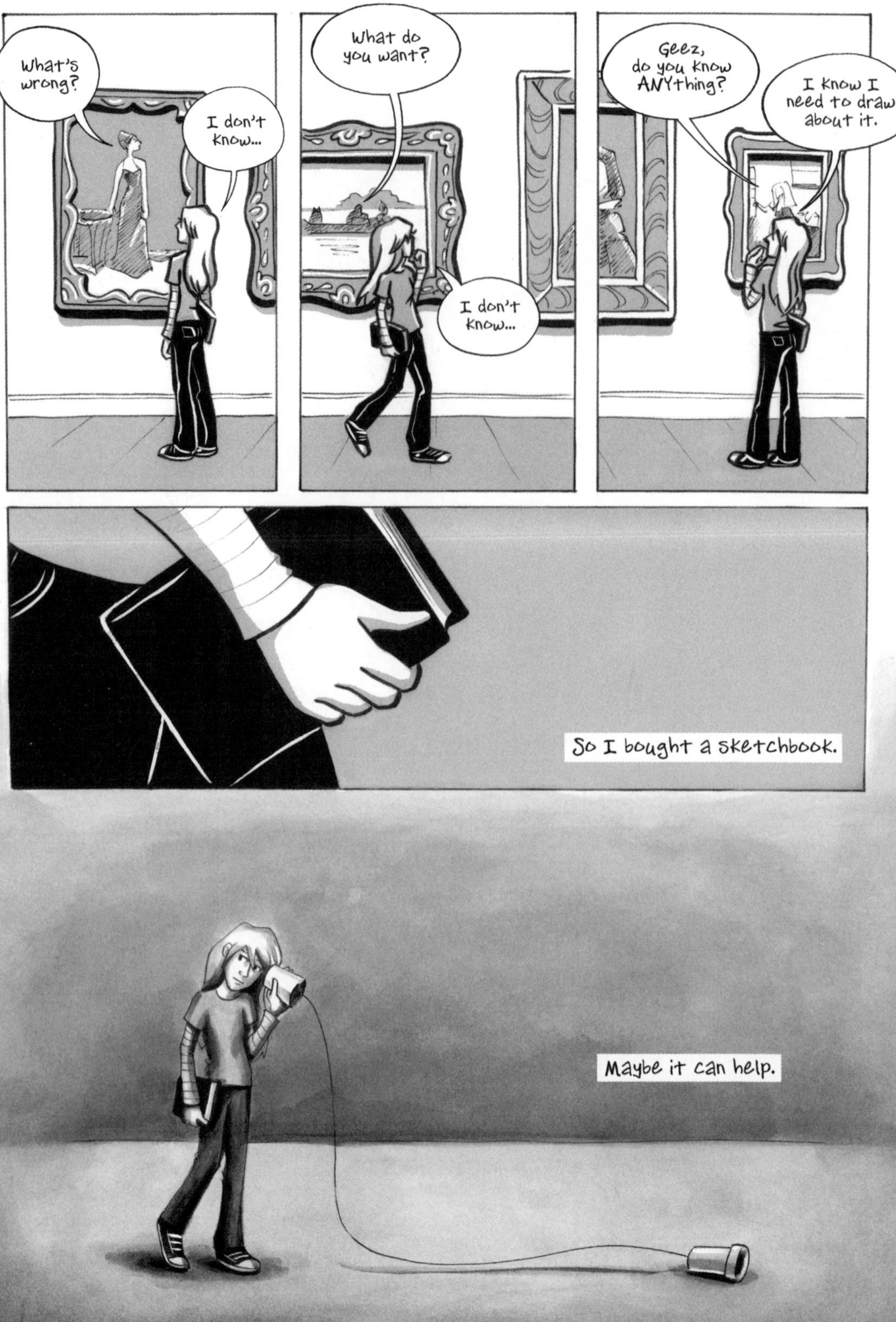
What's wrong?
I don't know...
What do you want?
I don't know...
Geez, do you know ANYthing?
I know I need to draw about it.
So I bought a sketchbook.
Maybe it can help.

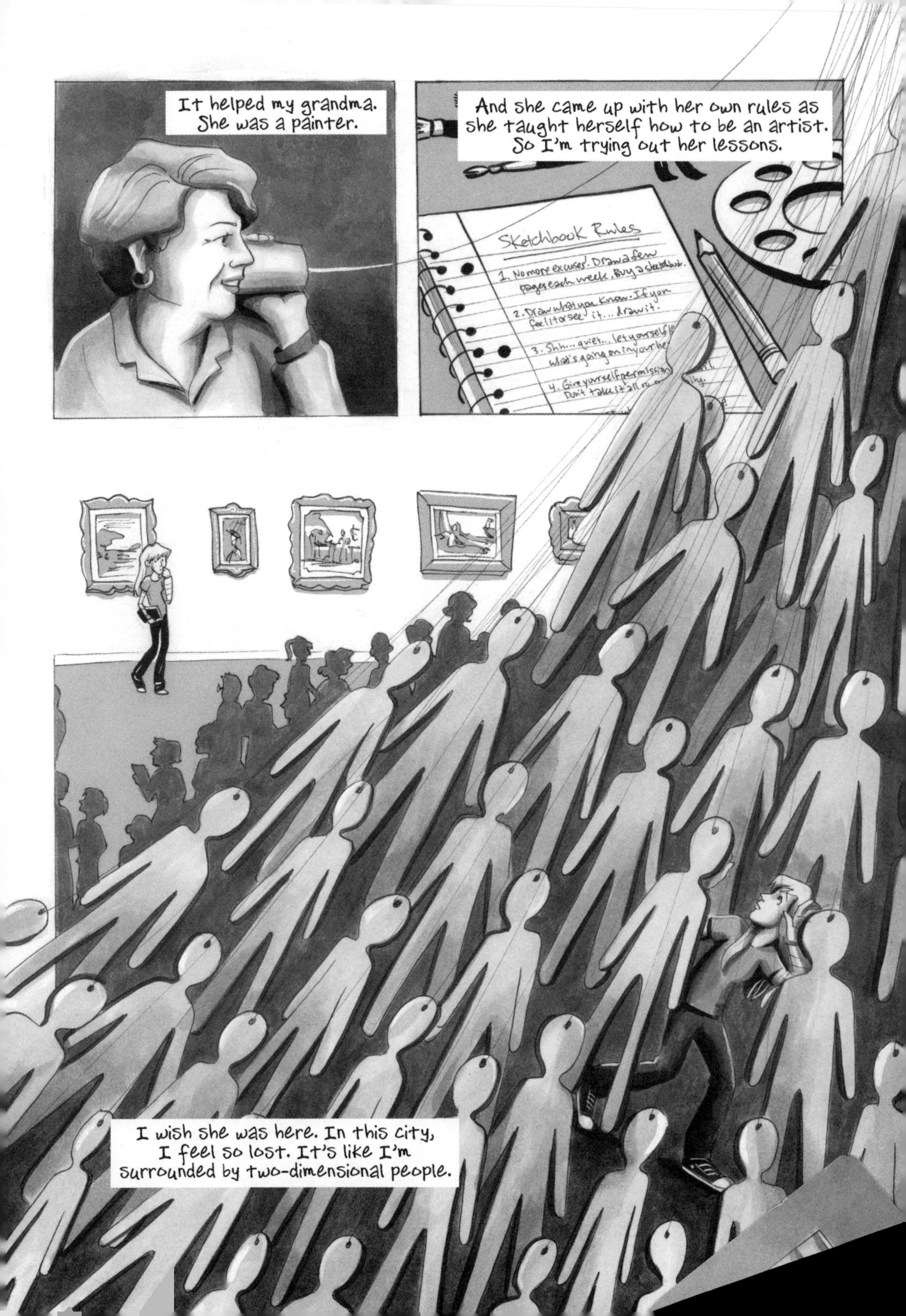
It helped my grandma. She was a painter.
And she came up with her own rules as she taught herself how to be an artist. So I'm trying out her lessons.
Sketchbook Rules
1. No more excuses! Draw a few pages each week. Buy a sketchbook.
2. Draw what you know. If you feel it or see it... draw it.
3. Shh... quiet... let yourself
what's going on in your
4. Give yourself permission
Don't take it all
I wish she was here. In this city, I feel so lost. It's like I'm surrounded by two-dimensional people.

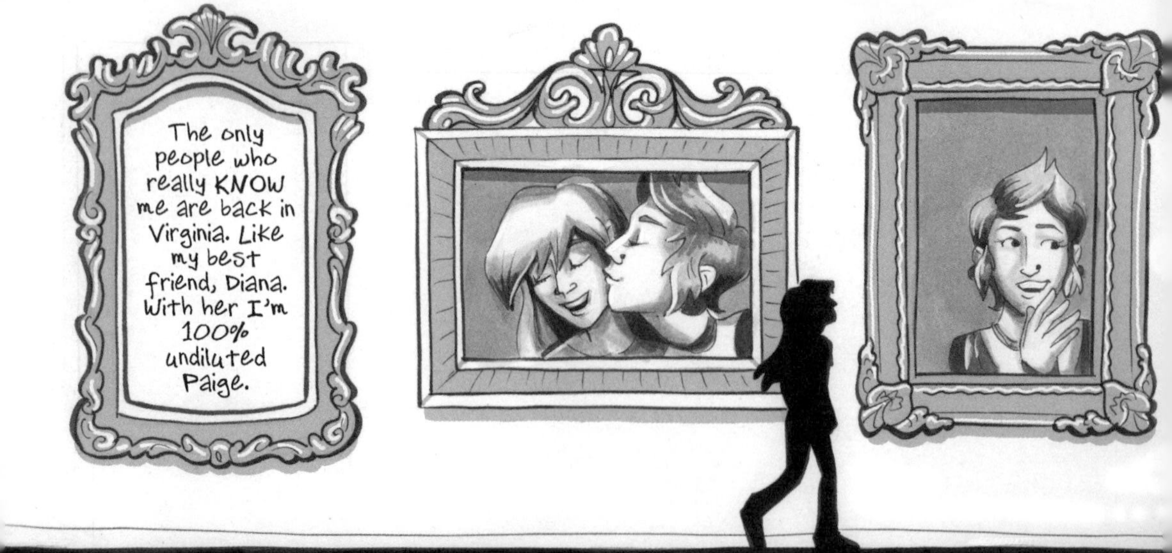
The only people who really KNOW me are back in Virginia. Like my best friend, Diana. With her I'm 100% undiluted Paige.

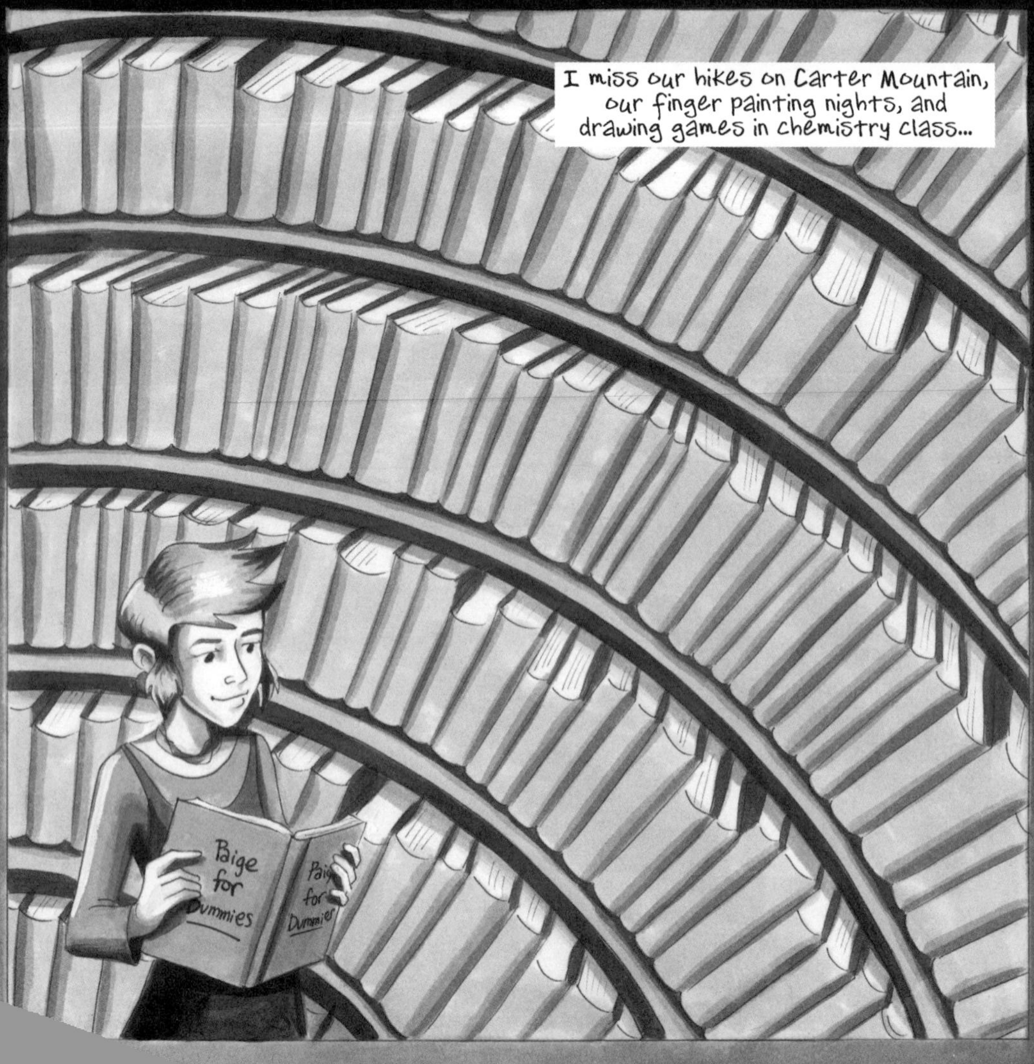
I miss our hikes on Carter Mountain, our finger painting nights, and drawing games in chemistry class...
Paige for Dummies
Paige for Dummies

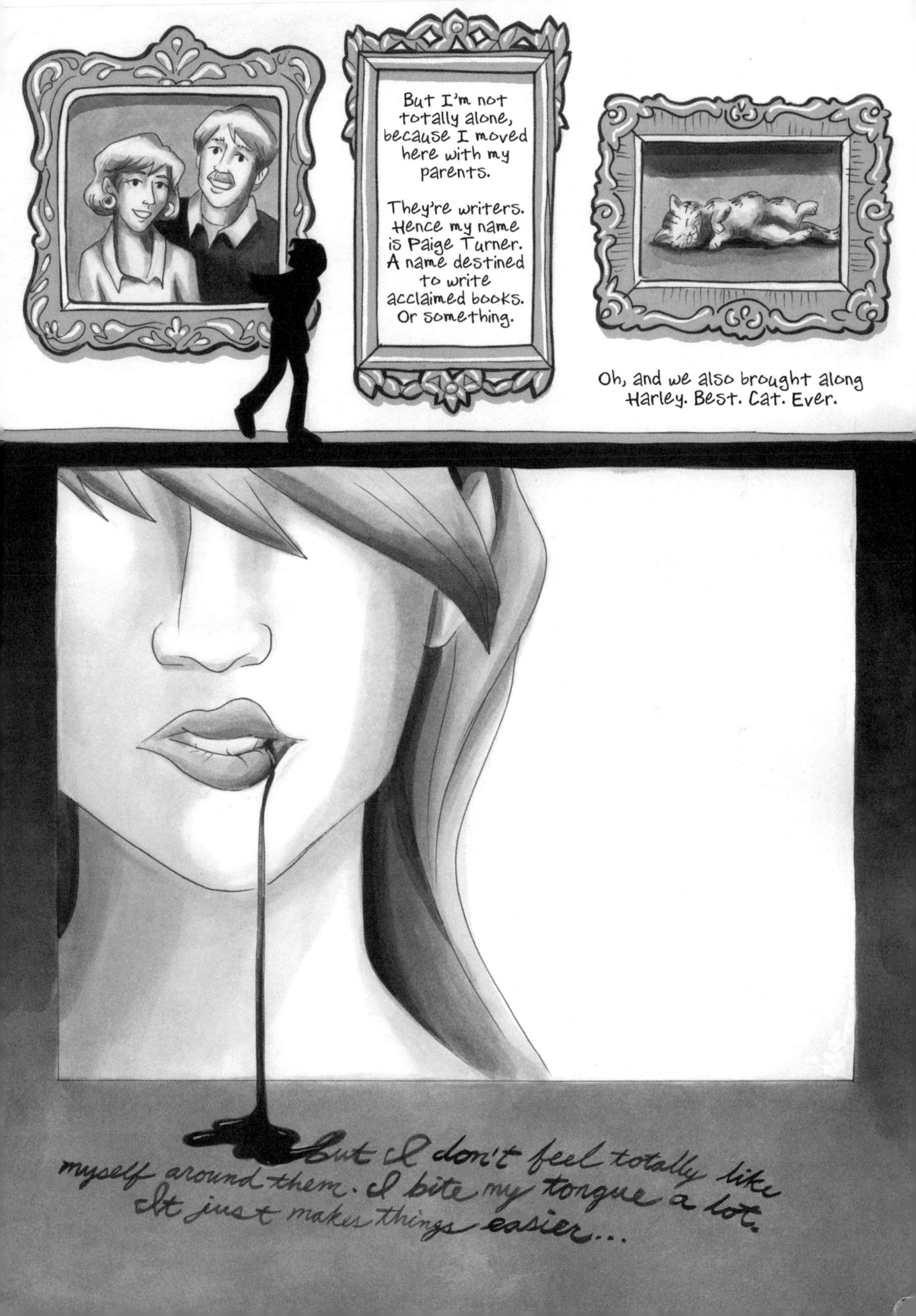

But I'm not totally alone, because I moved here with my parents.
They're writers. Hence my name is Paige Turner. A name destined to write acclaimed books. Or something.
Oh, and we also brought along Harley. Best. Cat. Ever.
But I don't feel totally like myself around them. I bite my tongue a lot. It just makes things easier...

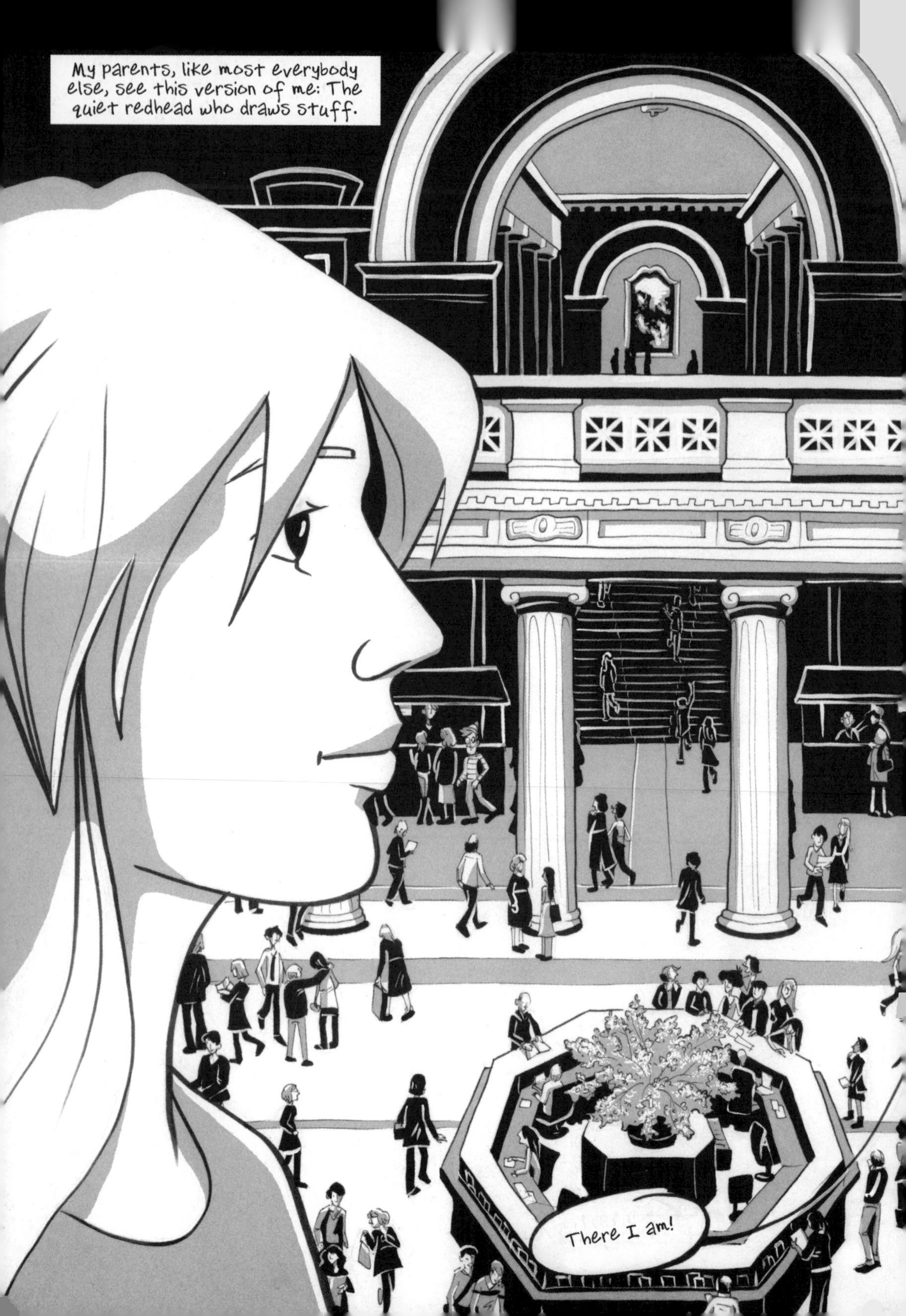
My parents, like most everybody else, see this version of me: The quiet redhead who draws stuff.
There I am!

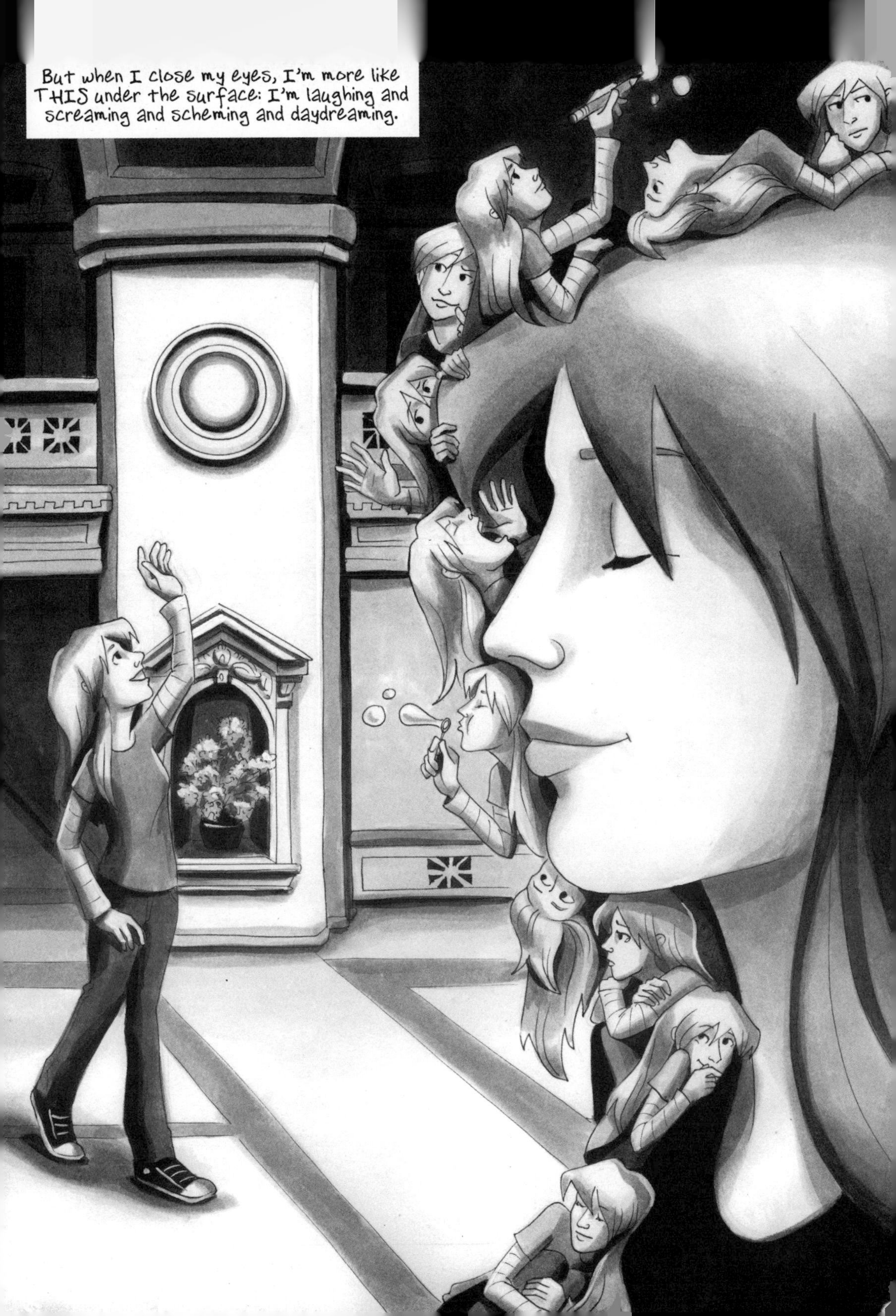
But when I close my eyes, I'm more like THIS under the surface: I'm laughing and screaming and scheming and daydreaming.

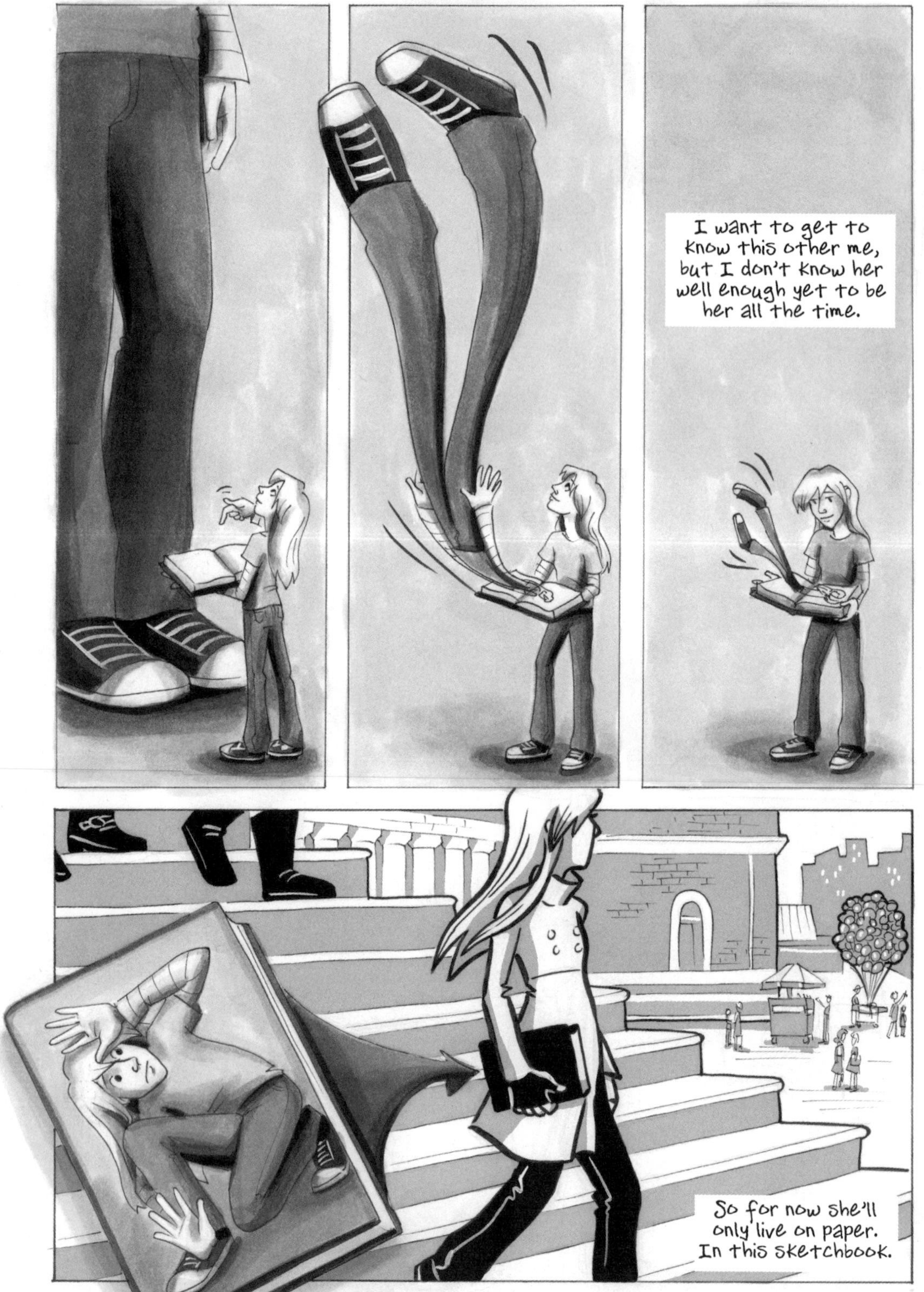
I want to get to know this other me, but I don't know her well enough yet to be her all the time.
So for now she'll only live on paper. In this sketchbook.

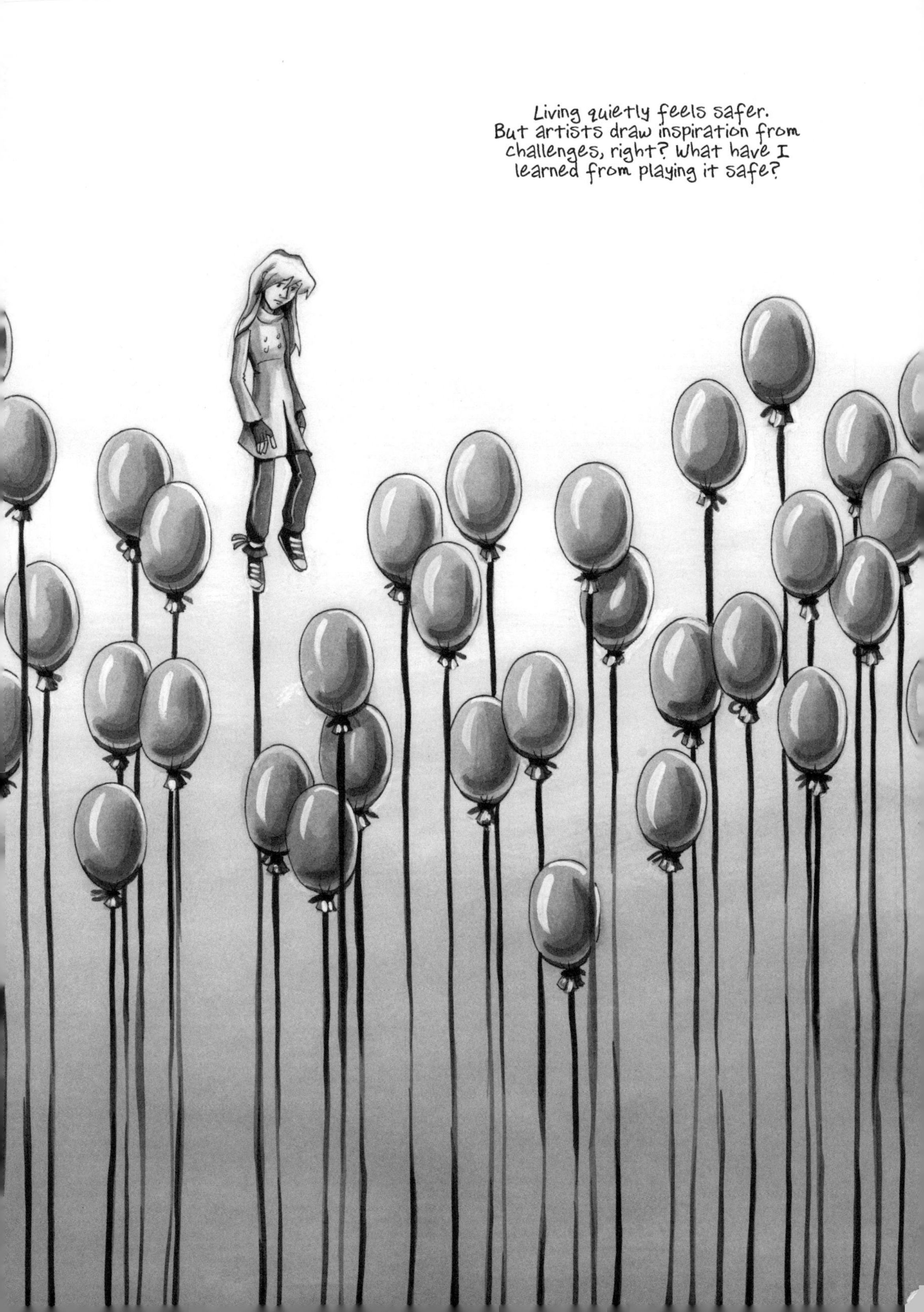
Living quietly feels safer. But artists draw inspiration from challenges, right? What have I learned from playing it safe?

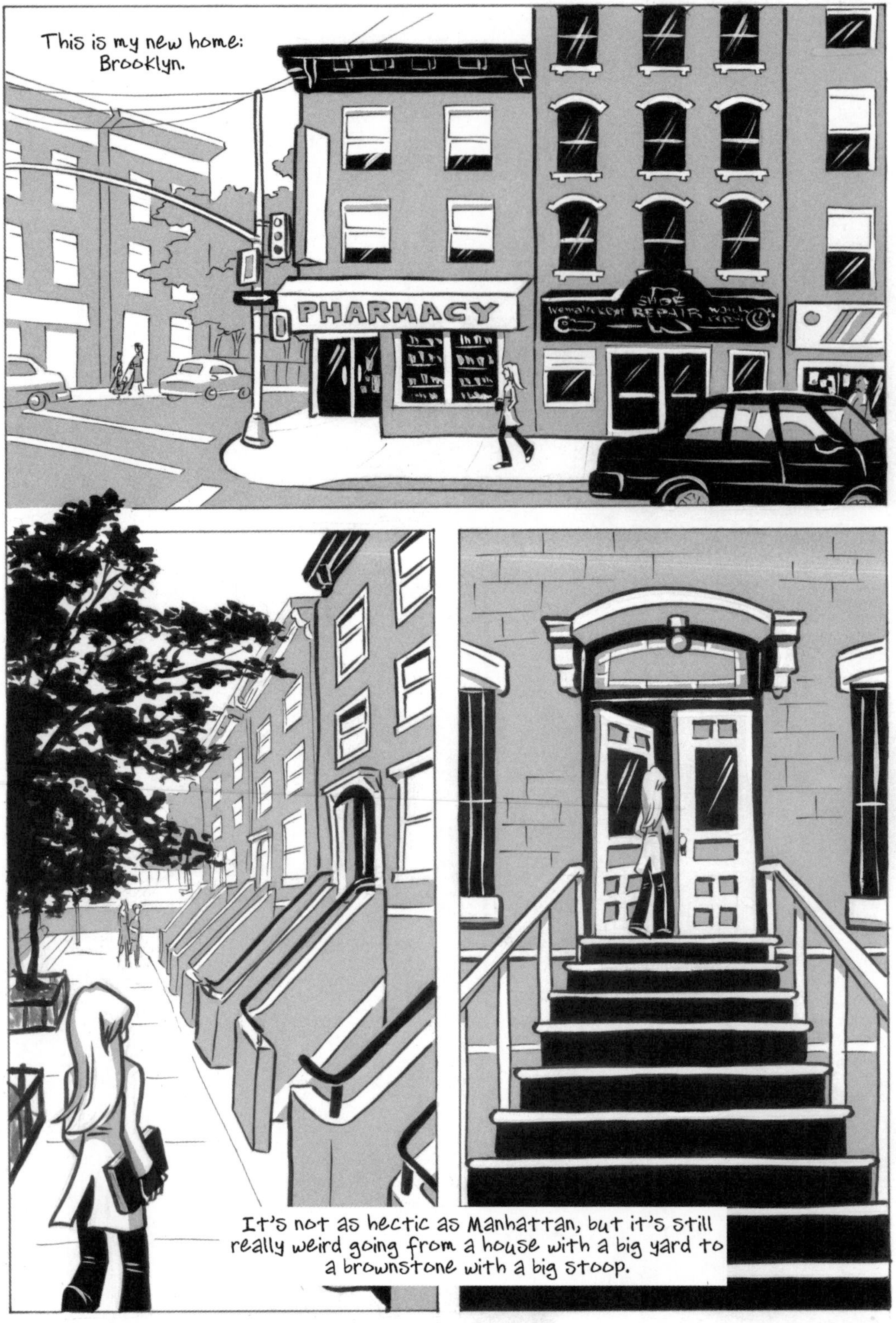
This is my new home: Brooklyn.
PHARMACY
SHOE REPAIR
It's not as hectic as Manhattan, but it's still really weird going from a house with a big yard to a brownstone with a big stoop.

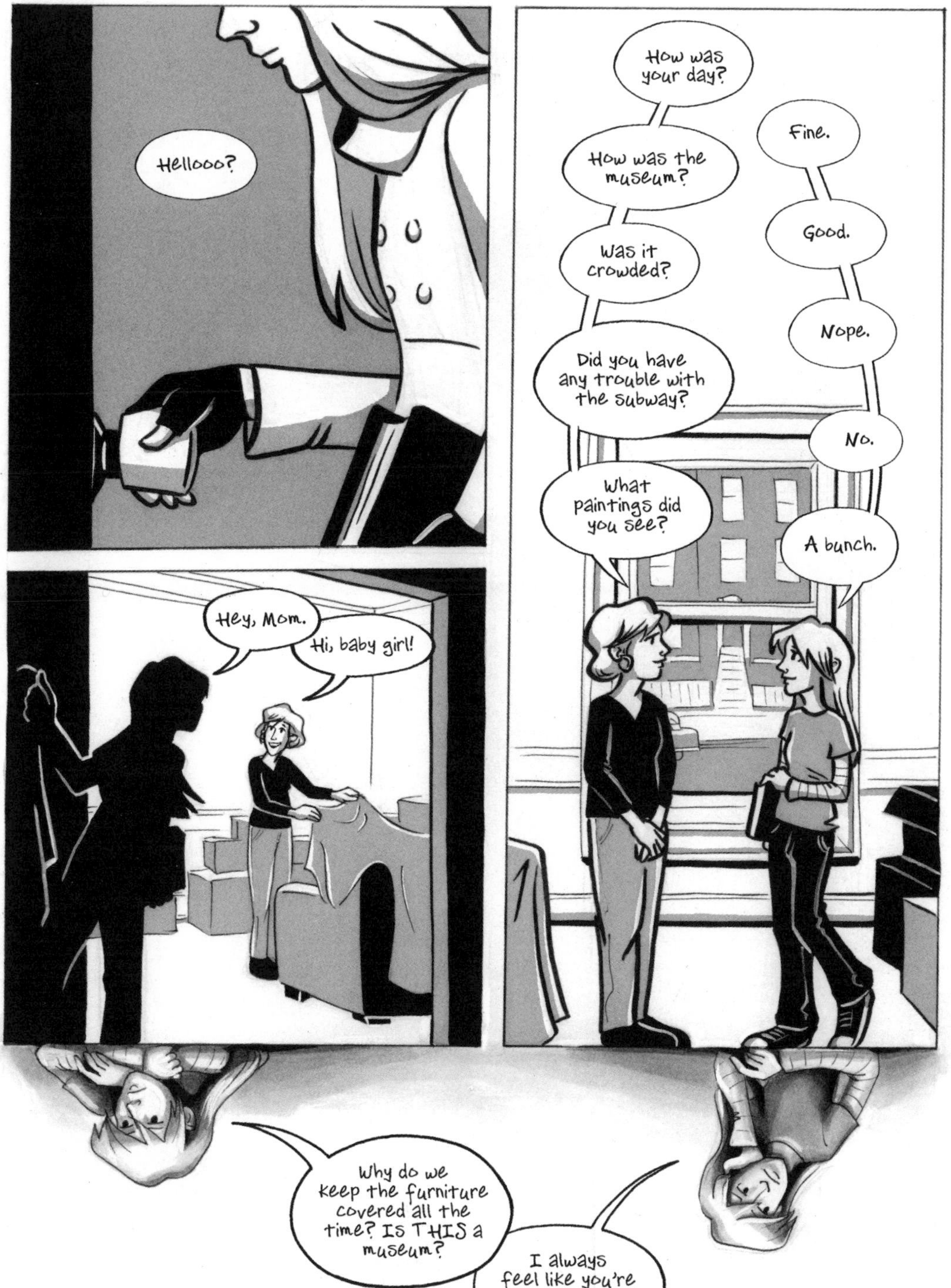
Hellooo?
Hey, Mom.
Hi, baby girl!
How was your day?
Fine.
How was the museum?
Good.
Was it crowded?
Nope.
Did you have any trouble with the subway?
No.
What paintings did you see?
A bunch.
Why do we keep the furniture covered all the time? IS THIS a museum?
I always feel like you're interviewing me...

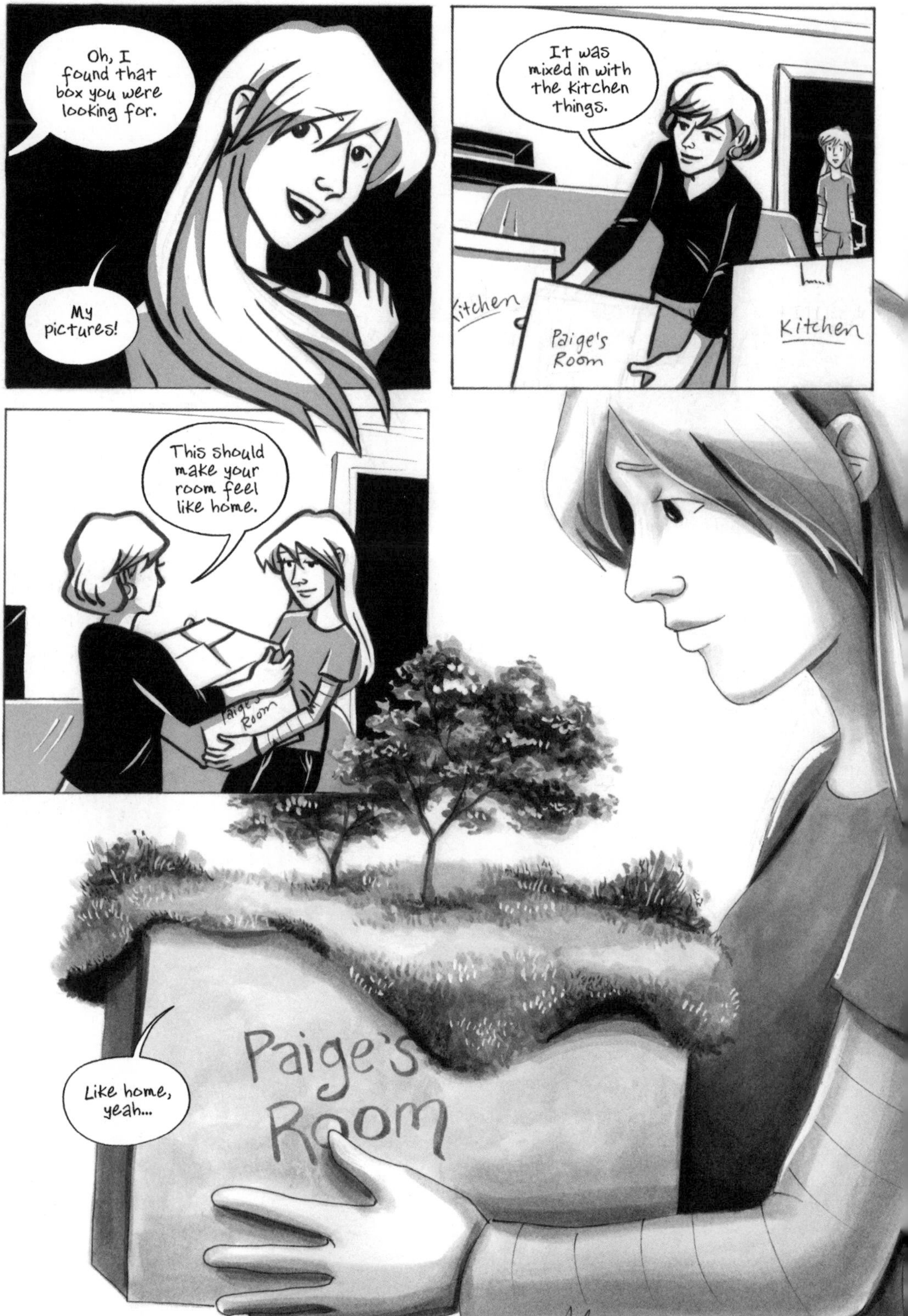
Oh, I found that box you were looking for.
My pictures!
It was mixed in with the kitchen things.
Kitchen
Paige's Room
Kitchen
This should make your room feel like home.
Paige's Room
Paige's Room
Like home, yeah...

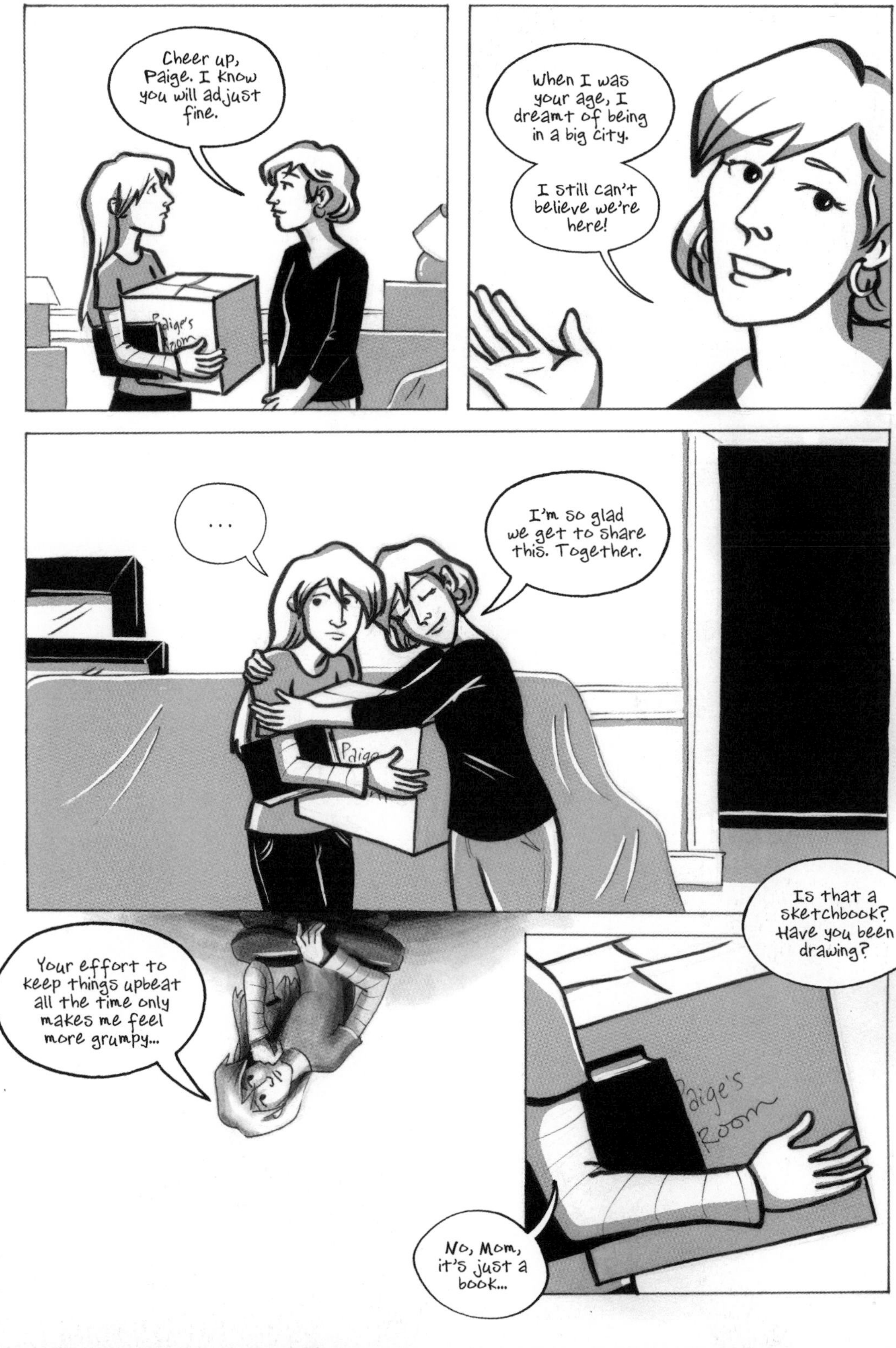
Cheer up, Paige. I know you will adjust fine.
When I was your age, I dreamt of being in a big city.
I still can't believe we're here!
...
I'm so glad we get to share this. Together.
Your effort to keep things upbeat all the time only makes me feel more grumpy...
Is that a sketchbook? Have you been drawing?
Paige's Room
No, Mom, it's just a book...

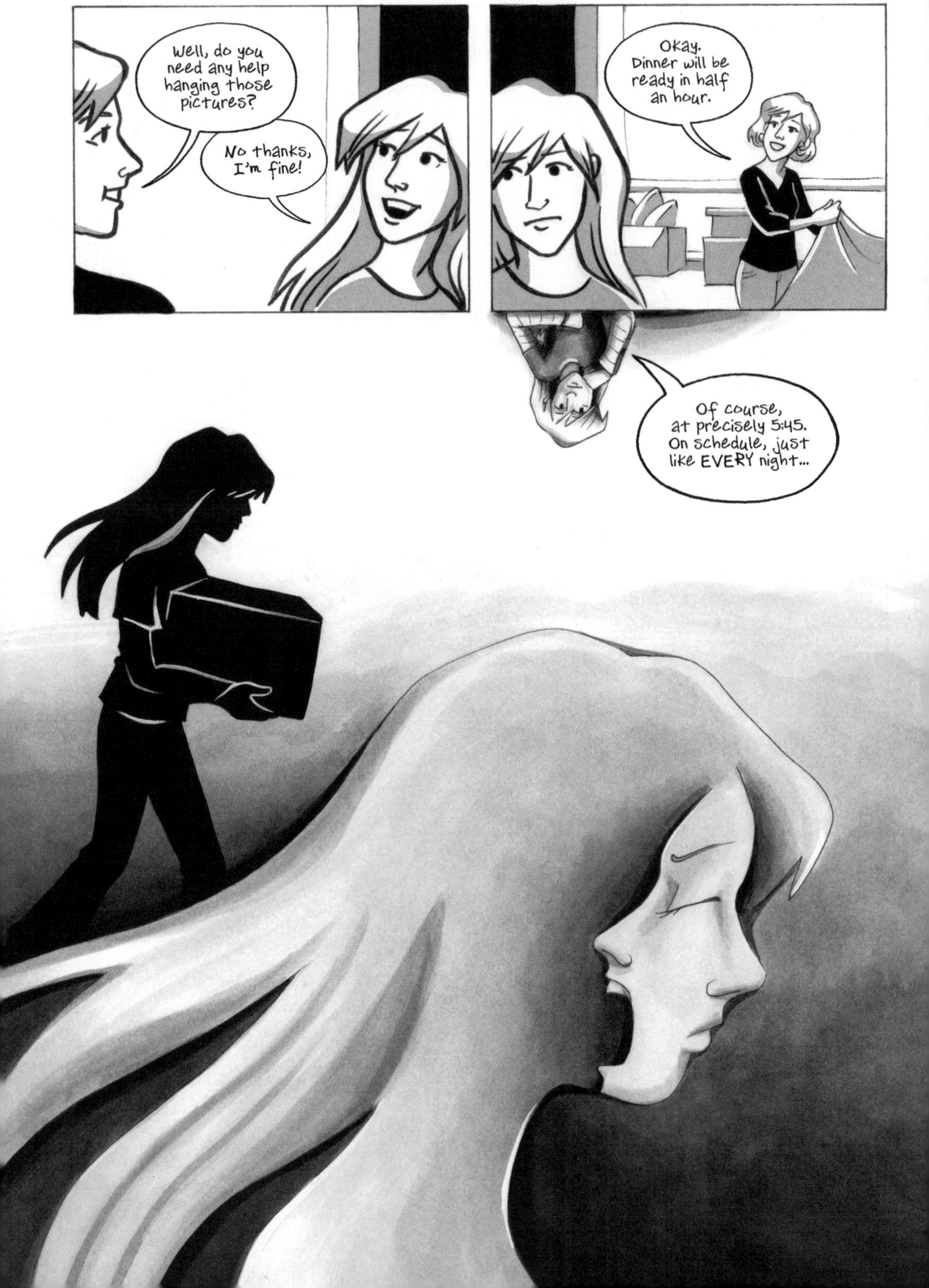
Well, do you need any help hanging those pictures?
No thanks, I'm fine!
Okay. Dinner will be ready in half an hour.
Of course, at precisely 5:45. On schedule, just like EVERY night...

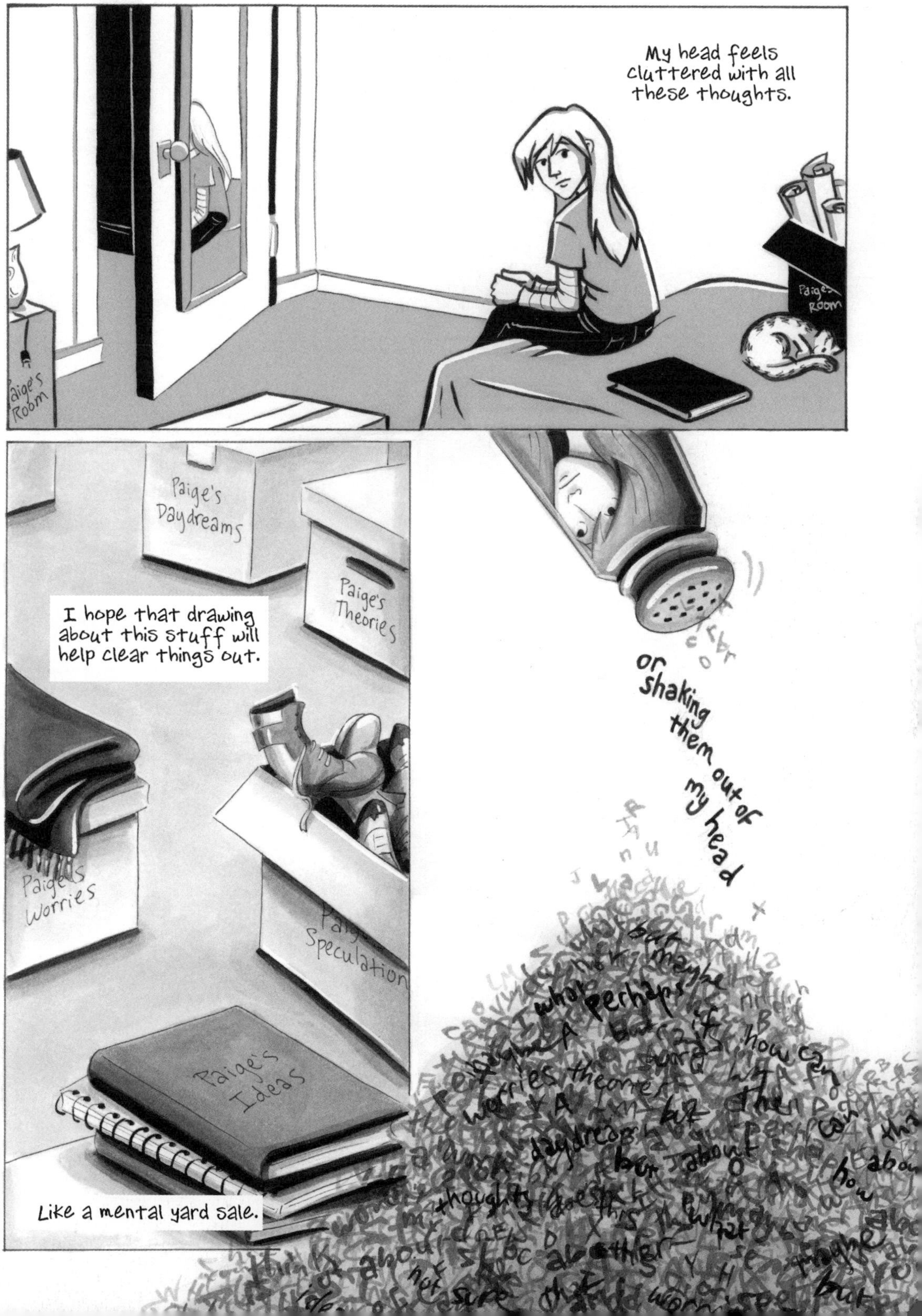

My head feels cluttered with all these thoughts.
Paige's Room
Paige's Room
Paige's Daydreams
Paige's Theories
I hope that drawing about this stuff will help clear things out.
Paige's Worries
Speculation
Paige's Ideas
Like a mental yard sale.
or shaking them out of my head

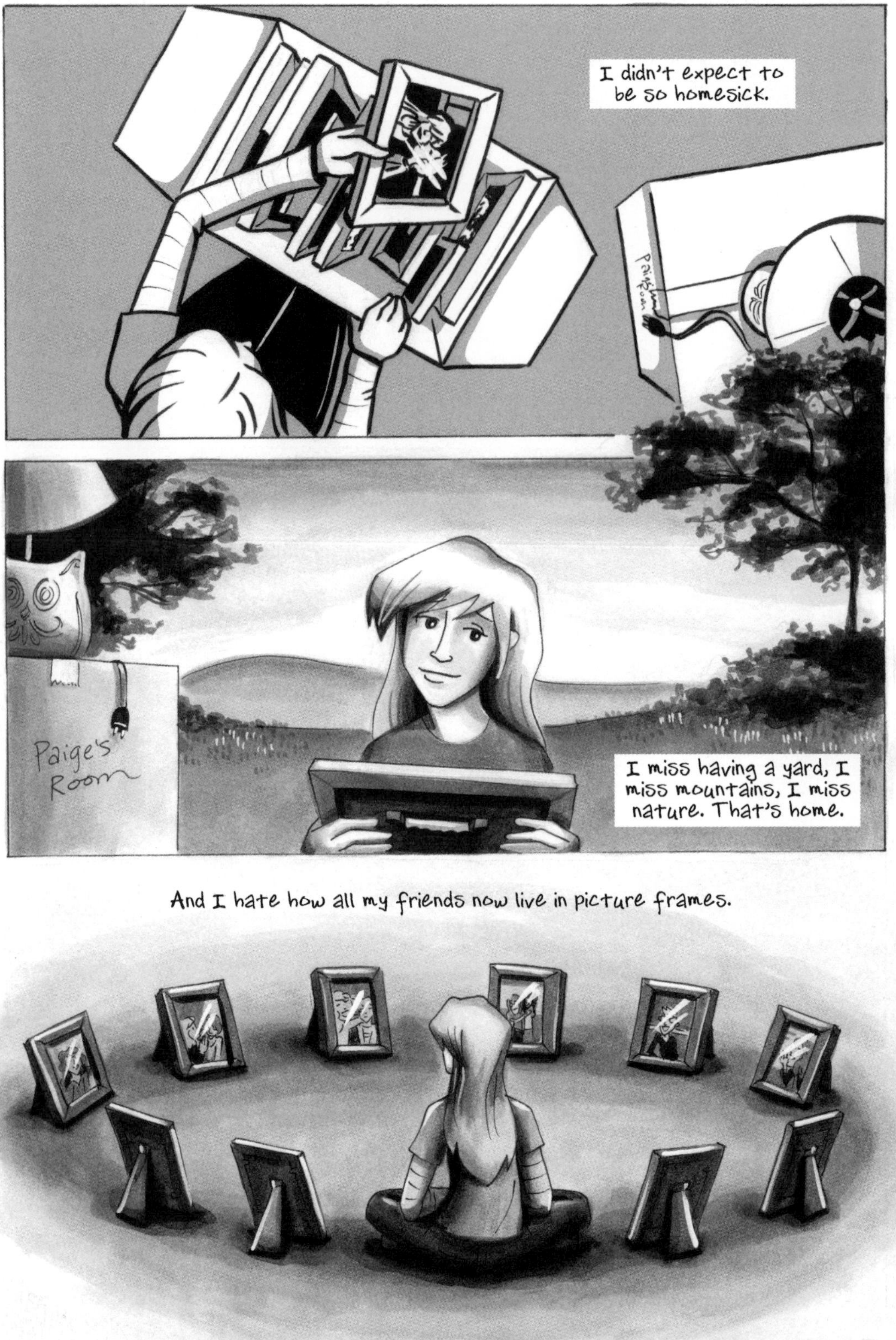
I didn't expect to be so homesick.
Paige's Room
Paige's Room
I miss having a yard, I miss mountains, I miss nature. That's home.
And I hate how all my friends now live in picture frames.

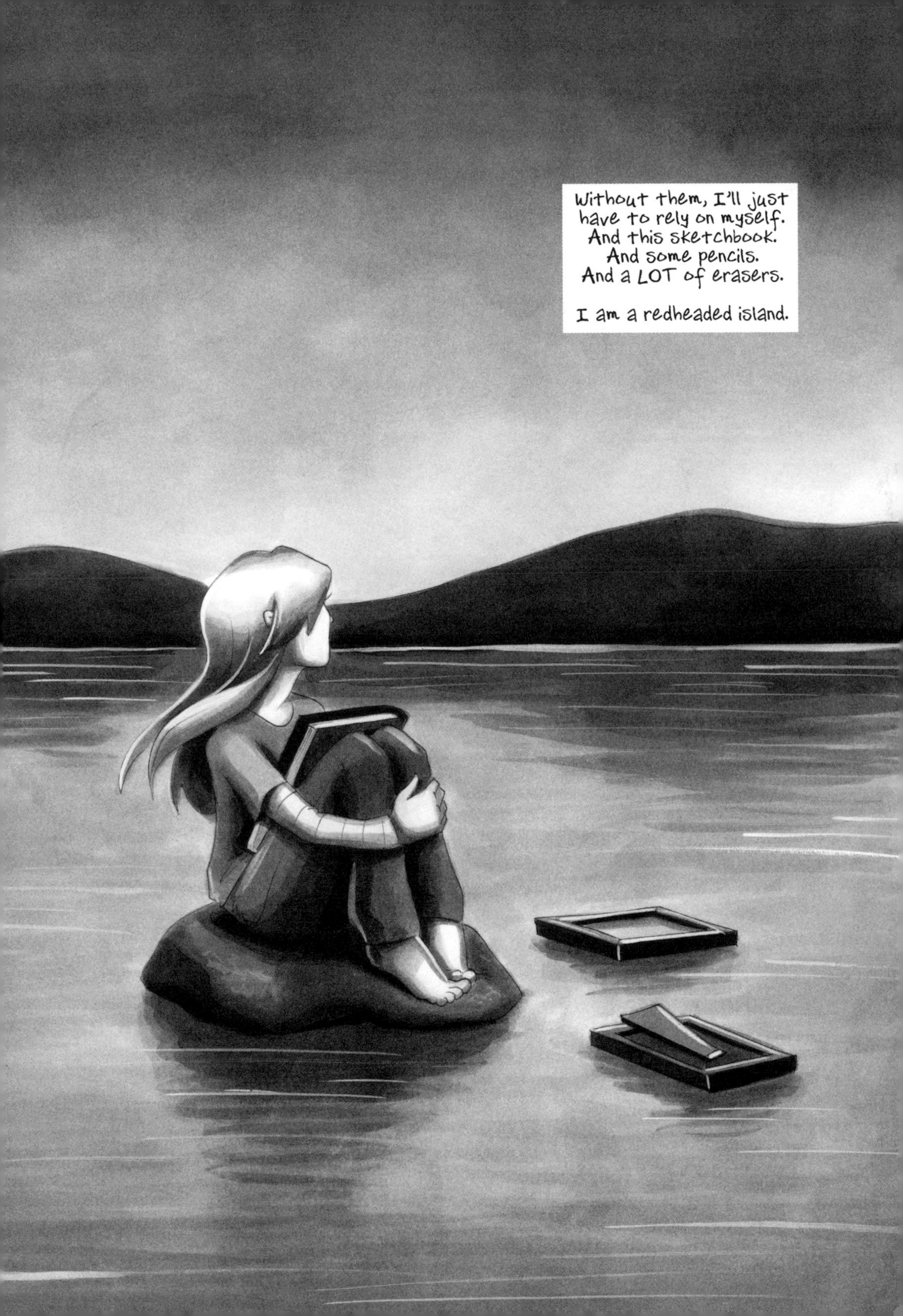
Without them, I'll just have to rely on myself. And this sketchbook. And some pencils. And a LOT of erasers.
I am a redheaded island.

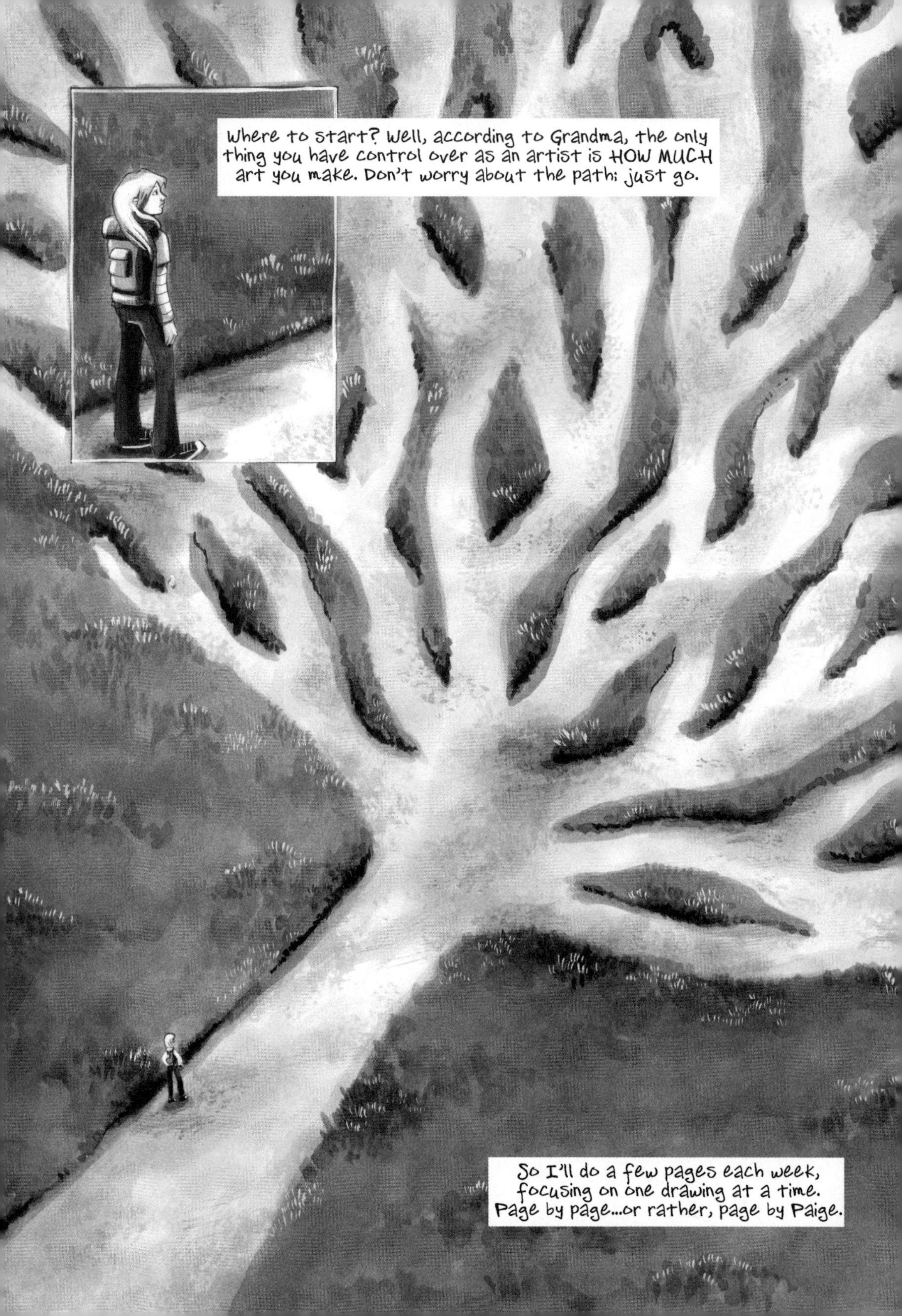
Where to start? Well, according to Grandma, the only thing you have control over as an artist is HOW MUCH art you make. Don't worry about the path; just go.
So I'll do a few pages each week, focusing on one drawing at a time. Page by page...or rather, page by Paige.

Rule #2

Draw what you <u>know</u>.
If you feel it or see it...
DRAW IT!

— Still December —

Okay, just draw.

Something.

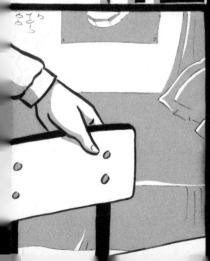

ANYTHING!!

What is THAT supposed to be?
What if my drawings really suck? I can't tear them out of the sketchbook, they'll stay there...
Shouldn't you be doing something more important?
Art is just silly and pointless, you know...
Grandma was a REAL artist; you're just pretending.
Who cares? Why bother?
You're going to fail, so why even try?
What if I have nothing to say? No good ideas at all?

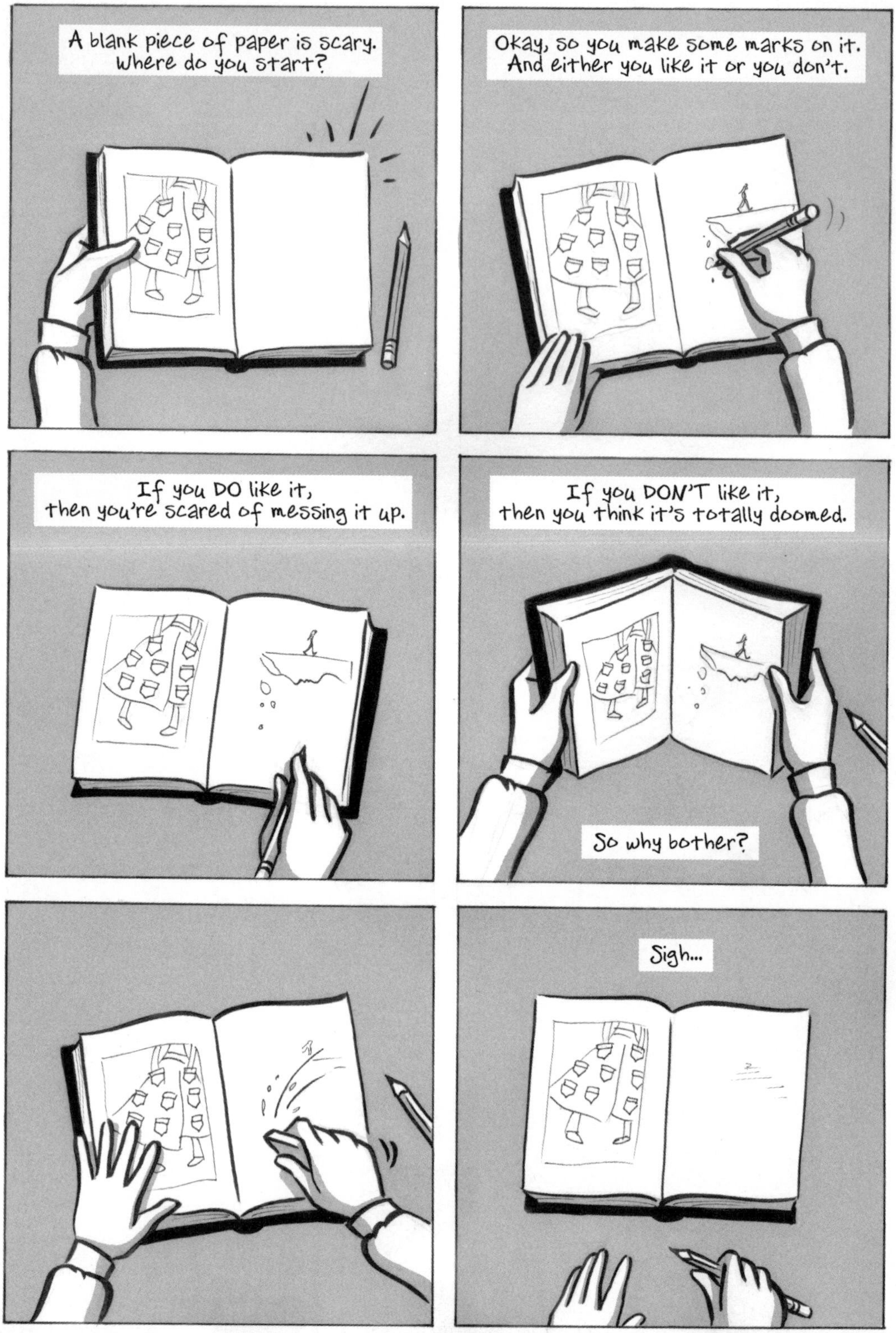
A blank piece of paper is scary. Where do you start?
Okay, so you make some marks on it. And either you like it or you don't.
If you DO like it, then you're scared of messing it up.
If you DON'T like it, then you think it's totally doomed.
So why bother?
Sigh...

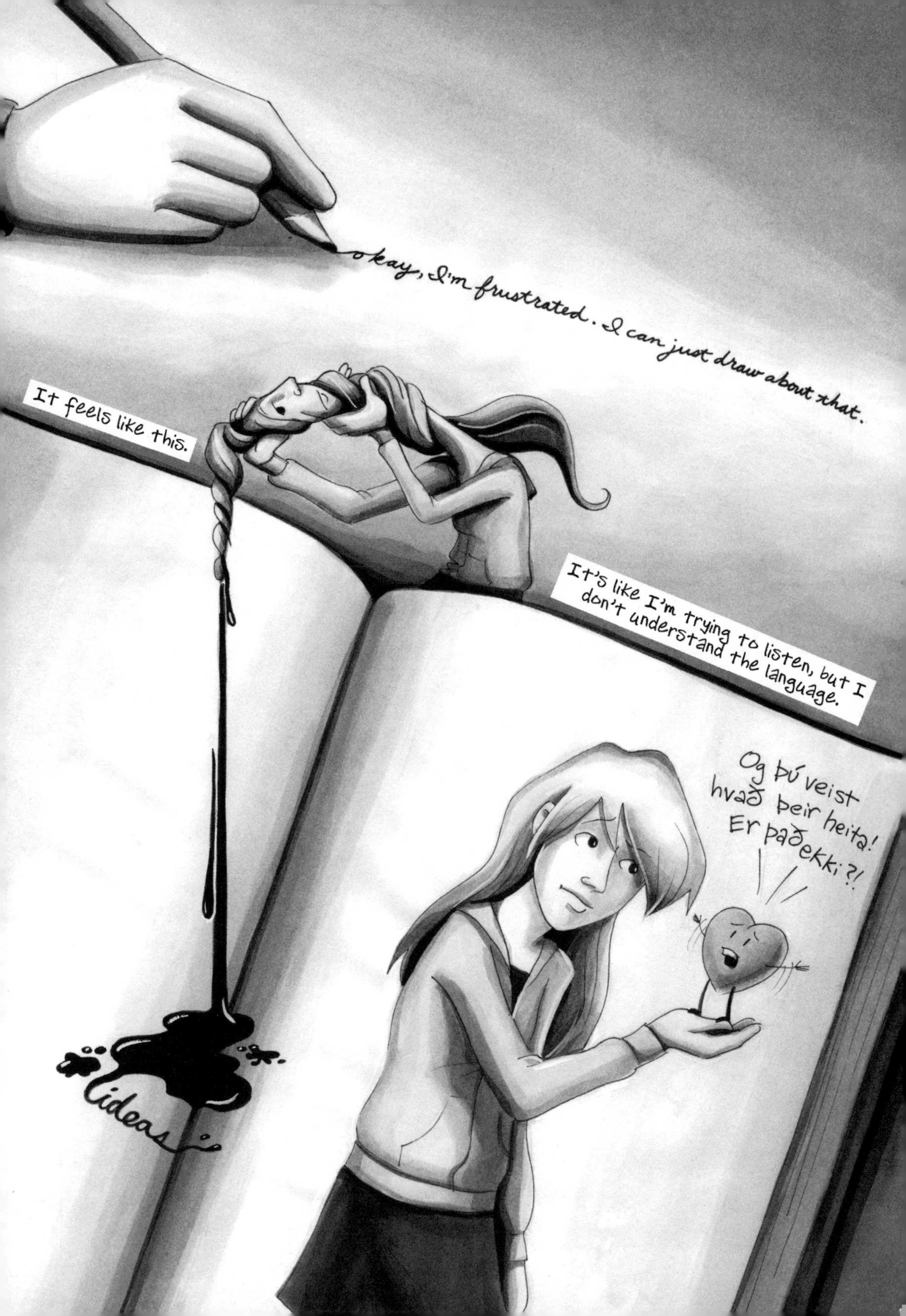

okay, I'm frustrated. I can just draw about that.
It feels like this.
It's like I'm trying to listen, but I don't understand the language.
Og þú veist hvað þeir heita! Er það ekki?!
ideas

I must be making this too hard.
I should draw what I know.
But what do I know?

So I went out for inspiration...

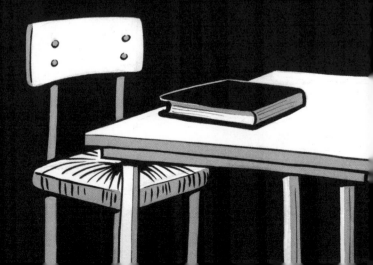

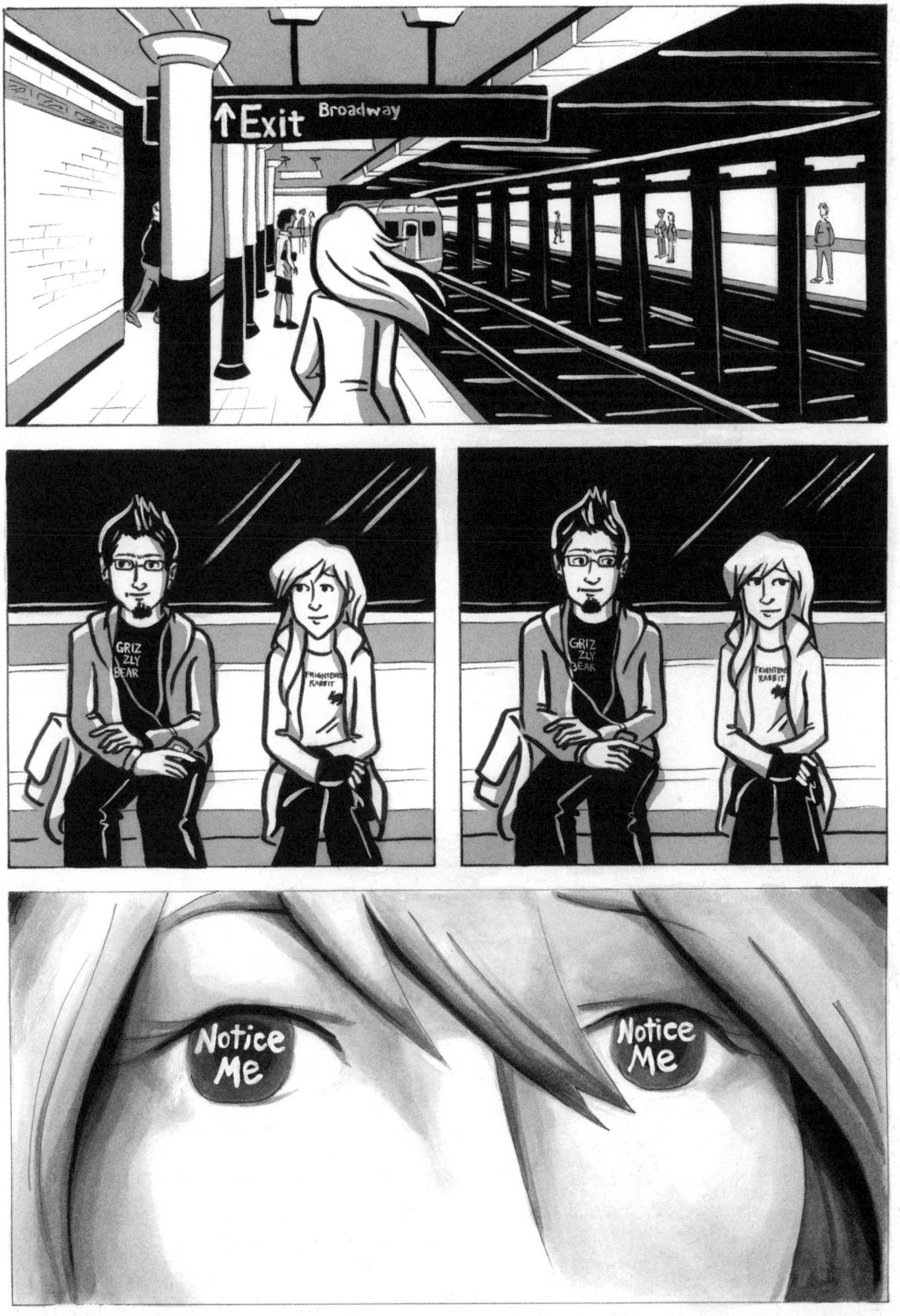
↑Exit
Broadway
GRIZ ZLY BEAR
GRIZ ZLY BEAR
Notice Me
Notice Me

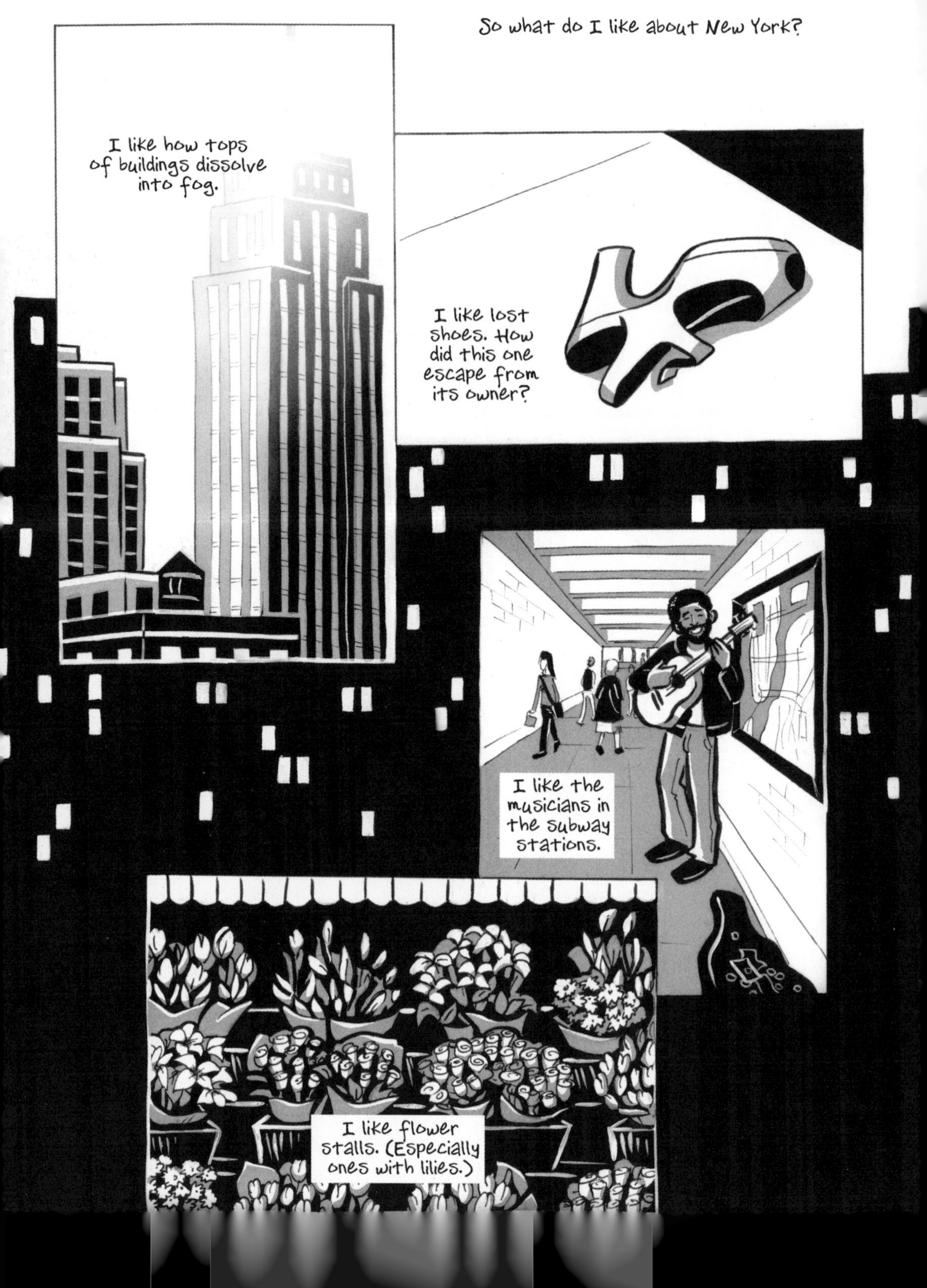
So what do I like about New York?
I like how tops of buildings dissolve into fog.
I like lost shoes. How did this one escape from its owner?
I like the musicians in the subway stations.
I like flower stalls. (Especially ones with lilies.)

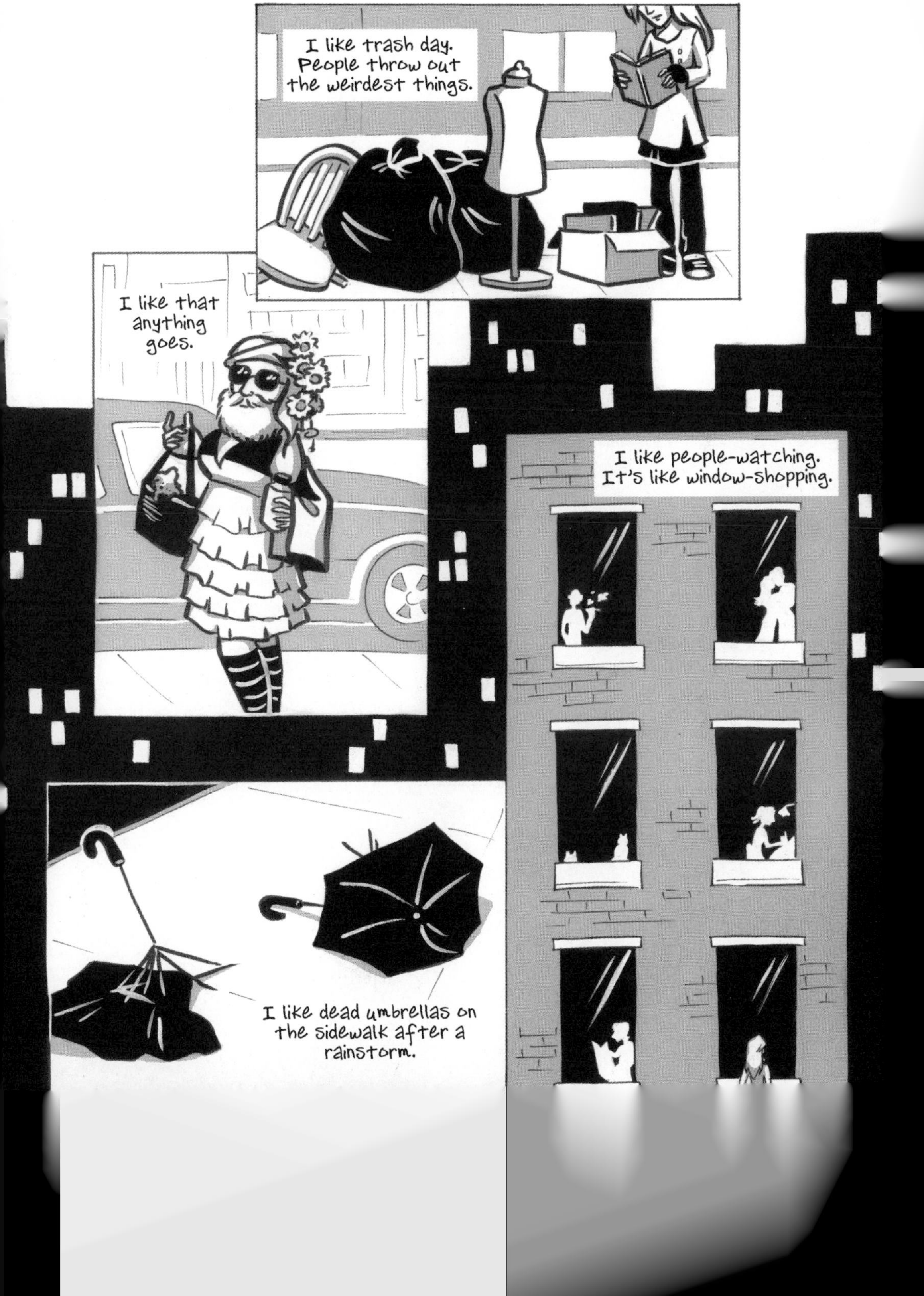
I like trash day. People throw out the weirdest things.
I like that anything goes.
I like people-watching. It's like window-shopping.
I like dead umbrellas on the sidewalk after a rainstorm.

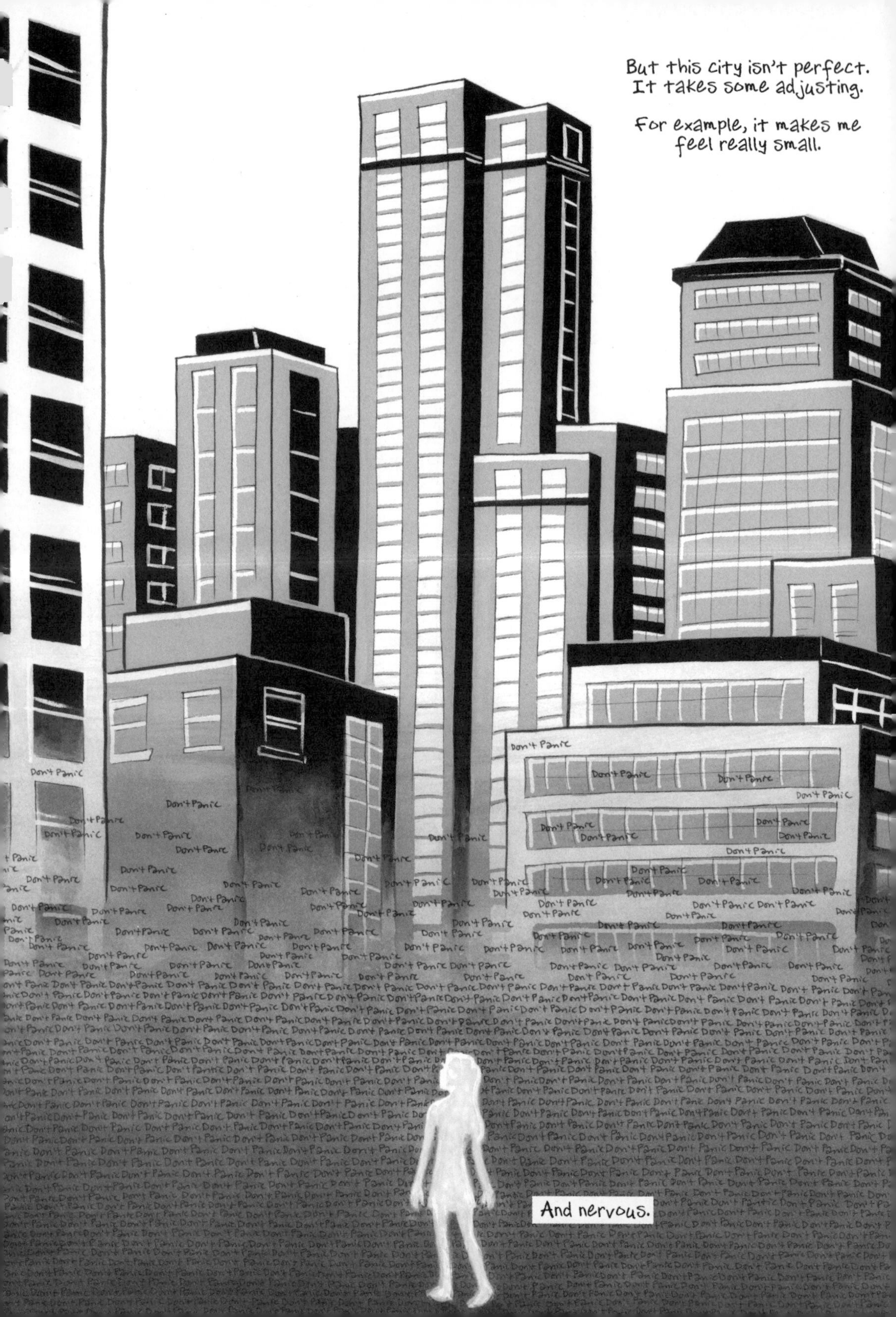
But this city isn't perfect. It takes some adjusting.
For example, it makes me feel really small.
Don't Panic
And nervous.

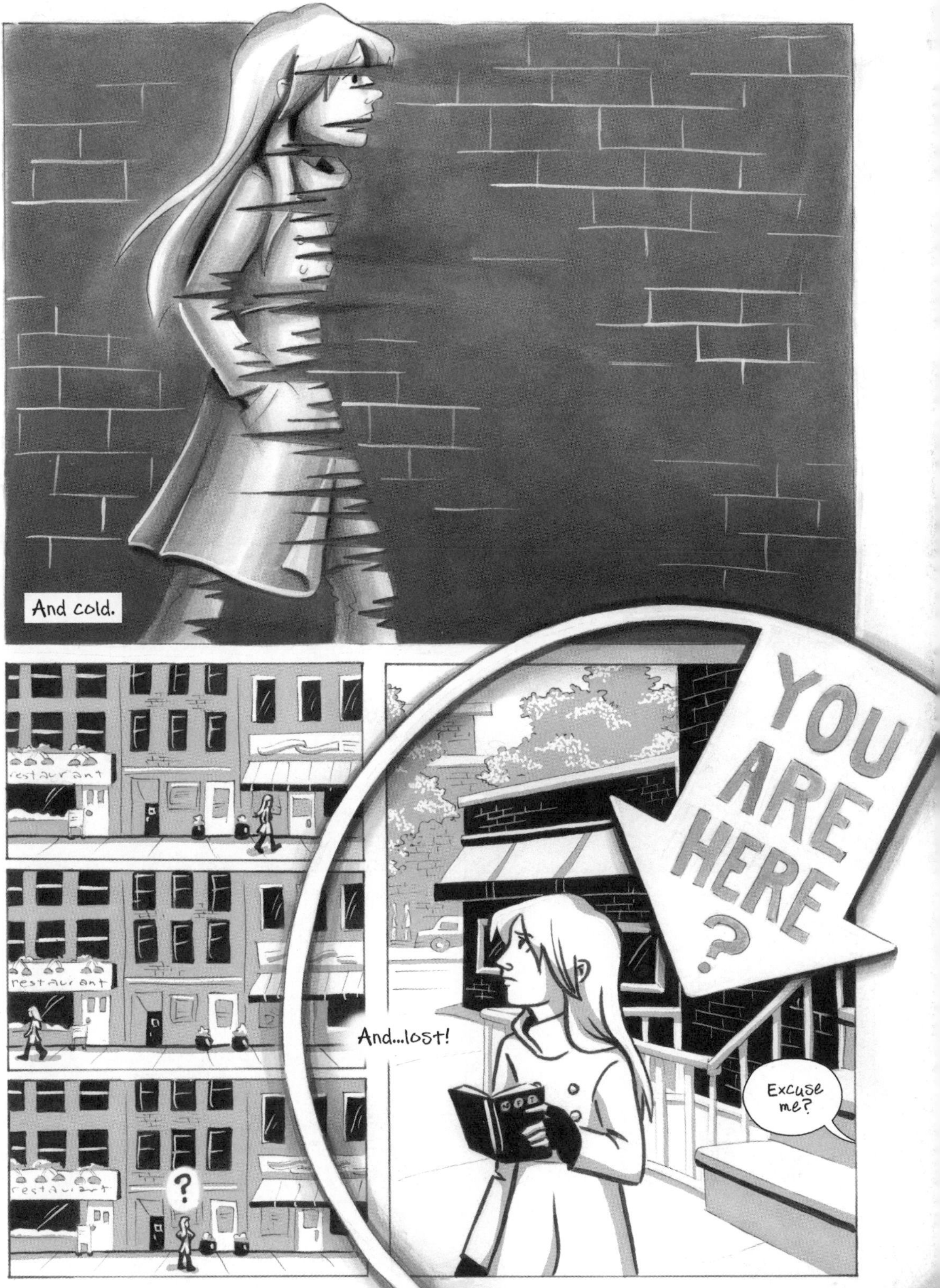
And cold.
restaurant
restaurant
restaurant
?
YOU ARE HERE ?
And...lost!
Excuse me?

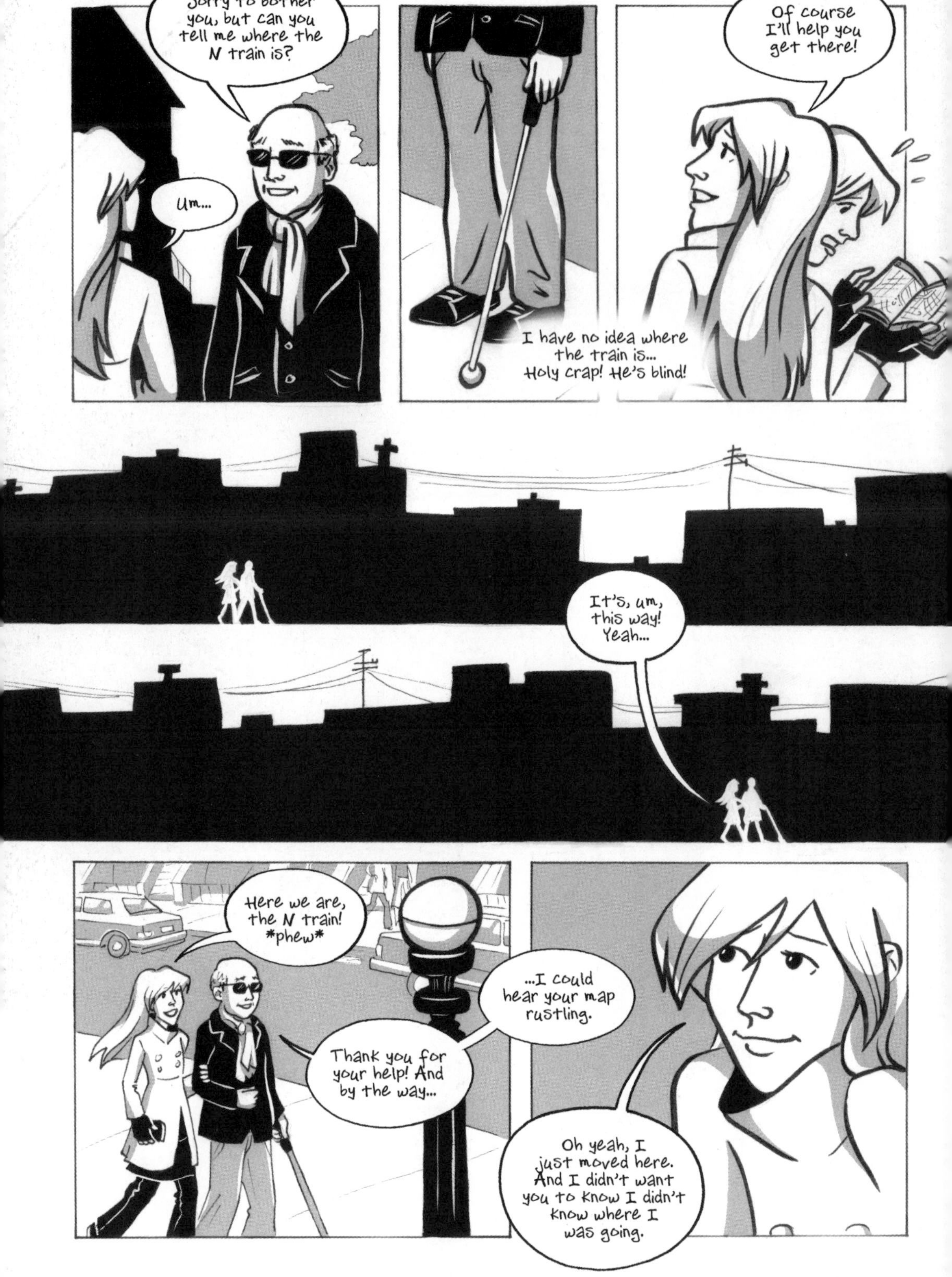
Sorry to bother you, but can you tell me where the N train is?
Um...
I have no idea where the train is... Holy crap! He's blind!
Of course I'll help you get there!
It's, um, this way! Yeah...
Here we are, the N train! *phew*
Thank you for your help! And by the way...
...I could hear your map rustling.
Oh yeah, I just moved here. And I didn't want you to know I didn't know where I was going.

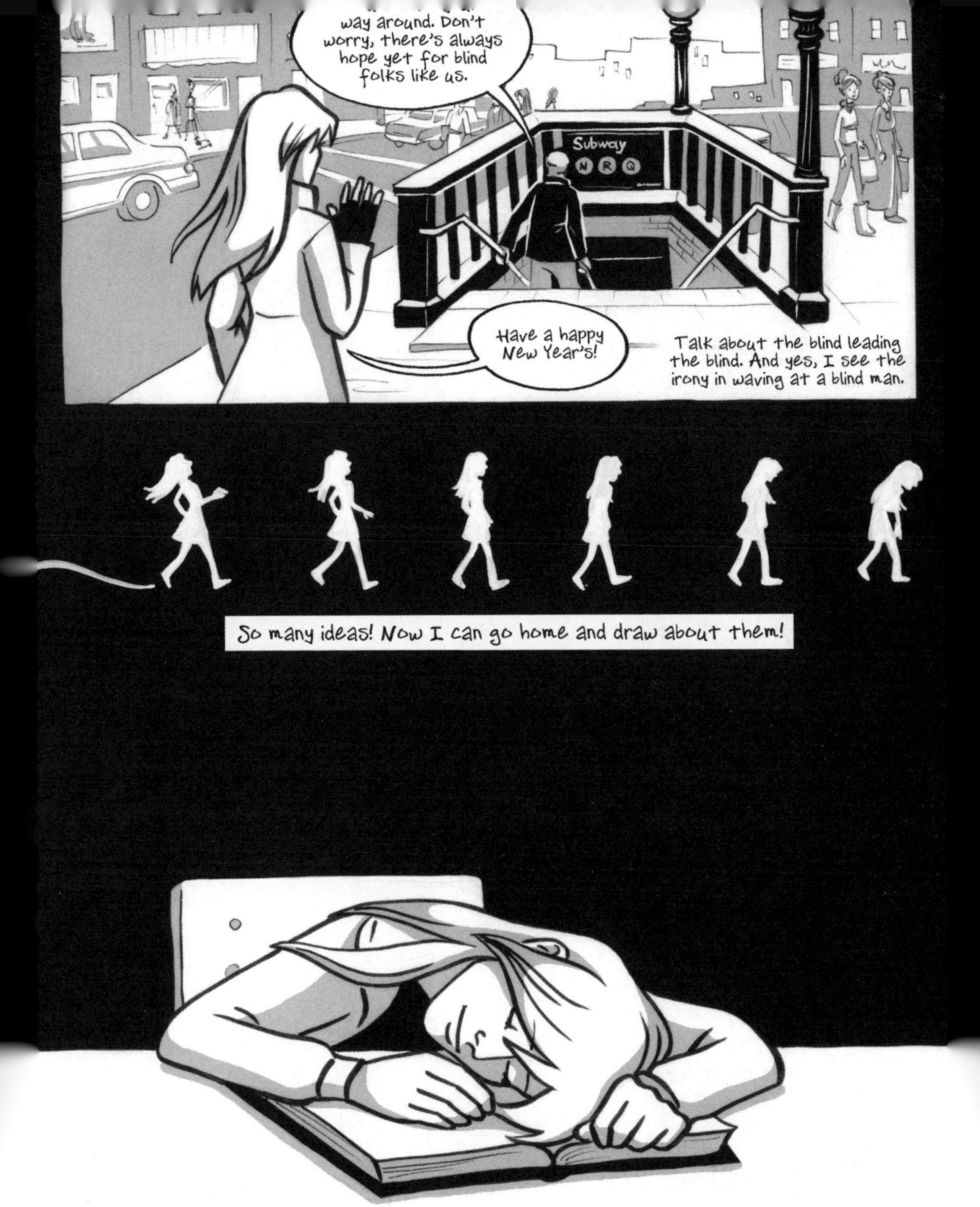
way around. Don't worry, there's always hope yet for blind folks like us.
Subway
N R Q
Have a happy New Year's!
Talk about the blind leading the blind. And yes, I see the irony in waving at a blind man.
So many ideas! Now I can go home and draw about them!

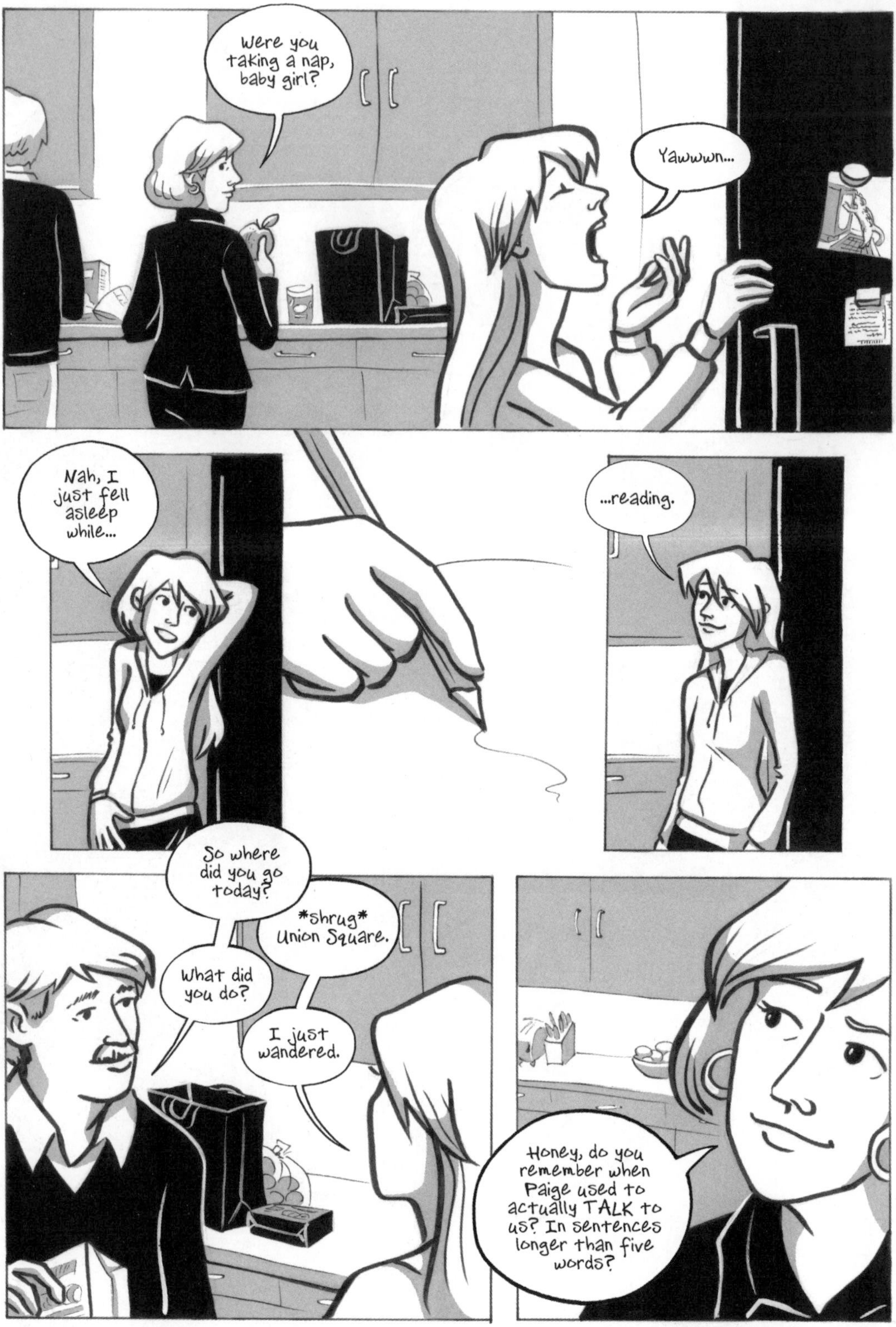
Were you taking a nap, baby girl?
Yawwwn...
Nah, I just fell asleep while...
...reading.
So where did you go today?
shrug Union Square.
What did you do?
I just wandered.
Honey, do you remember when Paige used to actually TALK to us? In sentences longer than five words?

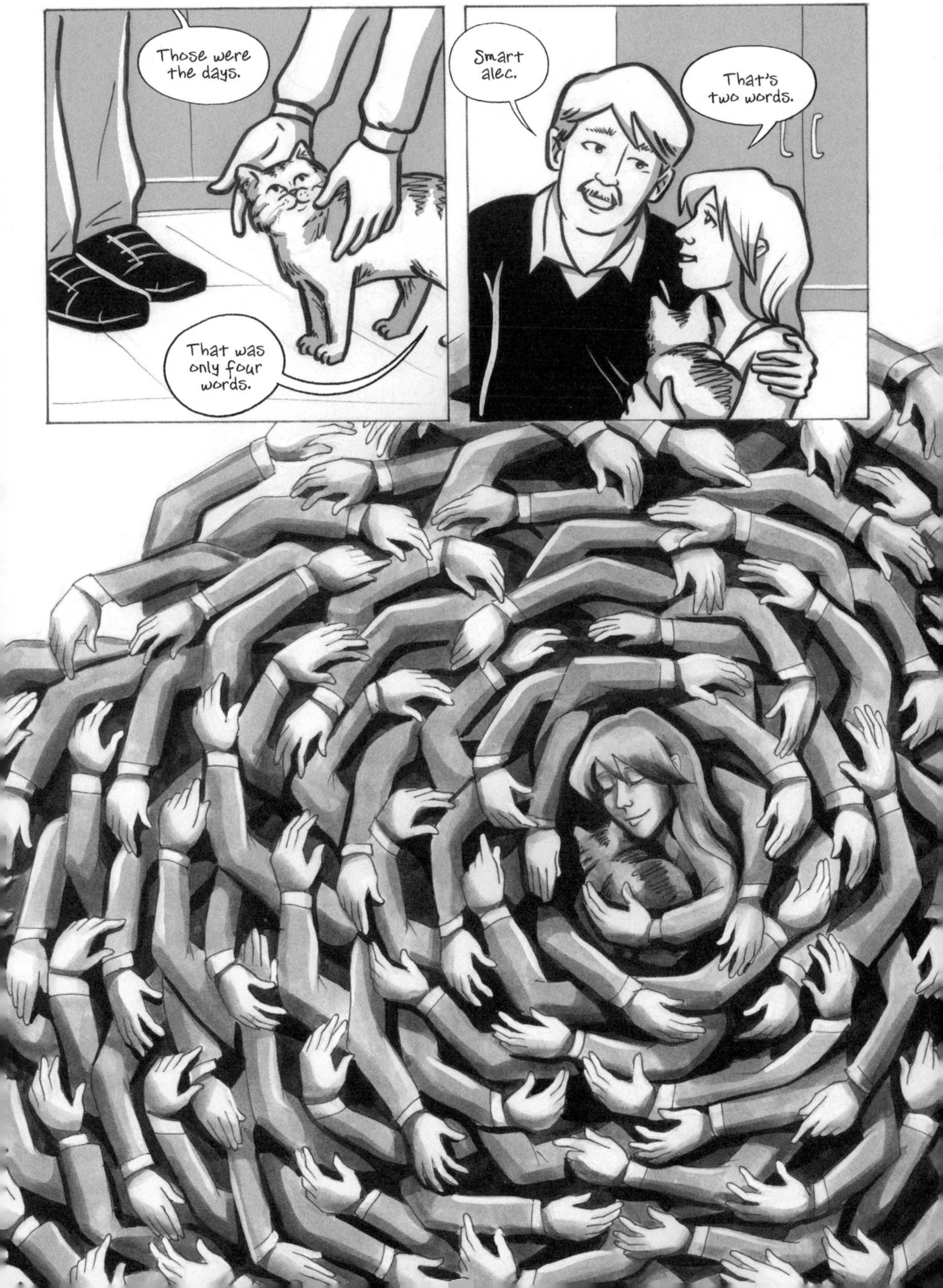
Those were the days.
That was only four words.
Smart alec.
That's two words.

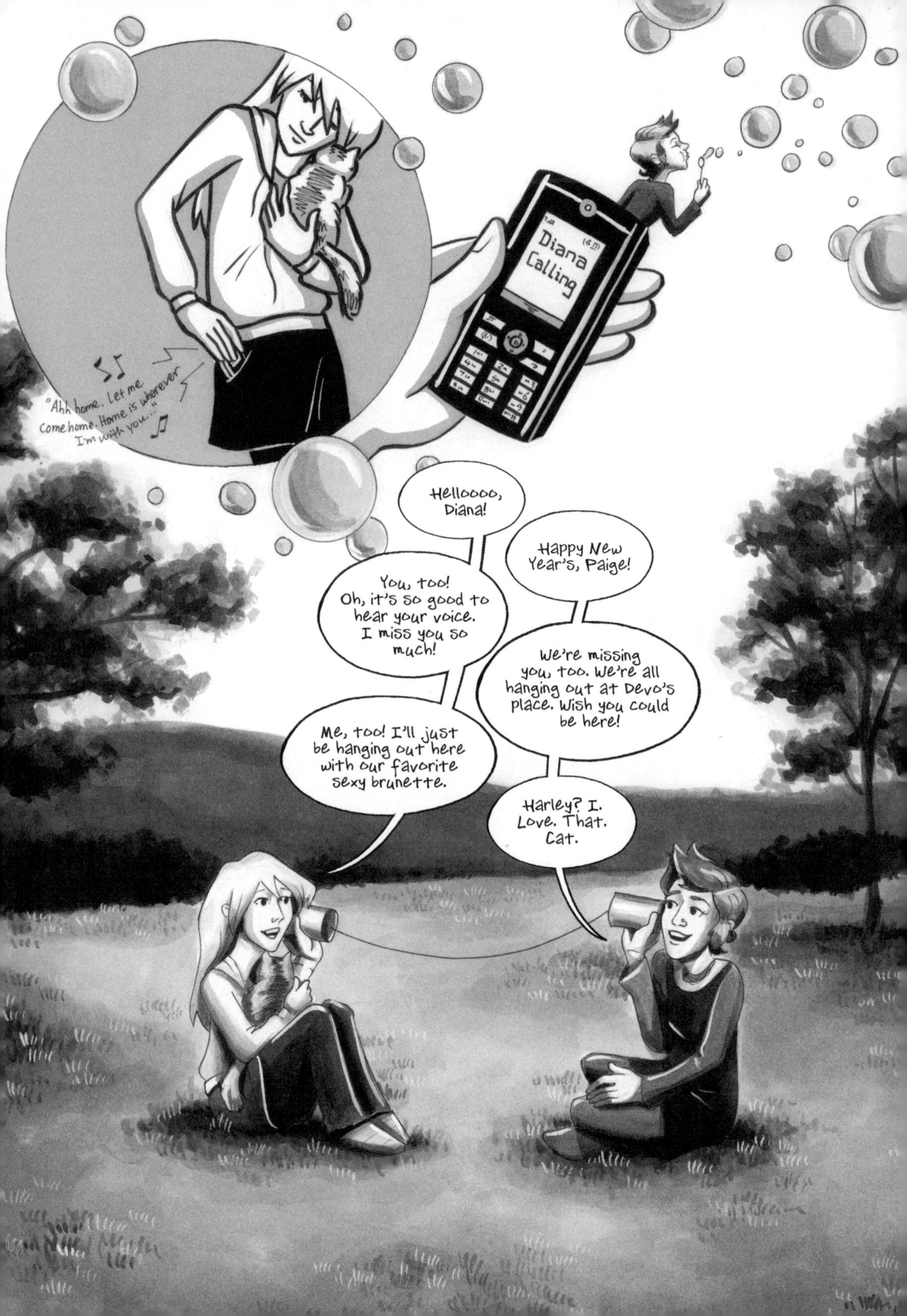
"Ahh home. Let me Come home. Home is wherever I'm with you..."
Diana Calling
Helloooo, Diana!
Happy New Year's, Paige!
You, too! Oh, it's so good to hear your voice. I miss you so much!
We're missing you, too. We're all hanging out at Devo's place. Wish you could be here!
Me, too! I'll just be hanging out here with our favorite sexy brunette.
Harley? I. Love. That. Cat.

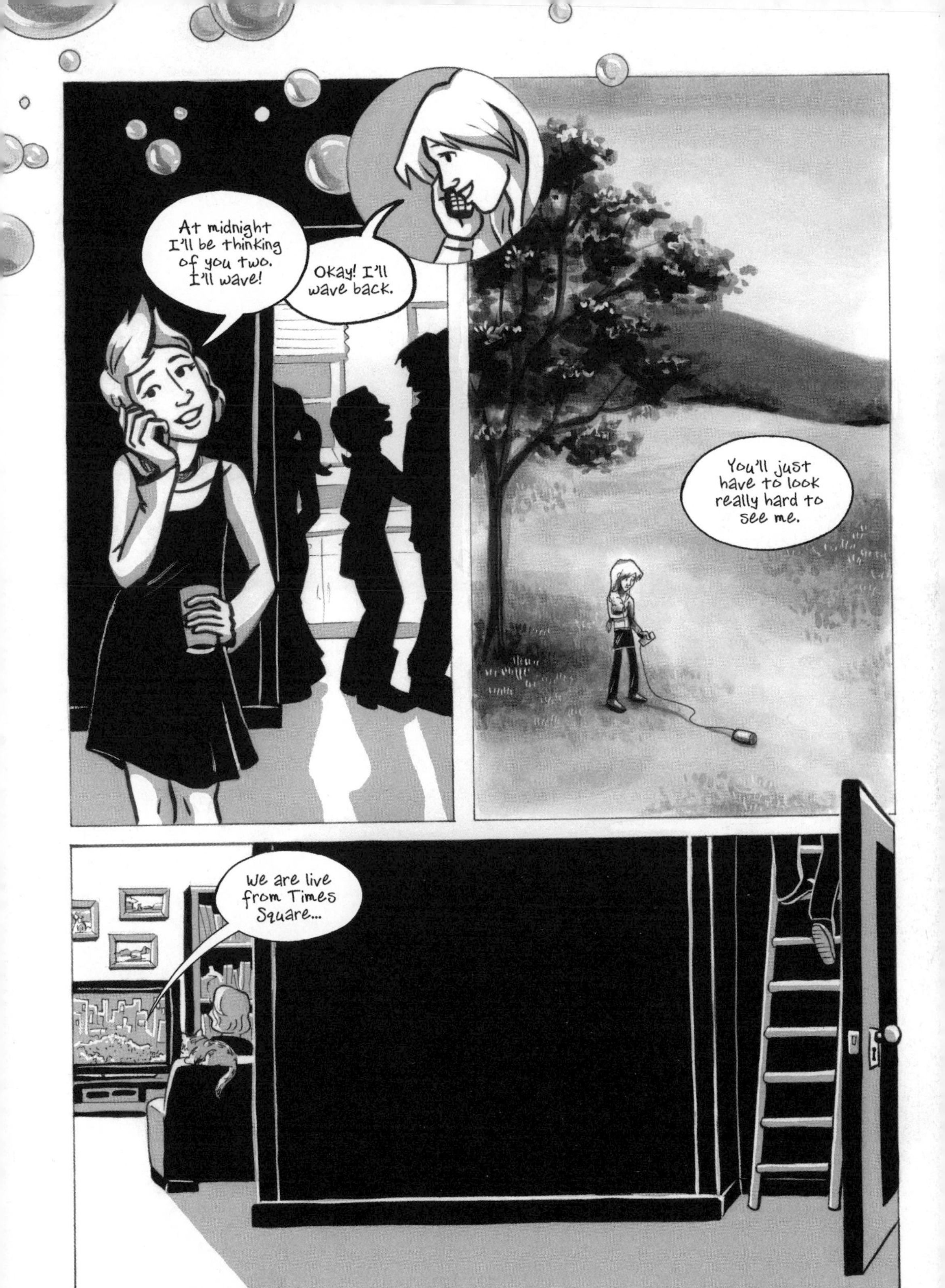
At midnight I'll be thinking of you two. I'll wave!
Okay! I'll wave back.
You'll just have to look really hard to see me.
We are live from Times Square...

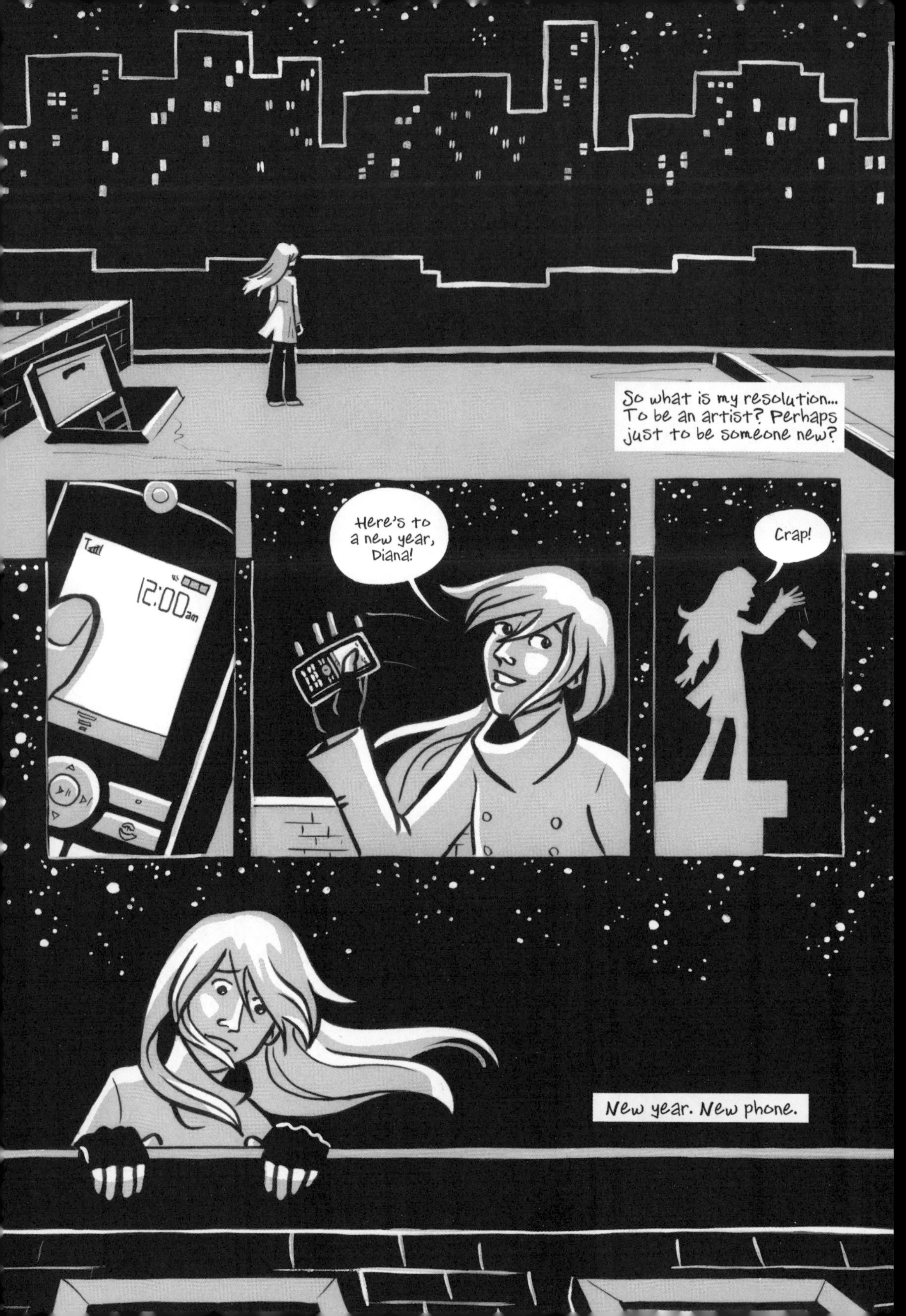
So what is my resolution... To be an artist? Perhaps just to be someone new?
12:00am
Here's to a new year, Diana!
Crap!
New year. New phone.

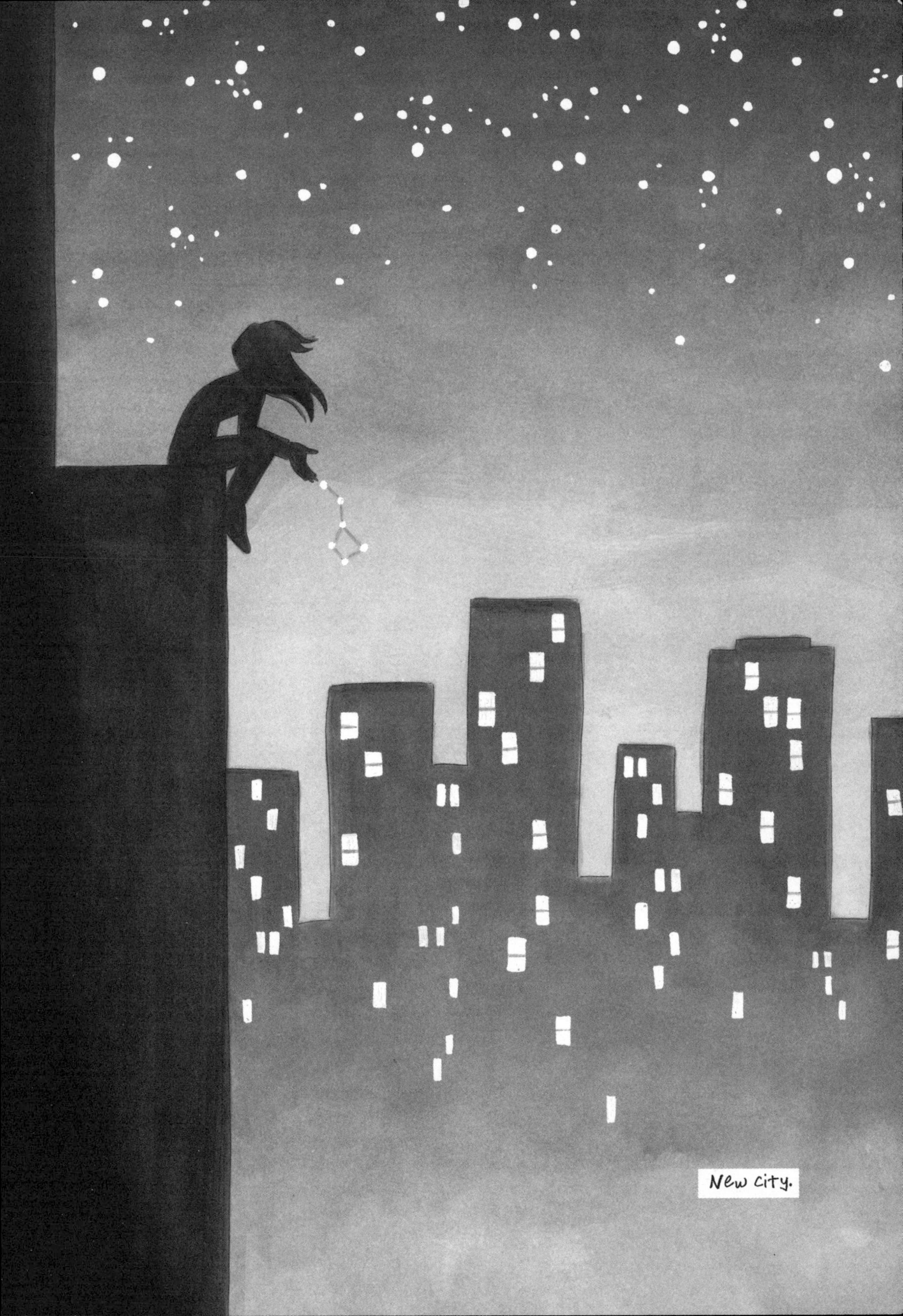
New city.

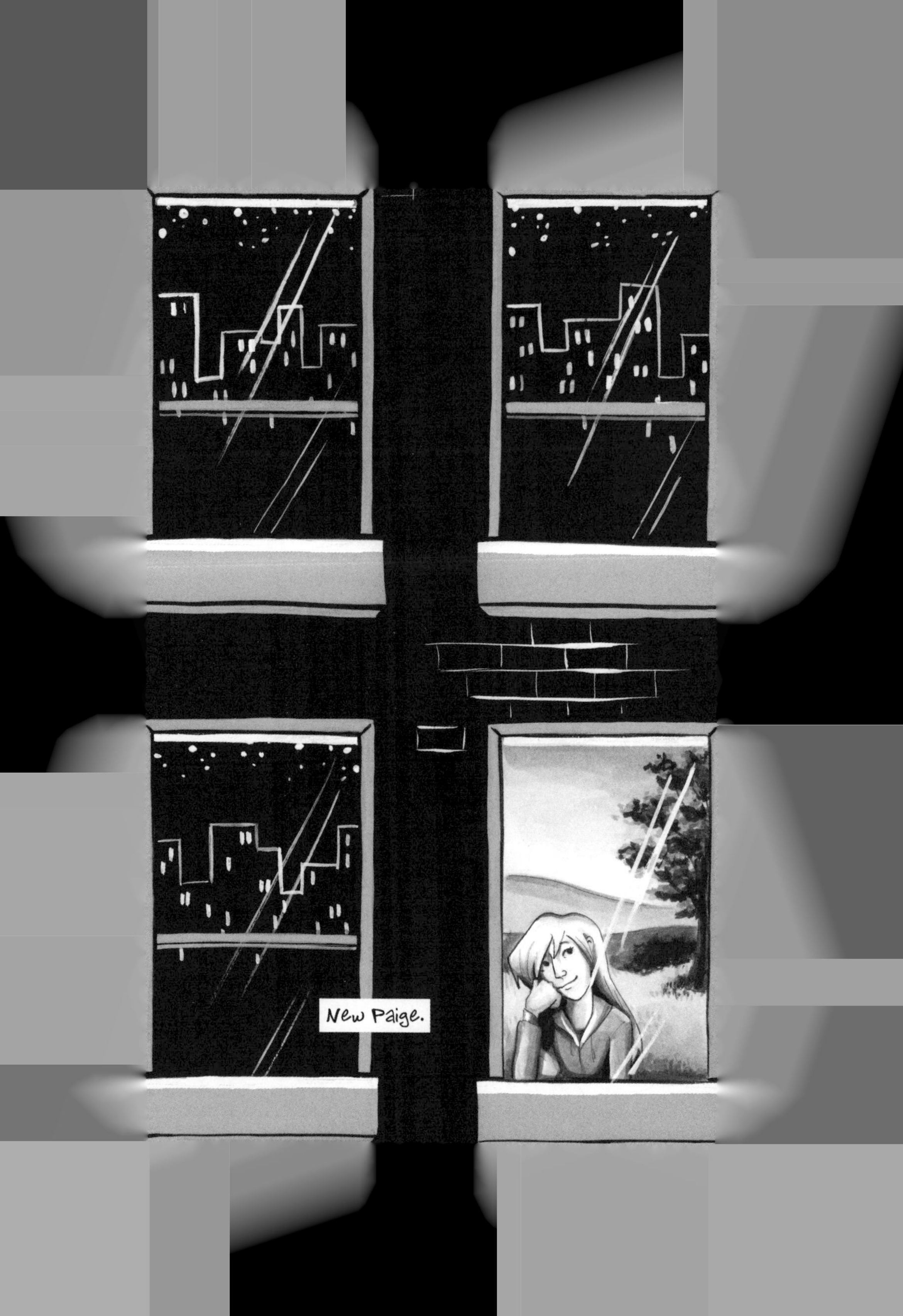
New Paige.

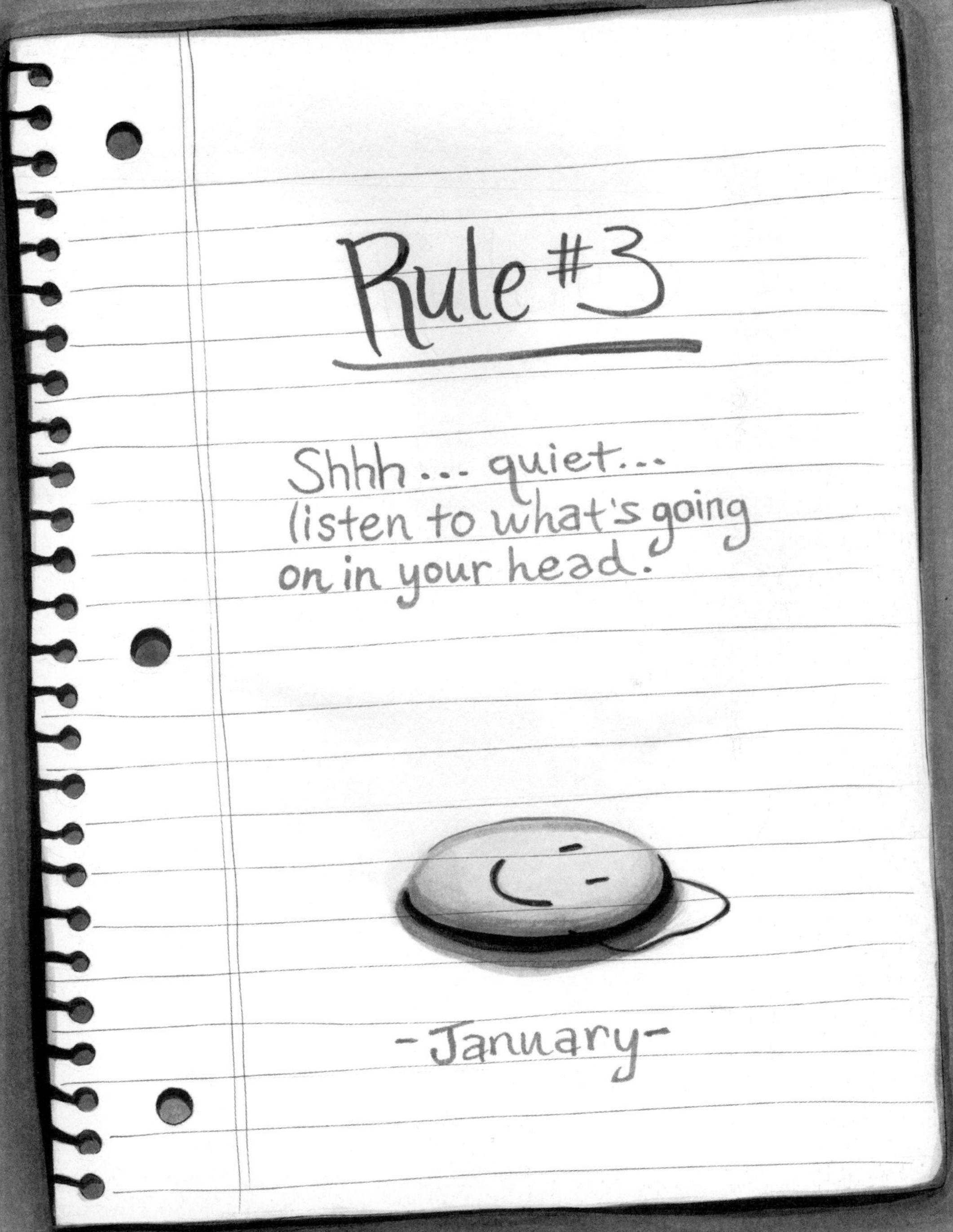
Rule #3
Shhh... quiet...
listen to what's going
on in your head.
-January-

I miss home
stop thinking!
I don't want to start a new school
what if...
try to get some Sleep!
what if I'm really behind?
Sigh.
I miss my old room
shhhh...
I'm not a city girl
what if no one talks to me?
what should I wear?
easier said than done, Grandma
I feel so alone
Don't be so nervous
Why did we move here?
Arrrg!
I don't belong here
shhh...
maybe
I should try counting sheep
It's so loud here
stop thinking
It's so cold here
Why did we have to move in the middle of the school year?
I wonder what Diana is doing
my feet are cold
There aren't enough trees
Why can't I turn my brain off
Shut up!
I miss Diana
I miss my friends
I feel alone, really alone
This sucks.
I miss trees, and mountains
try counting sheep
I don't Know
I can't help but worry about this
I miss my old school
This is unfair!
why did Dad have to get a new job?
Be quiet, me!
what's wrong with the old one
This is totally unfair
blah blah

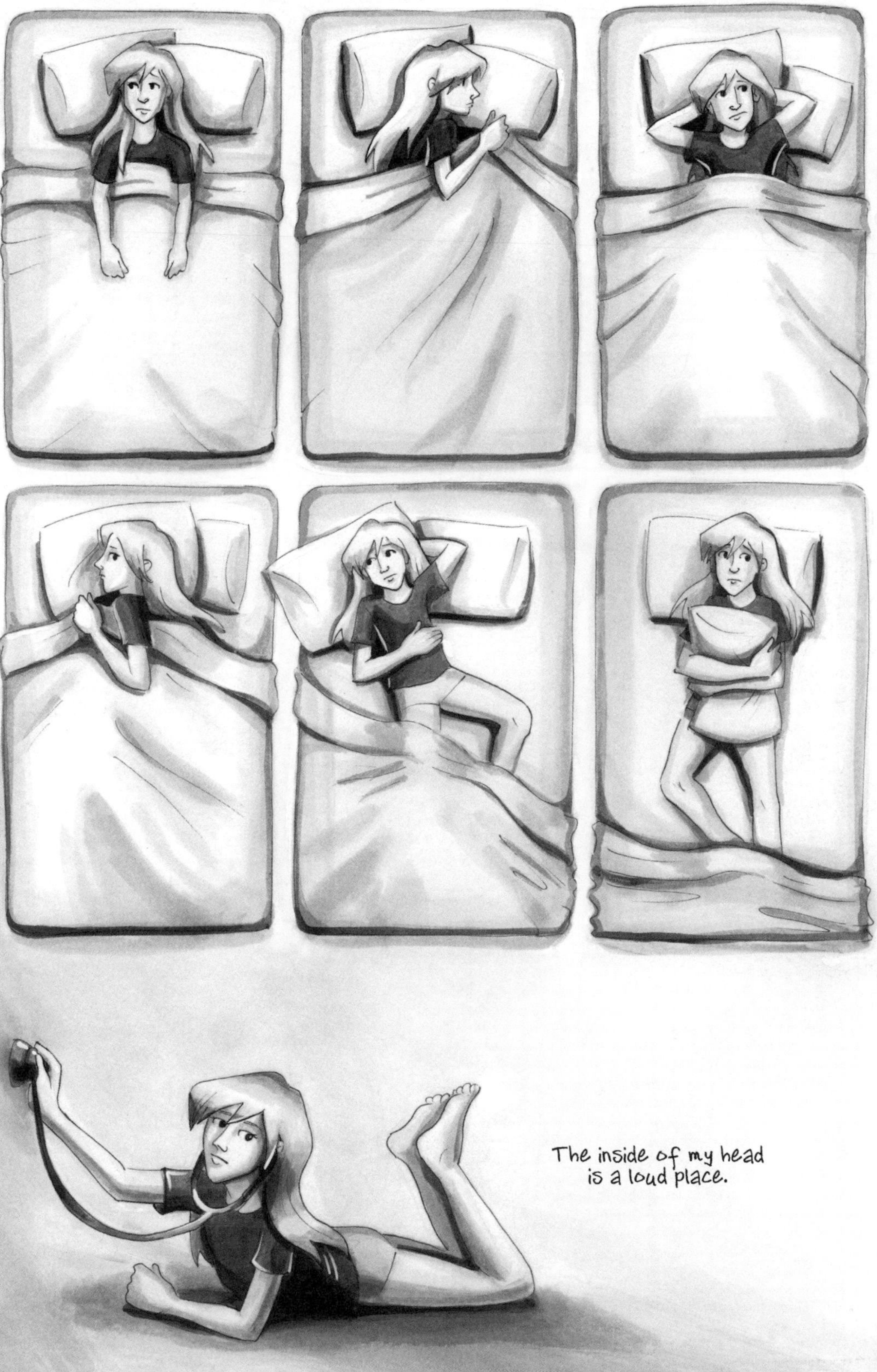
The inside of my head
is a loud place.

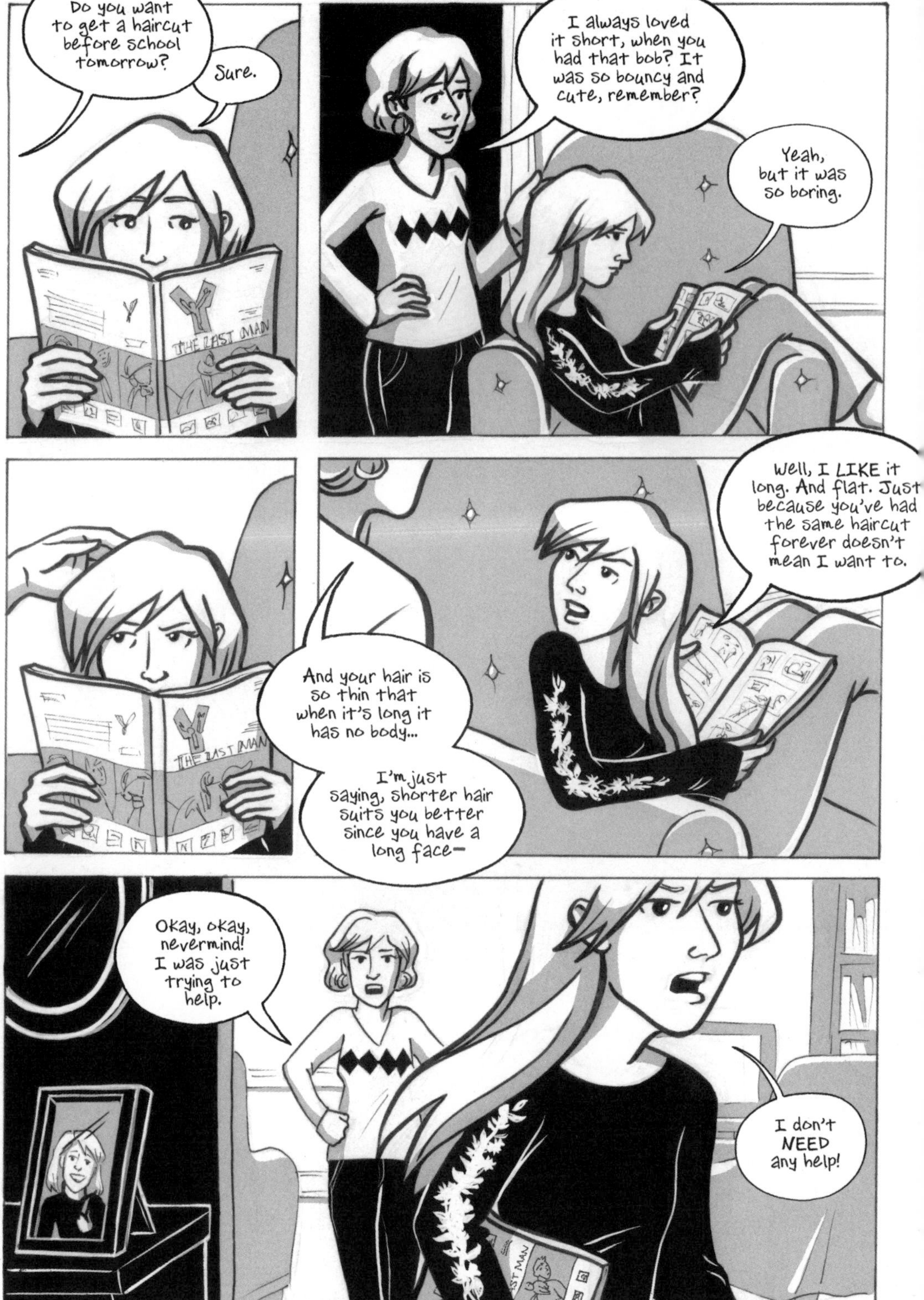

Do you want to get a haircut before school tomorrow?
Sure.
I always loved it short, when you had that bob? It was so bouncy and cute, remember?
Yeah, but it was so boring.
Well, I LIKE it long. And flat. Just because you've had the same haircut forever doesn't mean I want to.
And your hair is so thin that when it's long it has no body...
I'm just saying, shorter hair suits you better since you have a long face—
Okay, okay, nevermind! I was just trying to help.
I don't NEED any help!

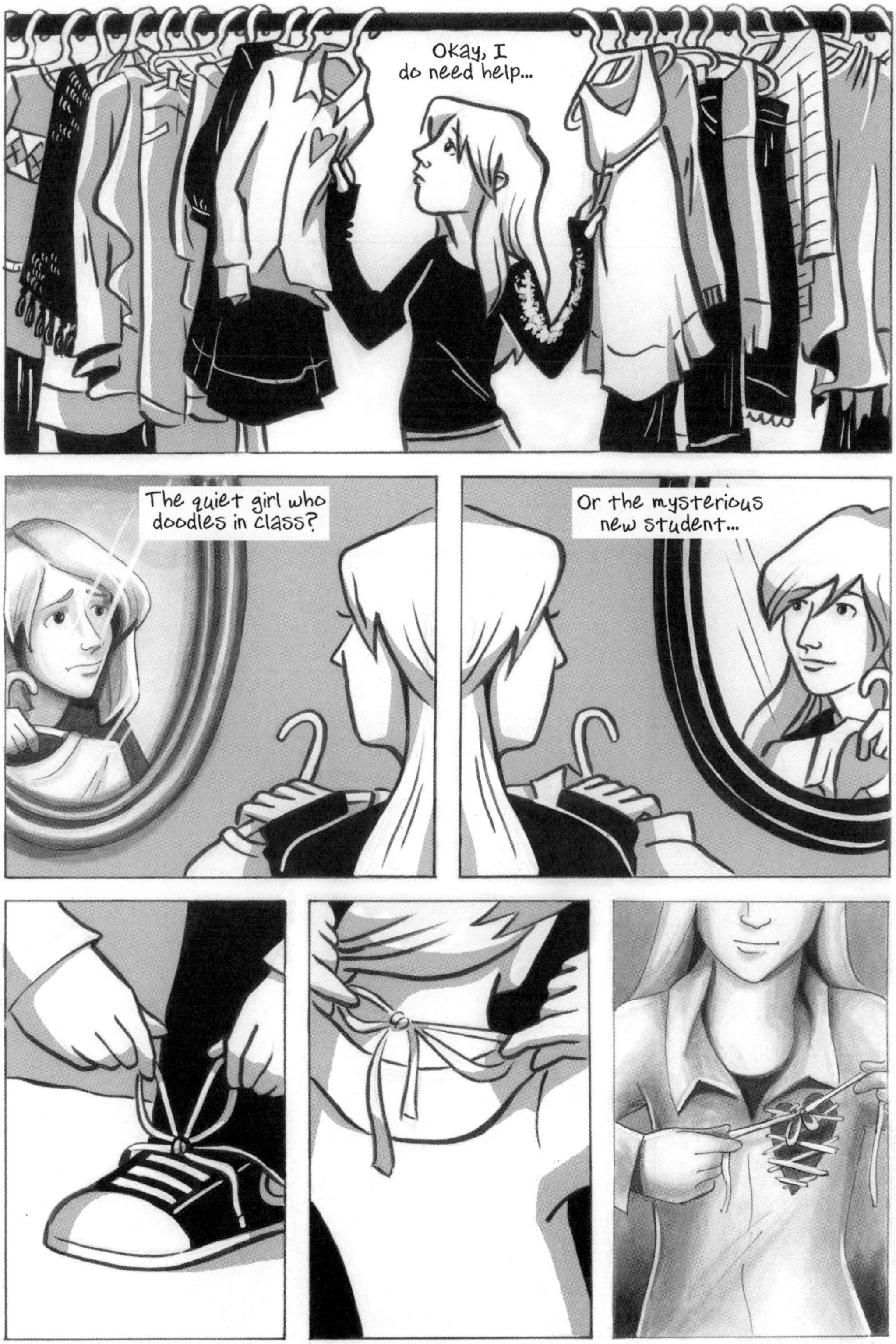
Okay, I do need help...
The quiet girl who doodles in class?
Or the mysterious new student...

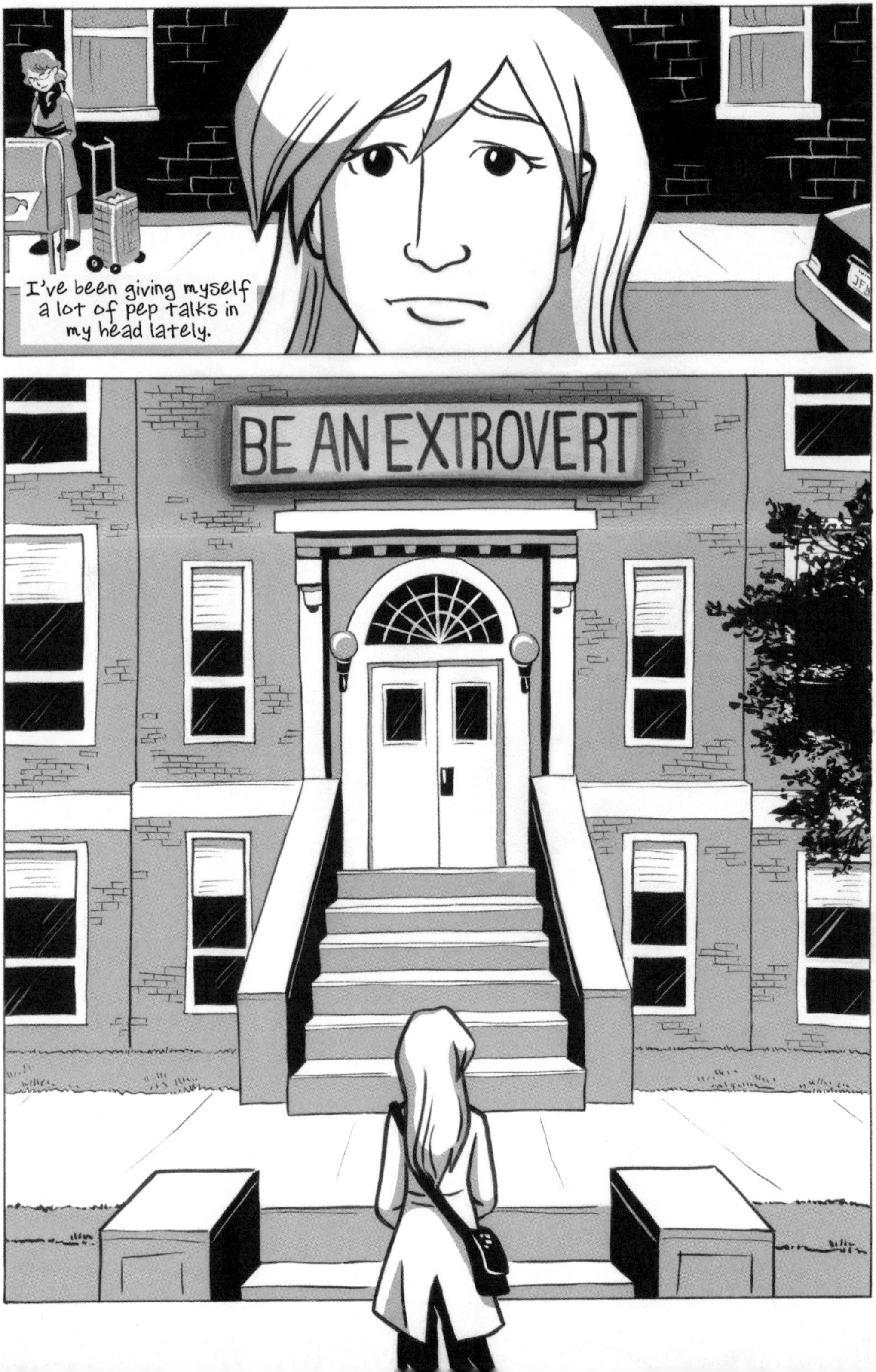
I've been giving myself a lot of pep talks in my head lately.
BE AN EXTROVERT

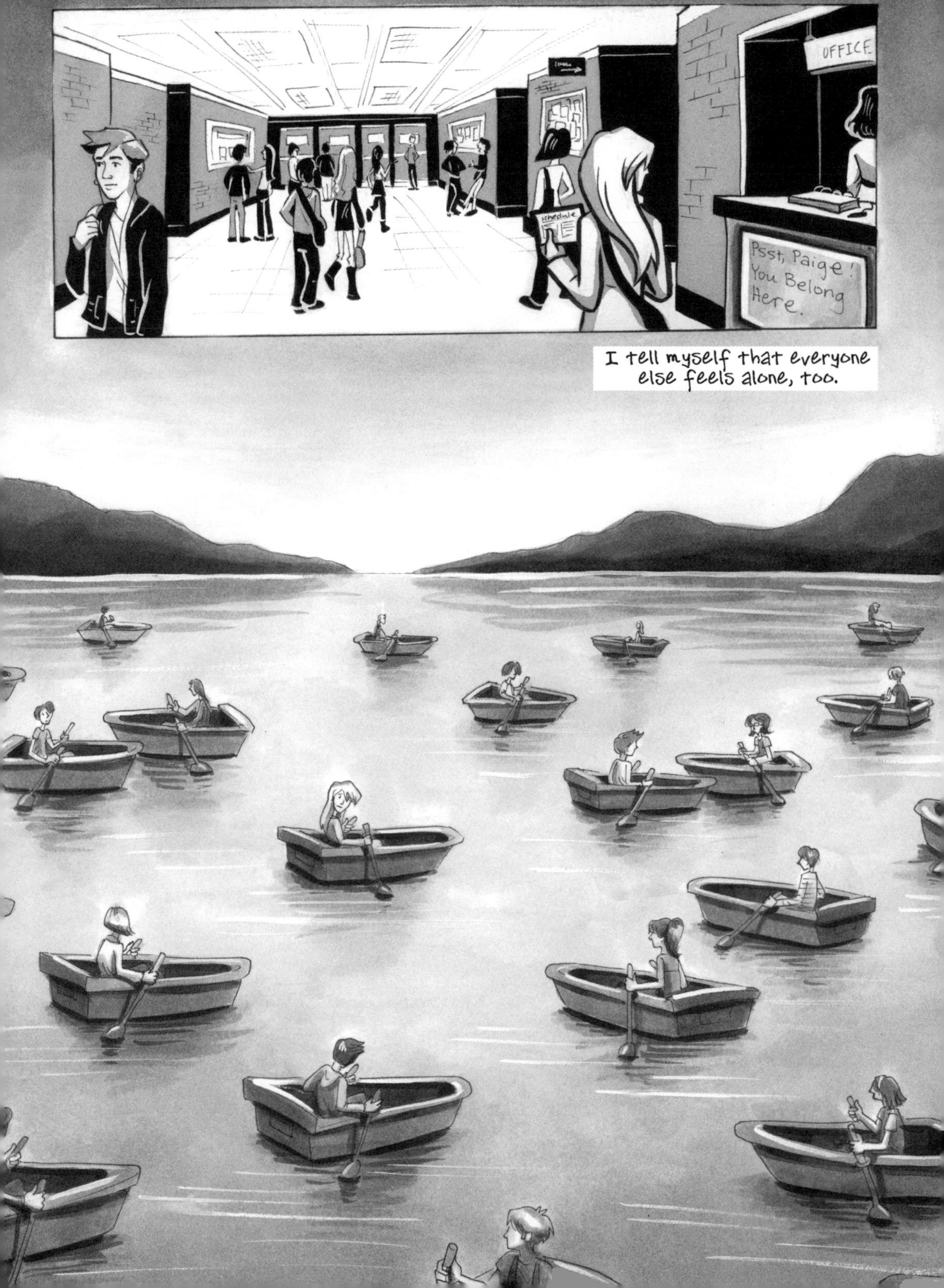
OFFICE
schedule
Psst, Paige! You Belong Here.
I tell myself that everyone else feels alone, too.

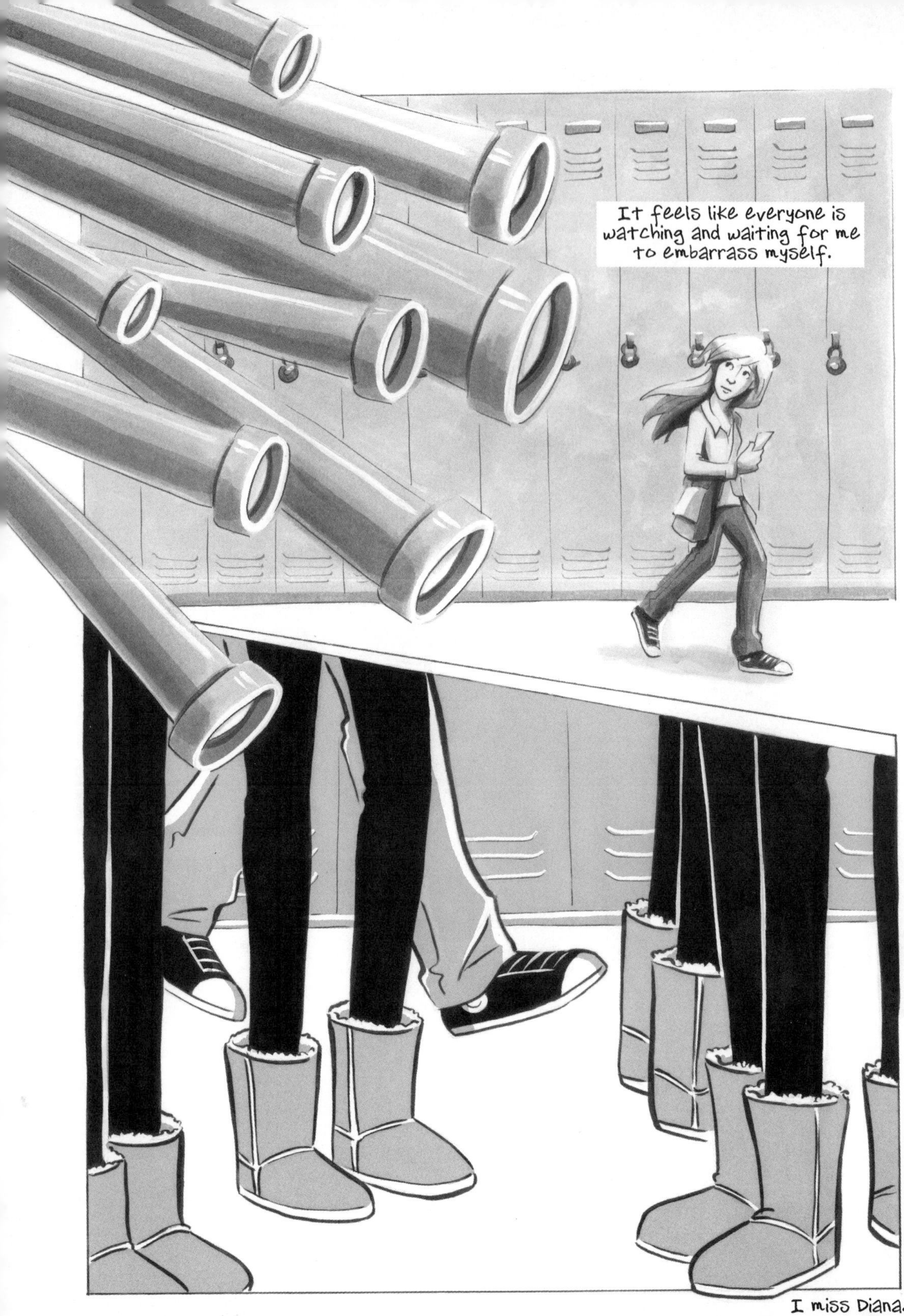
It feels like everyone is watching and waiting for me to embarrass myself.

I miss Diana.

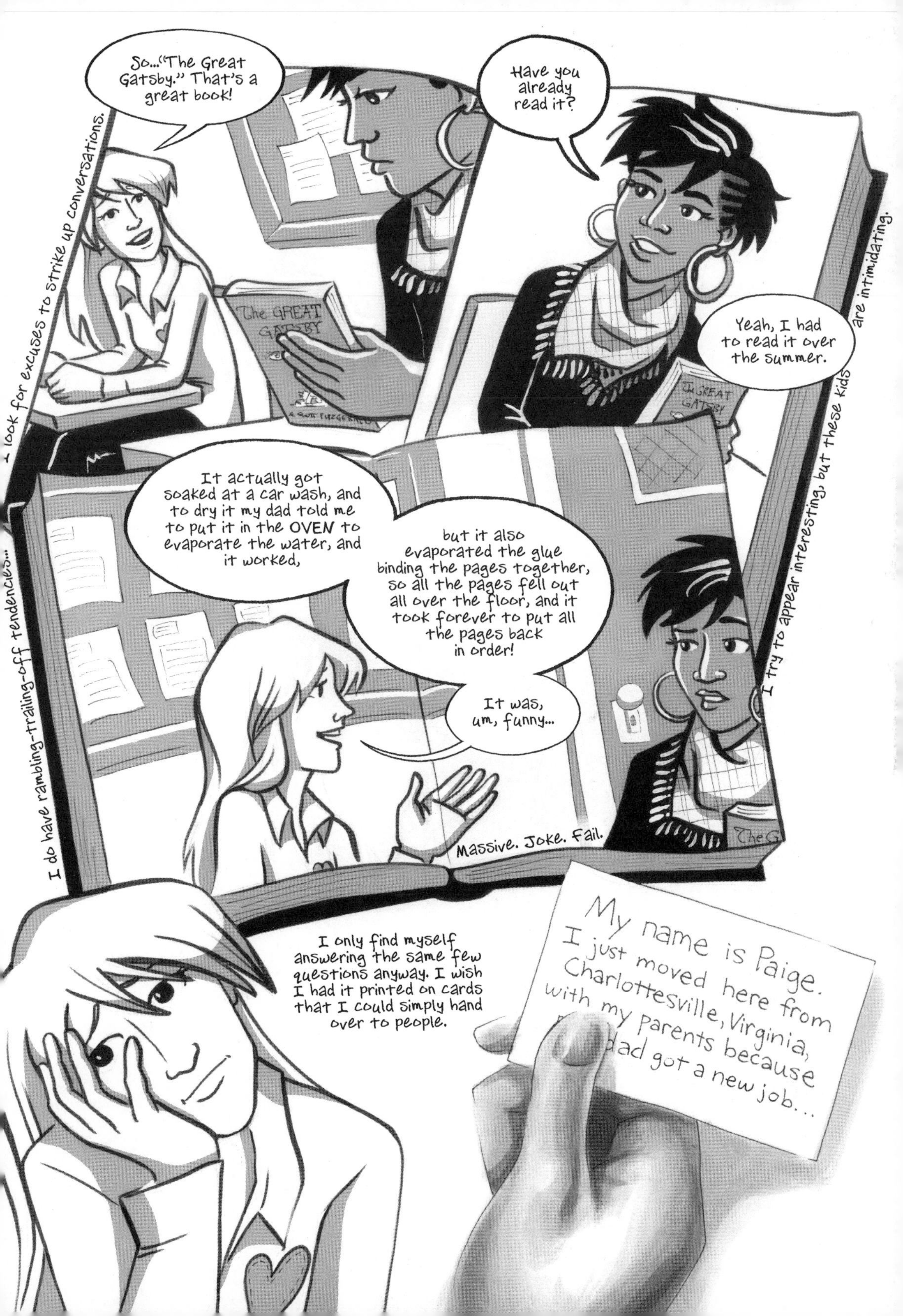
I look for excuses to strike up conversations.
So..."The Great Gatsby." That's a great book!
The GREAT GATSBY
Have you already read it?
I try to appear interesting, but these kids are intimidating.
Yeah, I had to read it over the summer.
The GREAT GATSBY
I do have rambling-trailing-off tendencies...
It actually got soaked at a car wash, and to dry it my dad told me to put it in the OVEN to evaporate the water, and it worked,
but it also evaporated the glue binding the pages together, so all the pages fell out all over the floor, and it took forever to put all the pages back in order!
It was, um, funny...
Massive. Joke. Fail.
I only find myself answering the same few questions anyway. I wish I had it printed on cards that I could simply hand over to people.
My name is Paige. I just moved here from Charlottesville, Virginia, with my parents because
dad got a new job...

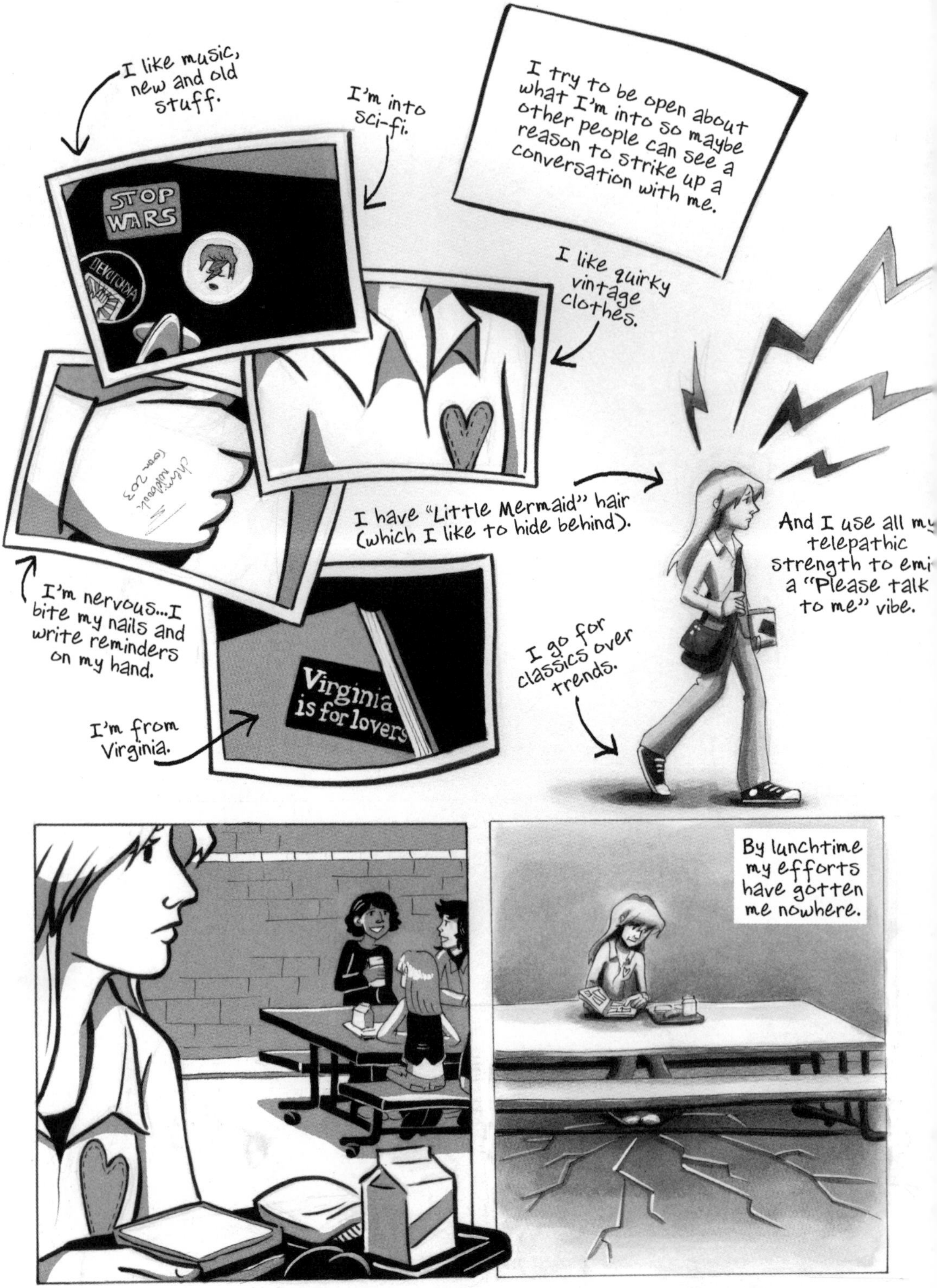

I like music, new and old stuff.
STOP WARS
I'm into sci-fi.
I try to be open about what I'm into so maybe other people can see a reason to strike up a conversation with me.
I like quirky vintage clothes.
I have "Little Mermaid" hair (which I like to hide behind).
And I use all m telepathic strength to emi a "Please talk to me" vibe.
I'm nervous...I bite my nails and write reminders on my hand.
I go for classics over trends.
I'm from Virginia.
Virginia is for lovers
By lunchtime my efforts have gotten me nowhere.

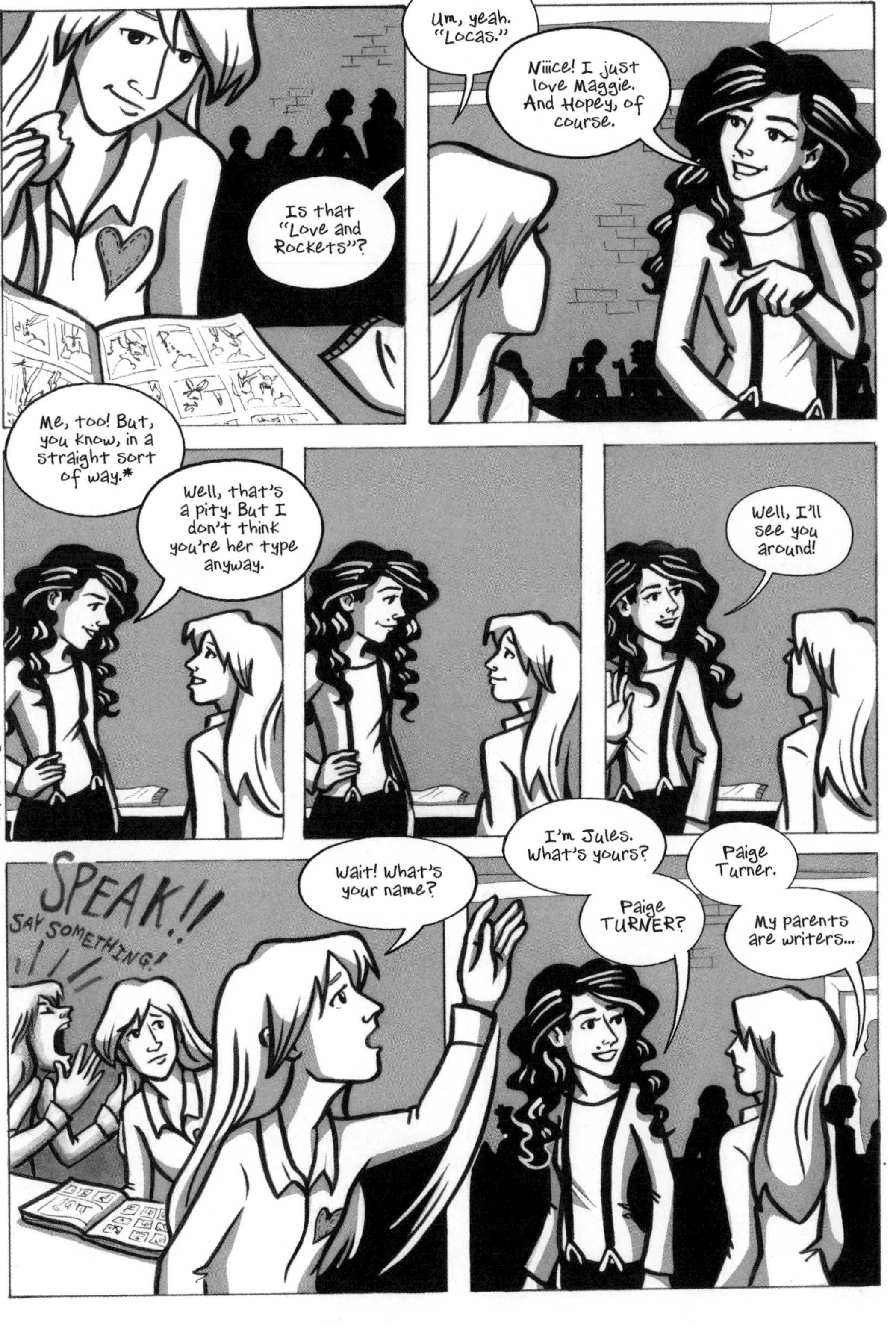
Is that "Love and Rockets"?
Um, yeah. "Locas."
Niiice! I just love Maggie. And Hopey, of course.
Me, too! But, you know, in a straight sort of way.*
Well, that's a pity. But I don't think you're her type anyway.
Well, I'll see you around!
SPEAK!!
SAY SOMETHING!
Wait! What's your name?
I'm Jules. What's yours?
Paige Turner.
Paige TURNER?
My parents are writers...

*Hopey is gay.

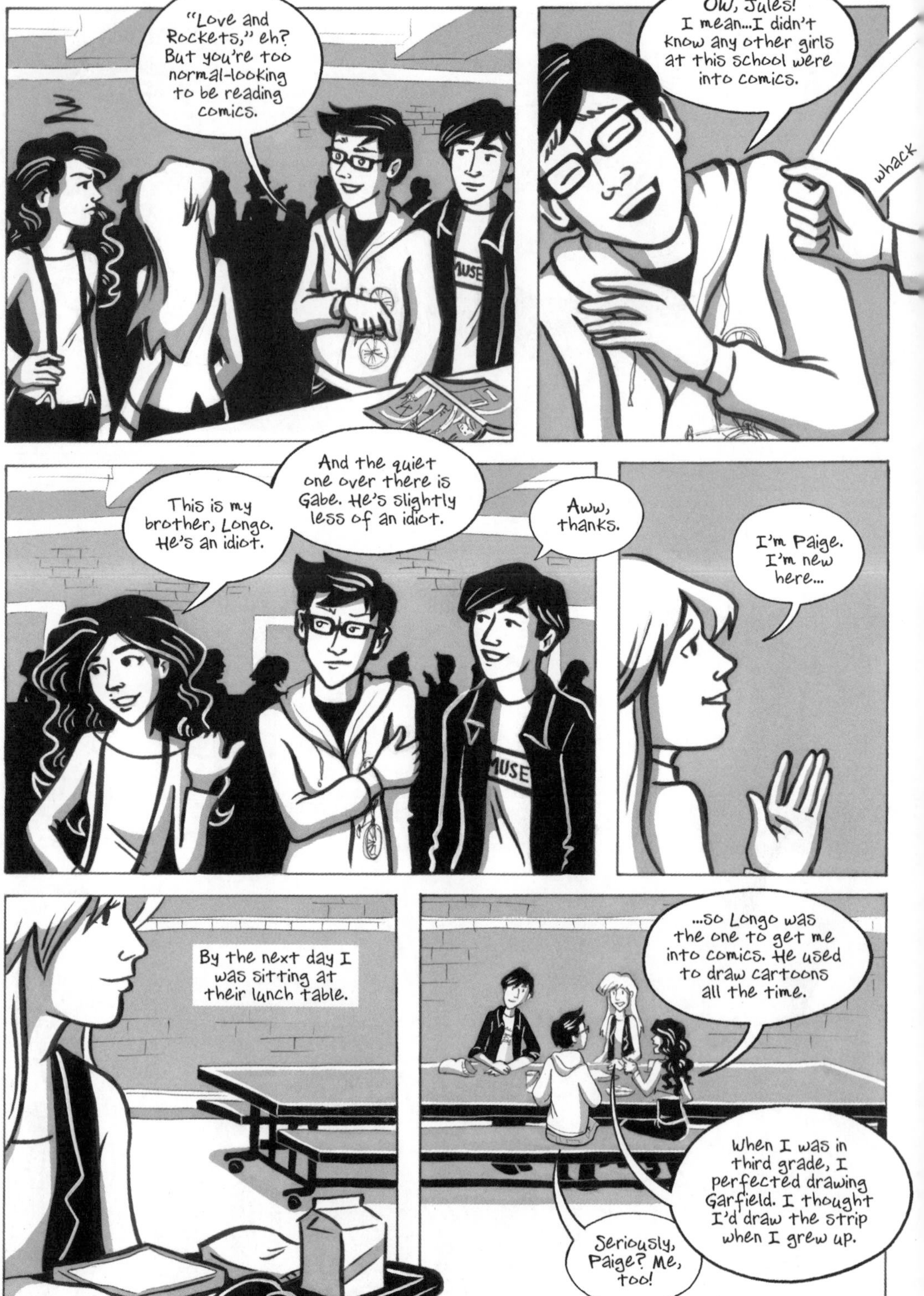
"Love and Rockets," eh? But you're too normal-looking to be reading comics.
OW, Jules! I mean...I didn't know any other girls at this school were into comics.
whack
This is my brother, Longo. He's an idiot.
And the quiet one over there is Gabe. He's slightly less of an idiot.
Aww, thanks.
I'm Paige. I'm new here...
By the next day I was sitting at their lunch table.
...so Longo was the one to get me into comics. He used to draw cartoons all the time.
When I was in third grade, I perfected drawing Garfield. I thought I'd draw the strip when I grew up.
Seriously, Paige? Me, too!

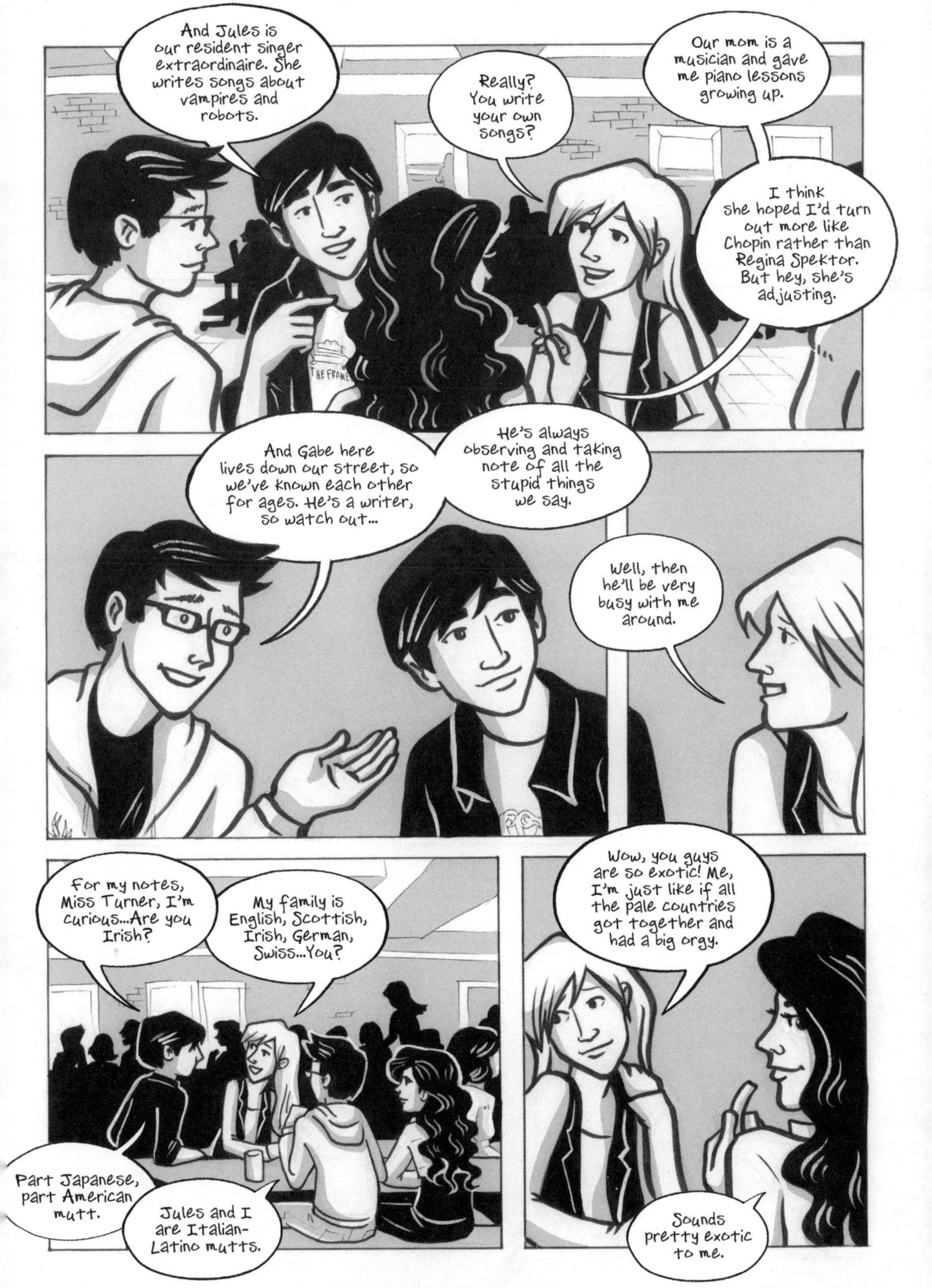
And Jules is our resident singer extraordinaire. She writes songs about vampires and robots.
Really? You write your own songs?
Our mom is a musician and gave me piano lessons growing up.
I think she hoped I'd turn out more like Chopin rather than Regina Spektor. But hey, she's adjusting.
THE FRAME
And Gabe here lives down our street, so we've known each other for ages. He's a writer, so watch out...
He's always observing and taking note of all the stupid things we say.
Well, then he'll be very busy with me around.
For my notes, Miss Turner, I'm curious...Are you Irish?
My family is English, Scottish, Irish, German, Swiss...You?
Part Japanese, part American mutt.
Jules and I are Italian-Latino mutts.
Wow, you guys are so exotic! Me, I'm just like if all the pale countries got together and had a big orgy.
Sounds pretty exotic to me.

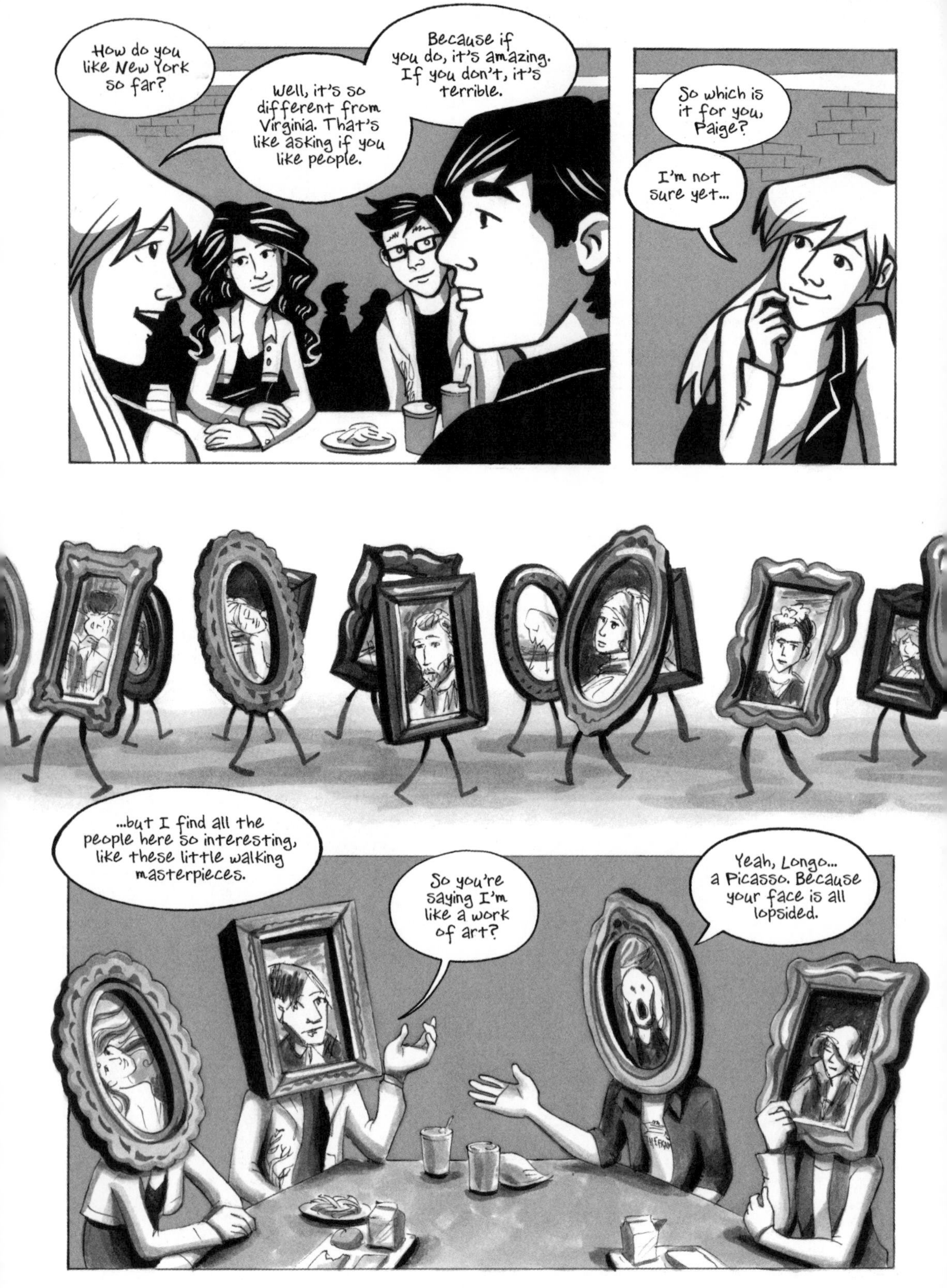
How do you like New York so far?
Well, it's so different from Virginia. That's like asking if you like people.
Because if you do, it's amazing. If you don't, it's terrible.
So which is it for you, Paige?
I'm not sure yet...
...but I find all the people here so interesting, like these little walking masterpieces.
So you're saying I'm like a work of art?
Yeah, Longo... a Picasso. Because your face is all lopsided.

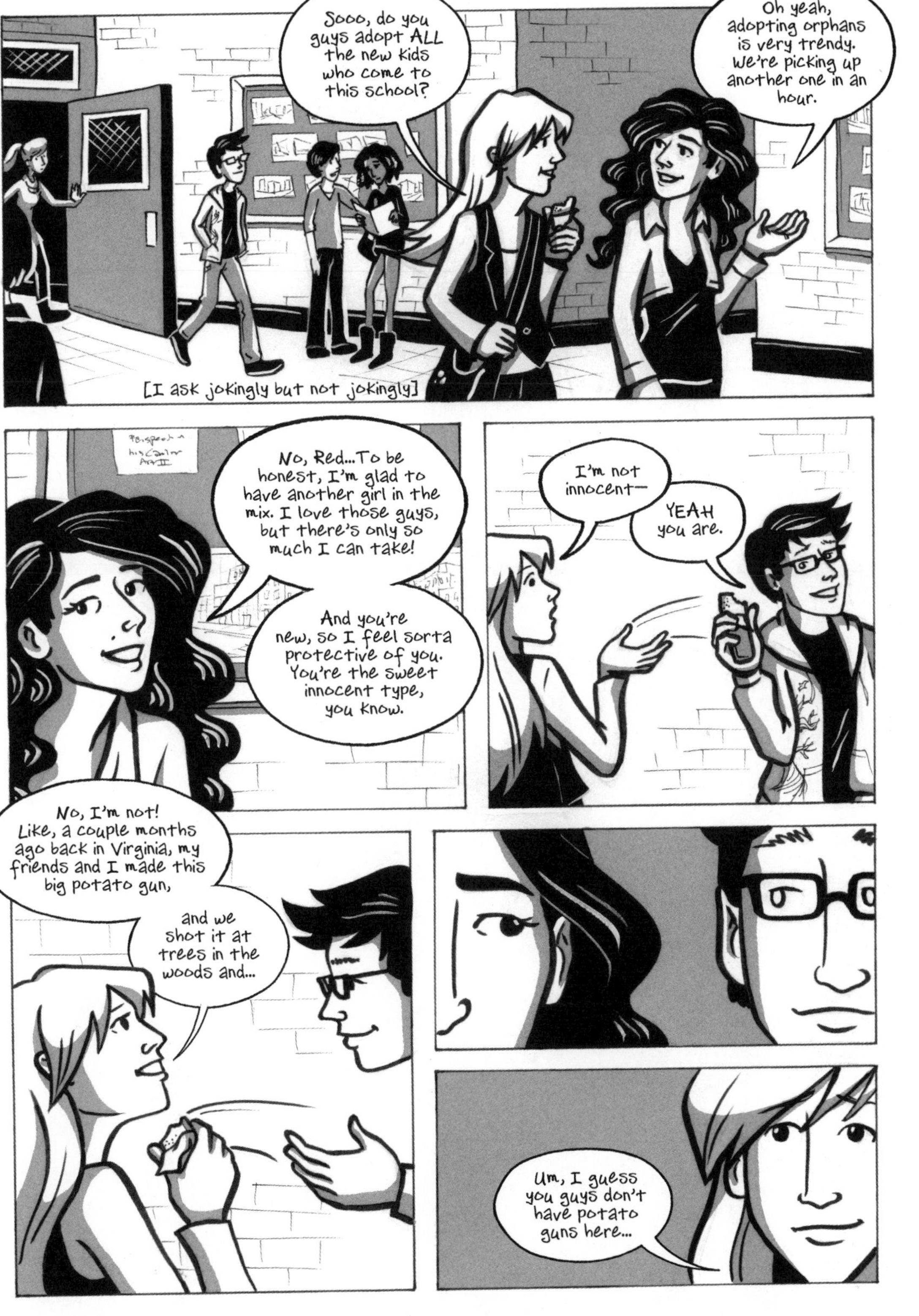

Sooo, do you guys adopt ALL the new kids who come to this school?
Oh yeah, adopting orphans is very trendy. We're picking up another one in an hour.
[I ask jokingly but not jokingly]
No, Red...To be honest, I'm glad to have another girl in the mix. I love those guys, but there's only so much I can take!
And you're new, so I feel sorta protective of you. You're the sweet innocent type, you know.
I'm not innocent—
YEAH you are.
No, I'm not! Like, a couple months ago back in Virginia, my friends and I made this big potato gun,
and we shot it at trees in the woods and...
Um, I guess you guys don't have potato guns here...

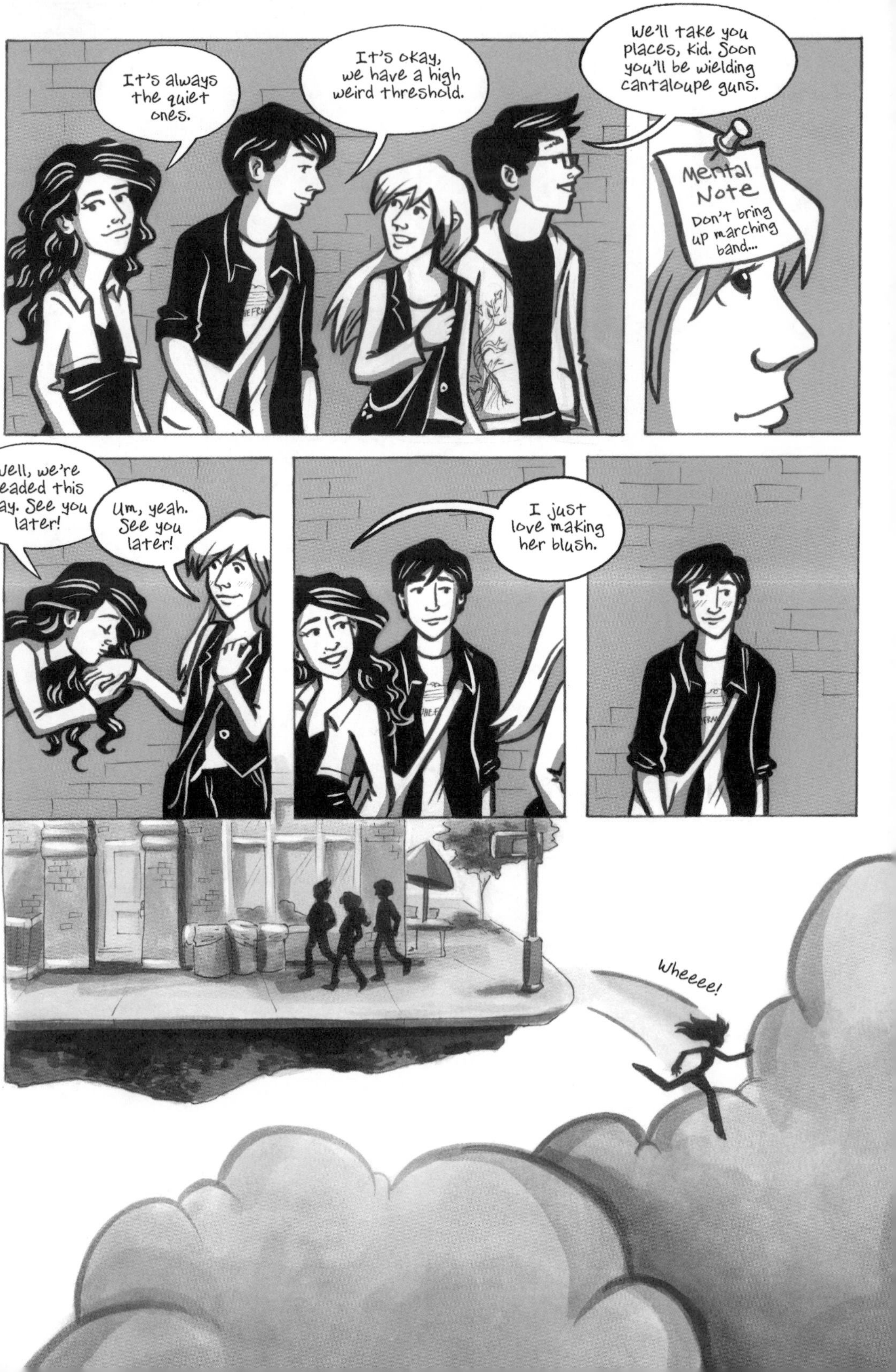
It's always the quiet ones.
It's okay, we have a high weird threshold.
We'll take you places, kid. Soon you'll be wielding cantaloupe guns.
Mental Note
Don't bring up marching band...
Well, we're headed this way. See you later!
Um, yeah. See you later!
I just love making her blush.
Wheeee!

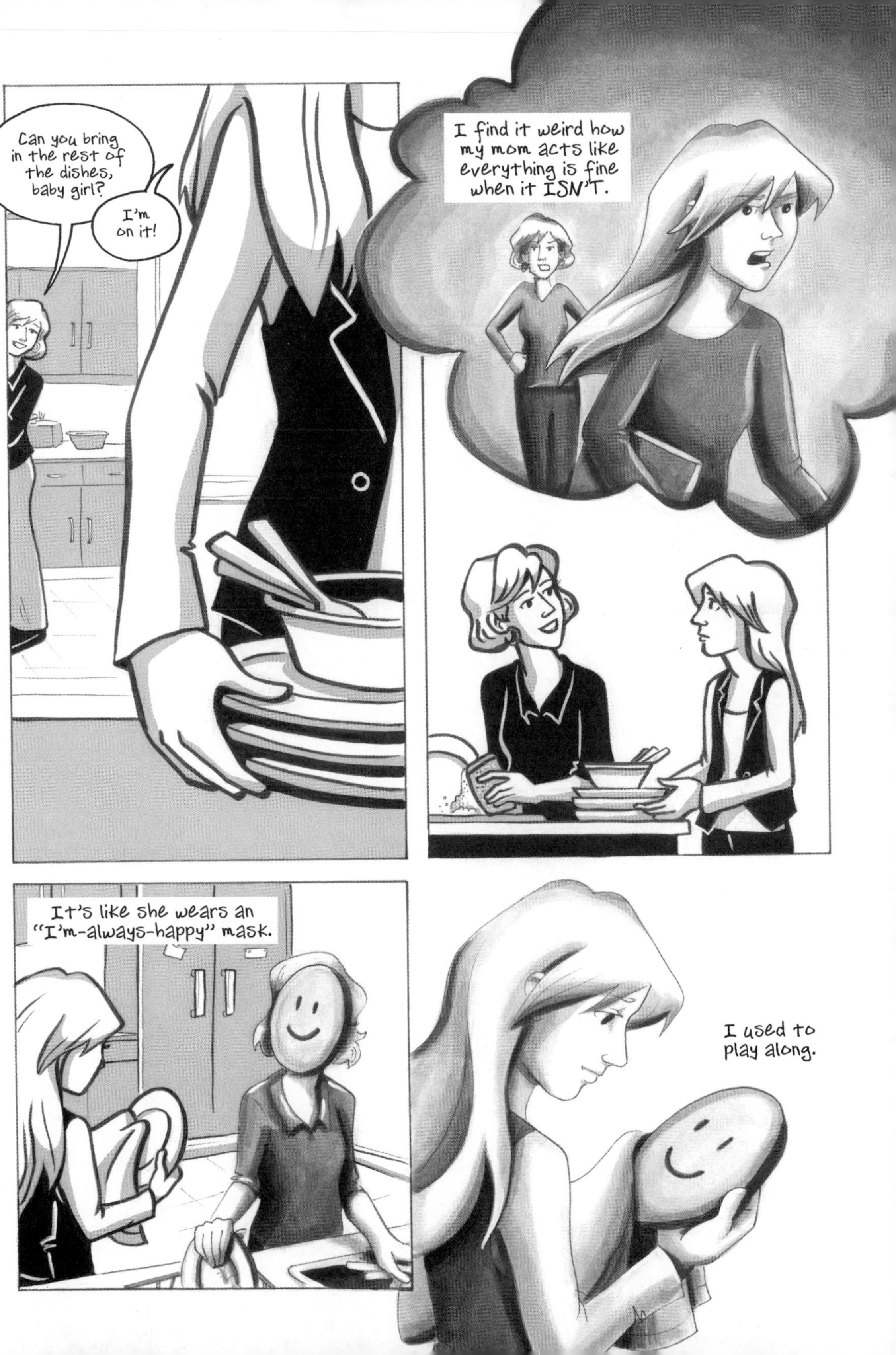
Can you bring in the rest of the dishes, baby girl?
I'm on it!
I find it weird how my mom acts like everything is fine when it ISN'T.
It's like she wears an "I'm-always-happy" mask.
I used to play along.

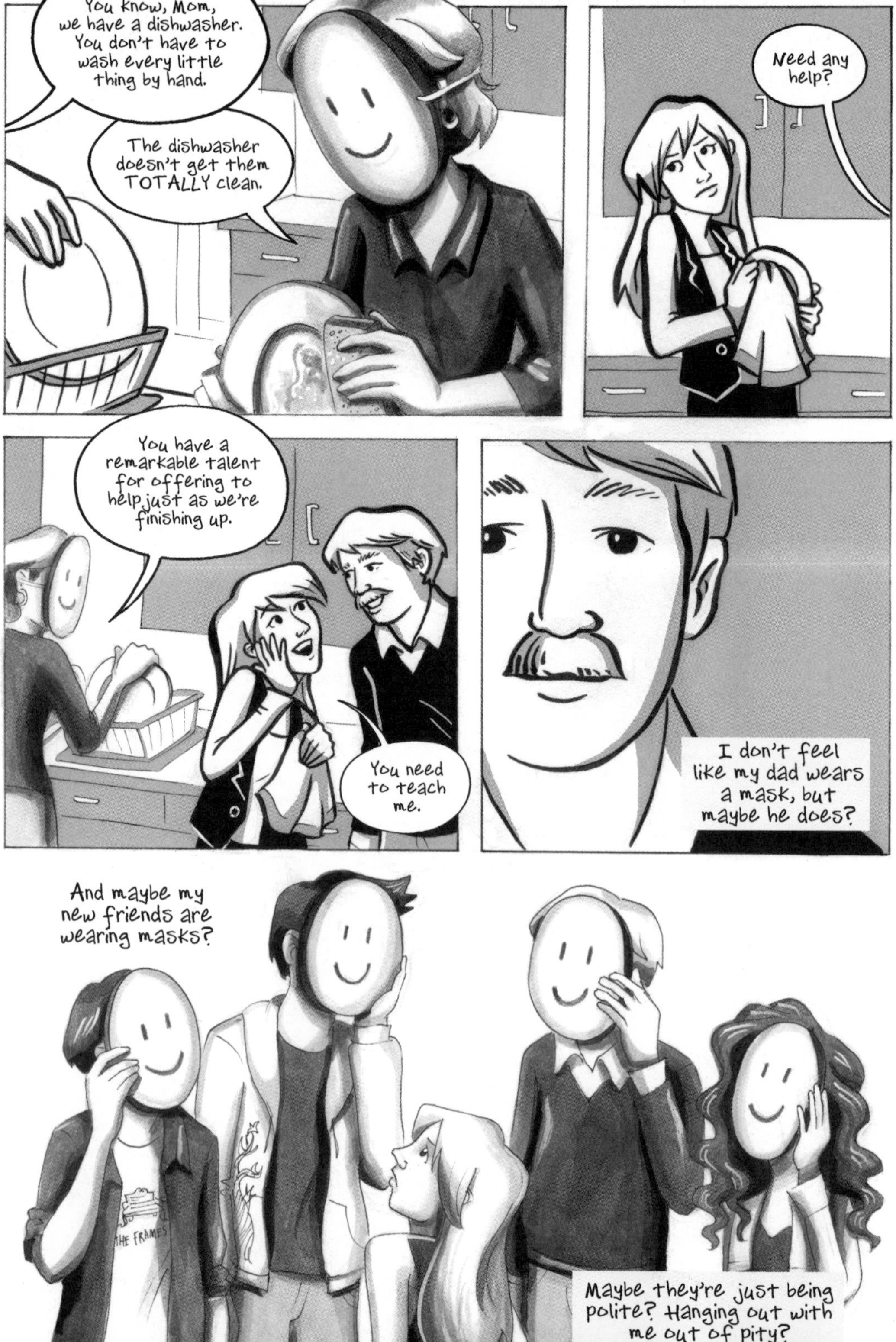
You know, Mom, we have a dishwasher. You don't have to wash every little thing by hand.
The dishwasher doesn't get them TOTALLY clean.
Need any help?
You have a remarkable talent for offering to help just as we're finishing up.
You need to teach me.
I don't feel like my dad wears a mask, but maybe he does?
And maybe my new friends are wearing masks?
THE FRAMES
Maybe they're just being polite? Hanging out with me out of pity?

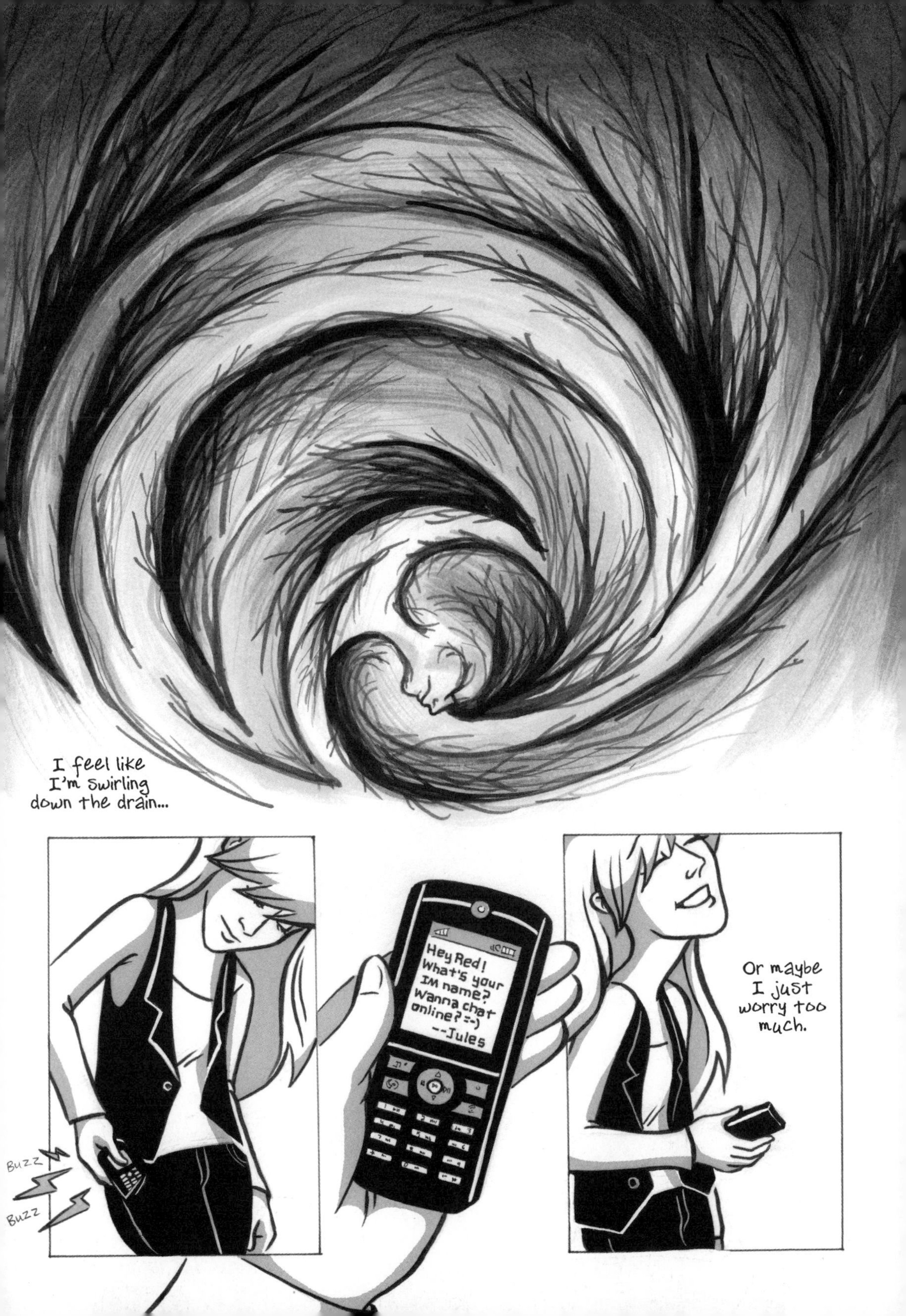

I feel like
I'm swirling
down the drain...
Buzz
Buzz
Hey Red!
What's your
IM name?
Wanna chat
online? :-)
--Jules
Or maybe
I just
worry too
much.

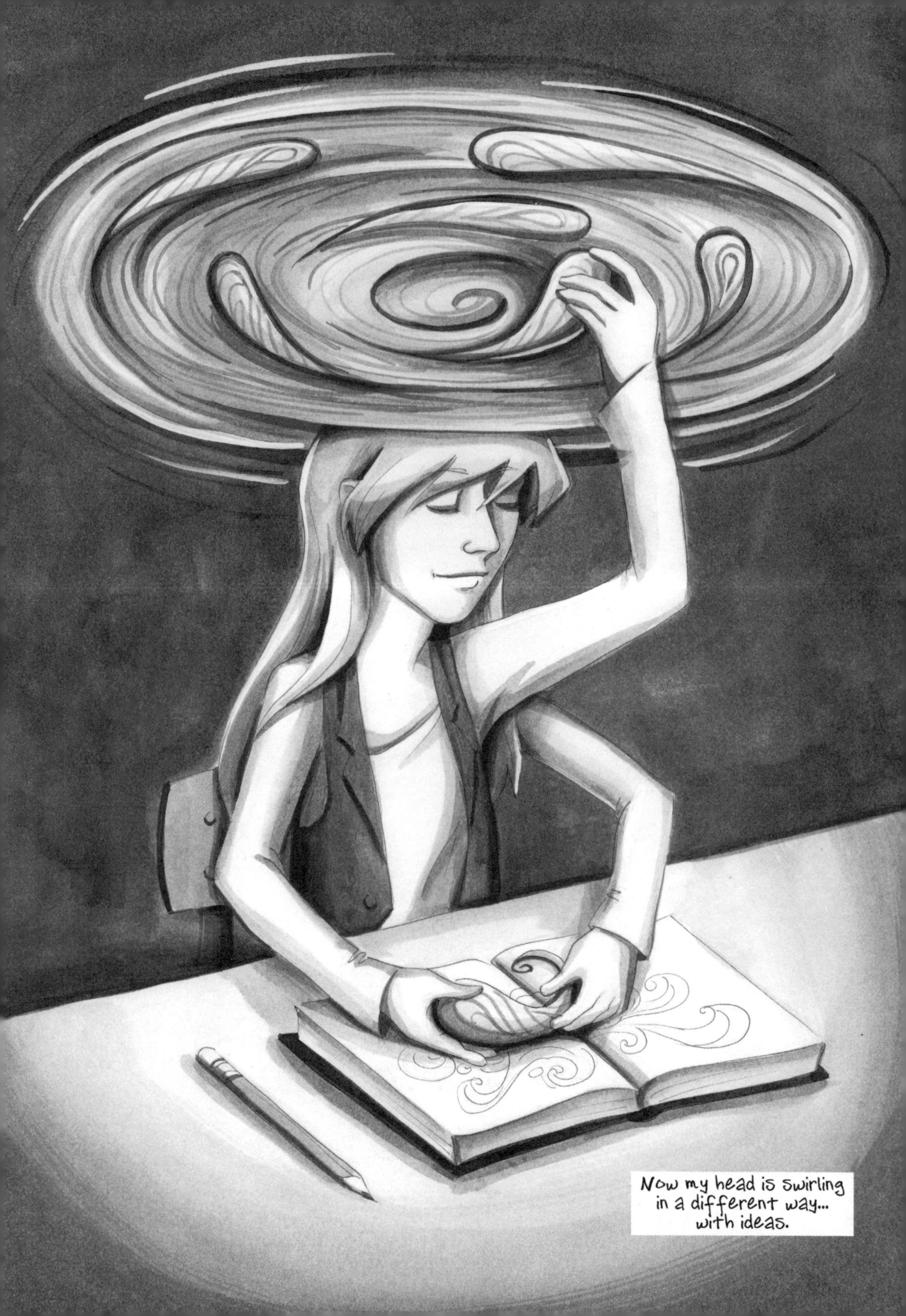
Now my head is swirling in a different way... with ideas.

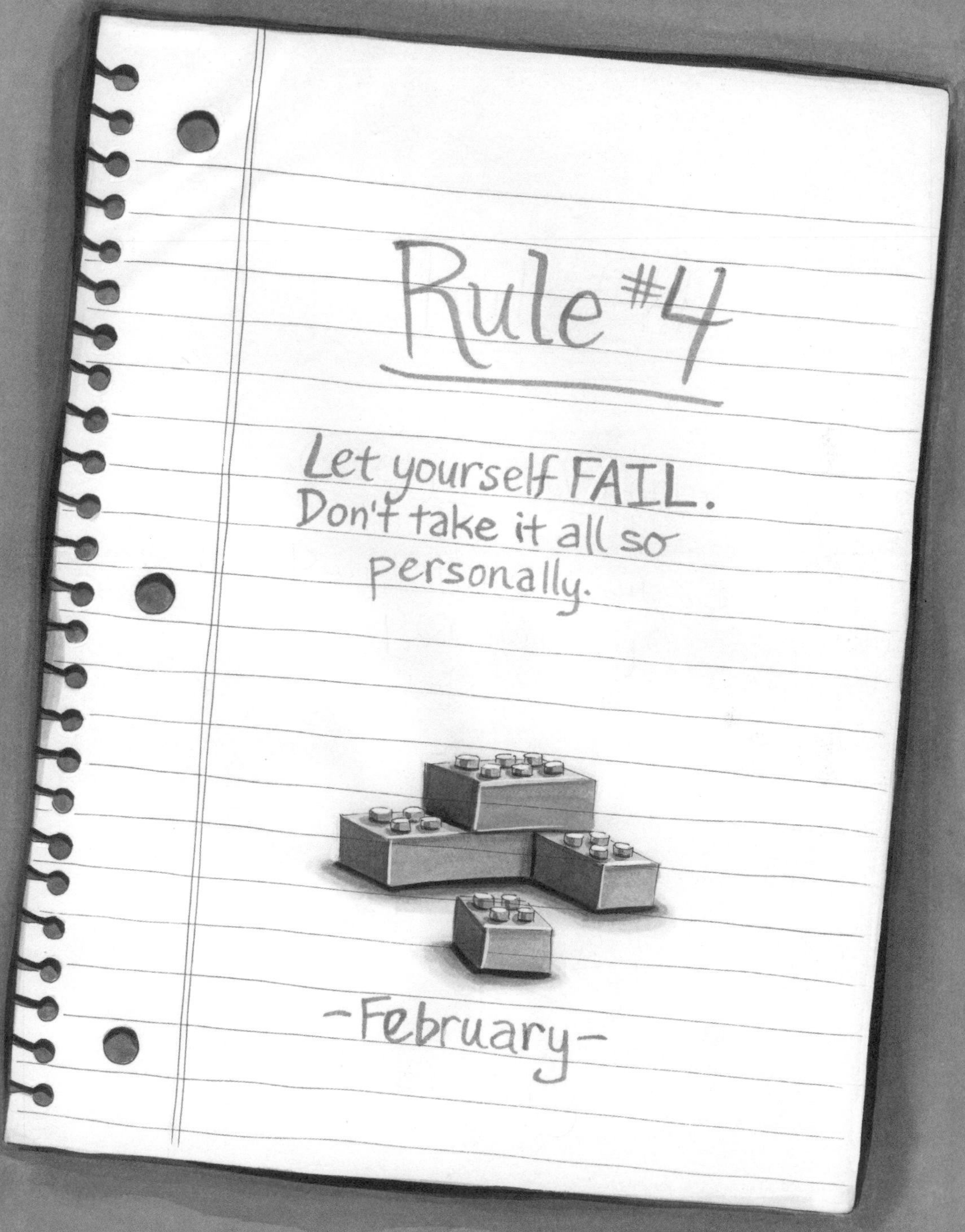
Rule #4
Let yourself FAIL.
Don't take it all so
personally.
-February-

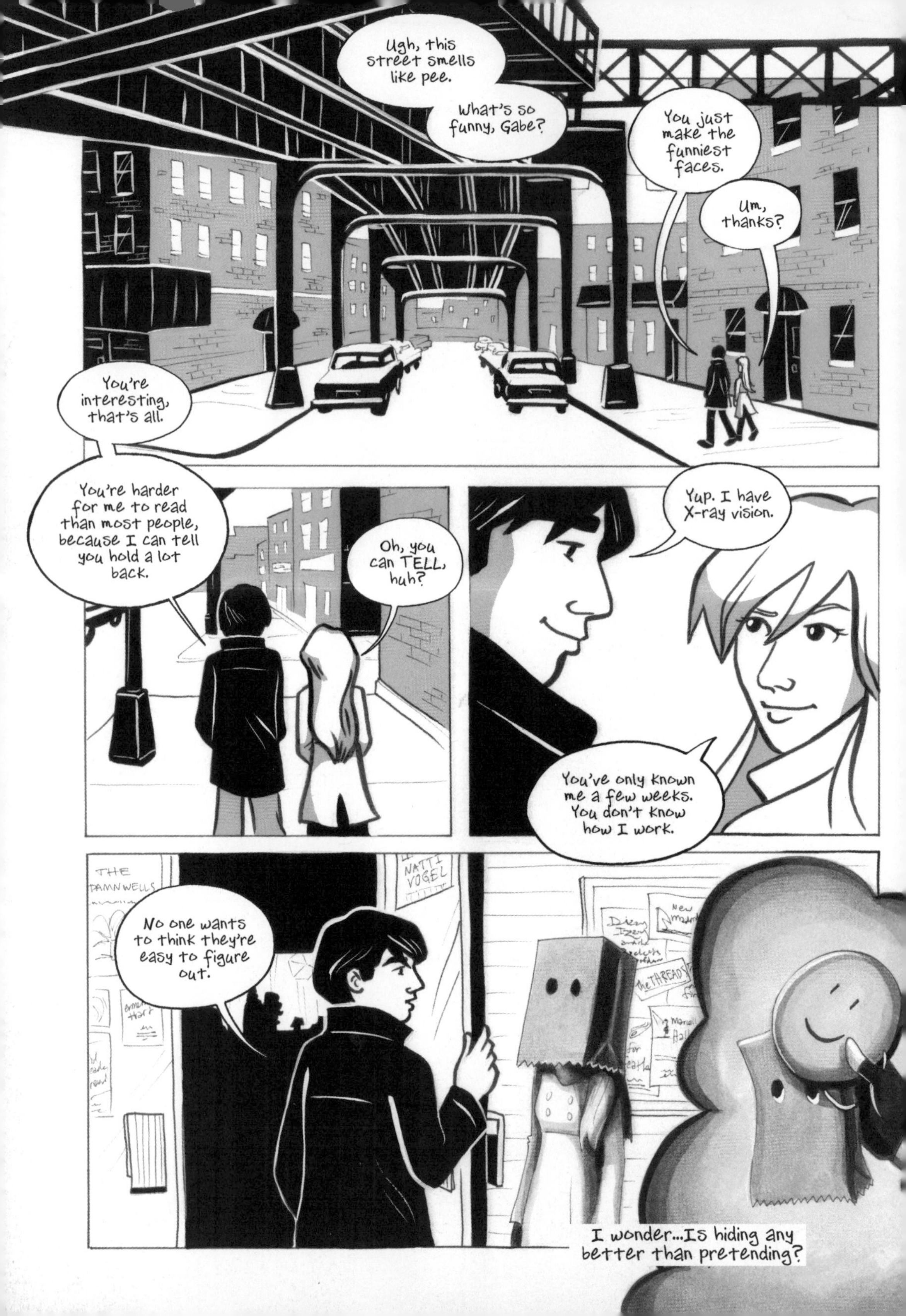

Ugh, this street smells like pee.
What's so funny, Gabe?
You just make the funniest faces.
Um, thanks?
You're interesting, that's all.
You're harder for me to read than most people, because I can tell you hold a lot back.
Oh, you can TELL, huh?
Yup. I have X-ray vision.
You've only known me a few weeks. You don't know how I work.
THE DAMNWELLS
NATTI VOGEL
No one wants to think they're easy to figure out.
the THREADS
I wonder...Is hiding any better than pretending?

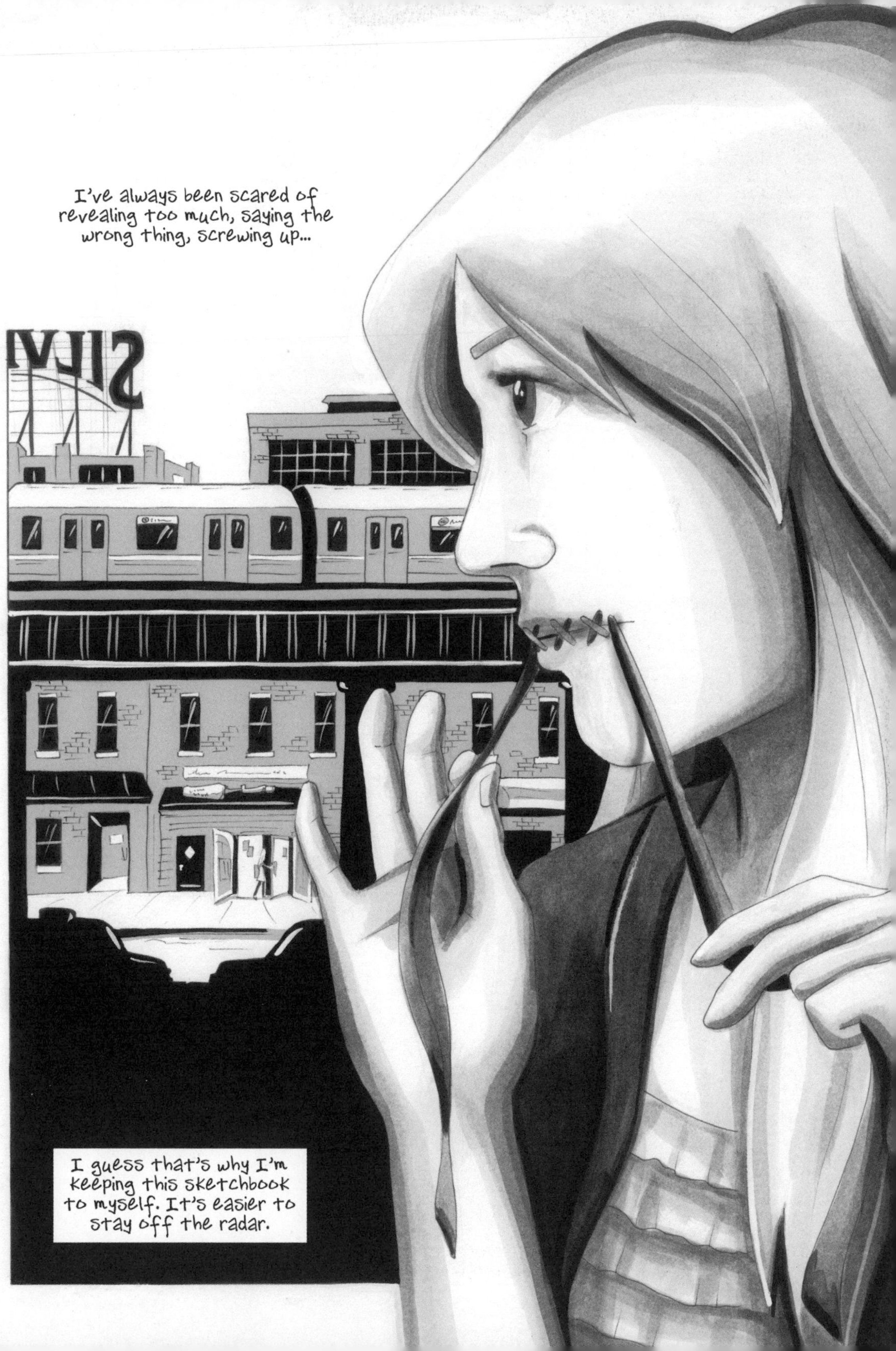
I've always been scared of revealing too much, saying the wrong thing, screwing up...
I guess that's why I'm keeping this sketchbook to myself. It's easier to stay off the radar.

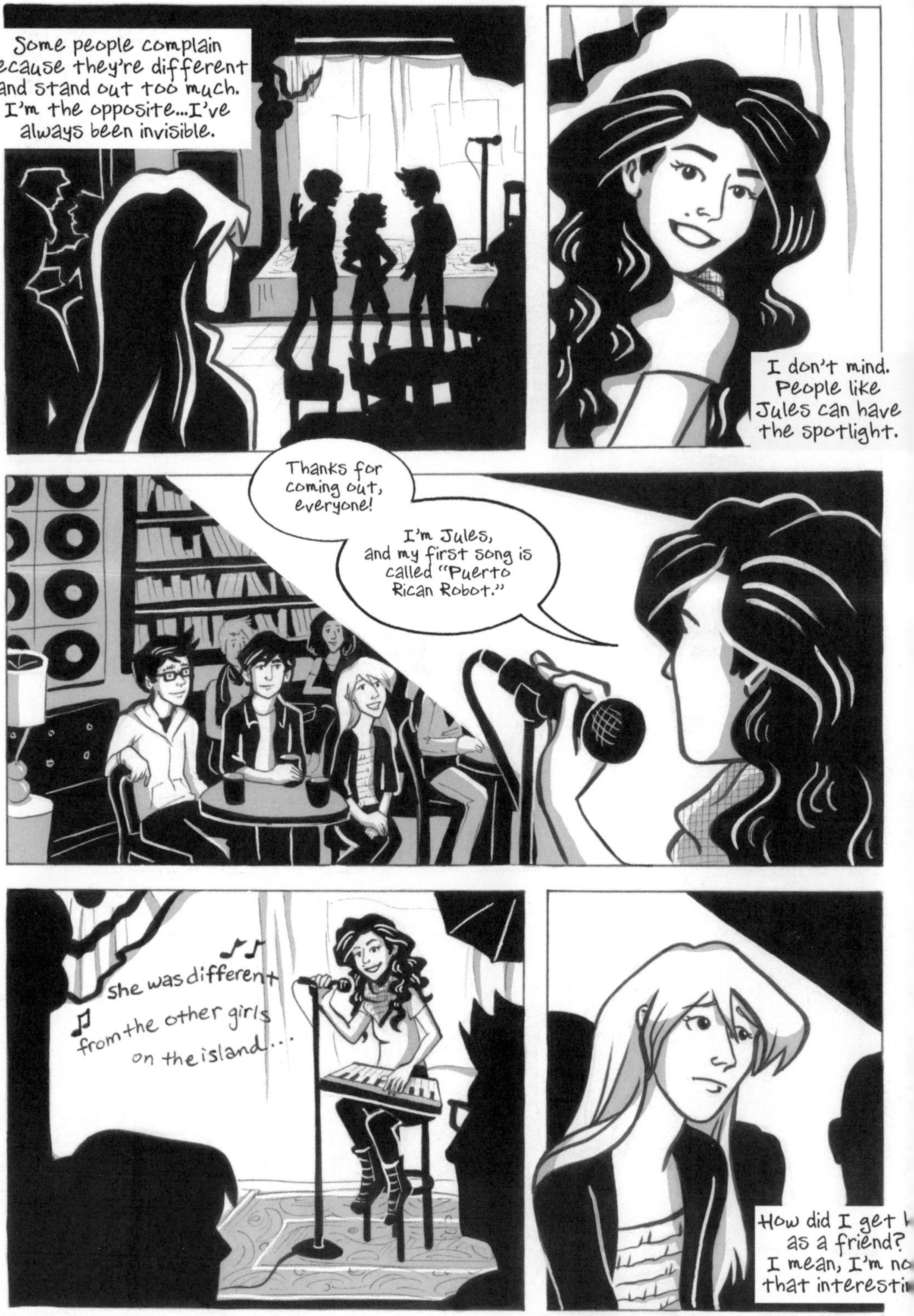

Some people complain because they're different and stand out too much. I'm the opposite...I've always been invisible.
I don't mind. People like Jules can have the spotlight.
Thanks for coming out, everyone!
I'm Jules, and my first song is called "Puerto Rican Robot."
she was different from the other girls on the island...
How did I get
as a friend?
I mean, I'm no
that interesti

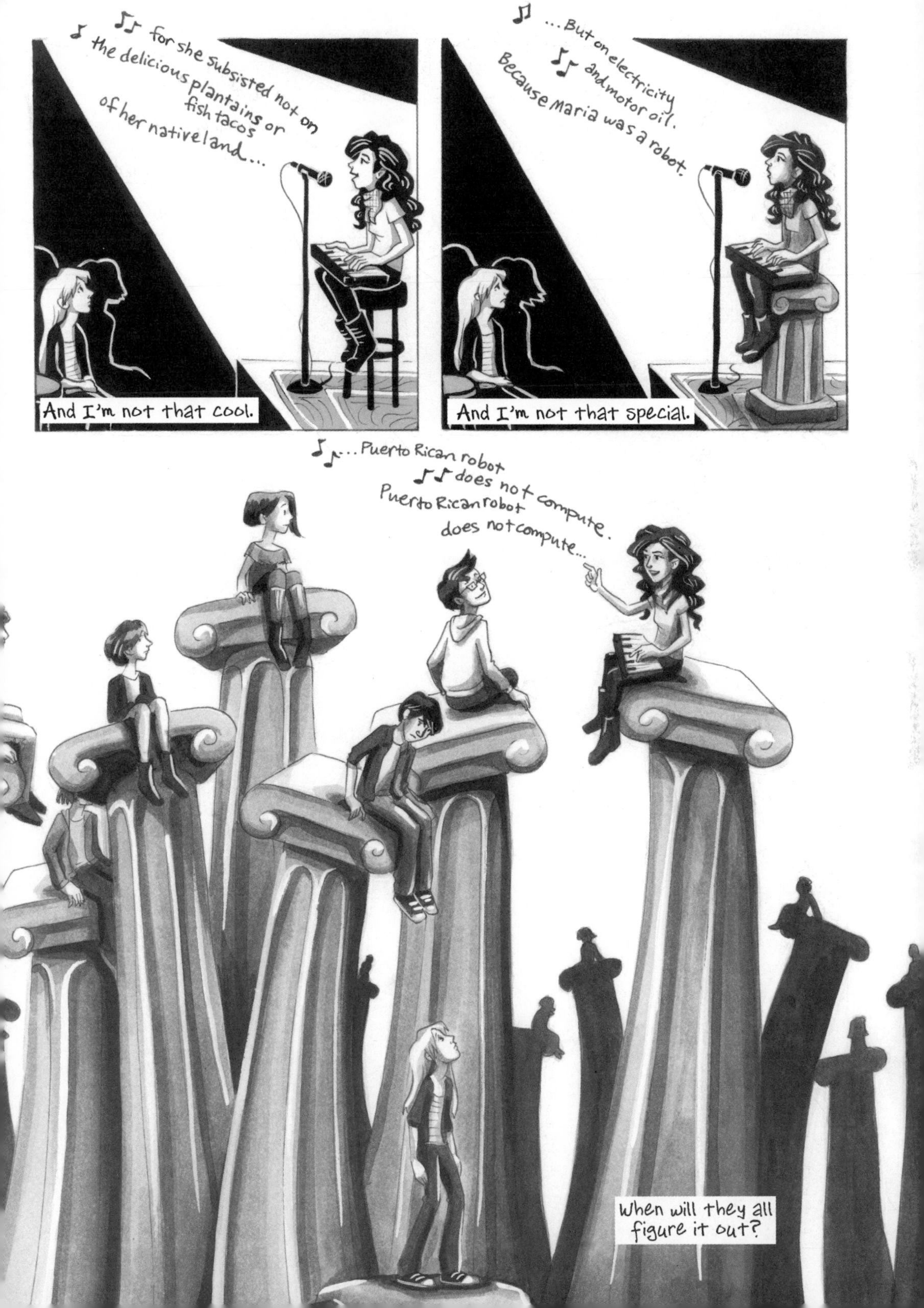
for she subsisted not on the delicious plantains or fish tacos of her native land...
And I'm not that cool.
...But on electricity and motor oil. Because Maria was a robot.
And I'm not that special.
...Puerto Rican robot does not compute. Puerto Rican robot does not compute...
When will they all figure it out?

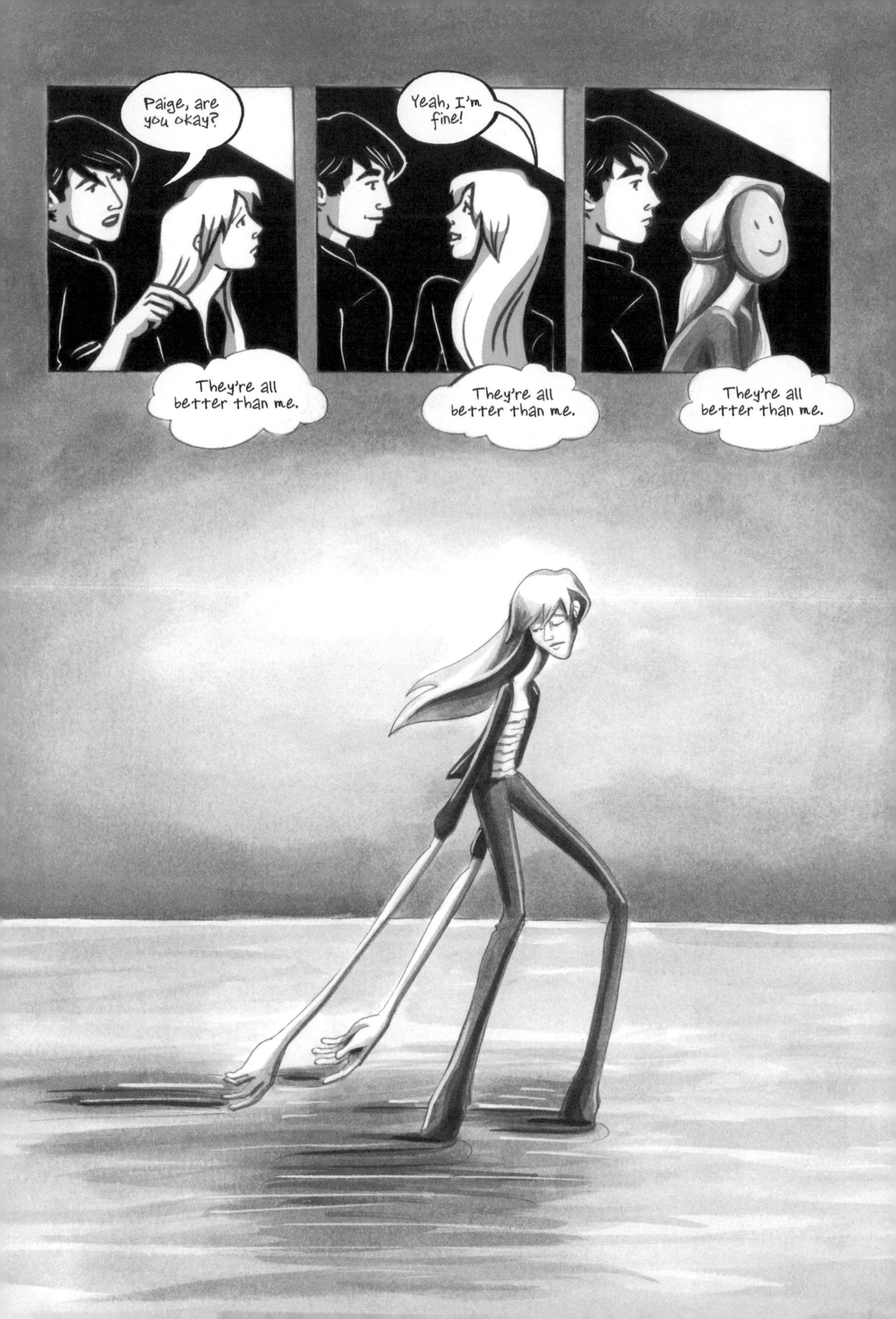
Paige, are you okay?
They're all better than me.
Yeah, I'm fine!
They're all better than me.
They're all better than me.

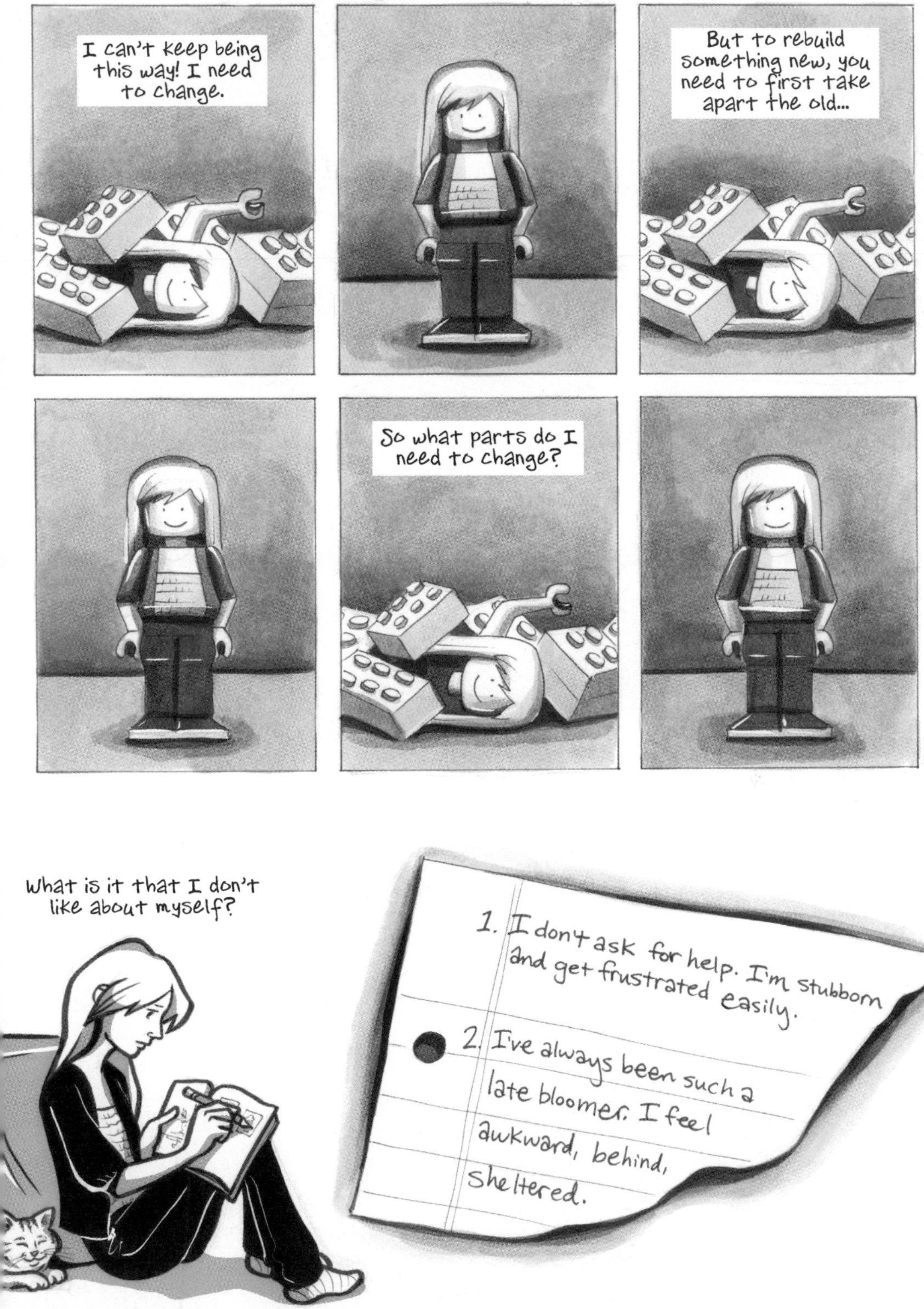
I can't keep being this way! I need to change.
But to rebuild something new, you need to first take apart the old...
So what parts do I need to change?
What is it that I don't like about myself?
1. I don't ask for help. I'm stubborn and get frustrated easily.
2. I've always been such a late bloomer. I feel awkward, behind, sheltered.

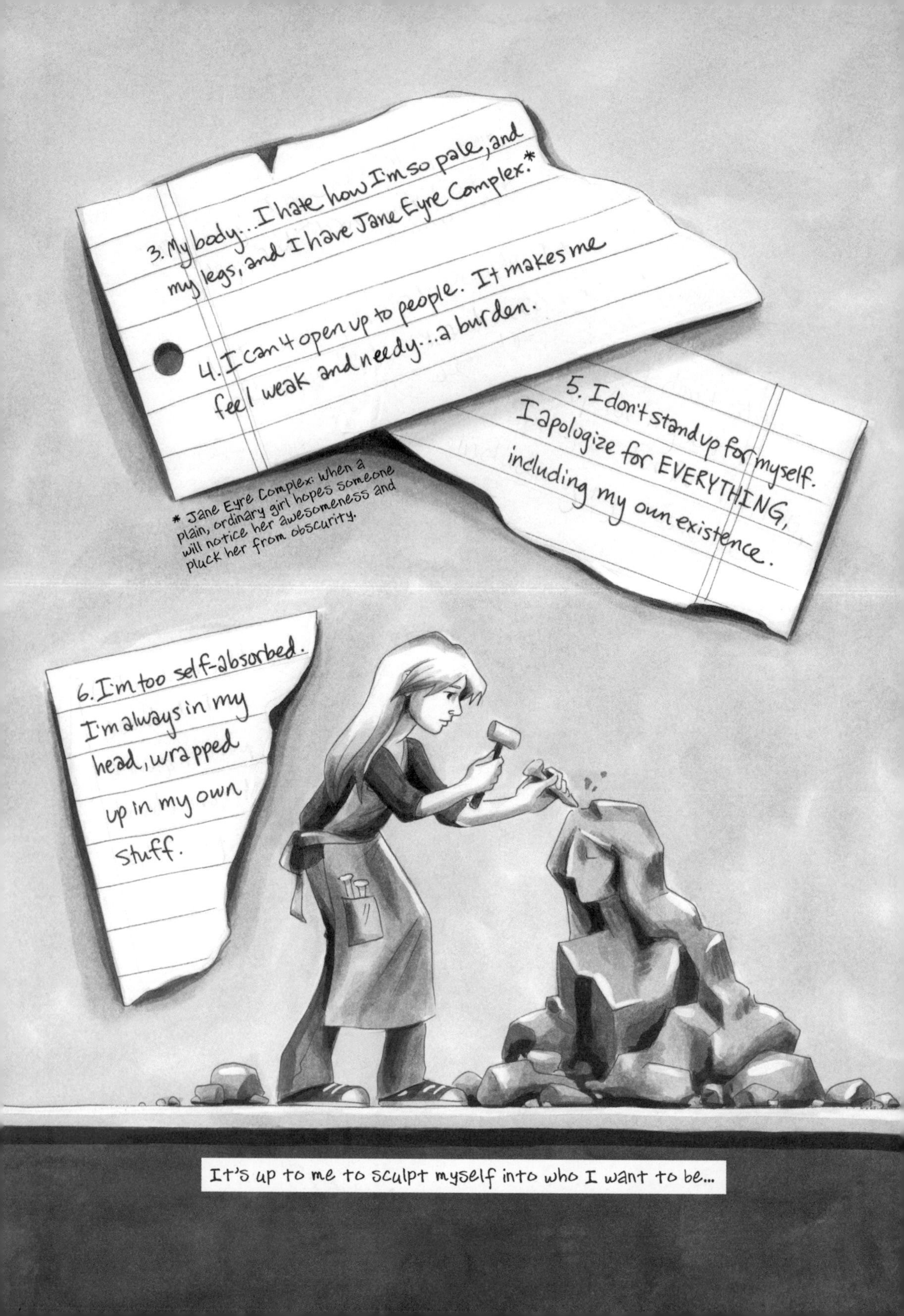
3. My body... I hate how I'm so pale, and my legs, and I have Jane Eyre Complex.*
4. I can't open up to people. It makes me feel weak and needy... a burden.
5. I don't stand up for myself. I apologize for EVERYTHING, including my own existence.
* Jane Eyre Complex: when a plain, ordinary girl hopes someone will notice her awesomeness and pluck her from obscurity.
6. I'm too self-absorbed. I'm always in my head, wrapped up in my own stuff.
It's up to me to sculpt myself into who I want to be...

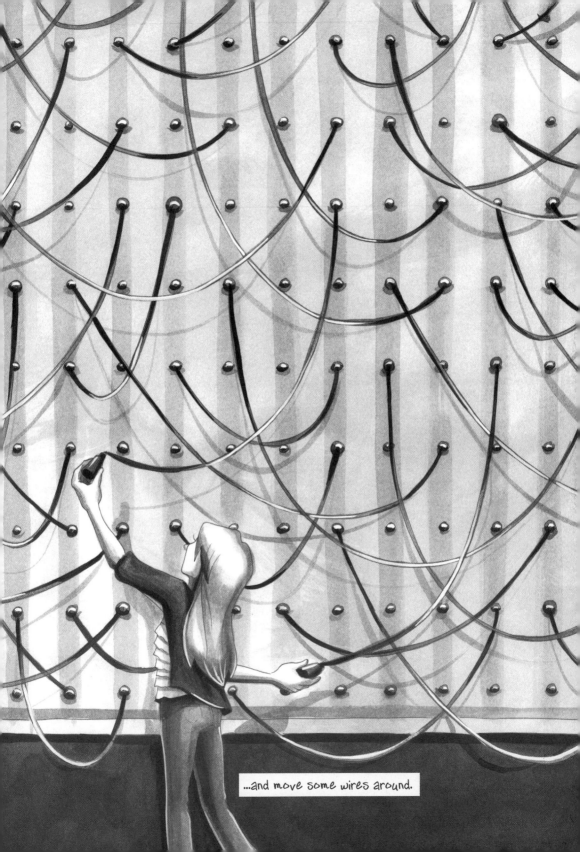

...and move some wires around.

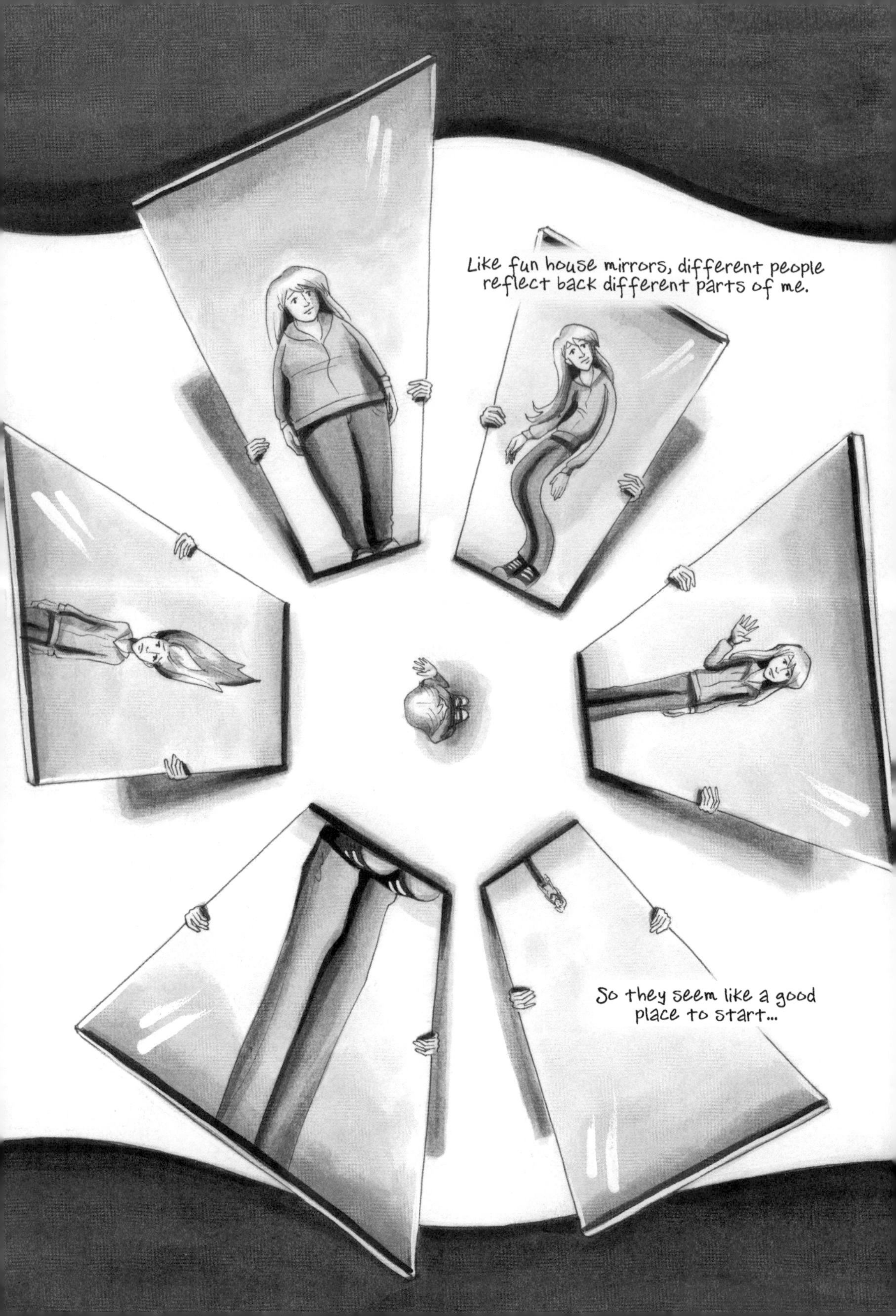
Like fun house mirrors, different people reflect back different parts of me.
So they seem like a good place to start...

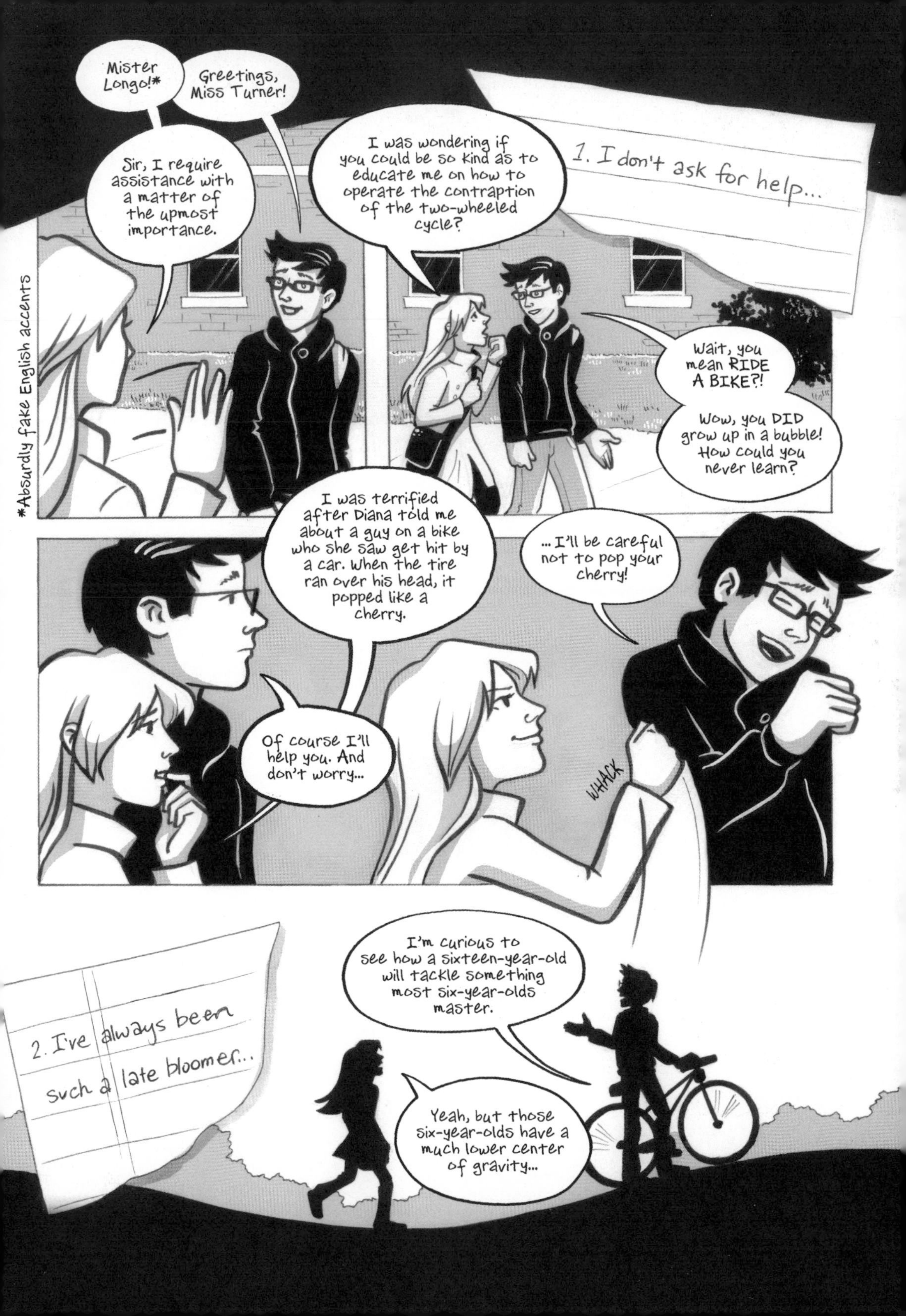
Mister Longo!*
Greetings, Miss Turner!
Sir, I require assistance with a matter of the upmost importance.
I was wondering if you could be so kind as to educate me on how to operate the contraption of the two-wheeled cycle?
1. I don't ask for help...
*Absurdly fake English accents
Wait, you mean RIDE A BIKE?!
Wow, you DID grow up in a bubble! How could you never learn?
I was terrified after Diana told me about a guy on a bike who she saw get hit by a car. When the tire ran over his head, it popped like a cherry.
Of course I'll help you. And don't worry...
... I'll be careful not to pop your cherry!
WHACK
2. I've always been such a late bloomer...
I'm curious to see how a sixteen-year-old will tackle something most six-year-olds master.
Yeah, but those six-year-olds have a much lower center of gravity...

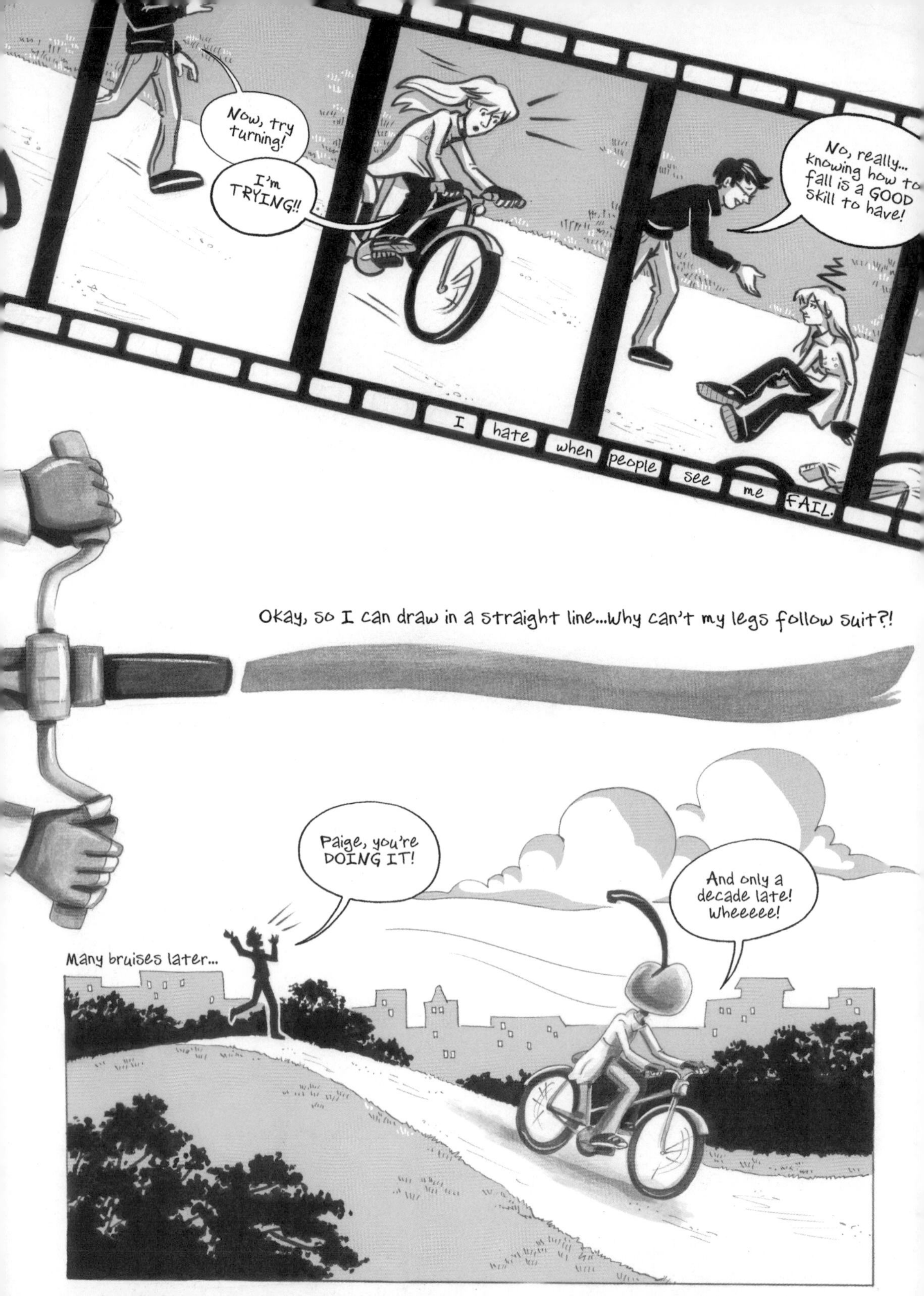

Now, try turning!
I'm TRYING!!
No, really... knowing how to fall is a GOOD skill to have!
I hate when people see me FAIL.
Okay, so I can draw in a straight line...Why can't my legs follow suit?!
Many bruises later...
Paige, you're DOING IT!
And only a decade late! Wheeeee!

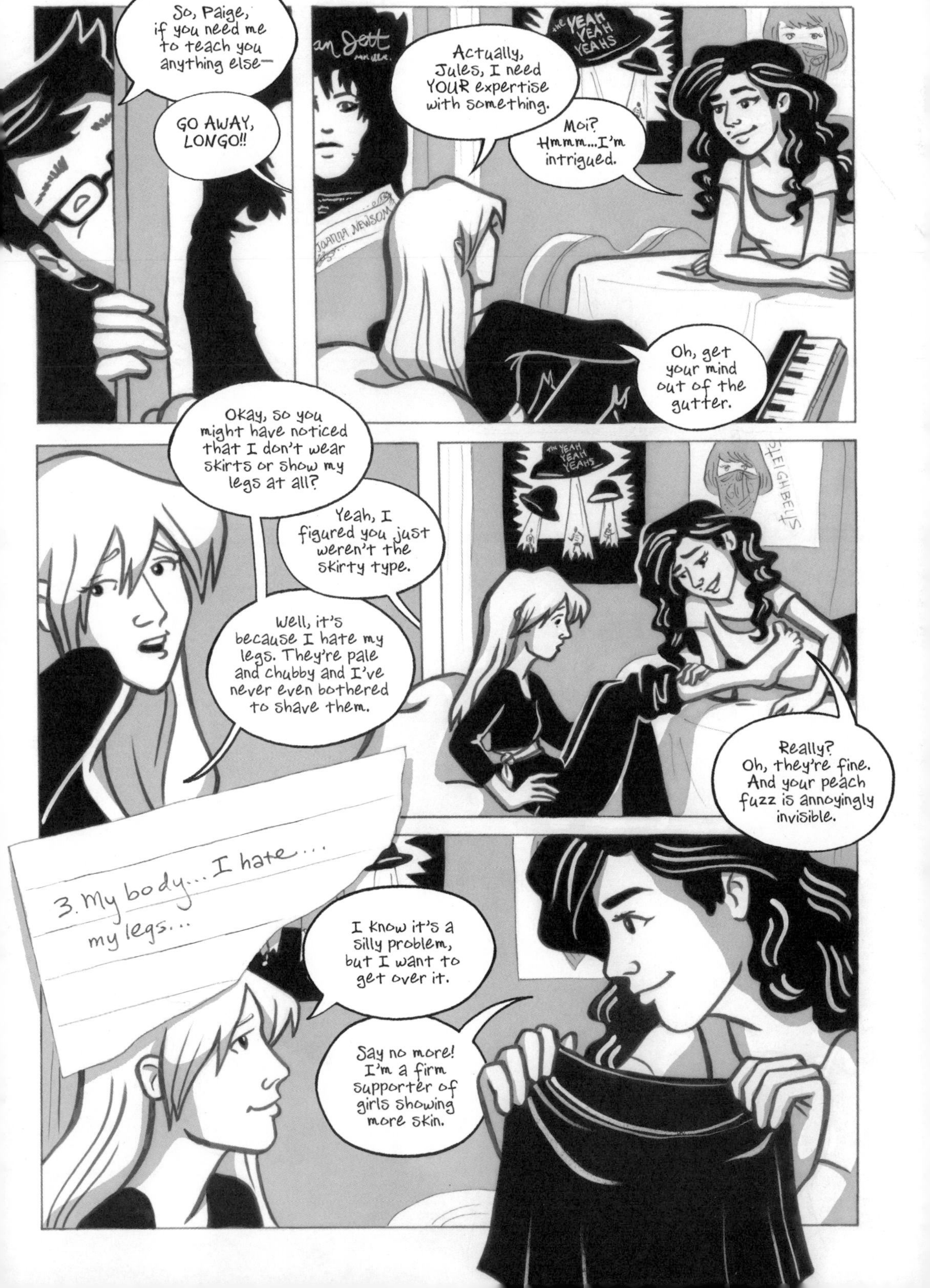
So, Paige, if you need me to teach you anything else—
GO AWAY, LONGO!!
Actually, Jules, I need YOUR expertise with something.
Moi? Hmmm...I'm intrigued.
Oh, get your mind out of the gutter.
THE YEAH YEAH YEAHS
JOANNA NEWSOM
Okay, so you might have noticed that I don't wear skirts or show my legs at all?
Yeah, I figured you just weren't the skirty type.
Well, it's because I hate my legs. They're pale and chubby and I've never even bothered to shave them.
Really? Oh, they're fine. And your peach fuzz is annoyingly invisible.
SLEIGH BELLS
3. My body... I hate... my legs...
I know it's a silly problem, but I want to get over it.
Say no more! I'm a firm supporter of girls showing more skin.

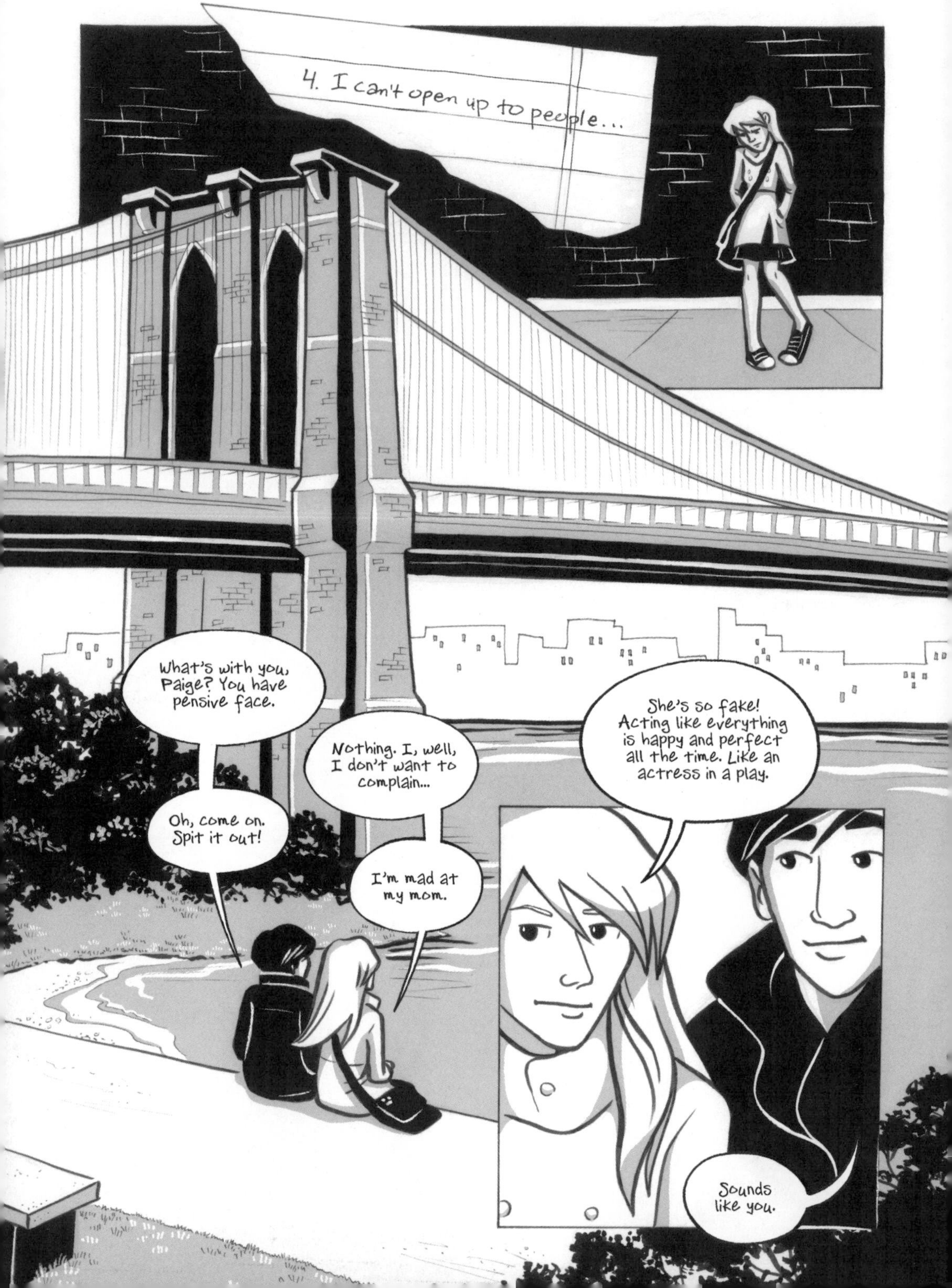
4. I can't open up to people...
What's with you, Paige? You have pensive face.
Oh, come on. Spit it out!
Nothing. I, well, I don't want to complain...
I'm mad at my mom.
She's so fake! Acting like everything is happy and perfect all the time. Like an actress in a play.
Sounds like you.

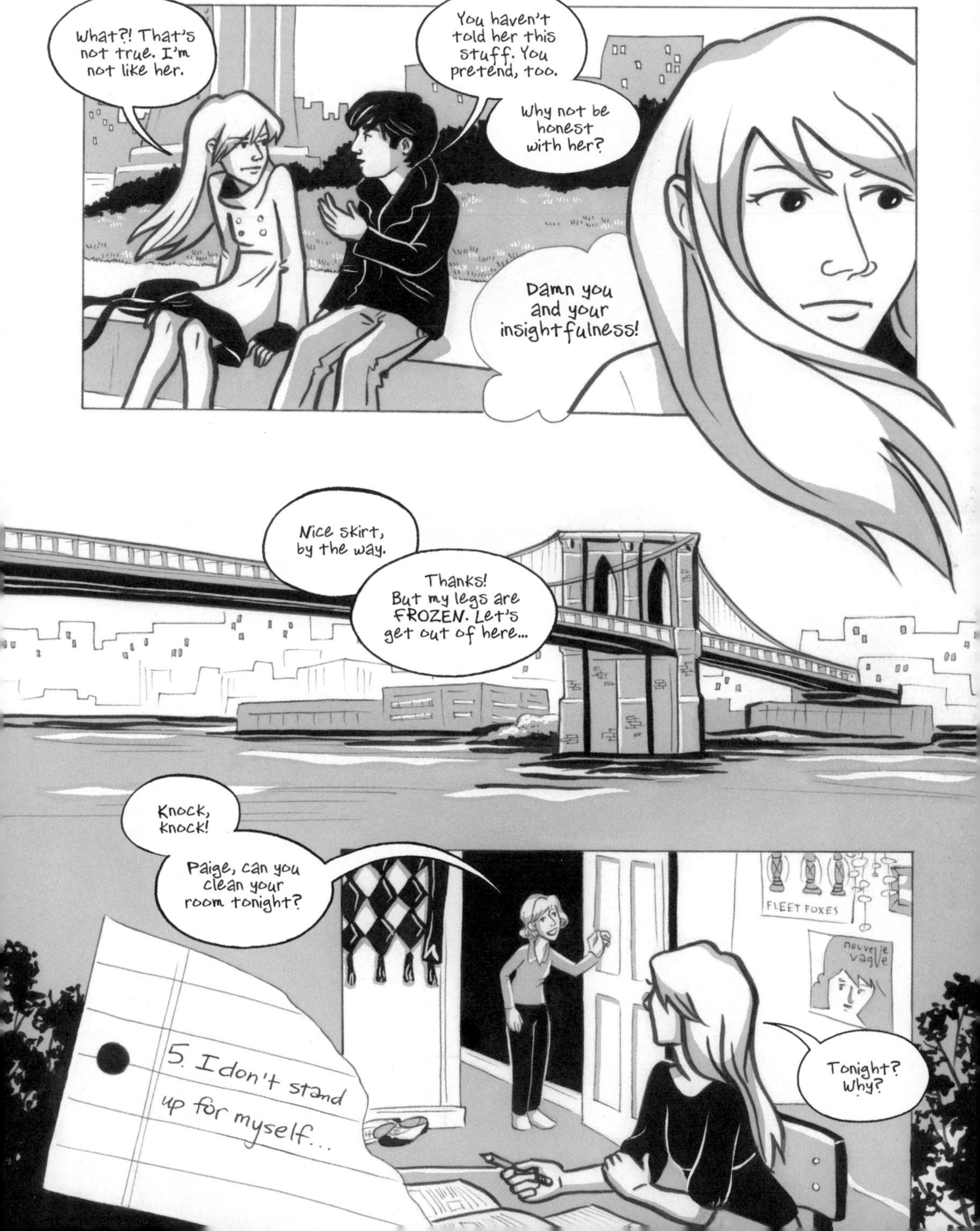
What?! That's not true. I'm not like her.
You haven't told her this stuff. You pretend, too.
Why not be honest with her?
Damn you and your insightfulness!
Nice skirt, by the way.
Thanks! But my legs are FROZEN. Let's get out of here...
Knock, knock!
Paige, can you clean your room tonight?
FLEET FOXES
nouvelle vague
5. I don't stand up for myself...
Tonight? Why?

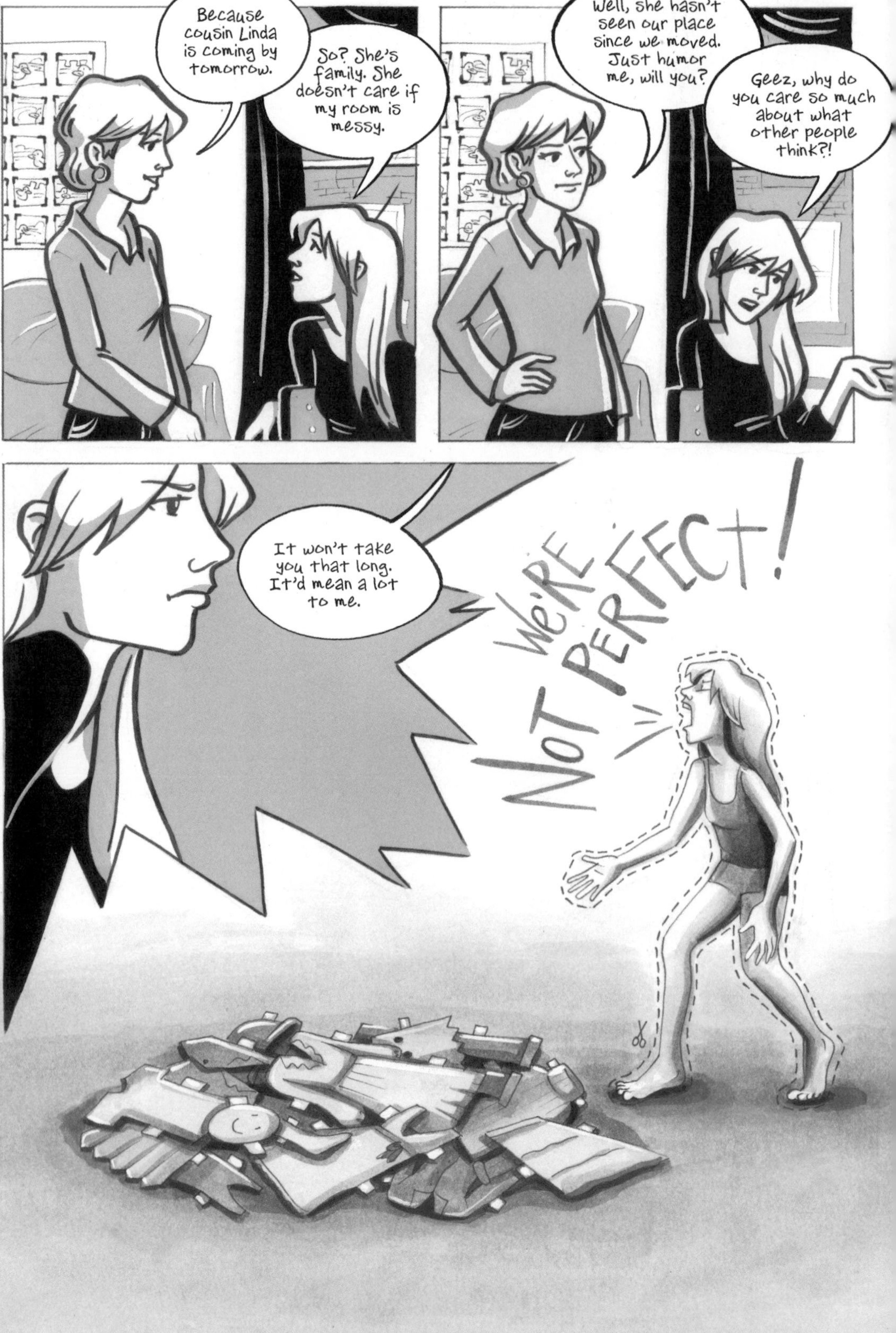

Because cousin Linda is coming by tomorrow.
So? She's family. She doesn't care if my room is messy.
Well, she hasn't seen our place since we moved. Just humor me, will you?
Geez, why do you care so much about what other people think?!
It won't take you that long. It'd mean a lot to me.
WE'RE NOT PERFECT!

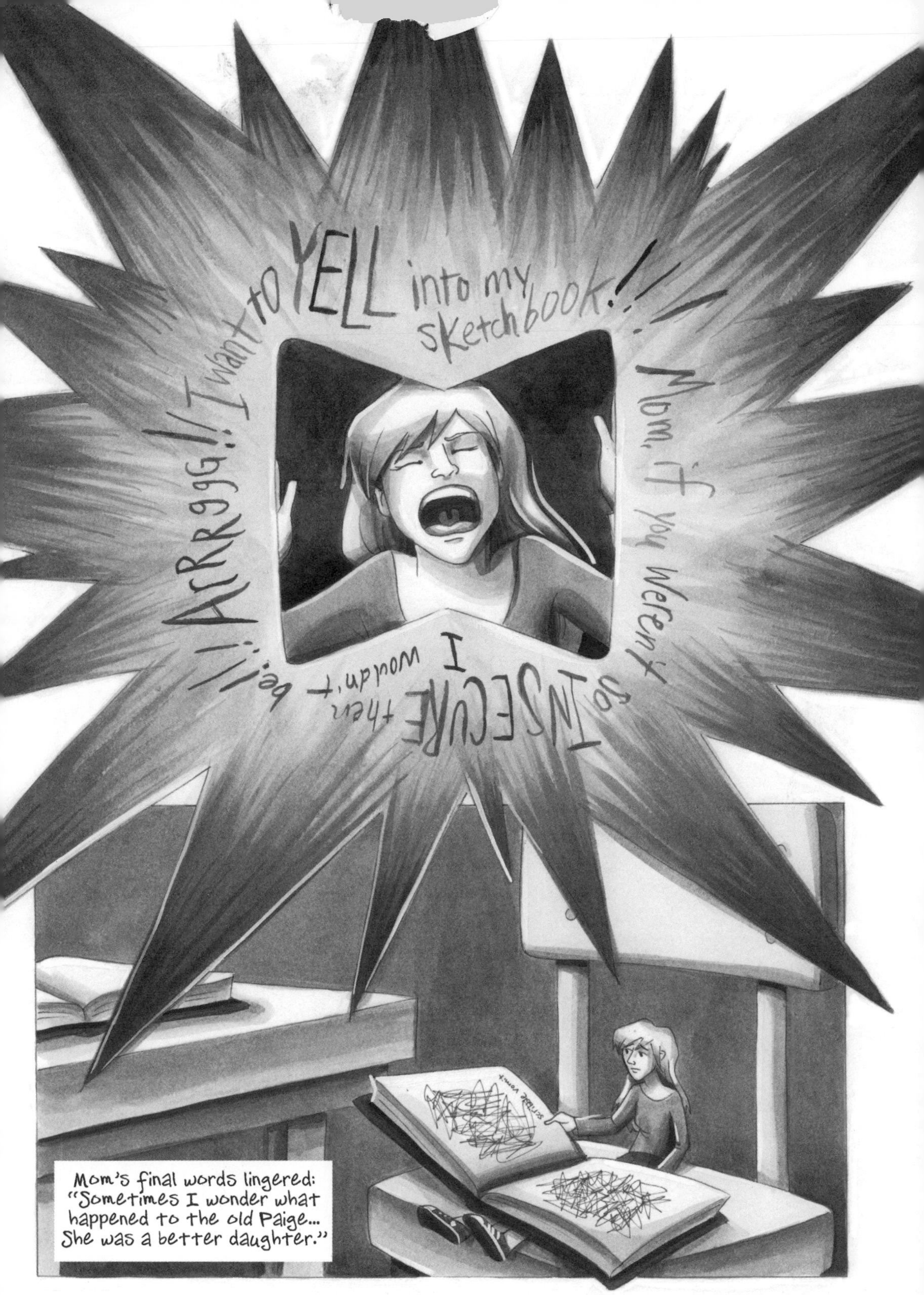
I want to YELL into my sketchbook!!!
Mom, if you weren't so INSECURE then I wouldn't be!!!
ARRRggg!!
Mom's final words lingered: "Sometimes I wonder what happened to the old Paige... She was a better daughter."

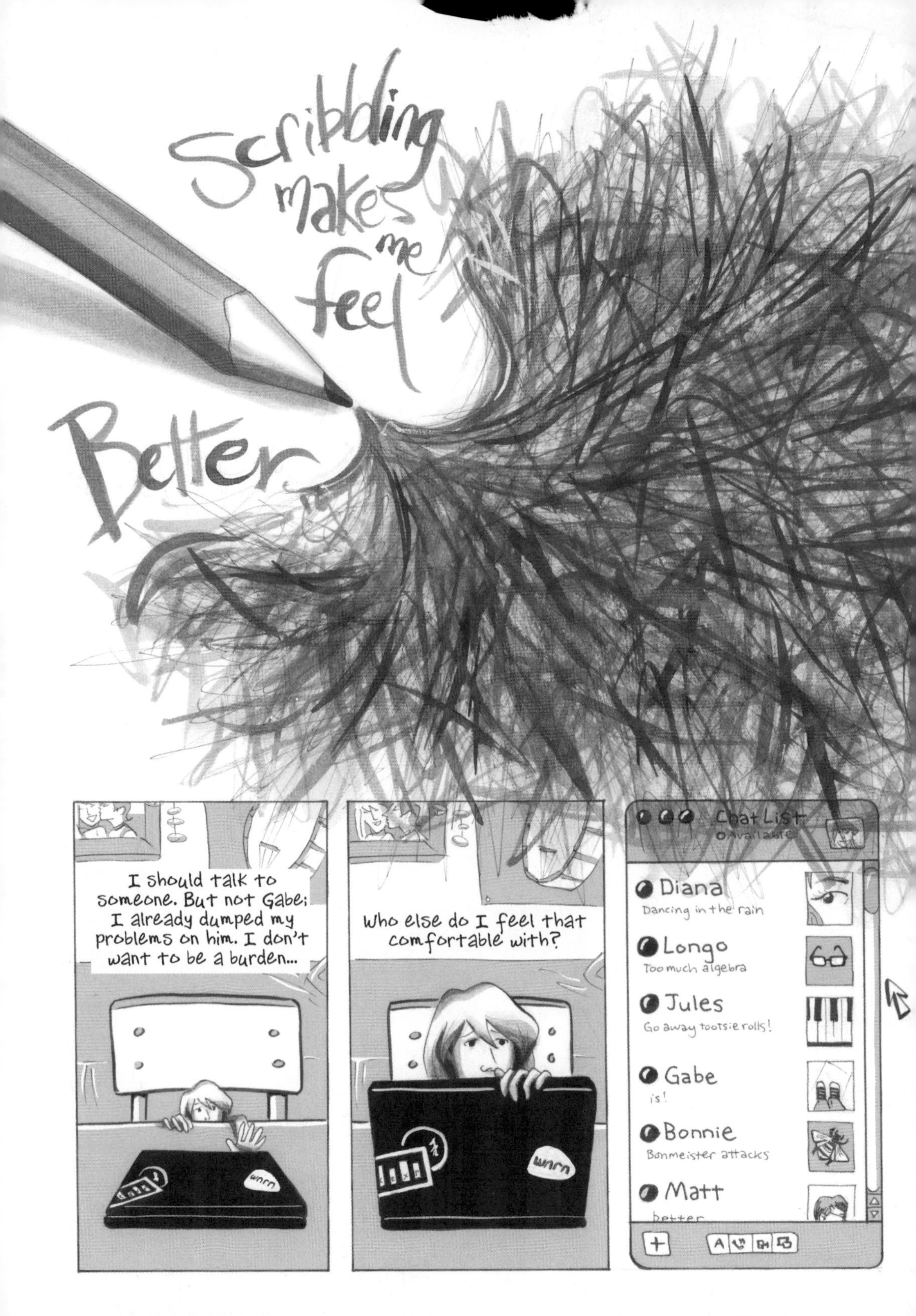
Scribbling makes me feel Better
I should talk to someone. But not Gabe; I already dumped my problems on him. I don't want to be a burden...
Who else do I feel that comfortable with?
Chat List
Available
Diana
Dancing in the rain
Longo
Too much algebra
Jules
Go away tootsie rolls!
Gabe
is!
Bonnie
Bonmeister attacks
Matt
better

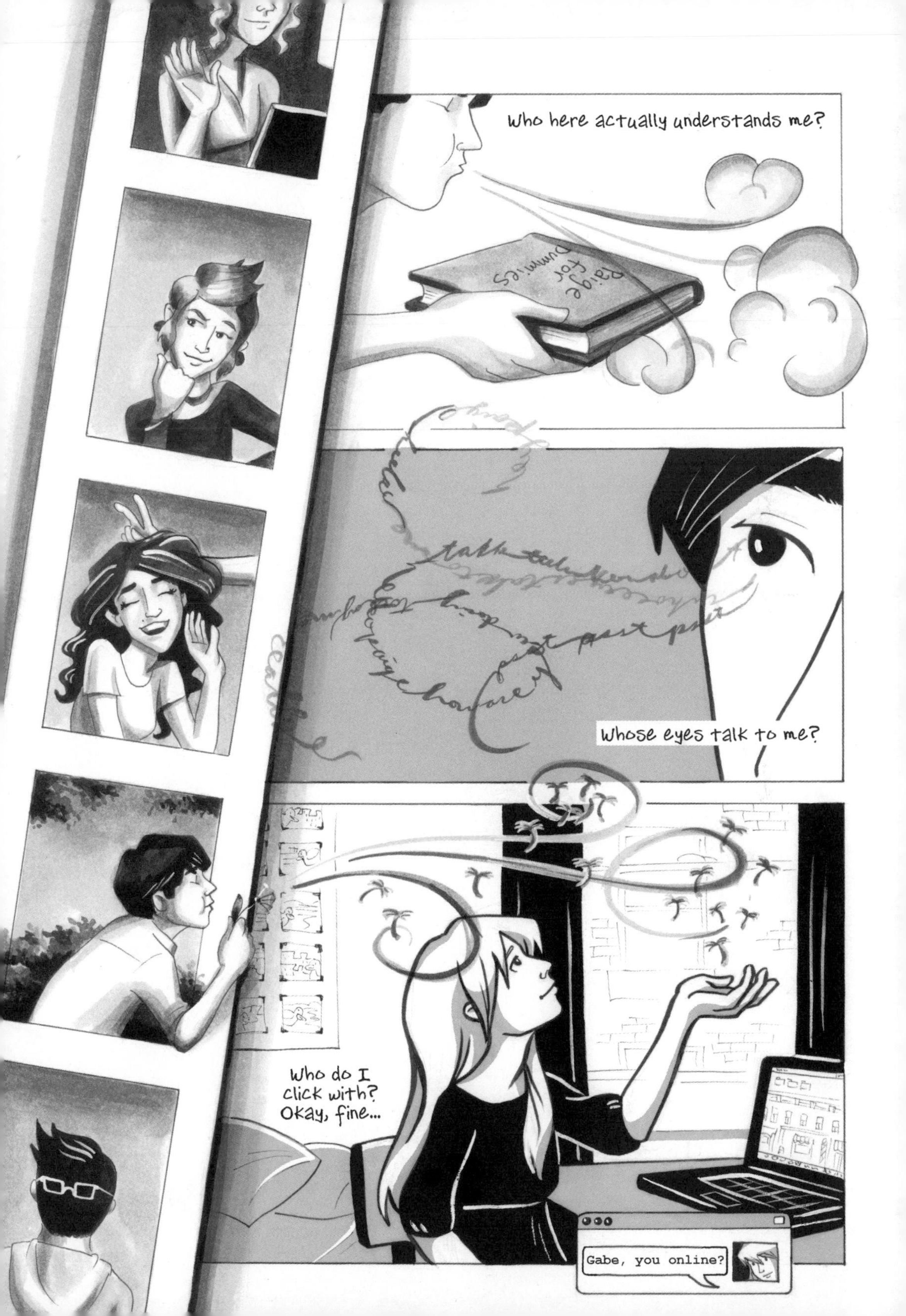
Who here actually understands me?
Paige for Dummies
Whose eyes talk to me?
Who do I click with? Okay, fine...
Gabe, you online?

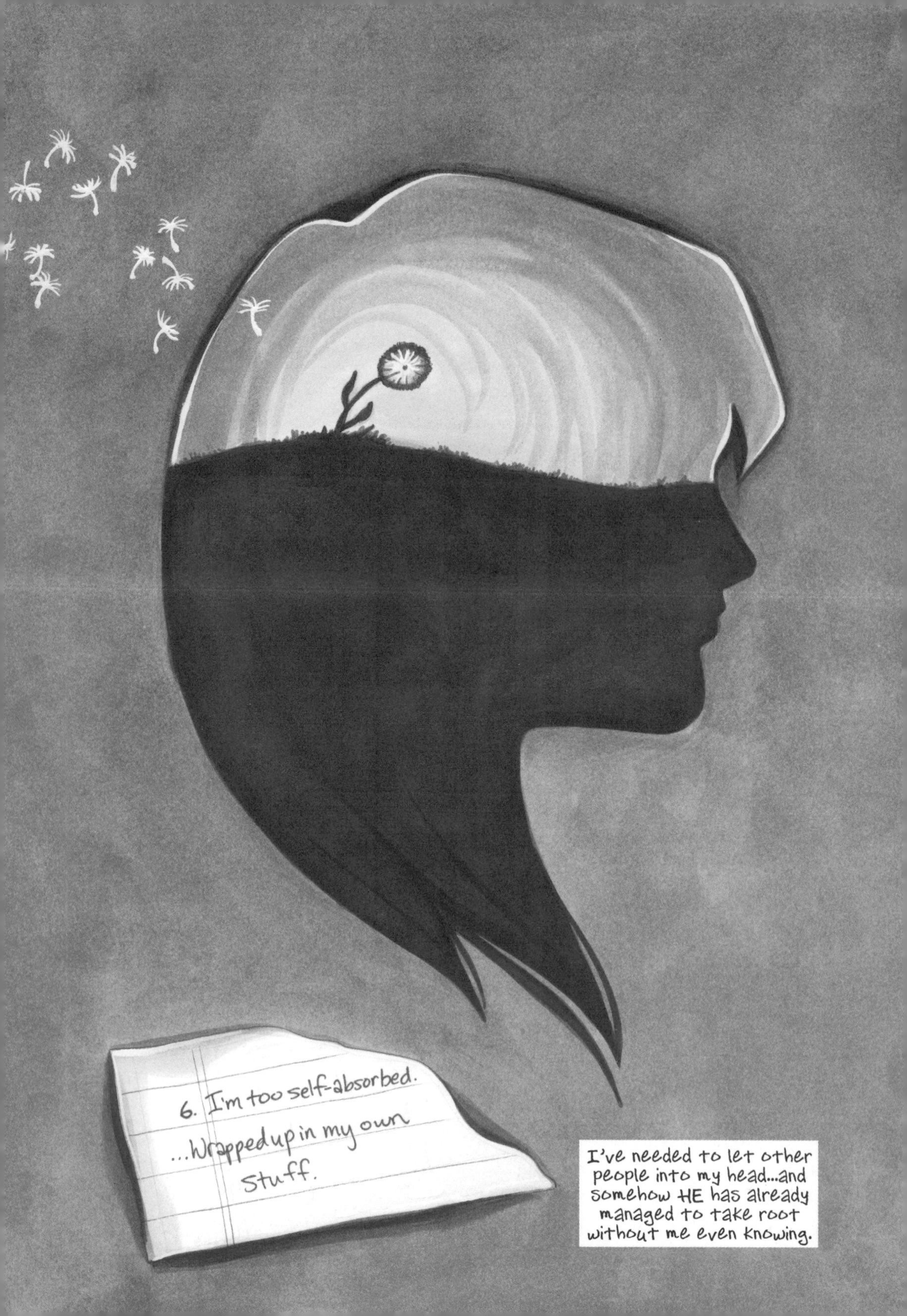
6. I'm too self-absorbed. ...Wrapped up in my own stuff.
I've needed to let other people into my head...and somehow HE has already managed to take root without me even knowing.

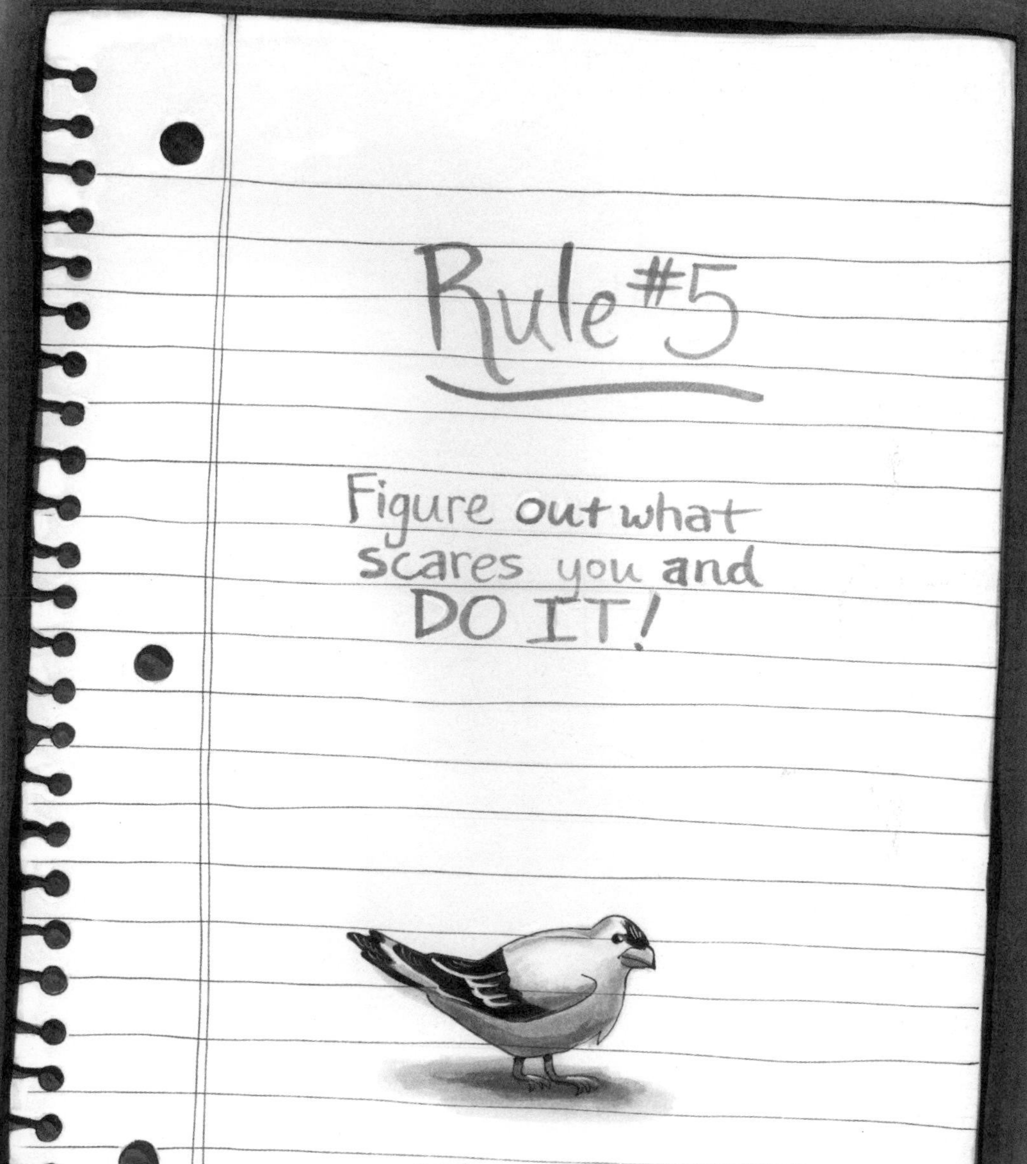
Rule #5
Figure out what scares you and DO IT!
-March-

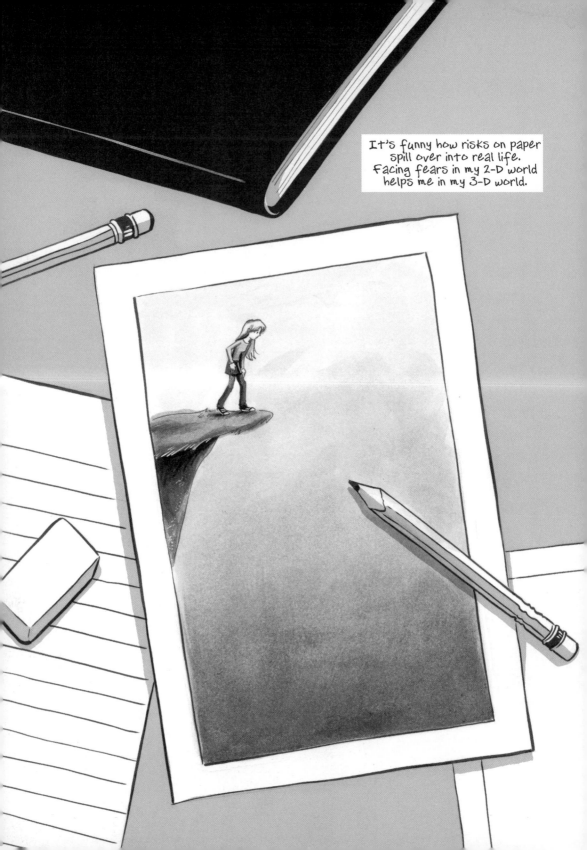

It's funny how risks on paper spill over into real life. Facing fears in my 2-D world helps me in my 3-D world.

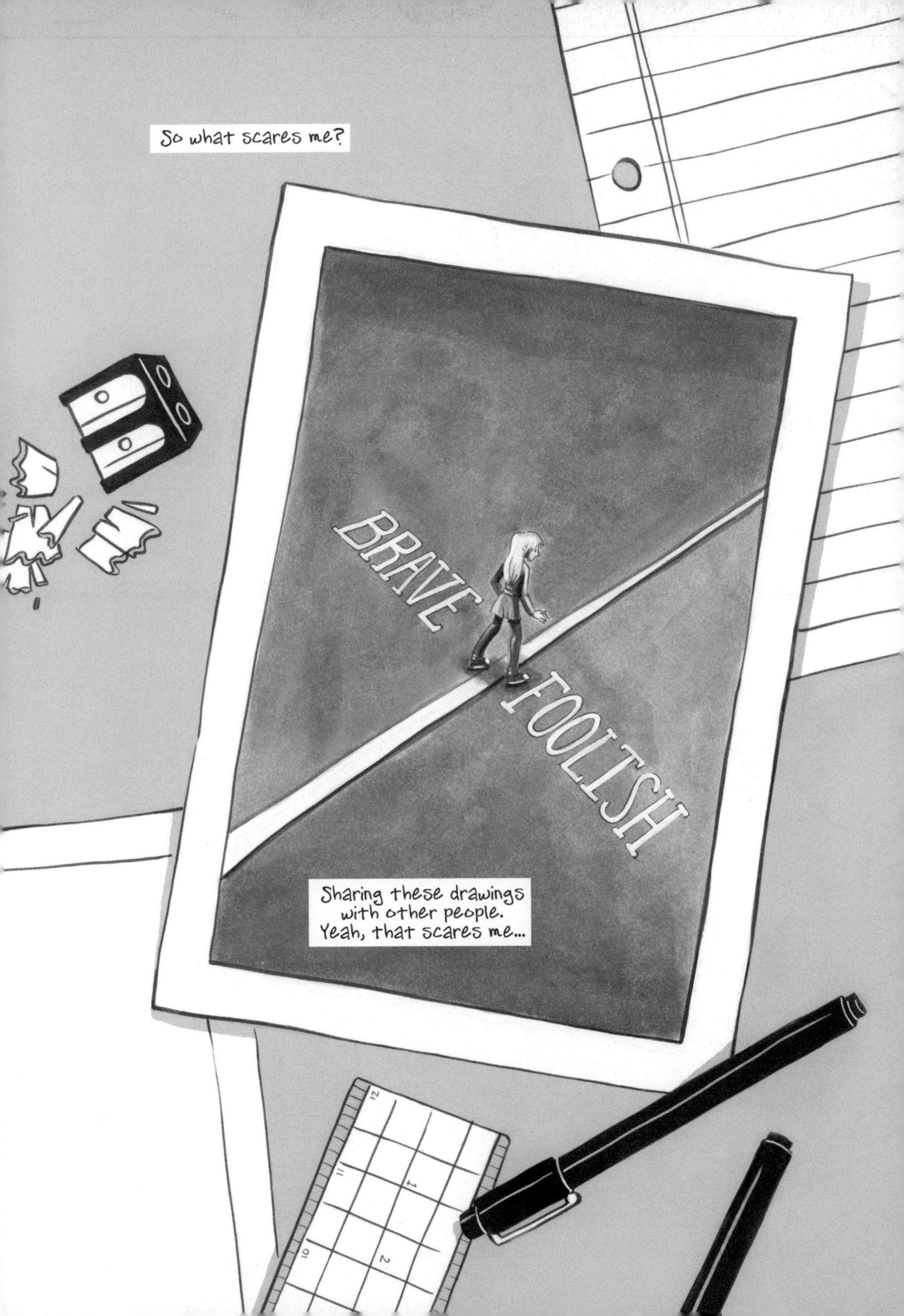
So what scares me?
BRAVE
FOOLISH
Sharing these drawings with other people. Yeah, that scares me...

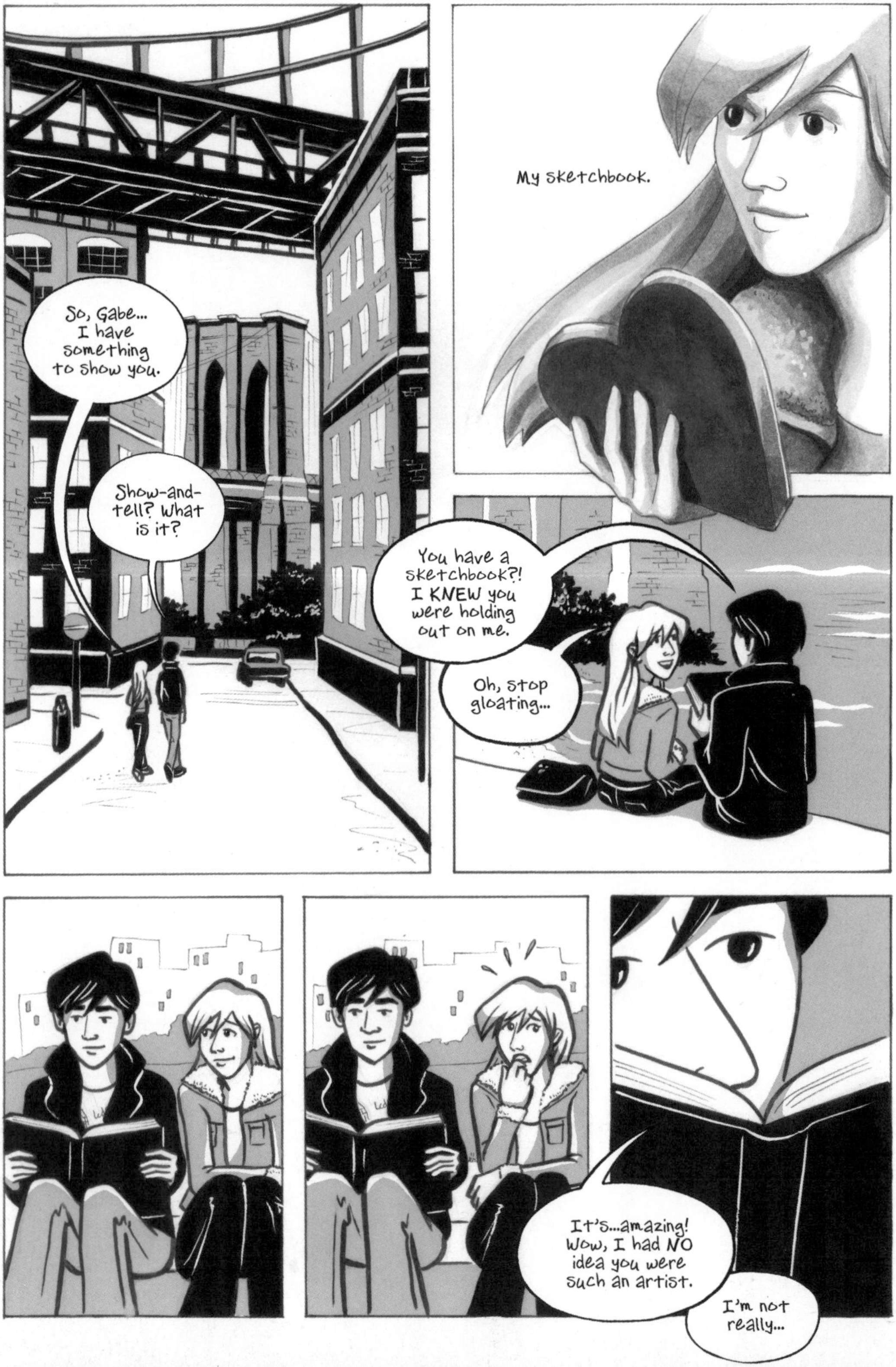
So, Gabe... I have something to show you.
Show-and-tell? What is it?
My sketchbook.
You have a sketchbook?! I KNEW you were holding out on me.
Oh, stop gloating...
It's...amazing! Wow, I had NO idea you were such an artist.
I'm not really...

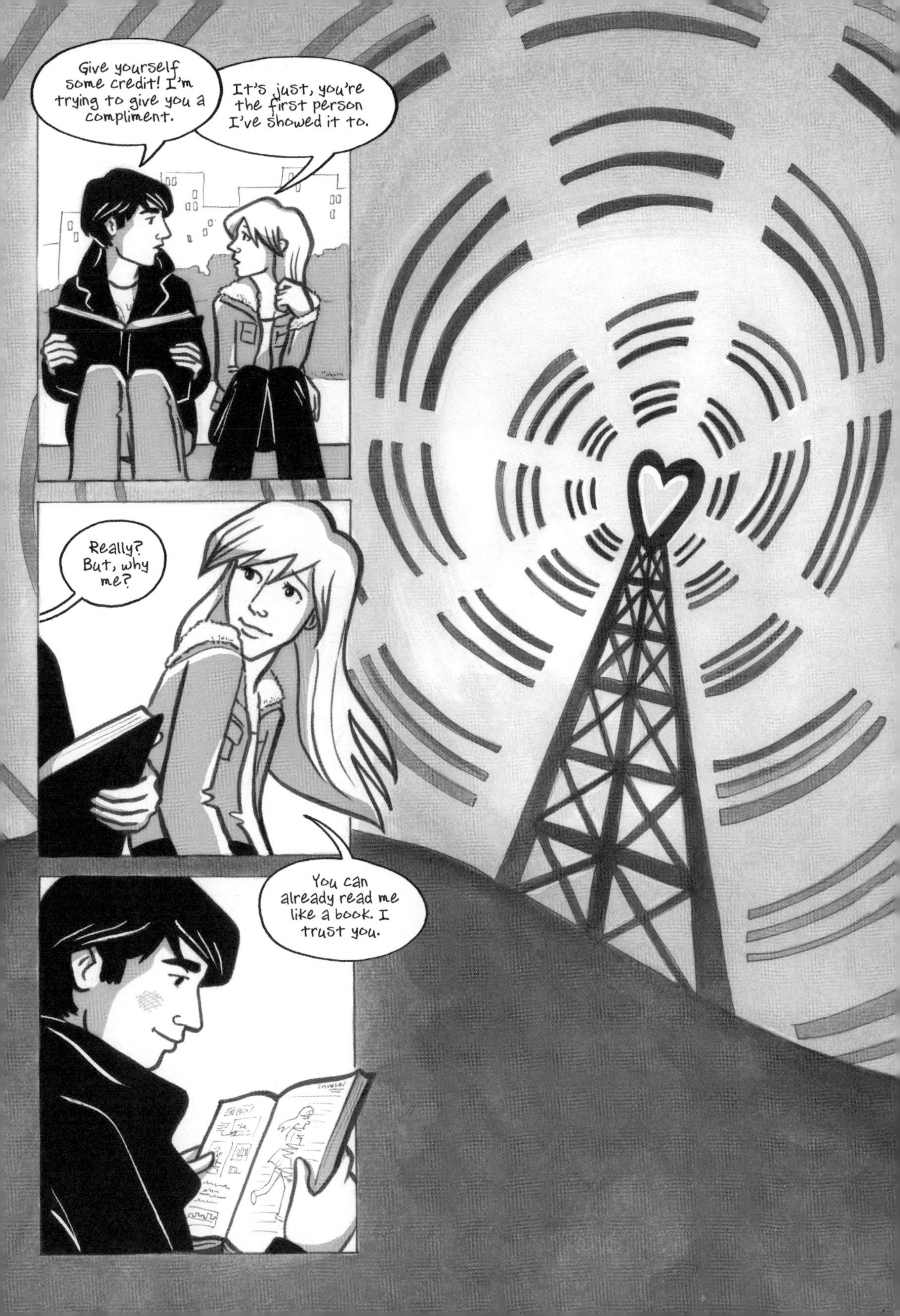
Give yourself some credit! I'm trying to give you a compliment.
It's just, you're the first person I've showed it to.
Really? But, why me?
You can already read me like a book. I trust you.

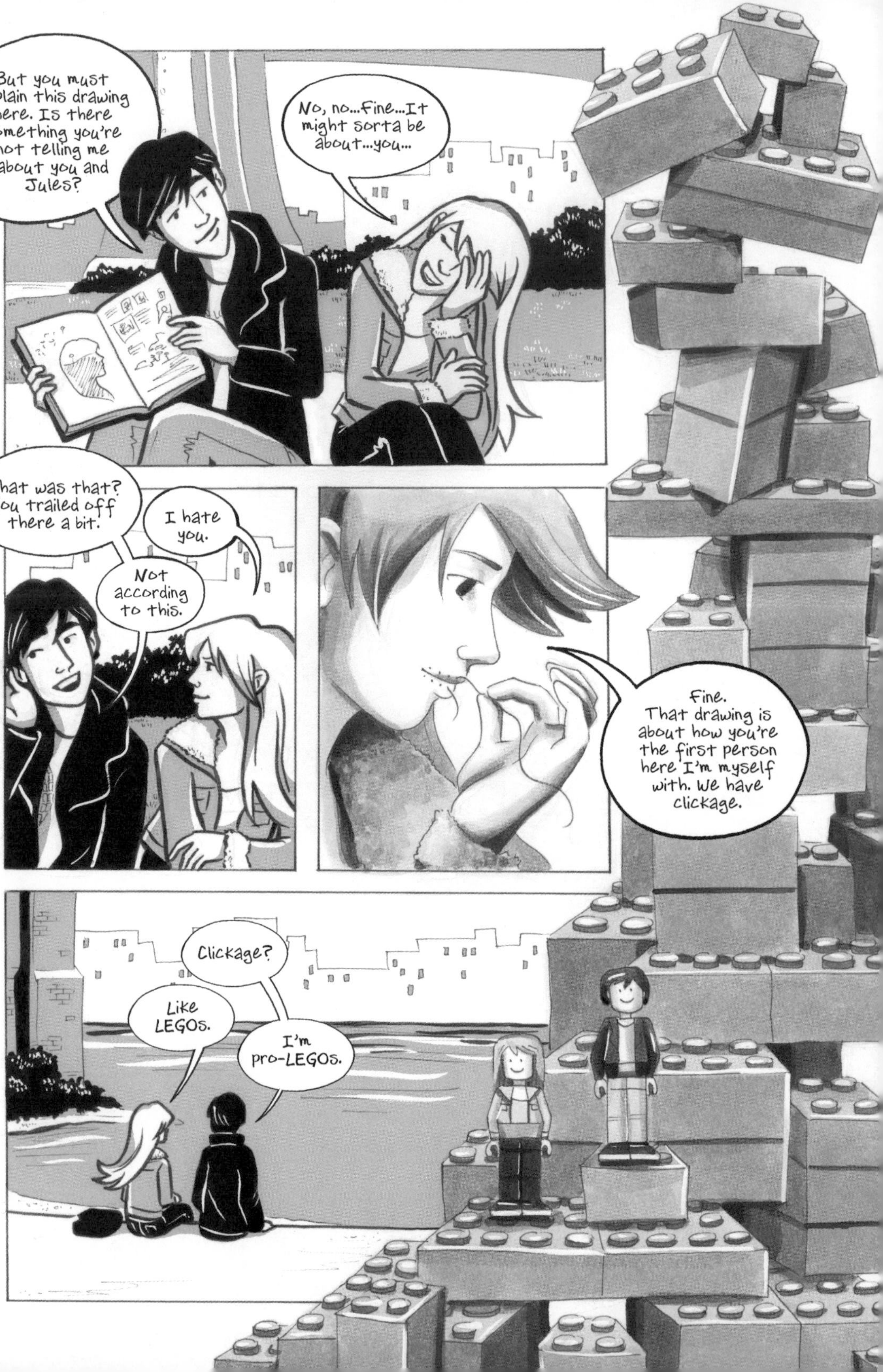

But you must explain this drawing here. Is there something you're not telling me about you and Jules?
No, no...fine...It might sorta be about...you...
What was that? You trailed off there a bit.
I hate you.
Not according to this.
Fine. That drawing is about how you're the first person here I'm myself with. We have clickage.
Clickage?
Like LEGOS.
I'm pro-LEGOS.

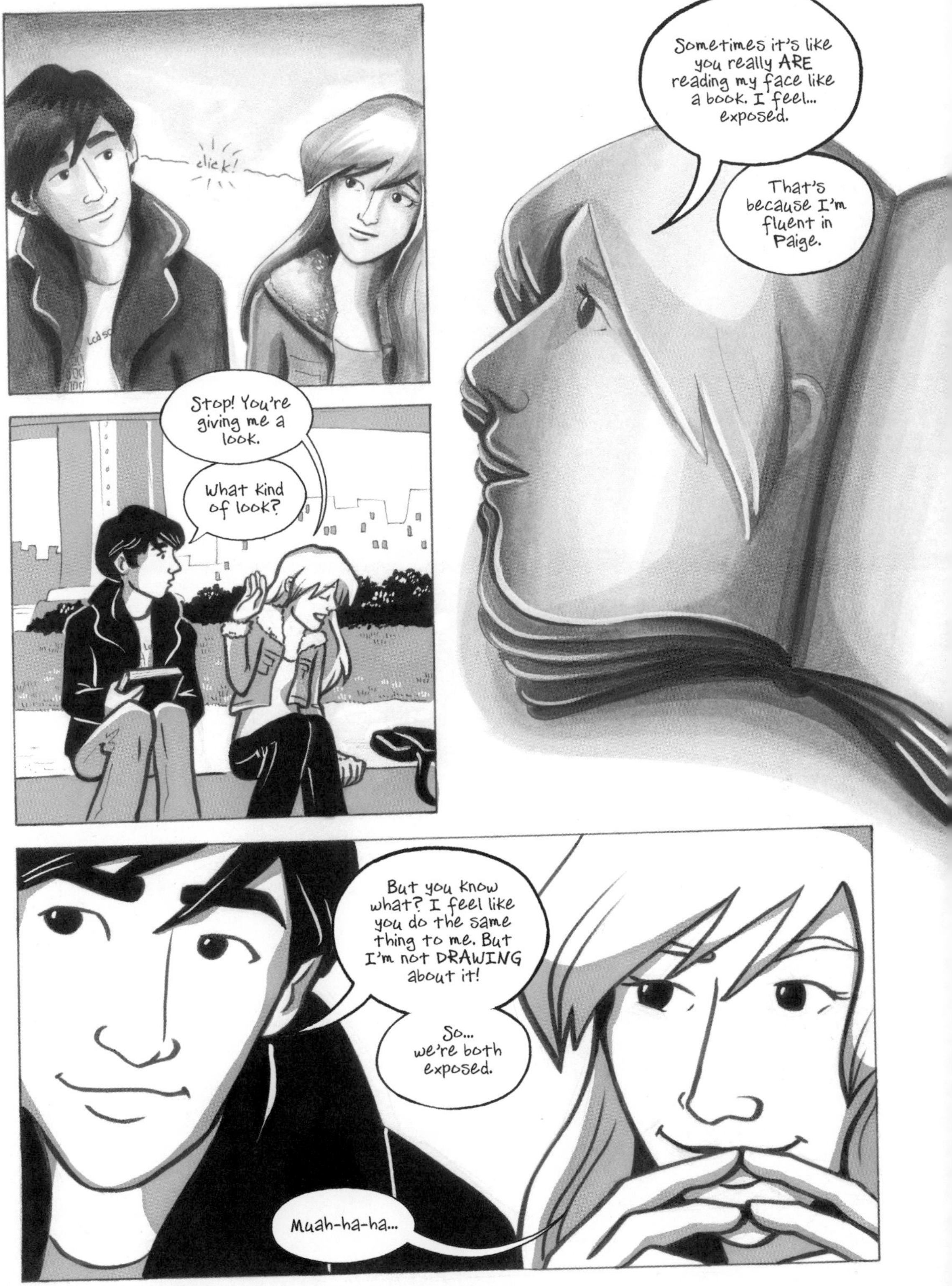
click!
Stop! You're giving me a look.
What kind of look?
Sometimes it's like you really ARE reading my face like a book. I feel... exposed.
That's because I'm fluent in Paige.
But you know what? I feel like you do the same thing to me. But I'm not DRAWING about it!
So... we're both exposed.
Muah-ha-ha...

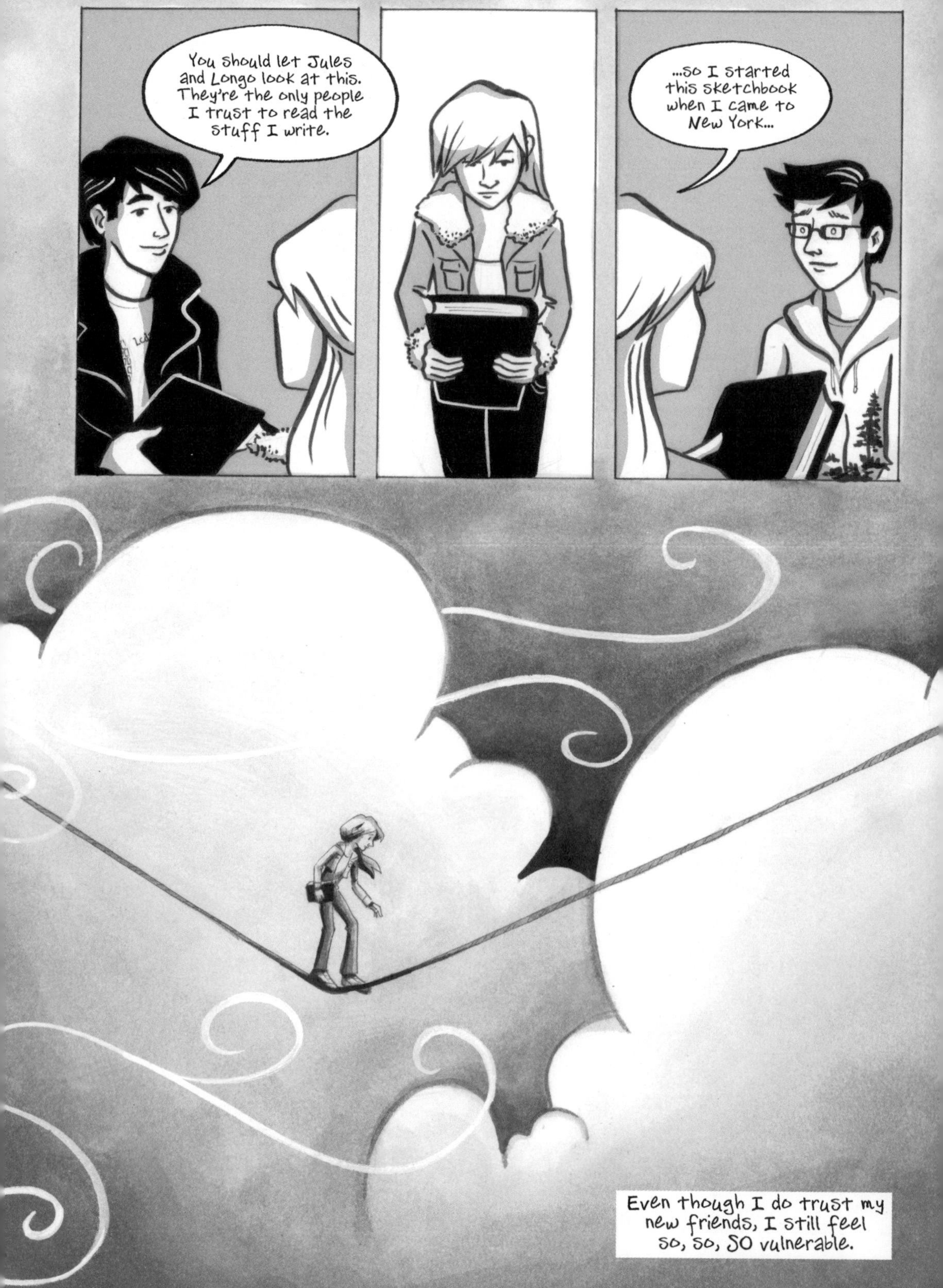
You should let Jules and Longo look at this. They're the only people I trust to read the stuff I write.
...so I started this sketchbook when I came to New York...
Even though I do trust my new friends, I still feel so, so, SO vulnerable.

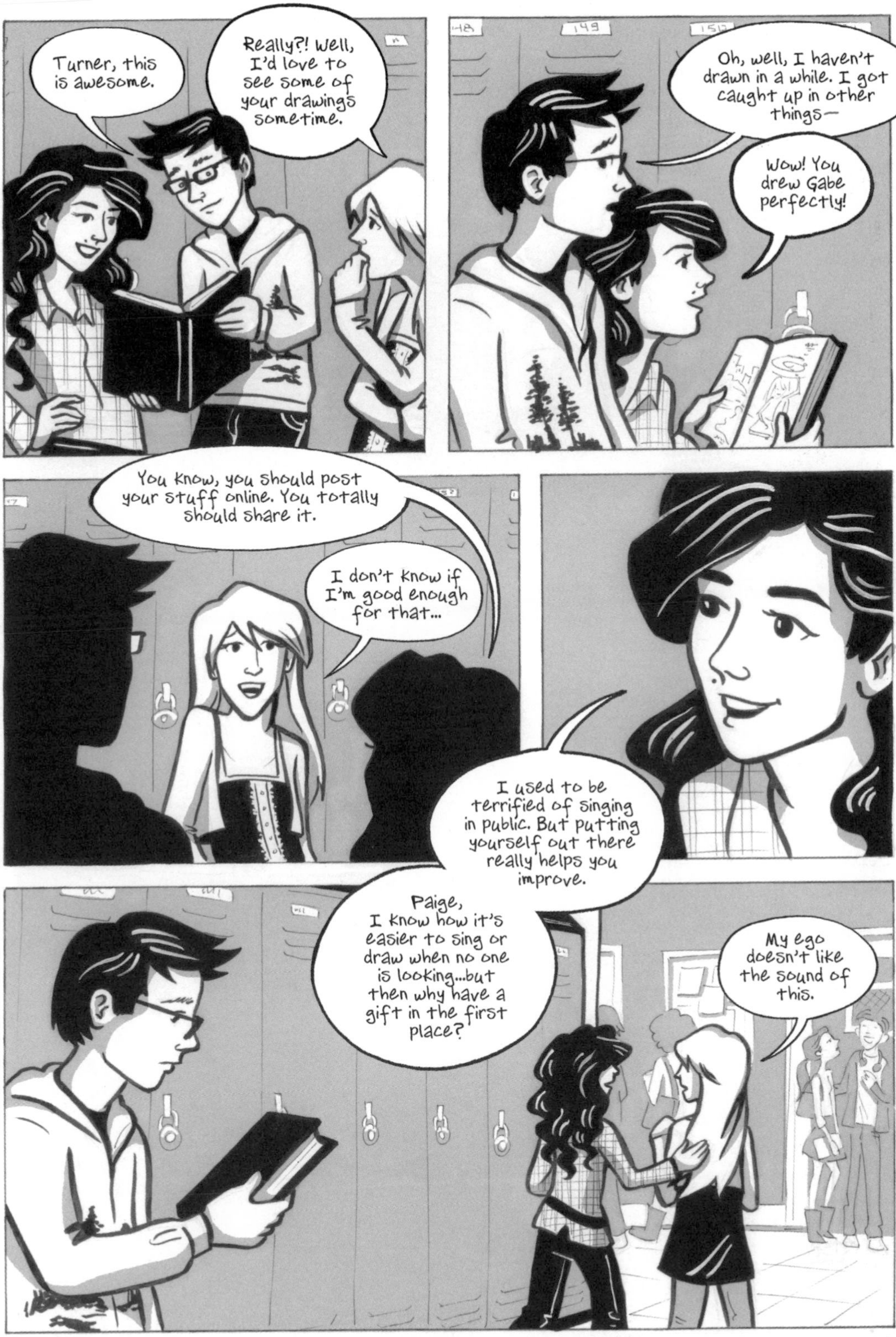
Turner, this is awesome.
Really?! Well, I'd love to see some of your drawings sometime.
Oh, well, I haven't drawn in a while. I got caught up in other things—
Wow! You drew Gabe perfectly!
You know, you should post your stuff online. You totally should share it.
I don't know if I'm good enough for that...
I used to be terrified of singing in public. But putting yourself out there really helps you improve.
Paige, I know how it's easier to sing or draw when no one is looking...but then why have a gift in the first place?
My ego doesn't like the sound of this.

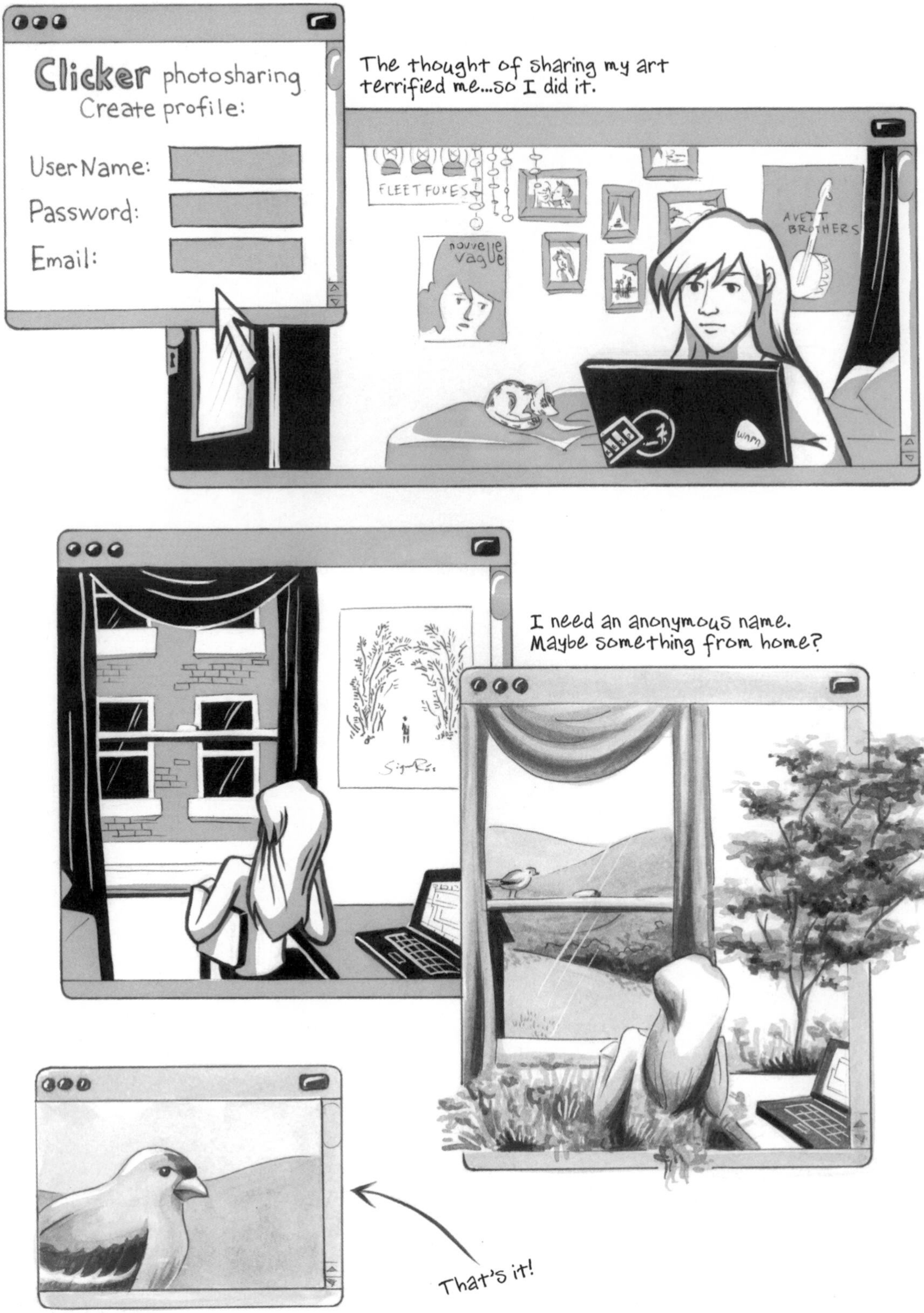
Clicker photosharing
Create profile:
UserName:
Password:
Email:
The thought of sharing my art terrified me...so I did it.
FLEET FOXES
nouvelle vague
AVETT BROTHERS
I need an anonymous name. Maybe something from home?
That's it!

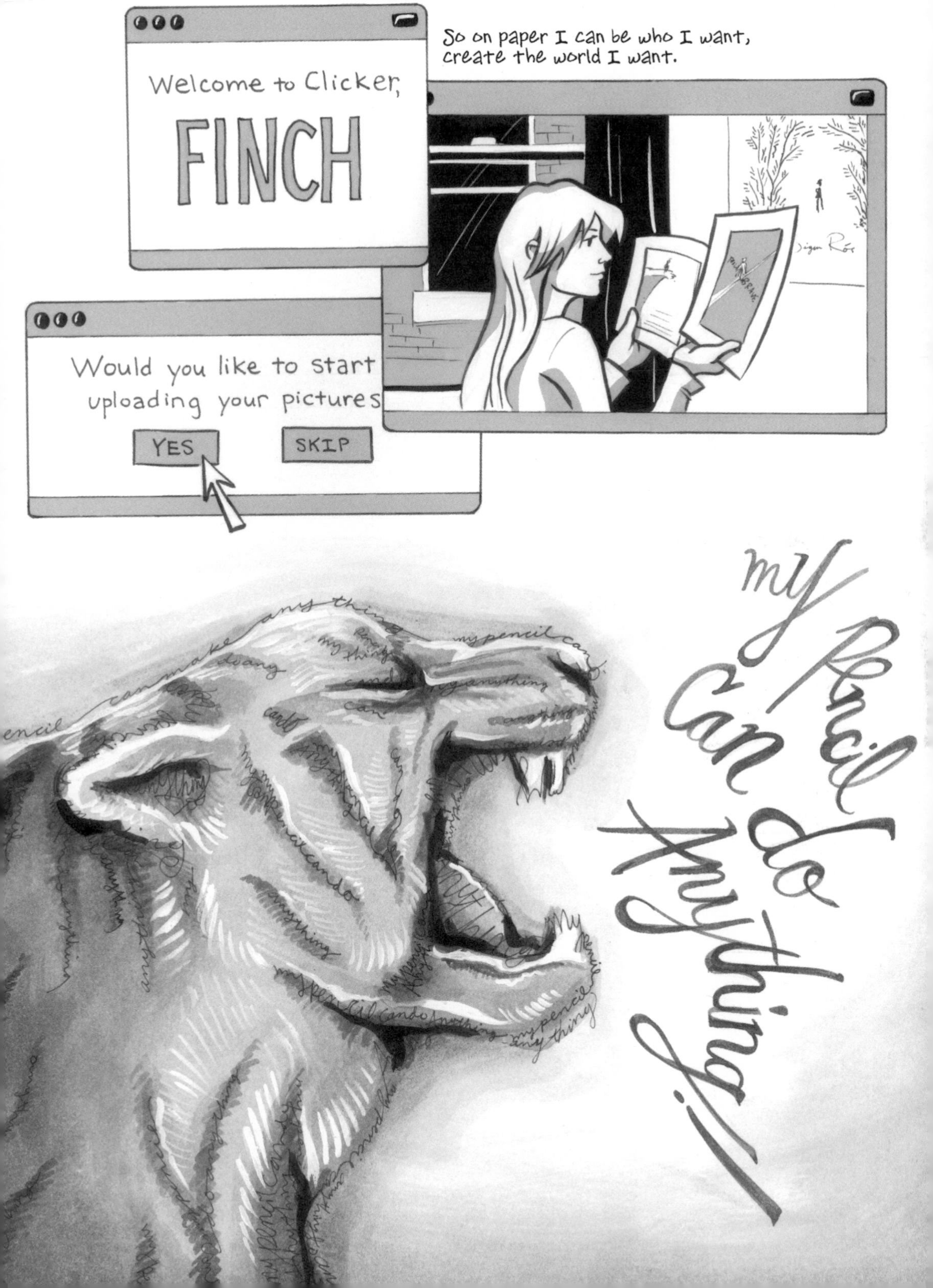
Welcome to Clicker,
FINCH
So on paper I can be who I want, create the world I want.
Would you like to start uploading your pictures
YES
SKIP
my pencil can do Anything!

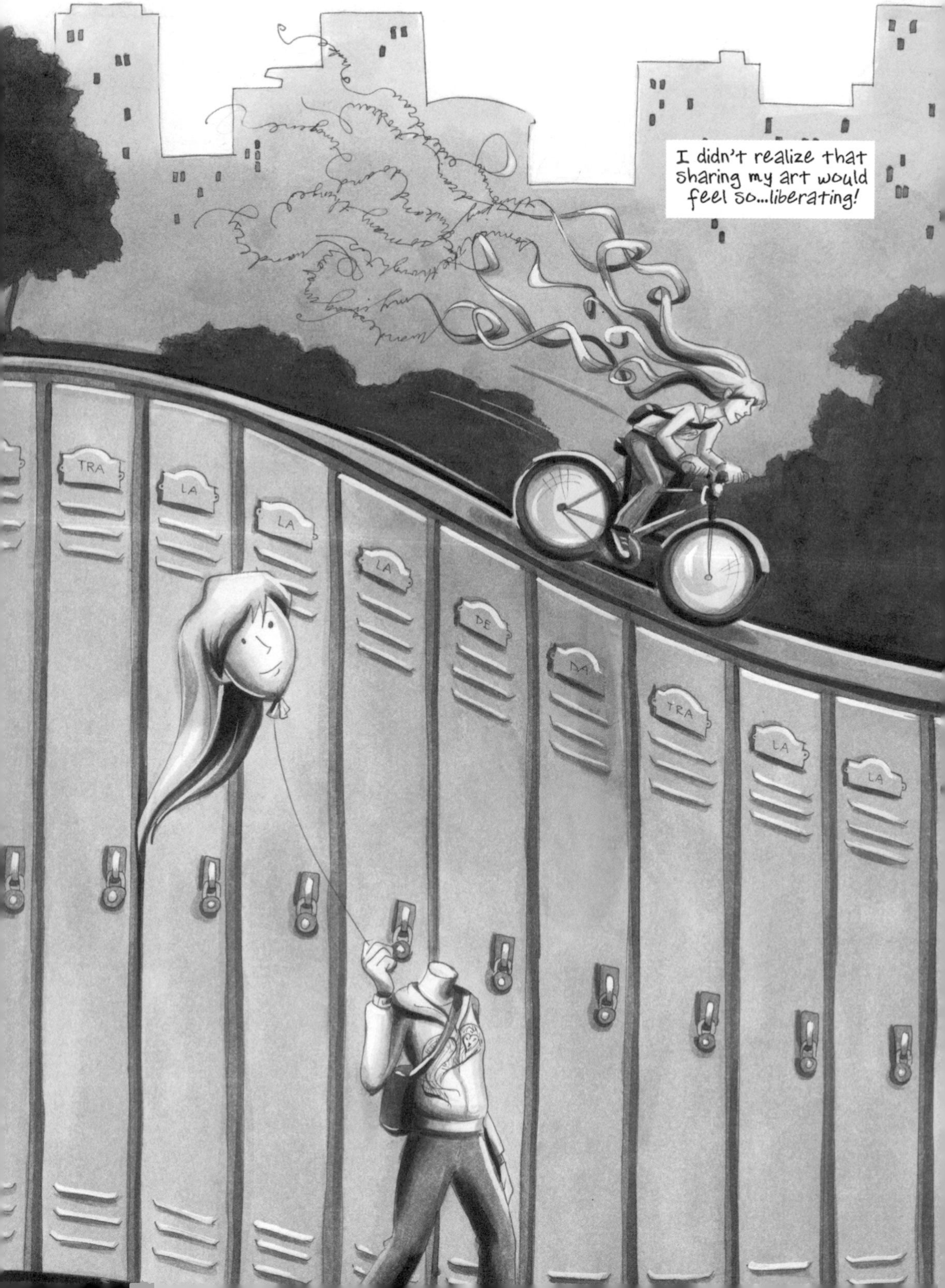
I didn't realize that sharing my art would feel so...liberating!
TRA LA LA LA DE DA TRA LA LA

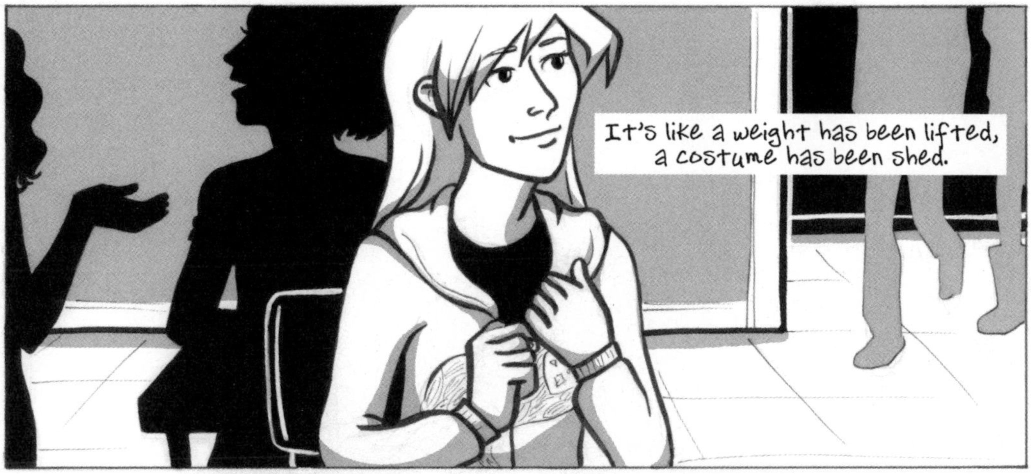
It's like a weight has been lifted, a costume has been shed.

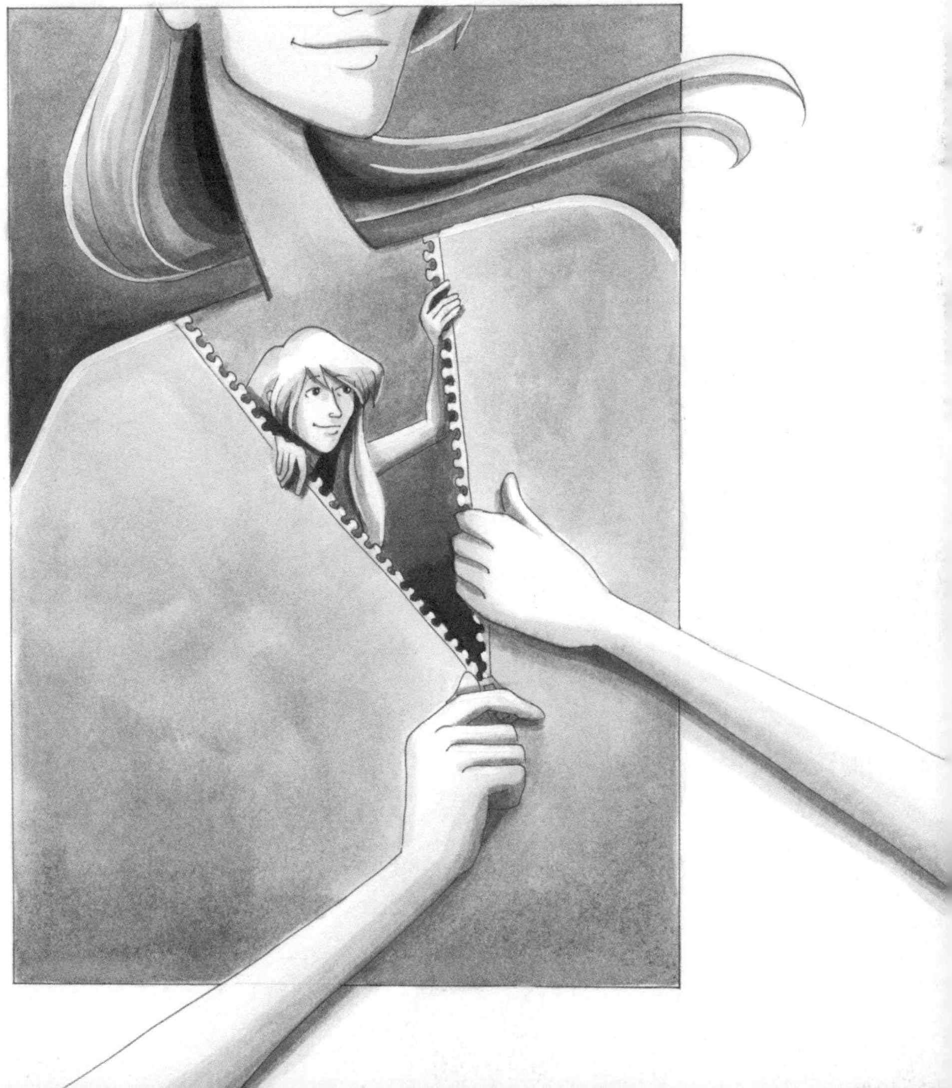

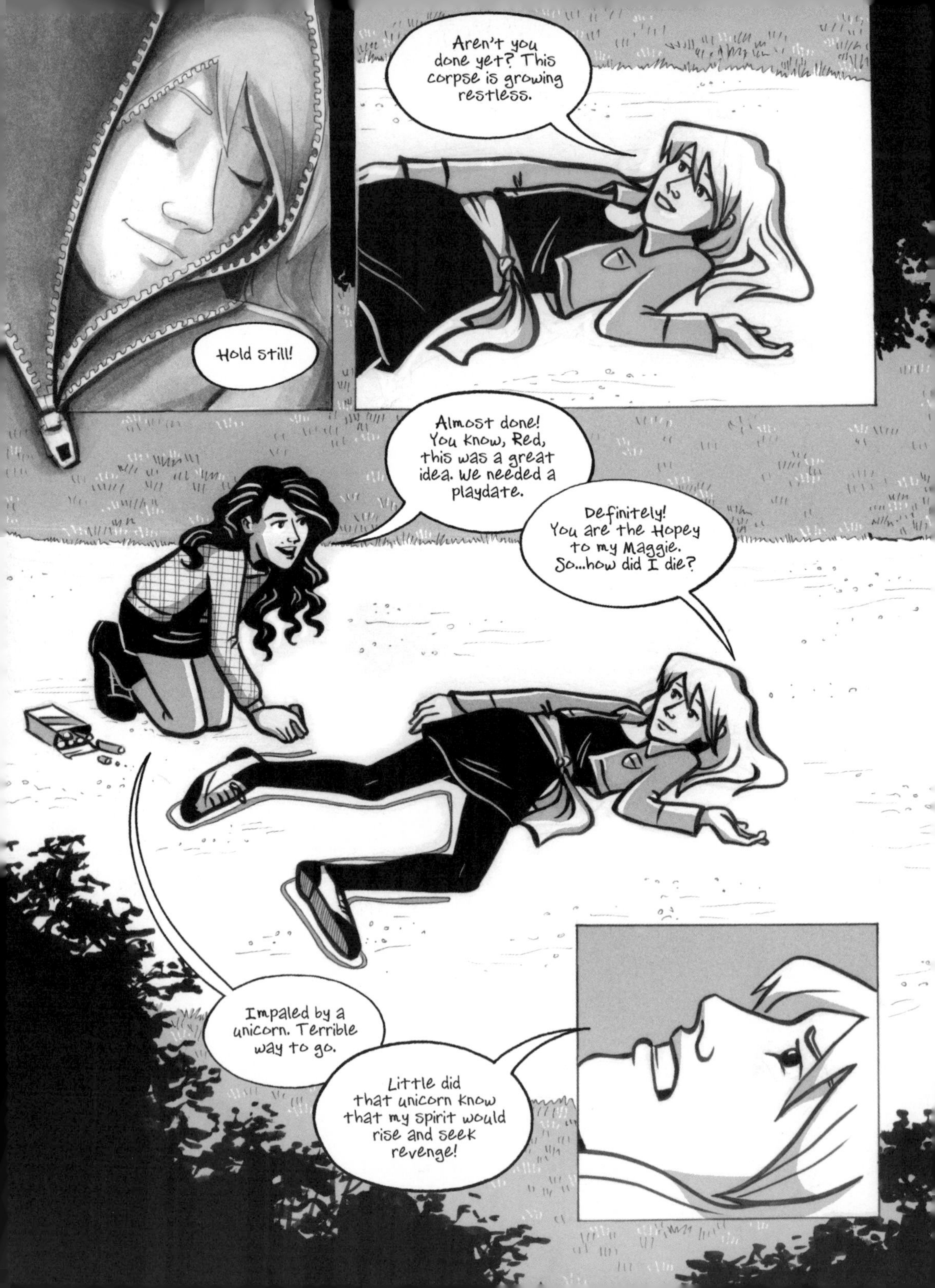
Hold still!
Aren't you done yet? This corpse is growing restless.
Almost done! You know, Red, this was a great idea. We needed a playdate.
Definitely! You are the Hopey to my Maggie. So...how did I die?
Impaled by a unicorn. Terrible way to go.
Little did that unicorn know that my spirit would rise and seek revenge!

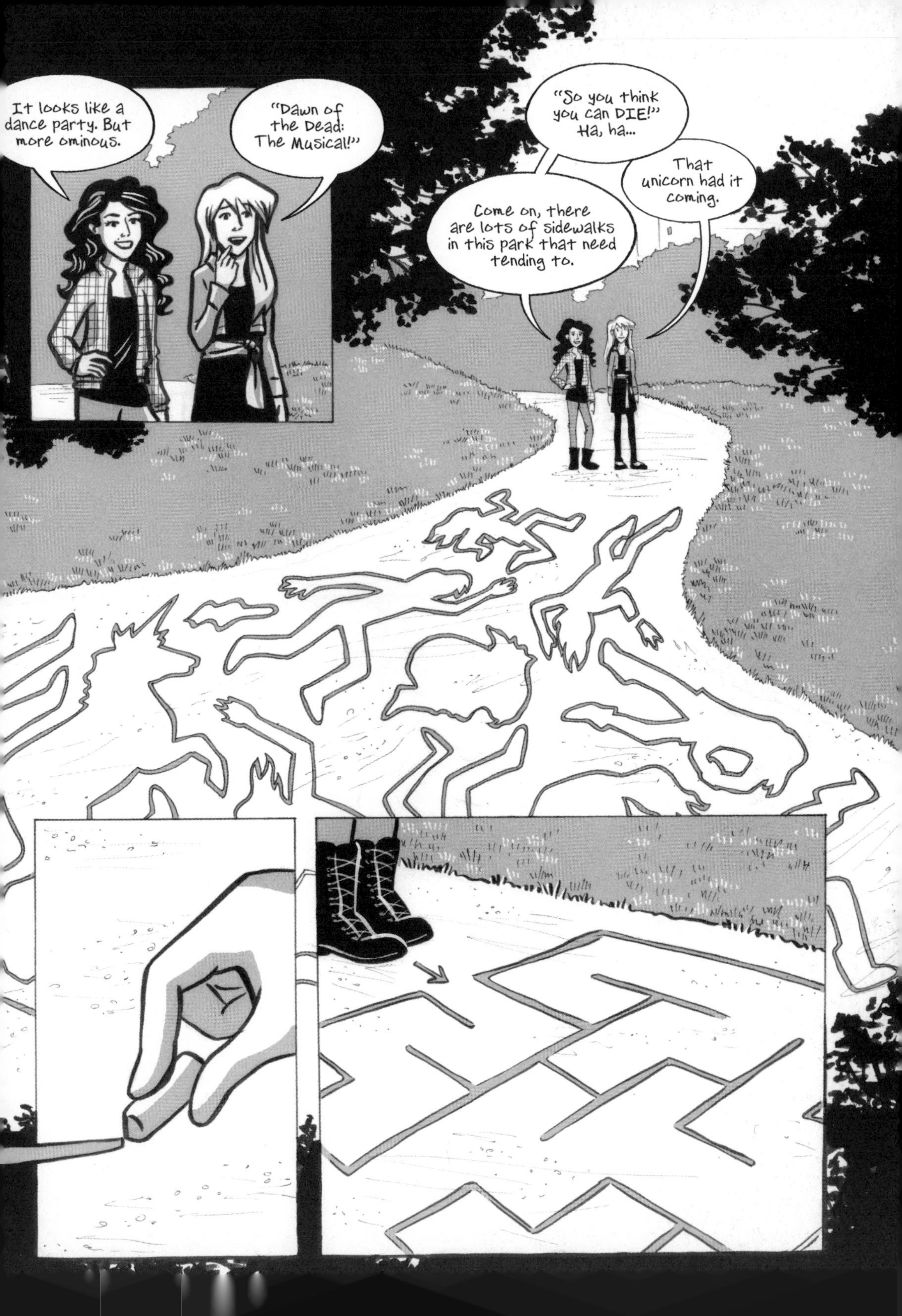

It looks like a dance party. But more ominous.
"Dawn of the Dead: The Musical!"
"So you think you can DIE!" Ha, ha...
That unicorn had it coming.
Come on, there are lots of sidewalks in this park that need tending to.

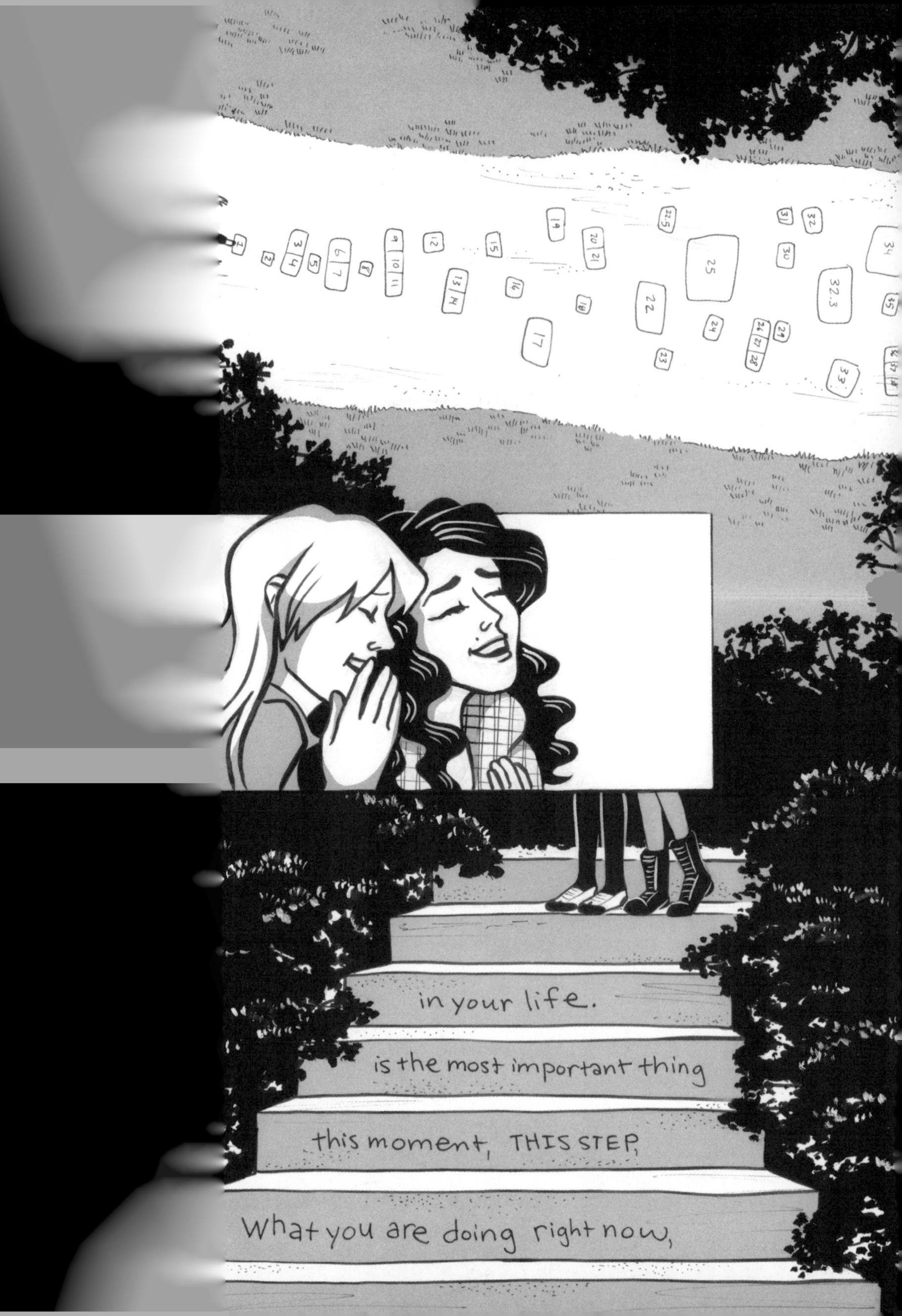
What you are doing right now,
this moment, THIS STEP,
is the most important thing
in your life.

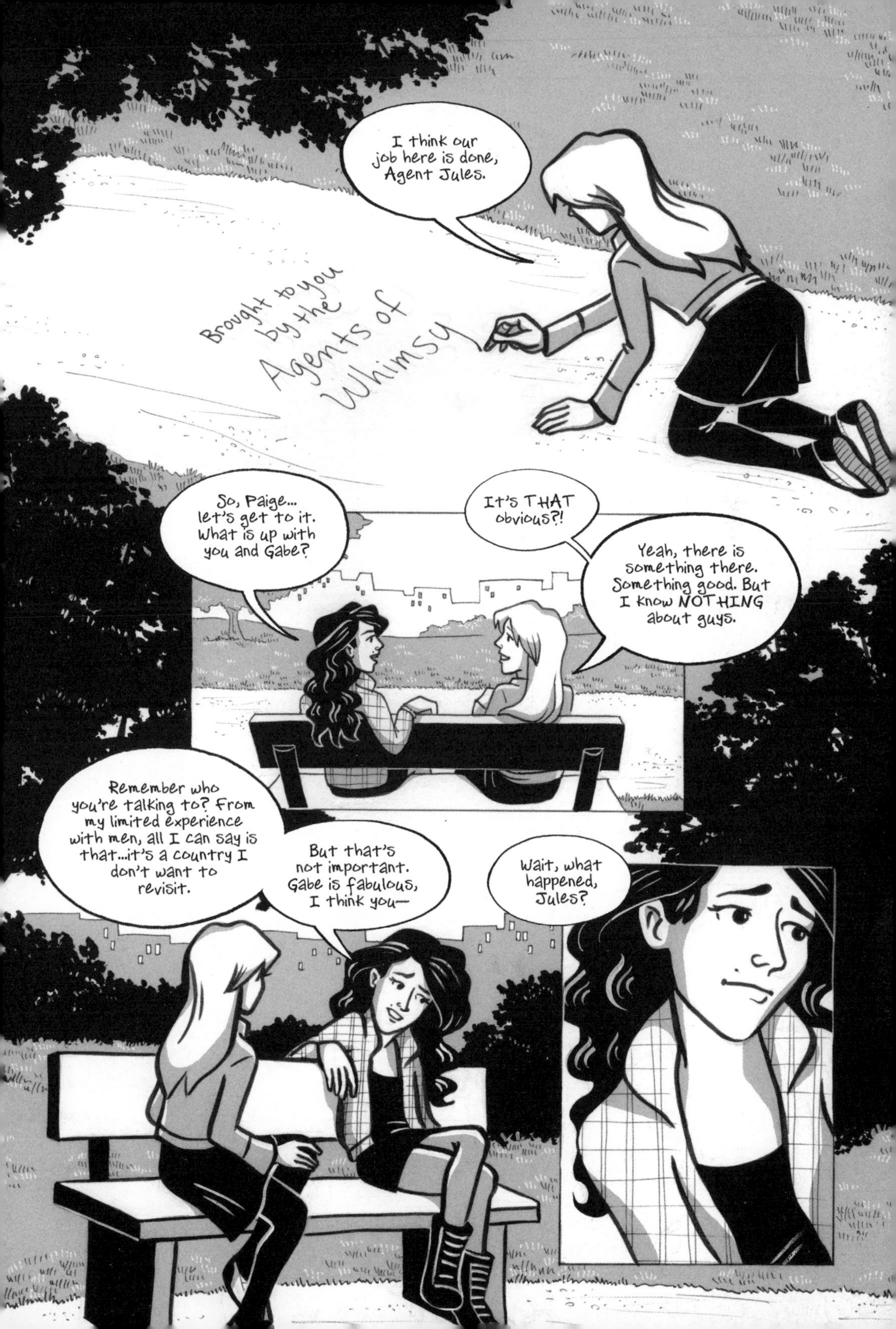

I think our job here is done, Agent Jules.
Brought to you by the Agents of Whimsy
So, Paige... let's get to it. What is up with you and Gabe?
It's THAT obvious?!
Yeah, there is something there. Something good. But I know NOTHING about guys.
Remember who you're talking to? From my limited experience with men, all I can say is that...it's a country I don't want to revisit.
But that's not important. Gabe is fabulous, I think you—
Wait, what happened, Jules?

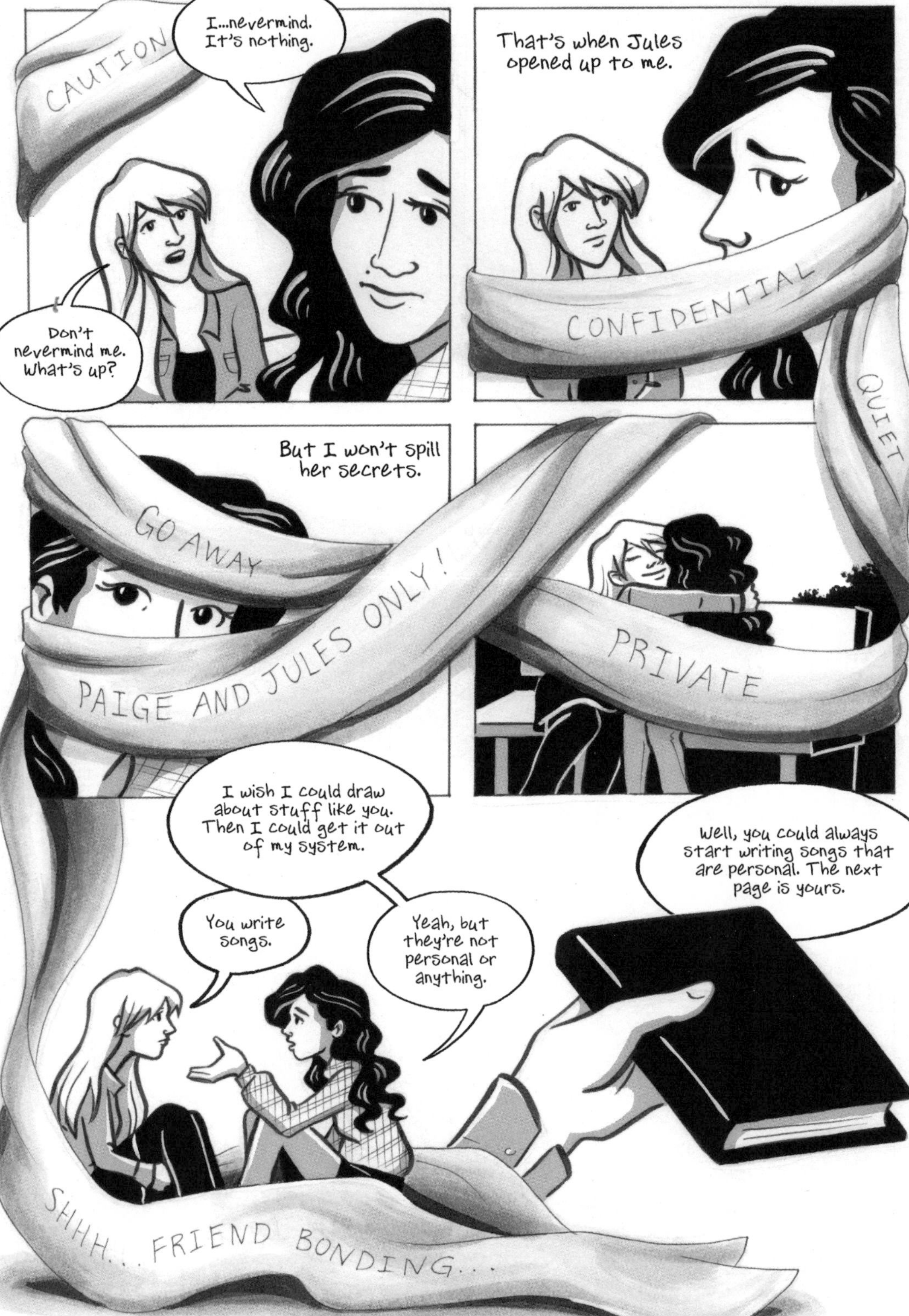
CAUTION
I...nevermind. It's nothing.
Don't nevermind me. What's up?
That's when Jules opened up to me.
CONFIDENTIAL
QUIET
But I won't spill her secrets.
GO AWAY
PAIGE AND JULES ONLY!
PRIVATE
I wish I could draw about stuff like you. Then I could get it out of my system.
You write songs.
Yeah, but they're not personal or anything.
Well, you could always start writing songs that are personal. The next page is yours.
SHHH...FRIEND BONDING...

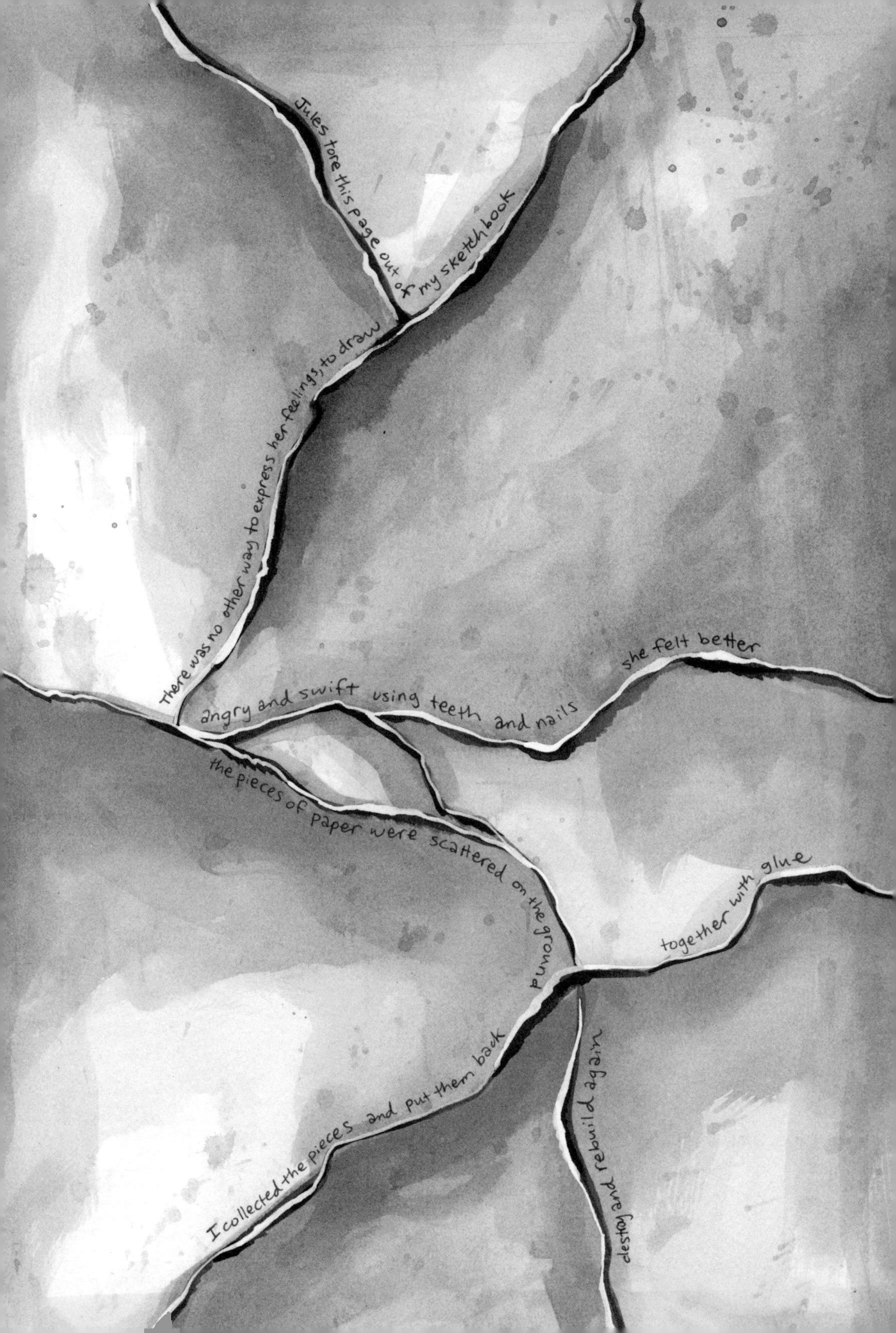
Jules tore this page out of my sketchbook
There was no other way to express her feelings, to draw
angry and swift using teeth and nails
she felt better
the pieces of paper were scattered on the ground
I collected the pieces and put them back
together with glue
destoy and rebuild again

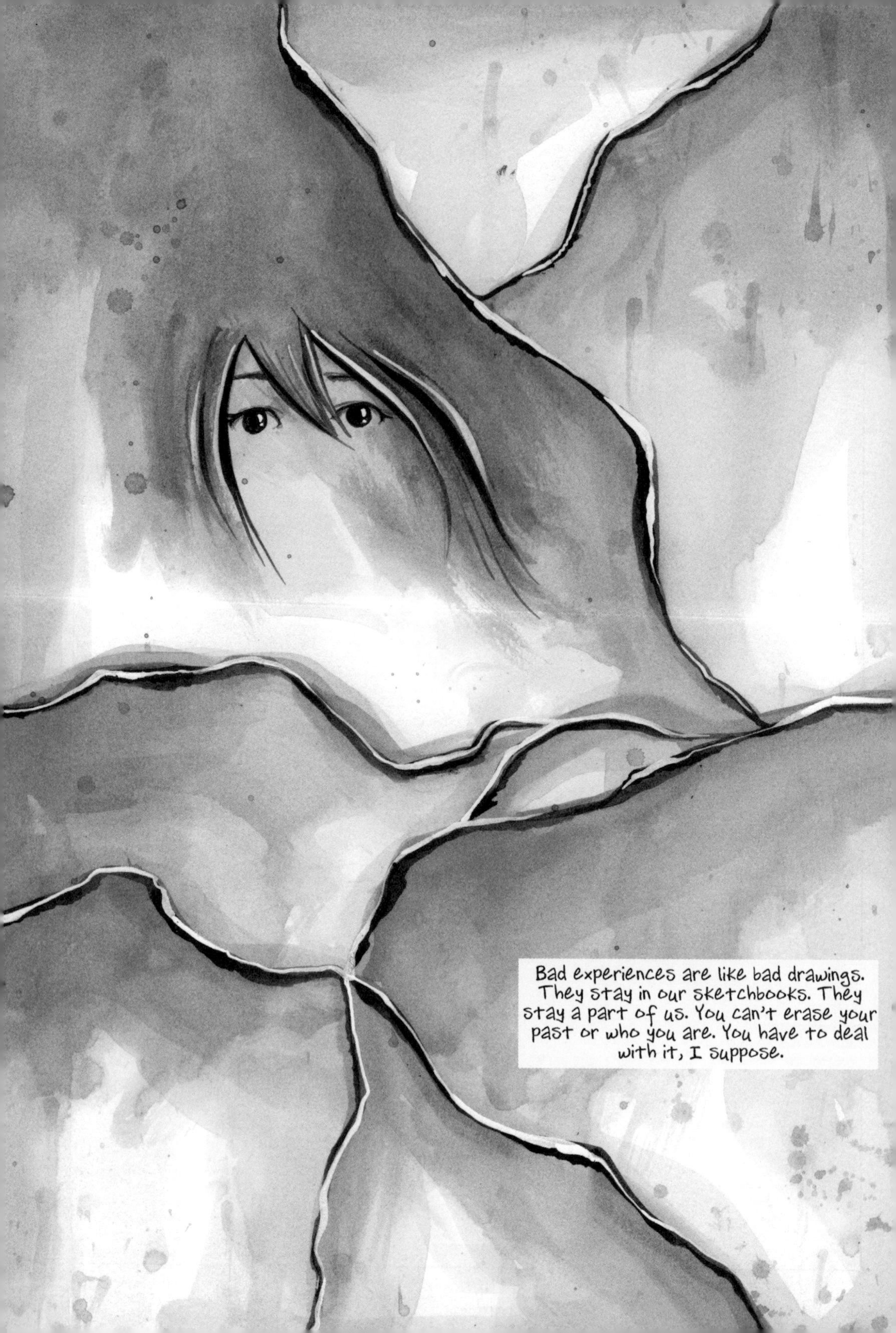
Bad experiences are like bad drawings. They stay in our sketchbooks. They stay a part of us. You can't erase your past or who you are. You have to deal with it, I suppose.

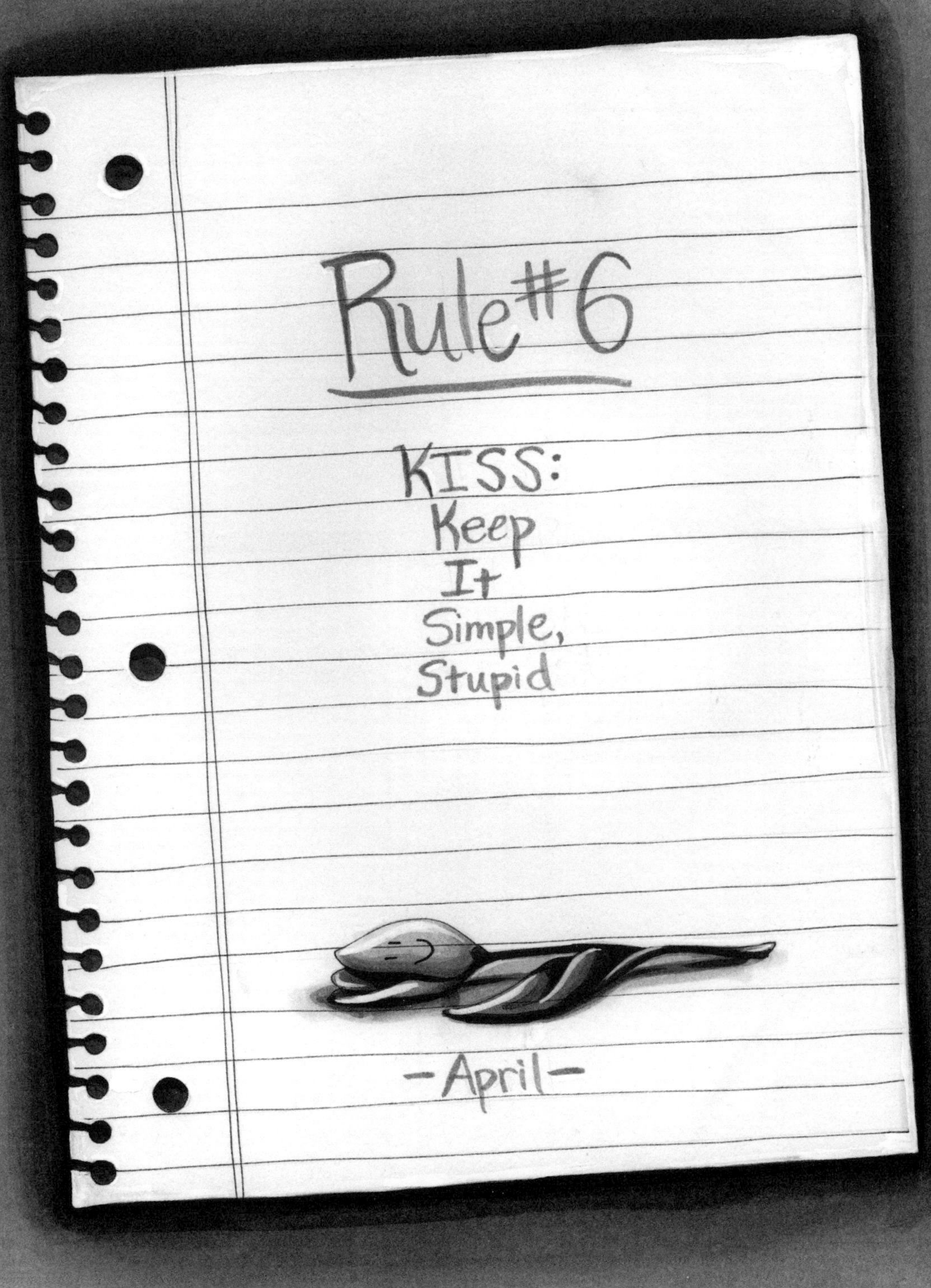
Rule #6
KISS:
Keep
It
Simple,
Stupid
-April-

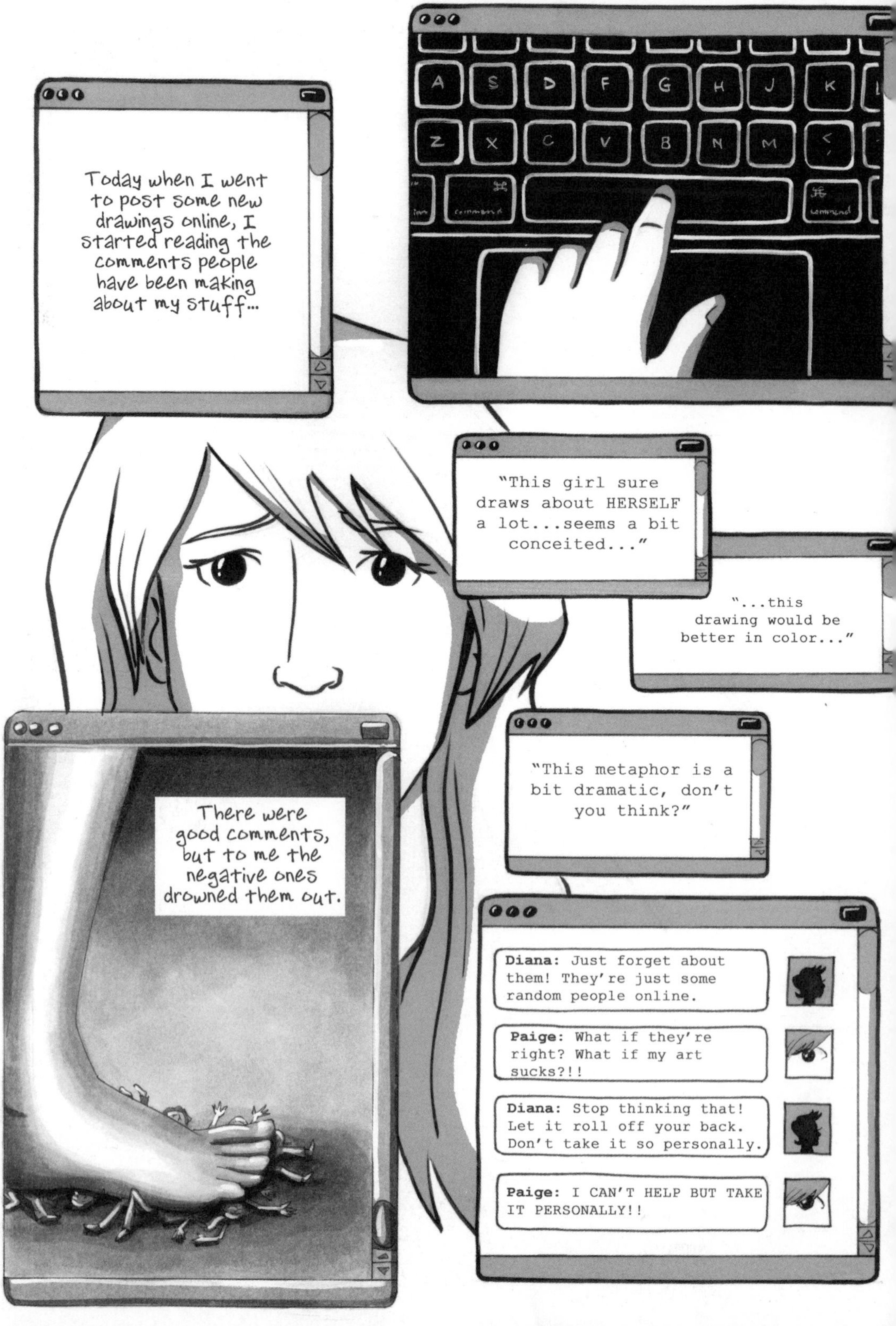

Today when I went to post some new drawings online, I started reading the comments people have been making about my stuff...
A
S
D
F
G
H
J
K
Z
X
C
V
B
N
M
"This girl sure draws about HERSELF a lot...seems a bit conceited..."
"...this drawing would be better in color..."
There were good comments, but to me the negative ones drowned them out.
"This metaphor is a bit dramatic, don't you think?"
Diana: Just forget about them! They're just some random people online.
Paige: What if they're right? What if my art sucks?!!
Diana: Stop thinking that! Let it roll off your back. Don't take it so personally.
Paige: I CAN'T HELP BUT TAKE IT PERSONALLY!!

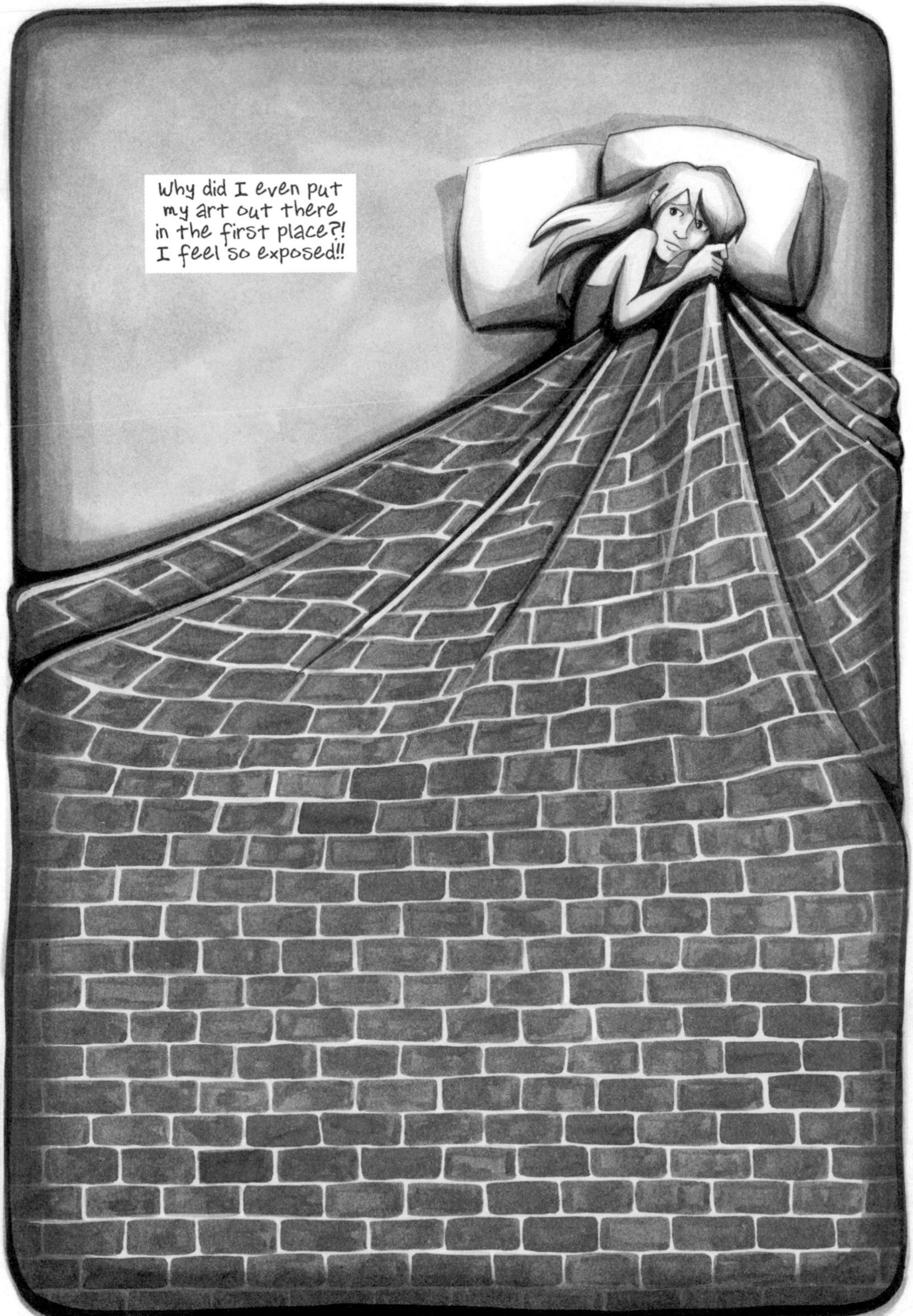
Why did I even put my art out there in the first place?! I feel so exposed!!

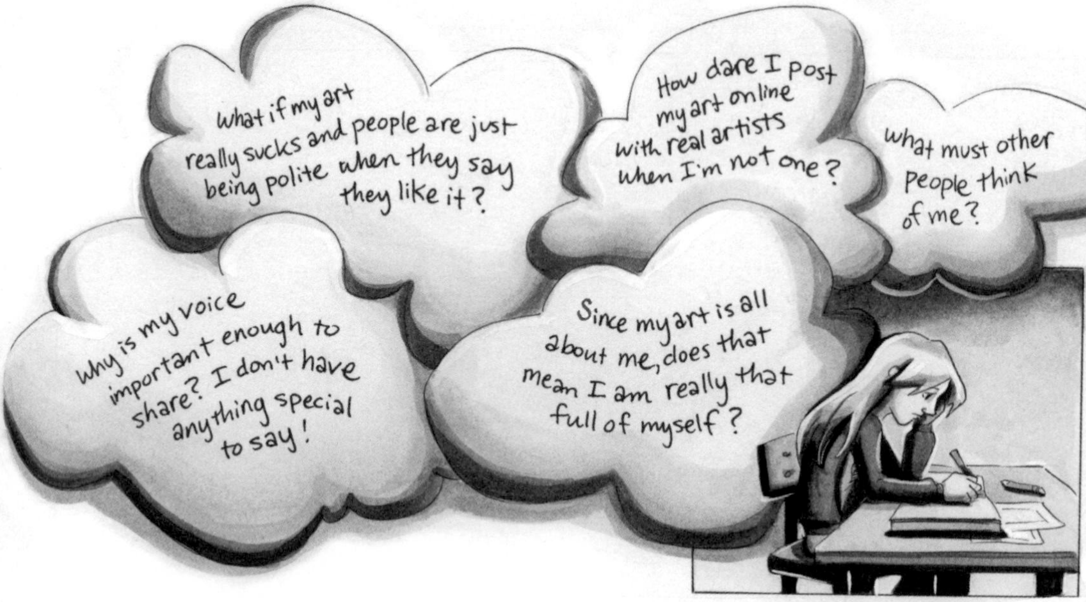
What if my art really sucks and people are just being polite when they say they like it?
How dare I post my art online with real artists when I'm not one?
What must other people think of me?
Why is my voice important enough to share? I don't have anything special to say!
Since my art is all about me, does that mean I am really that full of myself?

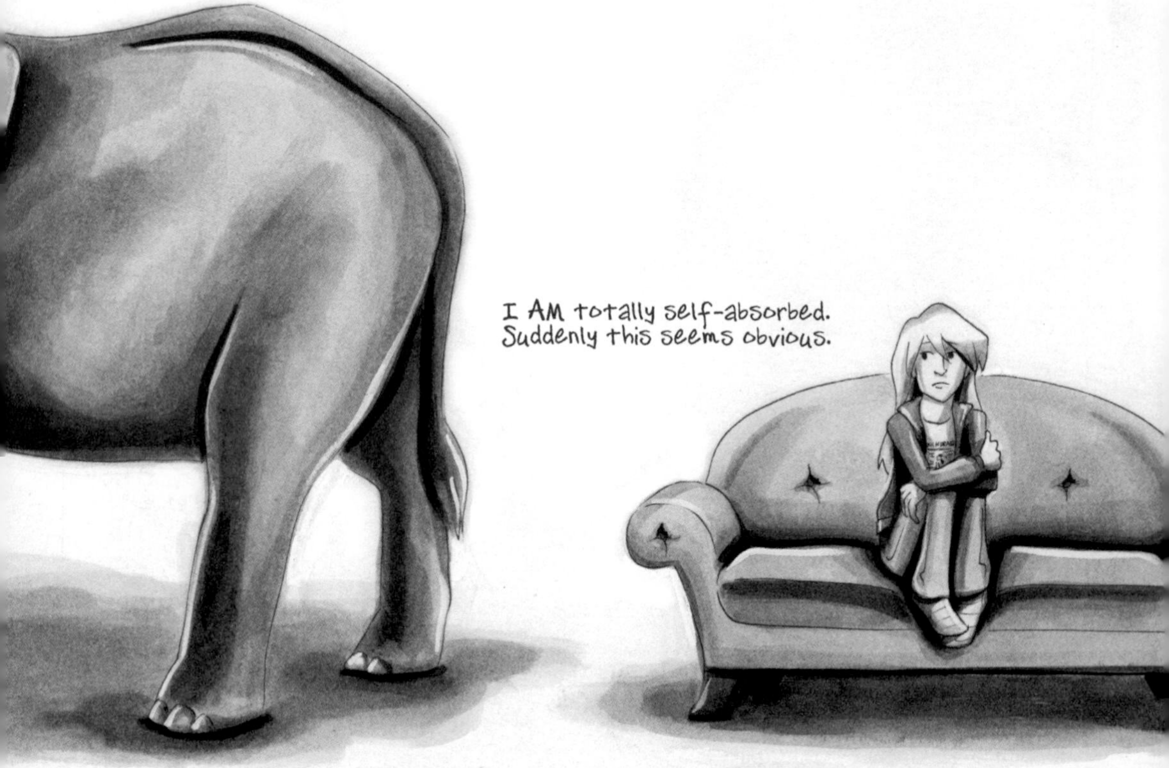
I AM totally self-absorbed. Suddenly this seems obvious.

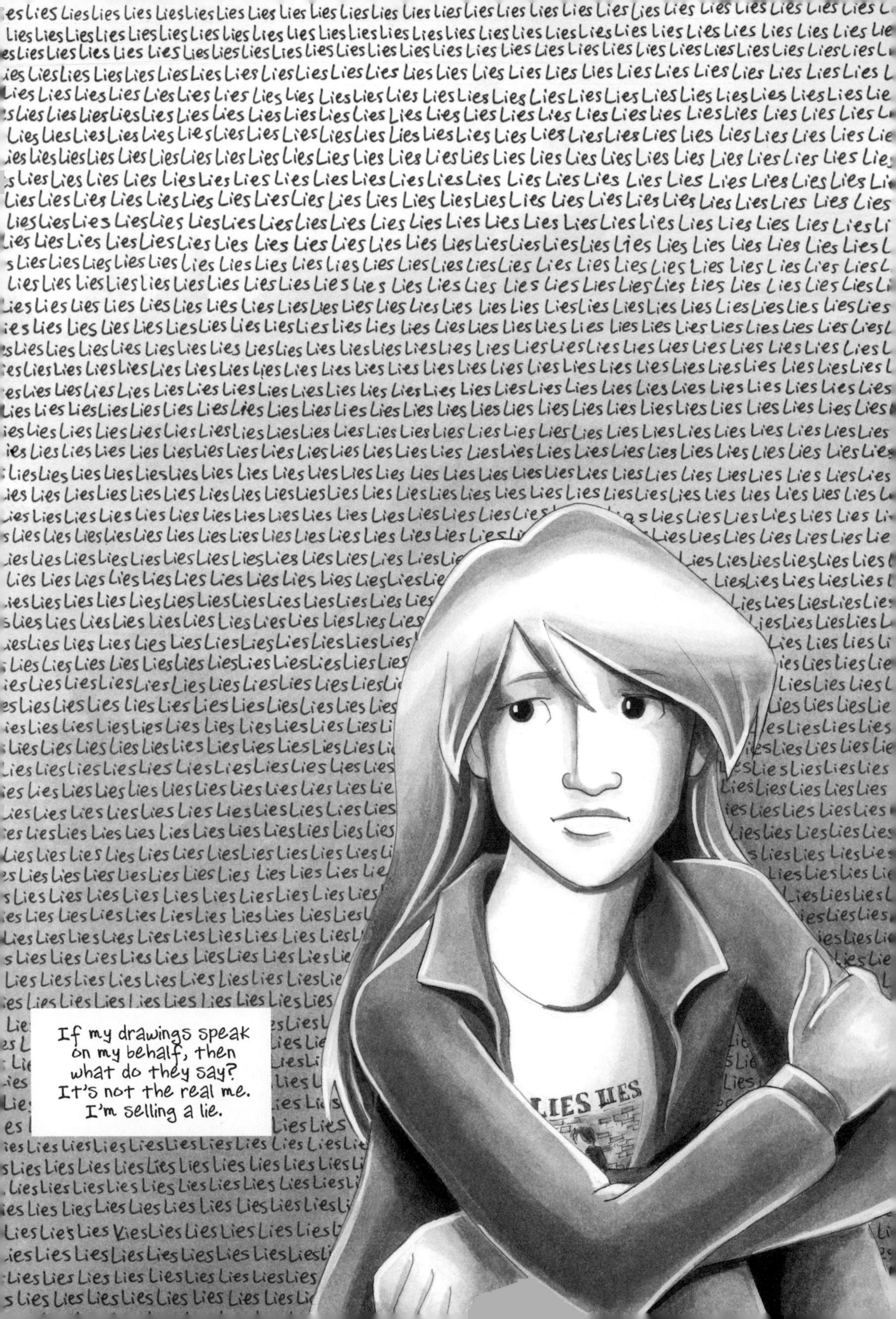
If my drawings speak on my behalf, then what do they say? It's not the real me. I'm selling a lie.
LIES LIES

I always do this. I make things more complicated than they really are.

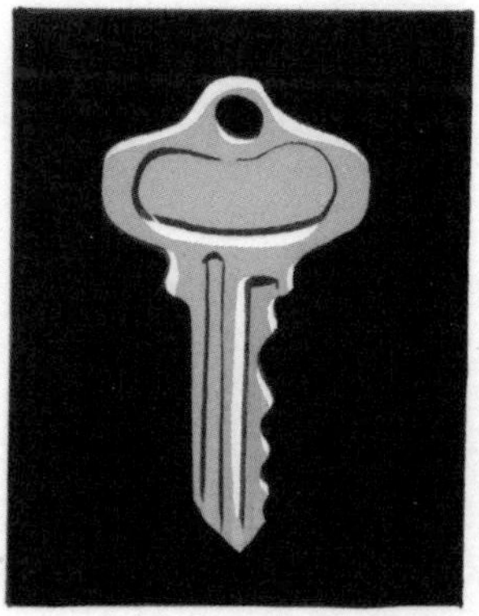

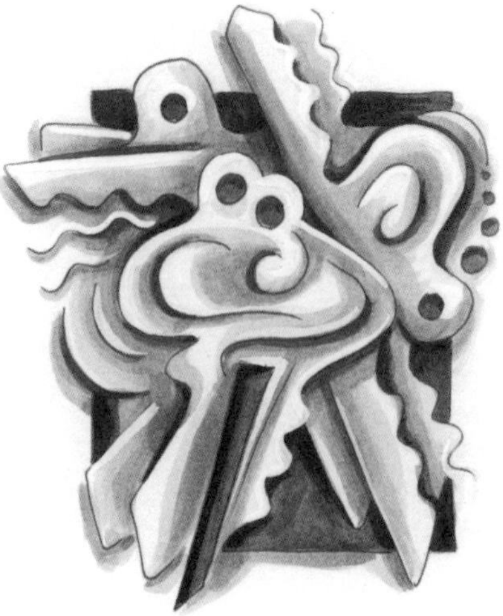

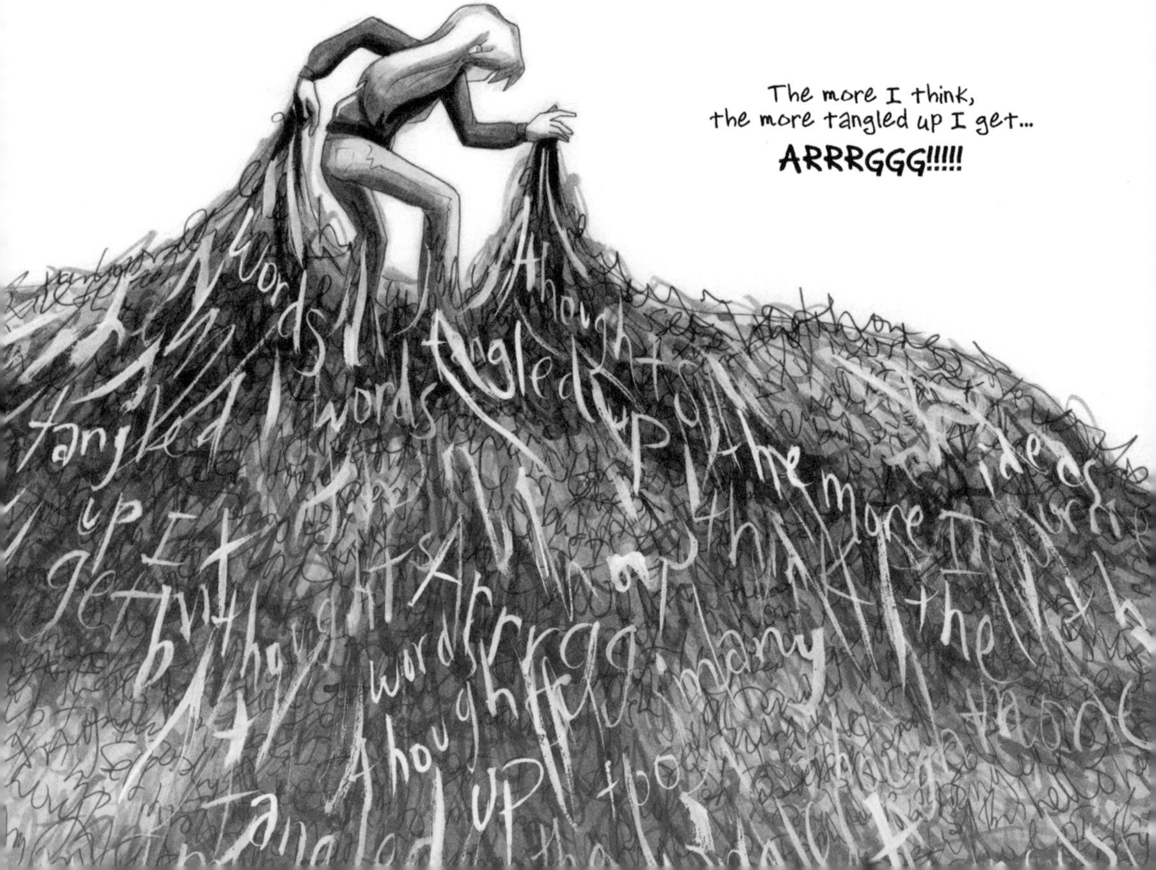

The more I think,
the more tangled up I get...
ARRRGGG!!!!!

And I didn't draw for a week.

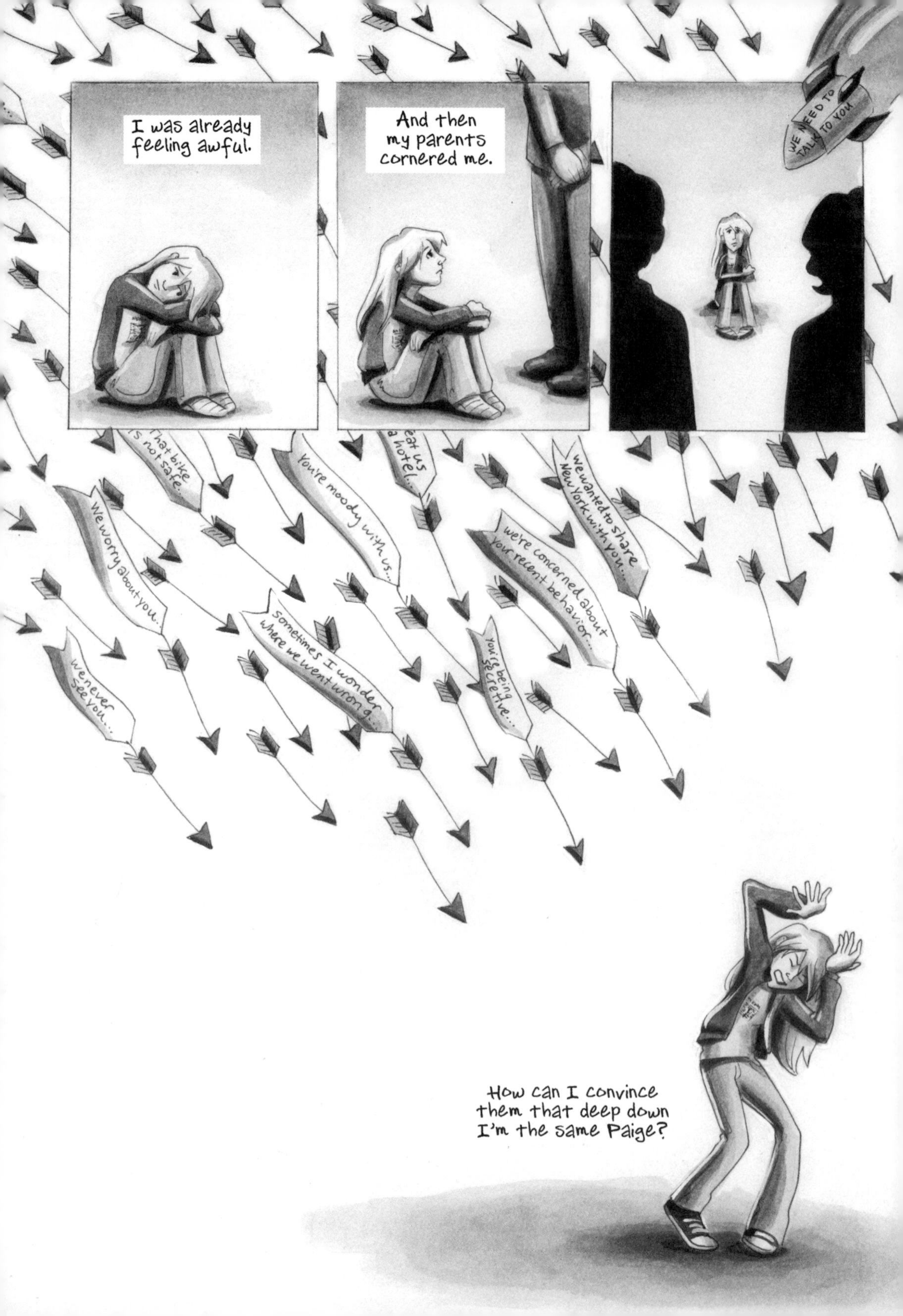
I was already feeling awful.
And then my parents cornered me.
WE NEED TO TALK TO YOU
That bike s not safe...
eat us a hotel...
You're moody with us...
We wanted to share New York with you...
We worry about you...
We're concerned about your recent behavior...
Sometimes I wonder where we went wrong...
You're being secretive...
We never see you...
How can I convince them that deep down I'm the same Paige?

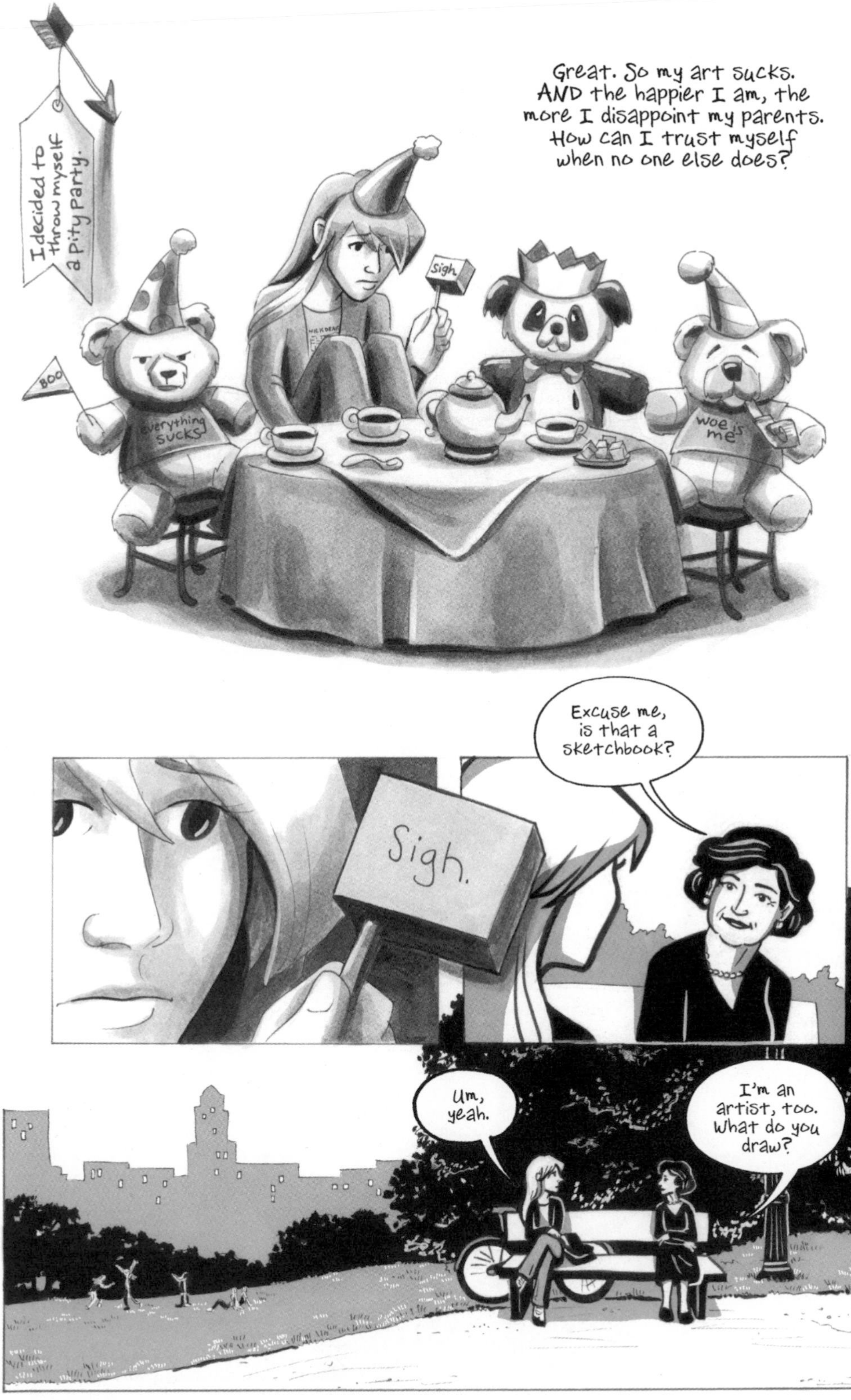
I decided to throw myself a pity party.
Great. So my art sucks. AND the happier I am, the more I disappoint my parents. How can I trust myself when no one else does?
Sigh.
BOO
everything sucks
woe is me
Sigh.
Excuse me, is that a sketchbook?
Um, yeah.
I'm an artist, too. What do you draw?

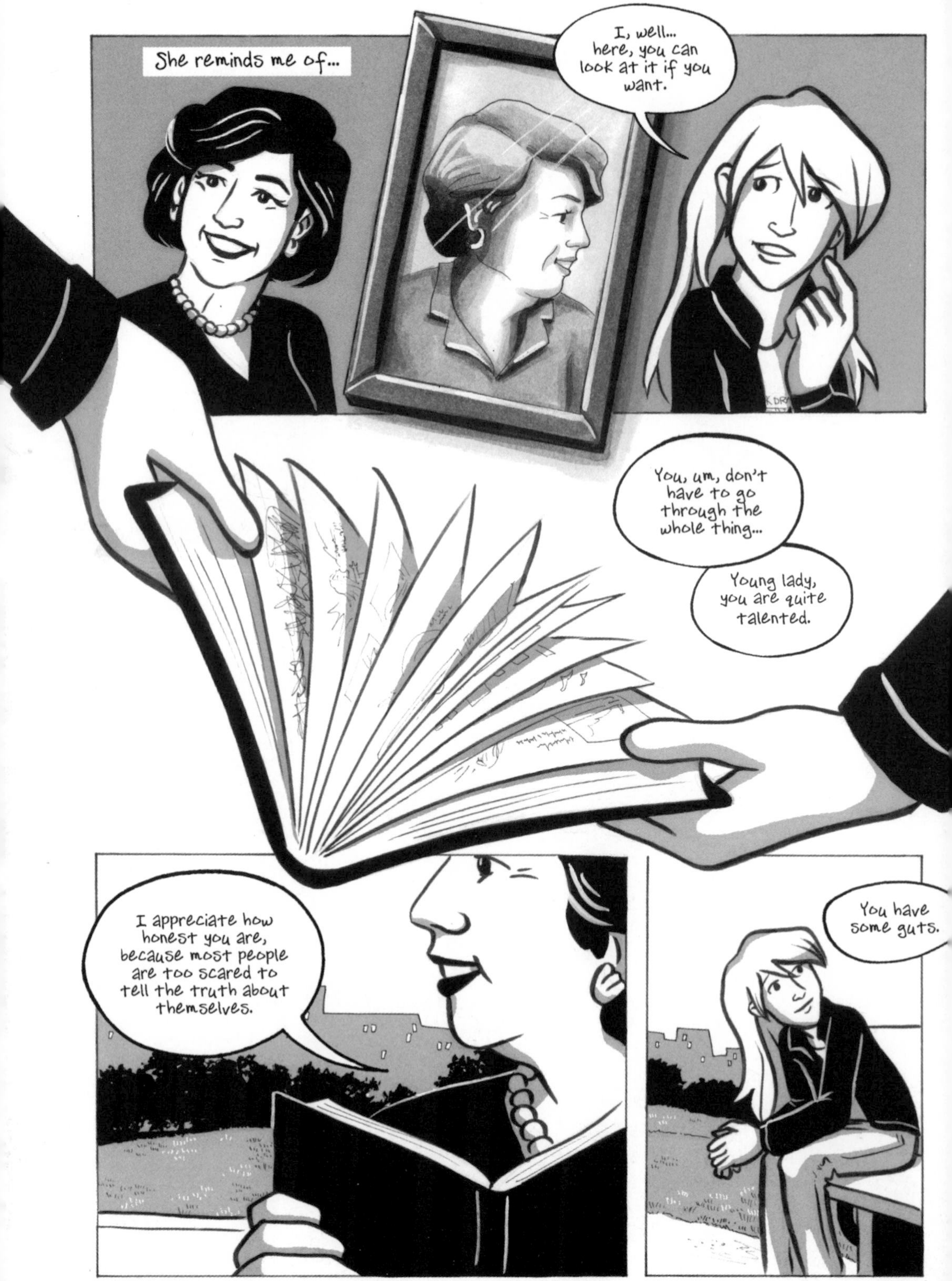
She reminds me of...
I, well... here, you can look at it if you want.
You, um, don't have to go through the whole thing...
Young lady, you are quite talented.
I appreciate how honest you are, because most people are too scared to tell the truth about themselves.
You have some guts.

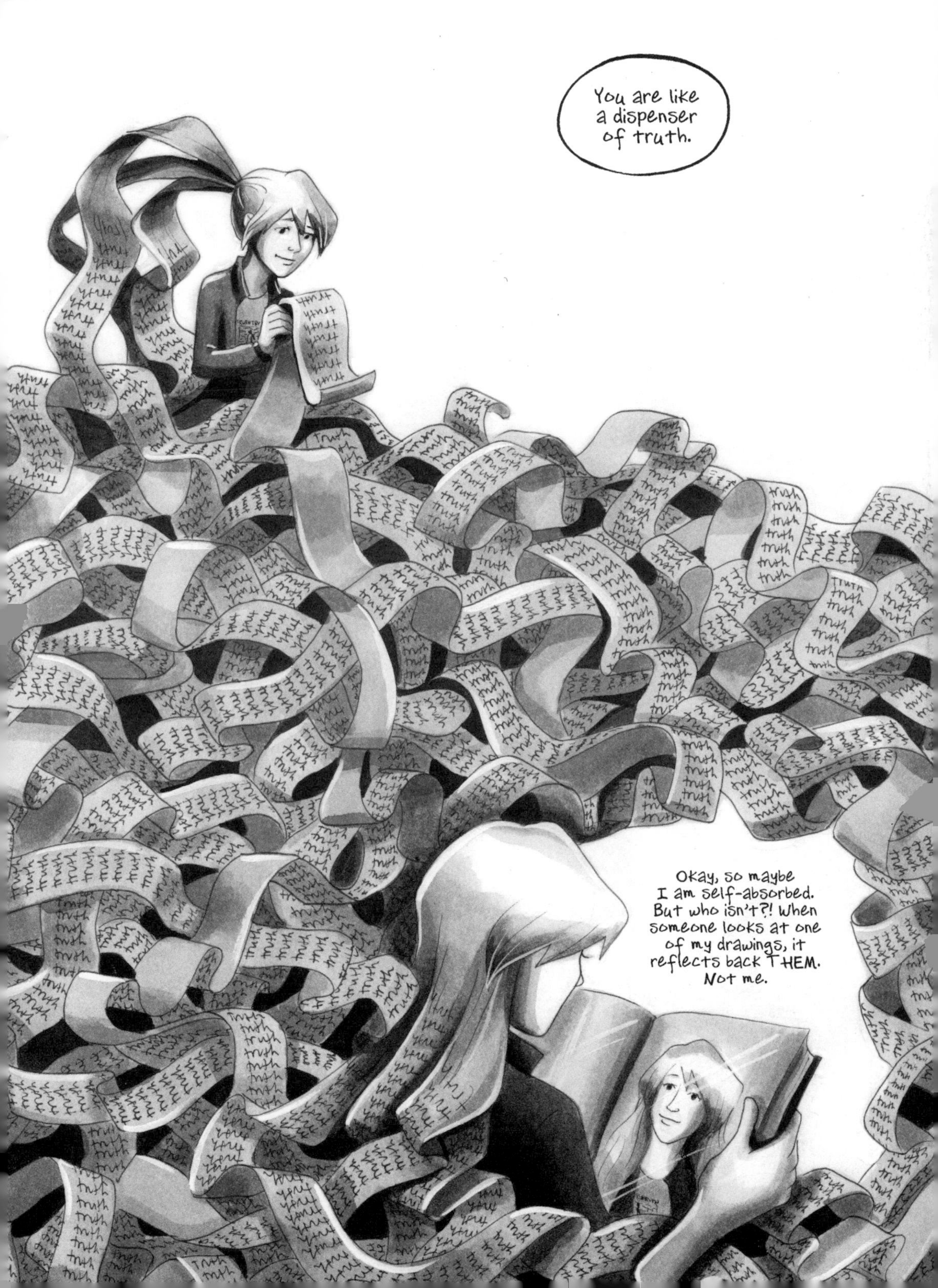
You are like a dispenser of truth.
Okay, so maybe I am self-absorbed. But who isn't?! When someone looks at one of my drawings, it reflects back THEM. Not me.

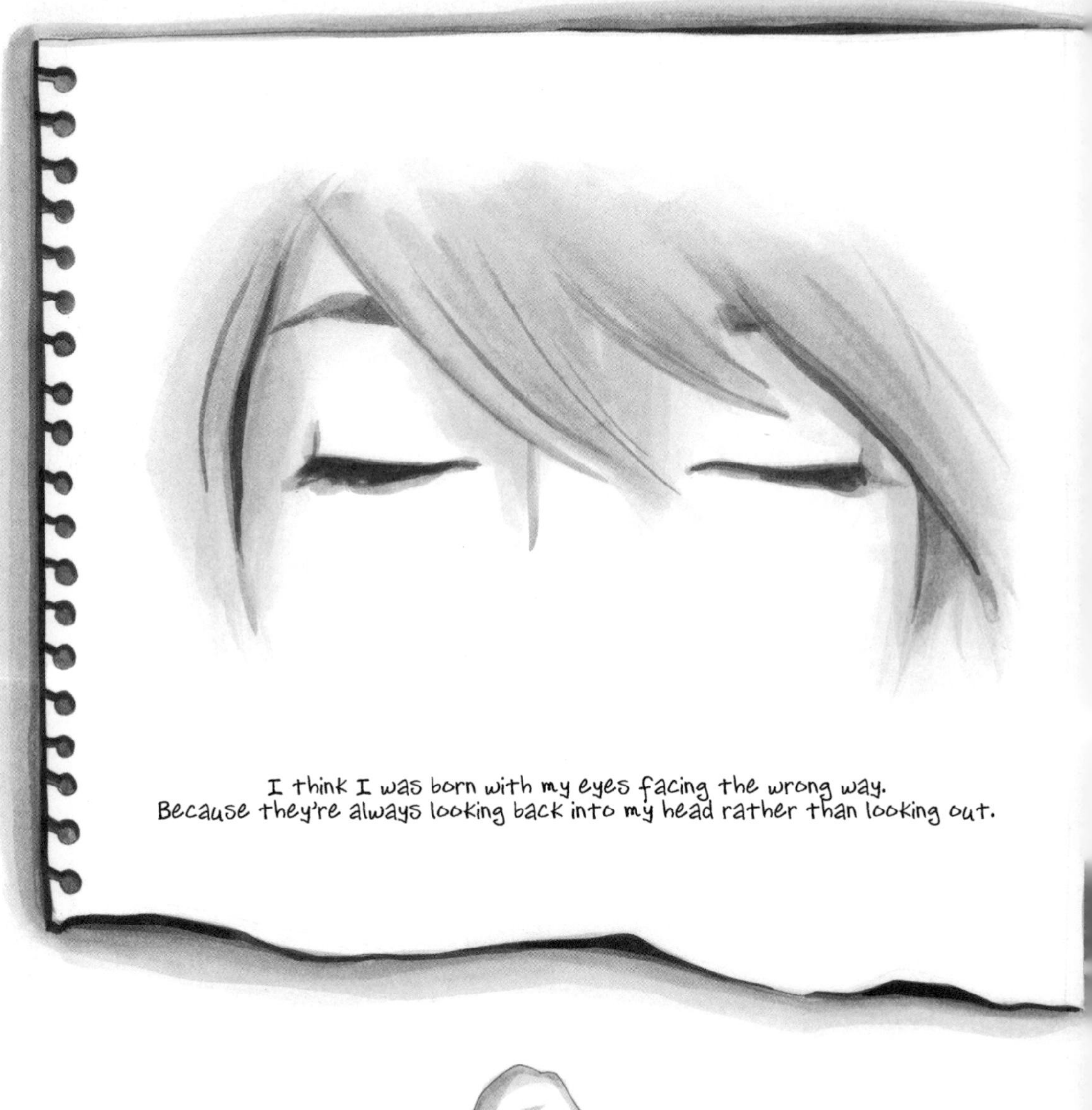
I think I was born with my eyes facing the wrong way.
Because they're always looking back into my head rather than looking out.

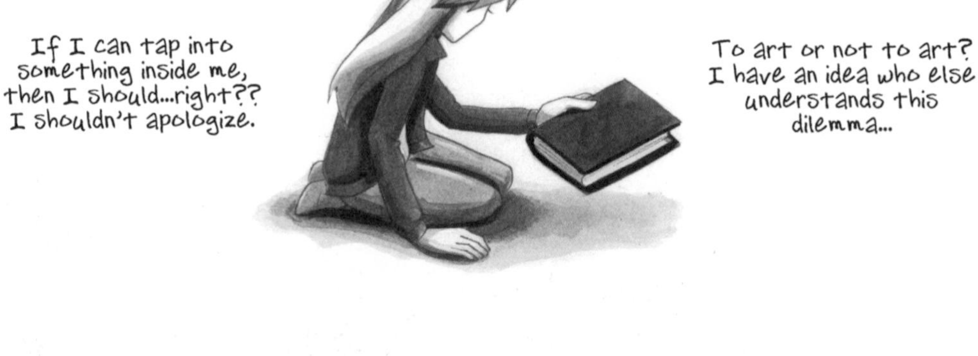
If I can tap into something inside me, then I should...right?? I shouldn't apologize.
To art or not to art? I have an idea who else understands this dilemma...

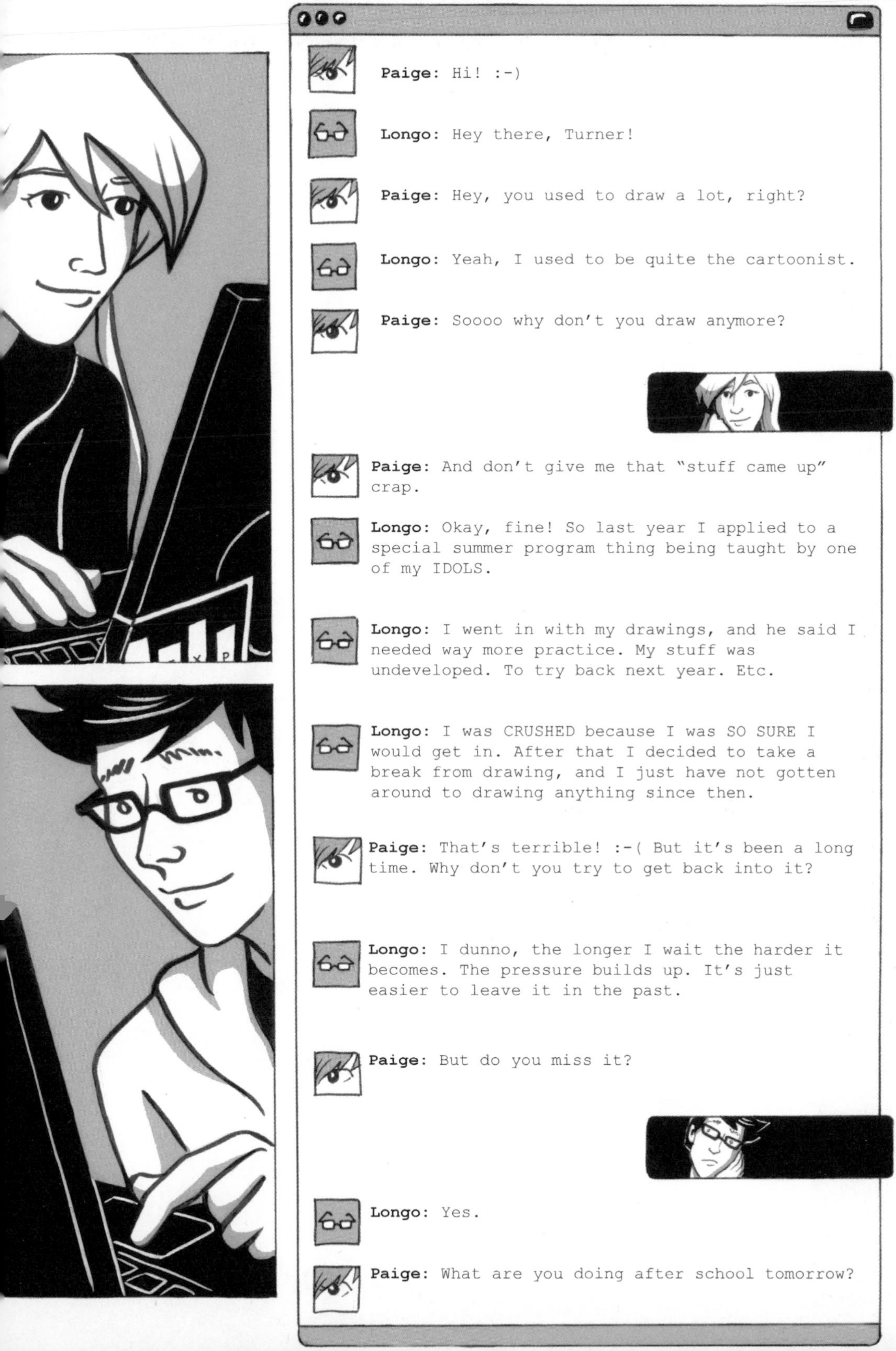
Paige: Hi! :-)
Longo: Hey there, Turner!
Paige: Hey, you used to draw a lot, right?
Longo: Yeah, I used to be quite the cartoonist.
Paige: Soooo why don't you draw anymore?
Paige: And don't give me that "stuff came up" crap.
Longo: Okay, fine! So last year I applied to a special summer program thing being taught by one of my IDOLS.
Longo: I went in with my drawings, and he said I needed way more practice. My stuff was undeveloped. To try back next year. Etc.
Longo: I was CRUSHED because I was SO SURE I would get in. After that I decided to take a break from drawing, and I just have not gotten around to drawing anything since then.
Paige: That's terrible! :-(But it's been a long time. Why don't you try to get back into it?
Longo: I dunno, the longer I wait the harder it becomes. The pressure builds up. It's just easier to leave it in the past.
Paige: But do you miss it?
Longo: Yes.
Paige: What are you doing after school tomorrow?

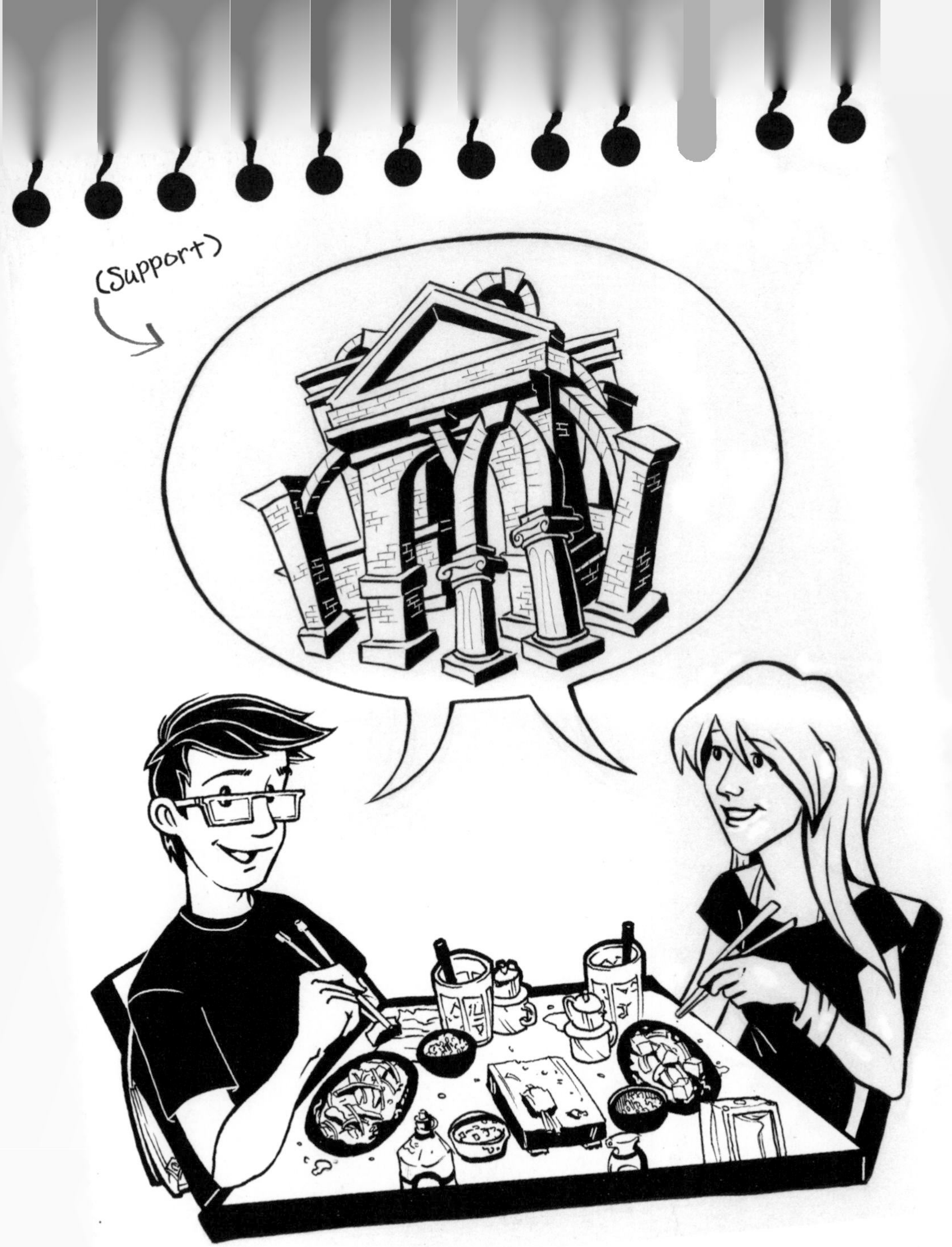
(Support)

(This is a drawing Longo and I made TOGETHER!)

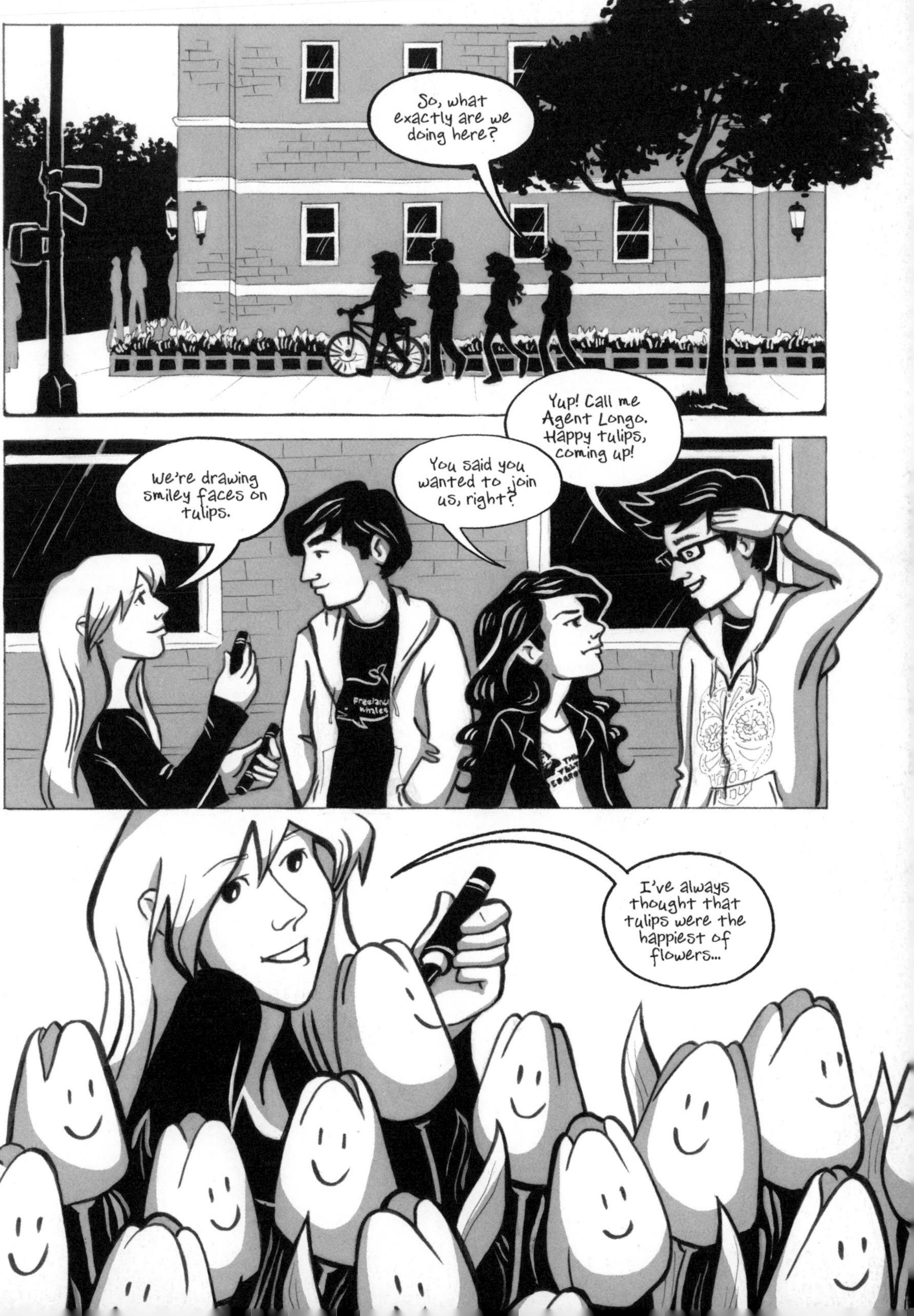

So, what exactly are we doing here?
We're drawing smiley faces on tulips.
You said you wanted to join us, right?
Yup! Call me Agent Longo. Happy tulips, coming up!
I've always thought that tulips were the happiest of flowers...

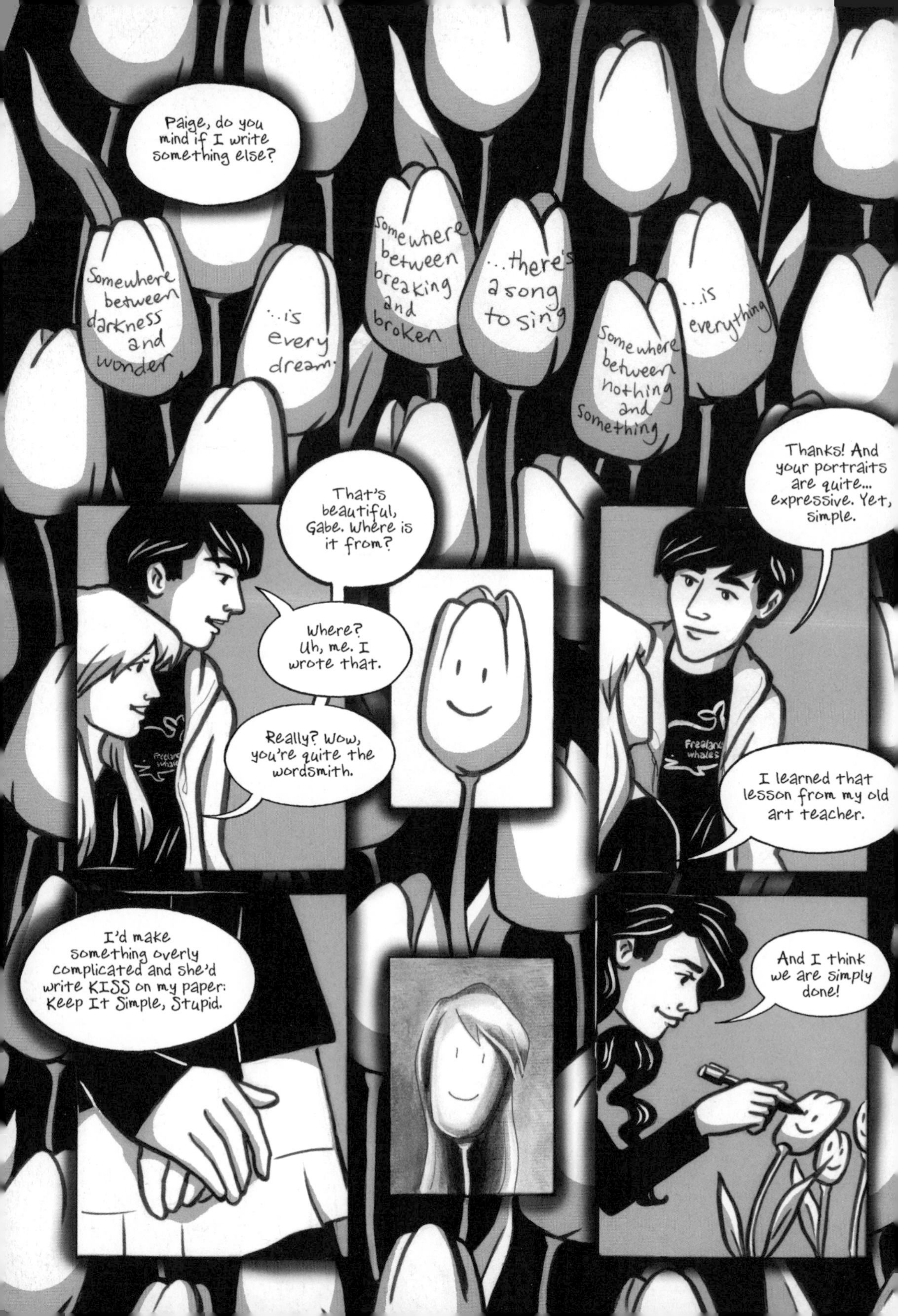

Paige, do you mind if I write something else?
Somewhere between darkness and wonder
...is every dream.
Somewhere between breaking and broken
...there's a song to sing
Somewhere between nothing and something
...is everything
That's beautiful, Gabe. Where is it from?
Where? Uh, me. I wrote that.
Really? Wow, you're quite the wordsmith.
Thanks! And your portraits are quite... expressive. Yet, simple.
I learned that lesson from my old art teacher.
I'd make something overly complicated and she'd write KISS on my paper: Keep It Simple, Stupid.
And I think we are simply done!

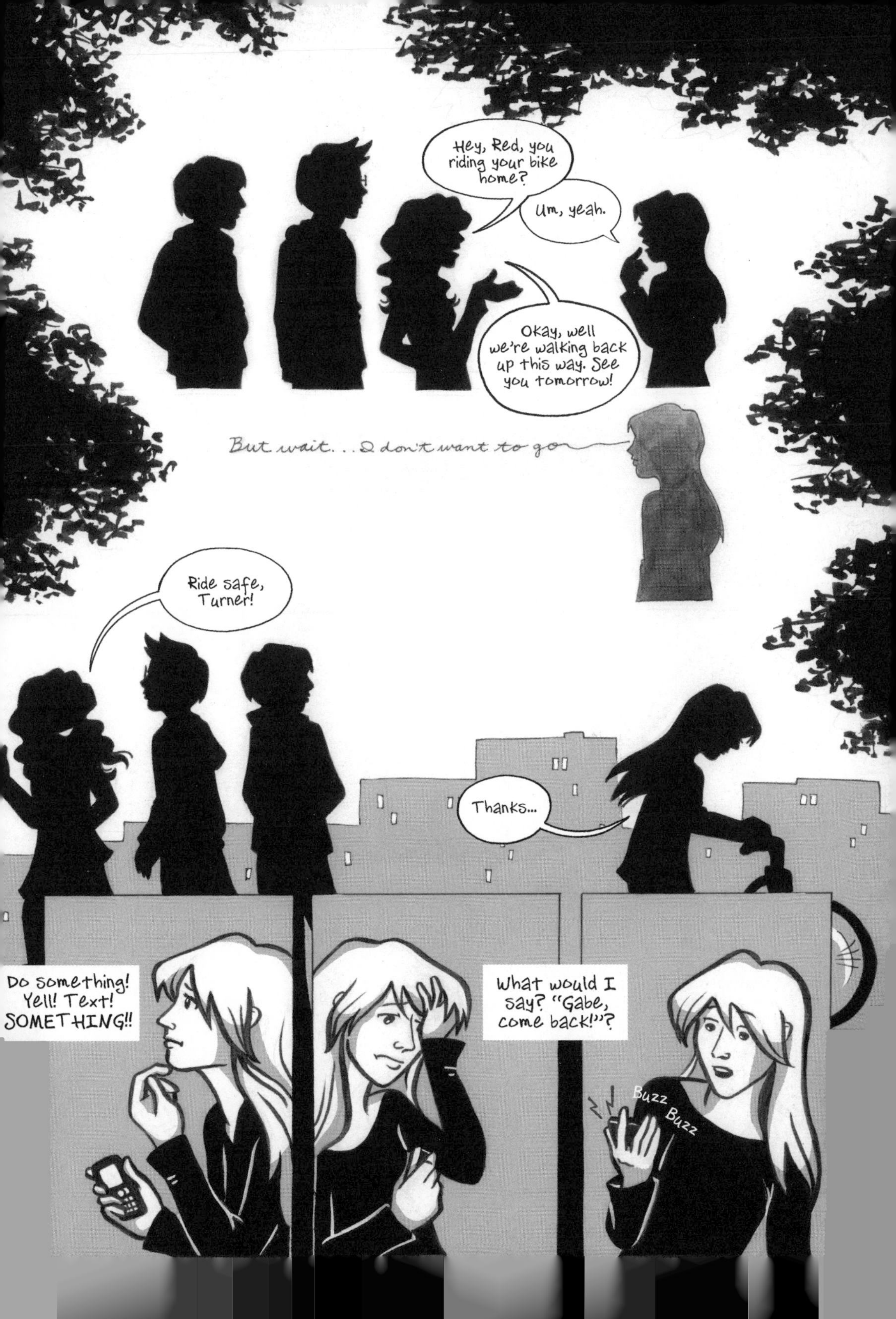

Hey, Red, you riding your bike home?
Um, yeah.
Okay, well we're walking back up this way. See you tomorrow!
But wait. . . I don't want to go
Ride safe, Turner!
Thanks...
Do something! Yell! Text! SOMETHING!!
What would I say? "Gabe, come back!"?
Buzz Buzz

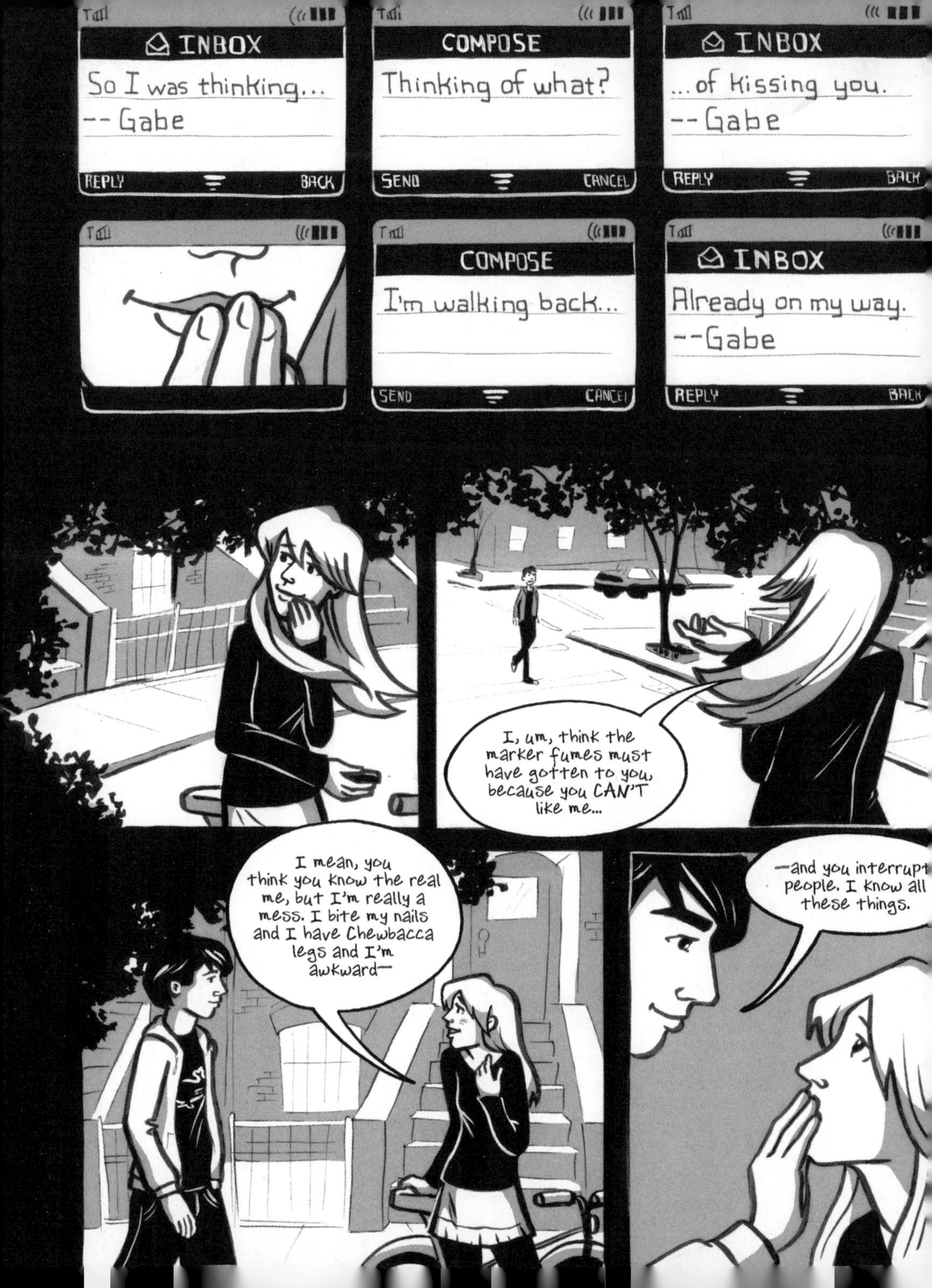

INBOX
So I was thinking...
--Gabe
REPLY
BACK
COMPOSE
Thinking of what?
SEND
CANCEL
INBOX
...of kissing you.
--Gabe
REPLY
BACK
COMPOSE
I'm walking back...
SEND
CANCEL
INBOX
Already on my way.
--Gabe
REPLY
BACK
I, um, think the marker fumes must have gotten to you, because you CAN'T like me...
I mean, you think you know the real me, but I'm really a mess. I bite my nails and I have Chewbacca legs and I'm awkward—
—and you interrupt people. I know all these things.

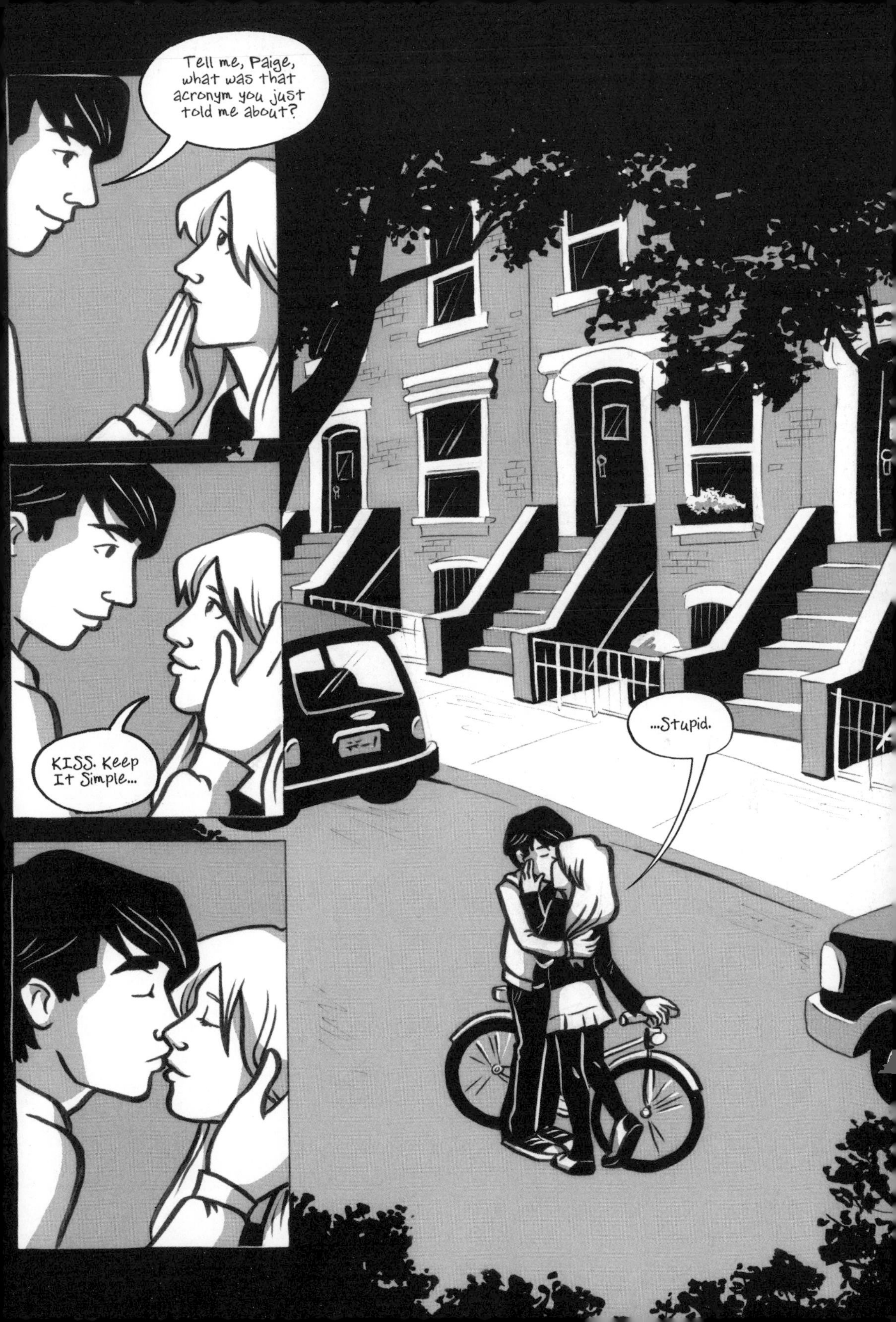
Tell me, Paige, what was that acronym you just told me about?
KISS. Keep It Simple...
...Stupid.

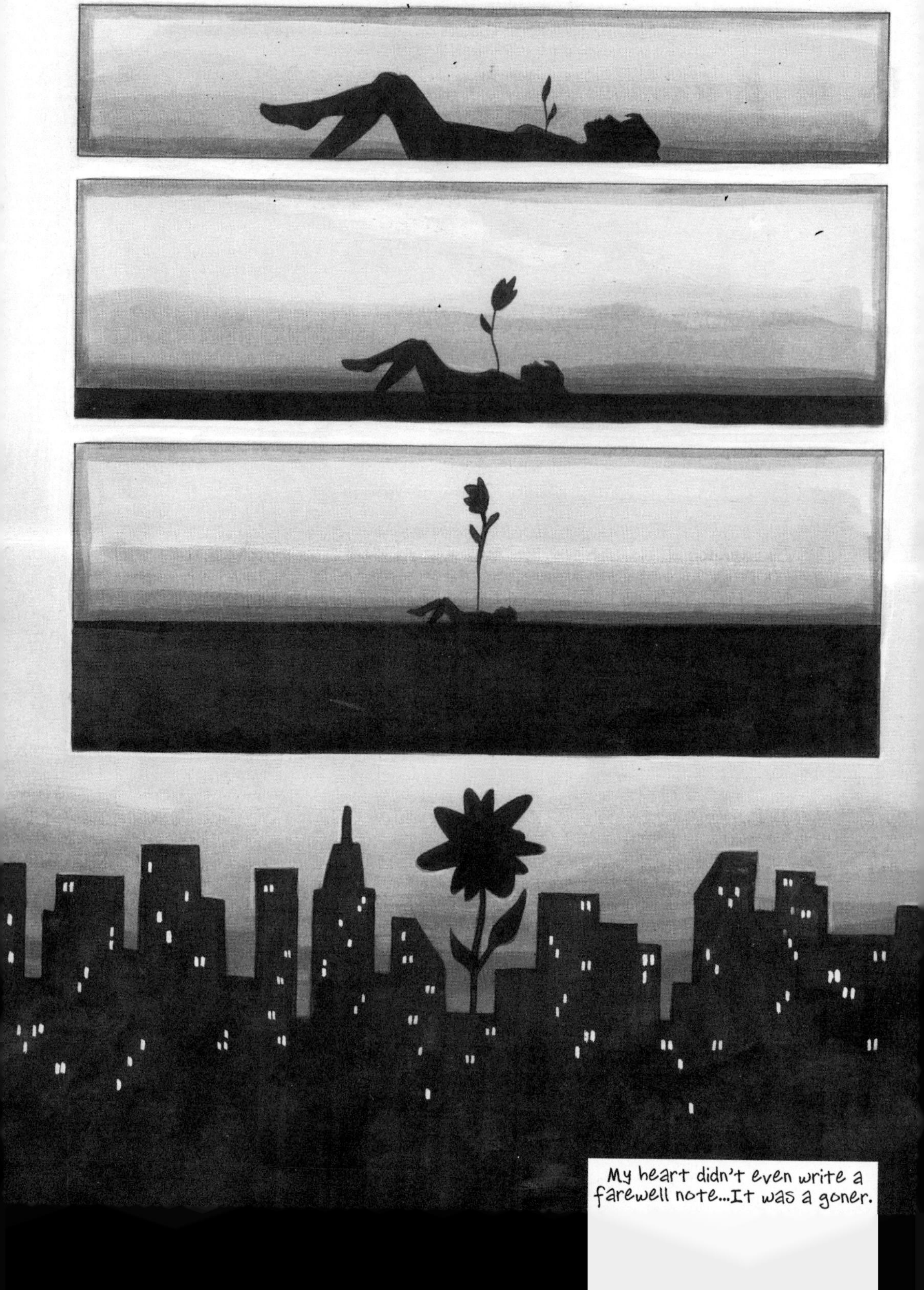
My heart didn't even write a farewell note...It was a goner.

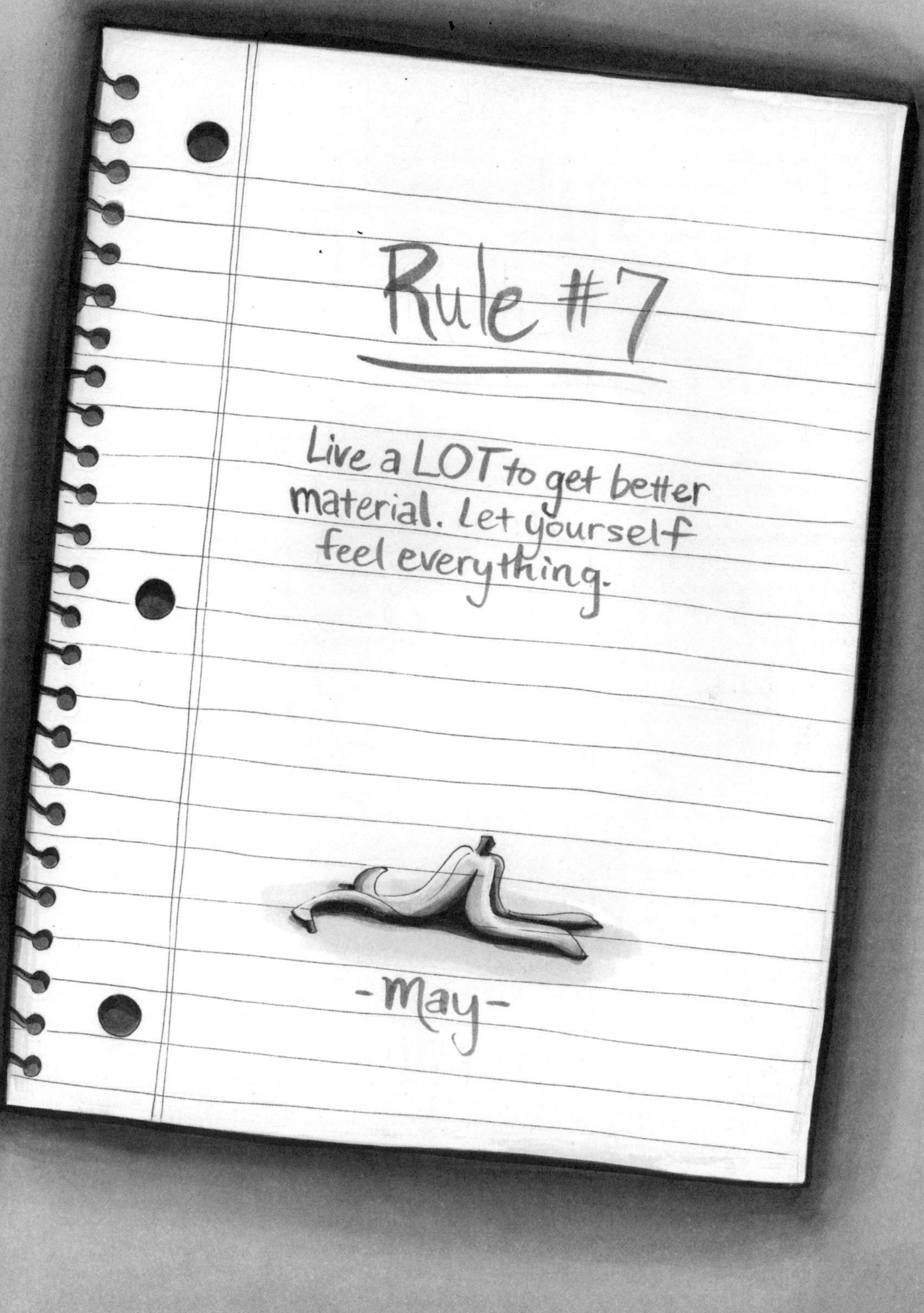
Rule #7
Live a LOT to get better material. Let yourself feel everything.
-May-

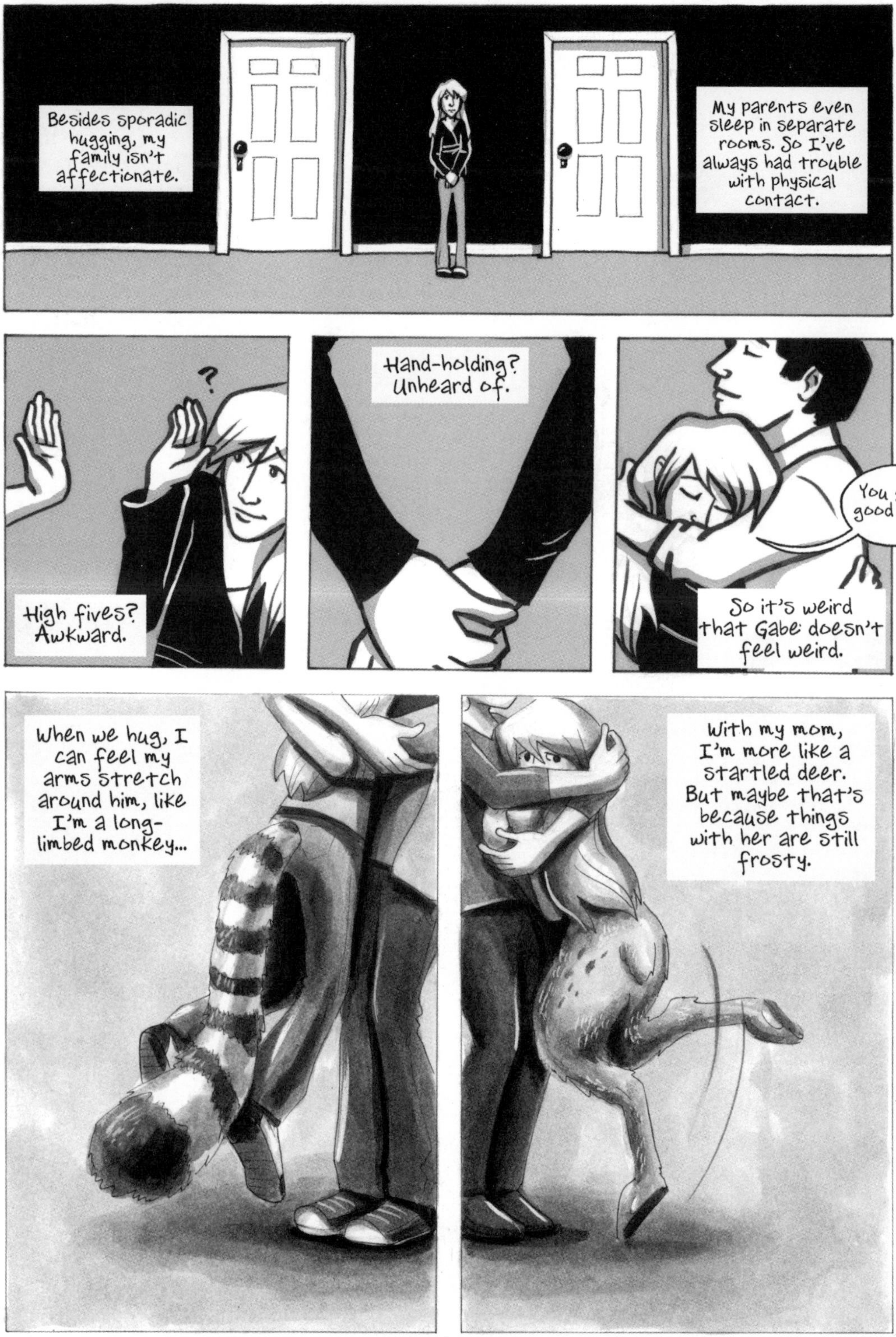
Besides sporadic hugging, my family isn't affectionate.
My parents even sleep in separate rooms. So I've always had trouble with physical contact.
?
High fives? Awkward.
Hand-holding? Unheard of.
So it's weird that Gabe doesn't feel weird.
When we hug, I can feel my arms stretch around him, like I'm a long-limbed monkey...
With my mom, I'm more like a startled deer. But maybe that's because things with her are still frosty.

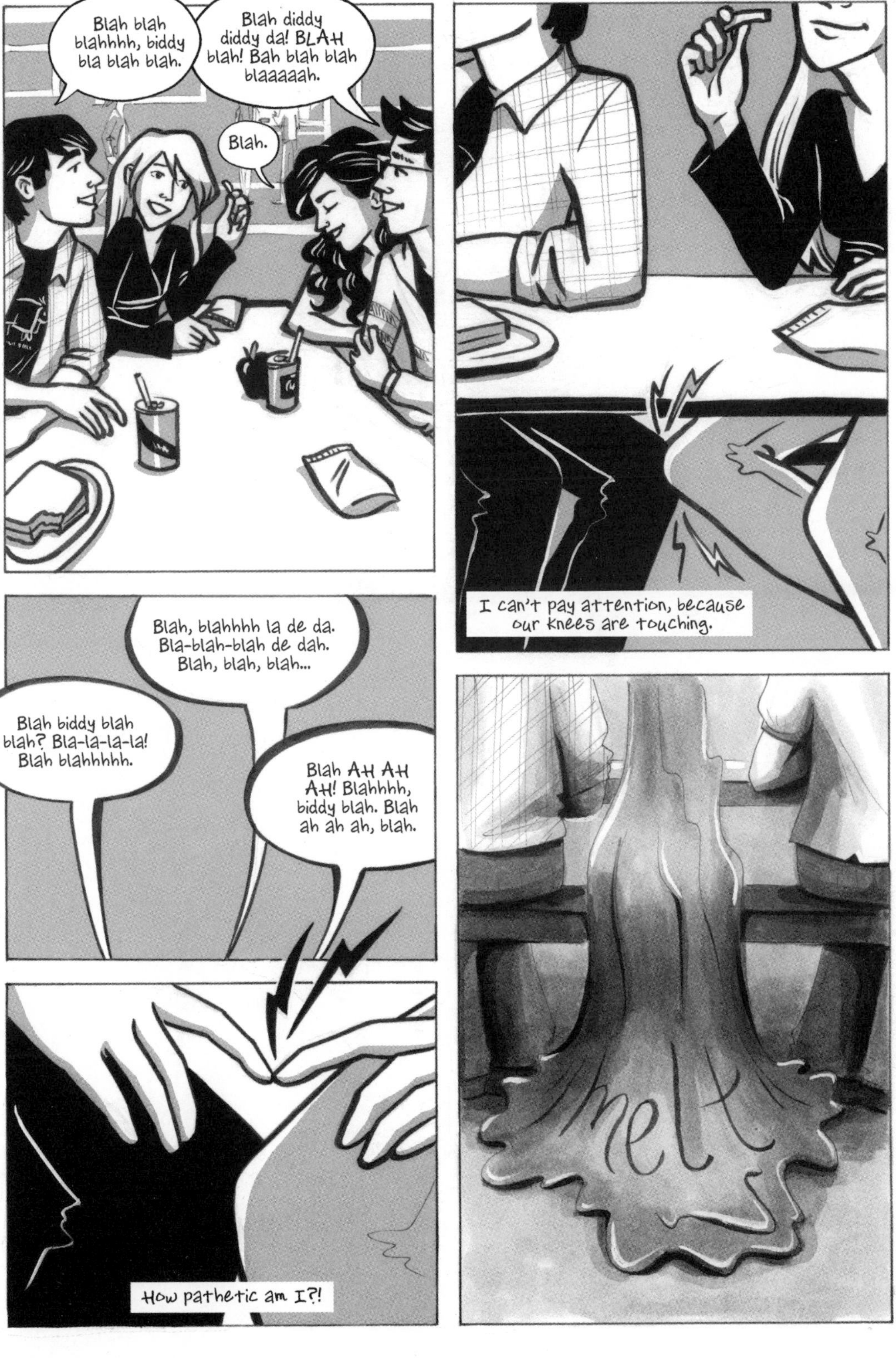
Blah blah blahhhh, biddy bla blah blah.
Blah diddy diddy da! BLAH blah! Bah blah blah blaaaaah.
Blah.
I can't pay attention, because our knees are touching.
Blah, blahhhh la de da. Bla-blah-blah de dah. Blah, blah, blah...
Blah biddy blah blah? Bla-la-la-la! Blah blahhhhh.
Blah AH AH AH! Blahhhh, biddy blah. Blah ah ah ah, blah.
How pathetic am I?!
melt

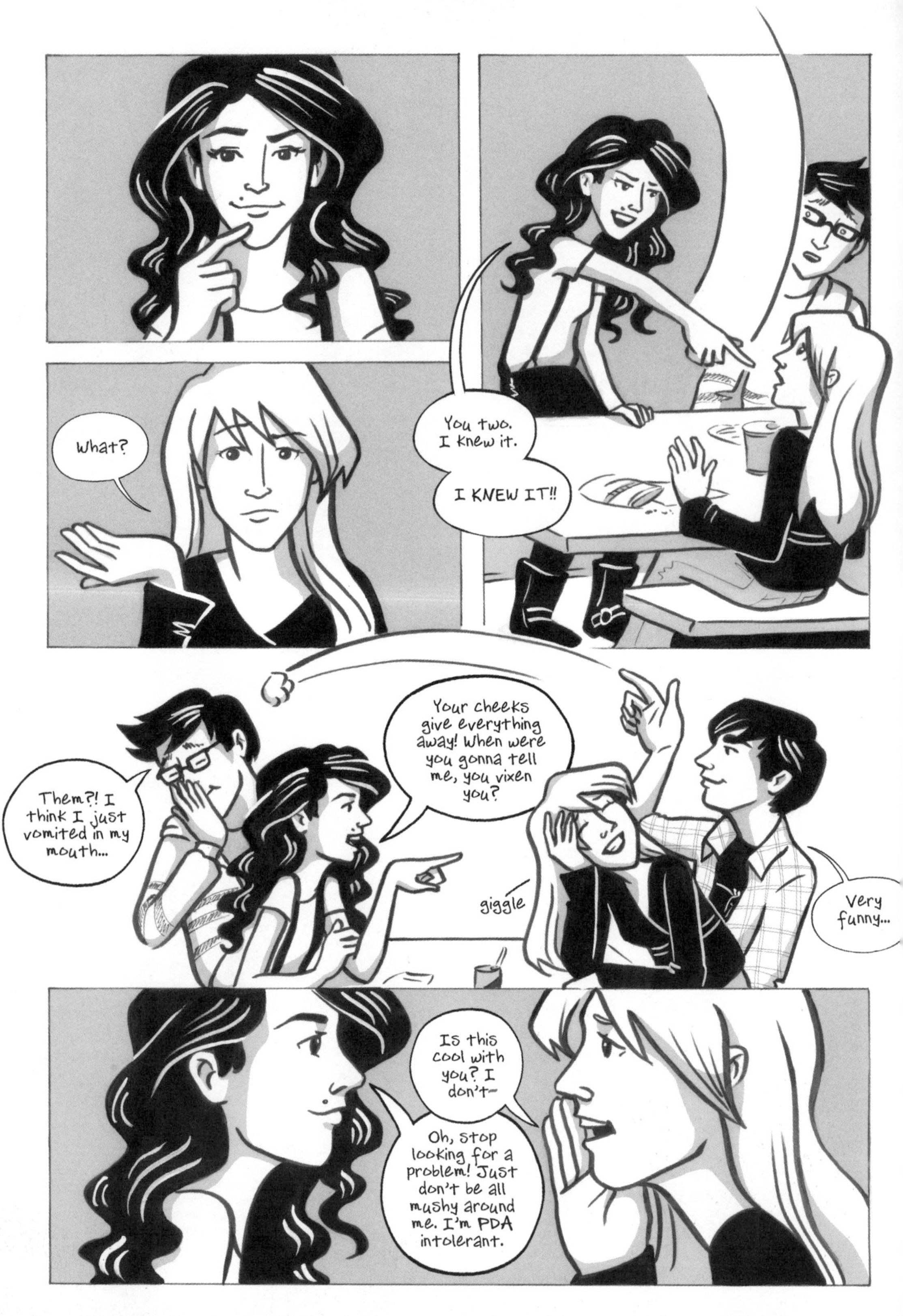
What?
You two. I knew it.
I KNEW IT!!
Them?! I think I just vomited in my mouth...
Your cheeks give everything away! When were you gonna tell me, you vixen you?
giggle
Very funny...
Is this cool with you? I don't—
Oh, stop looking for a problem! Just don't be all mushy around me. I'm PDA intolerant.

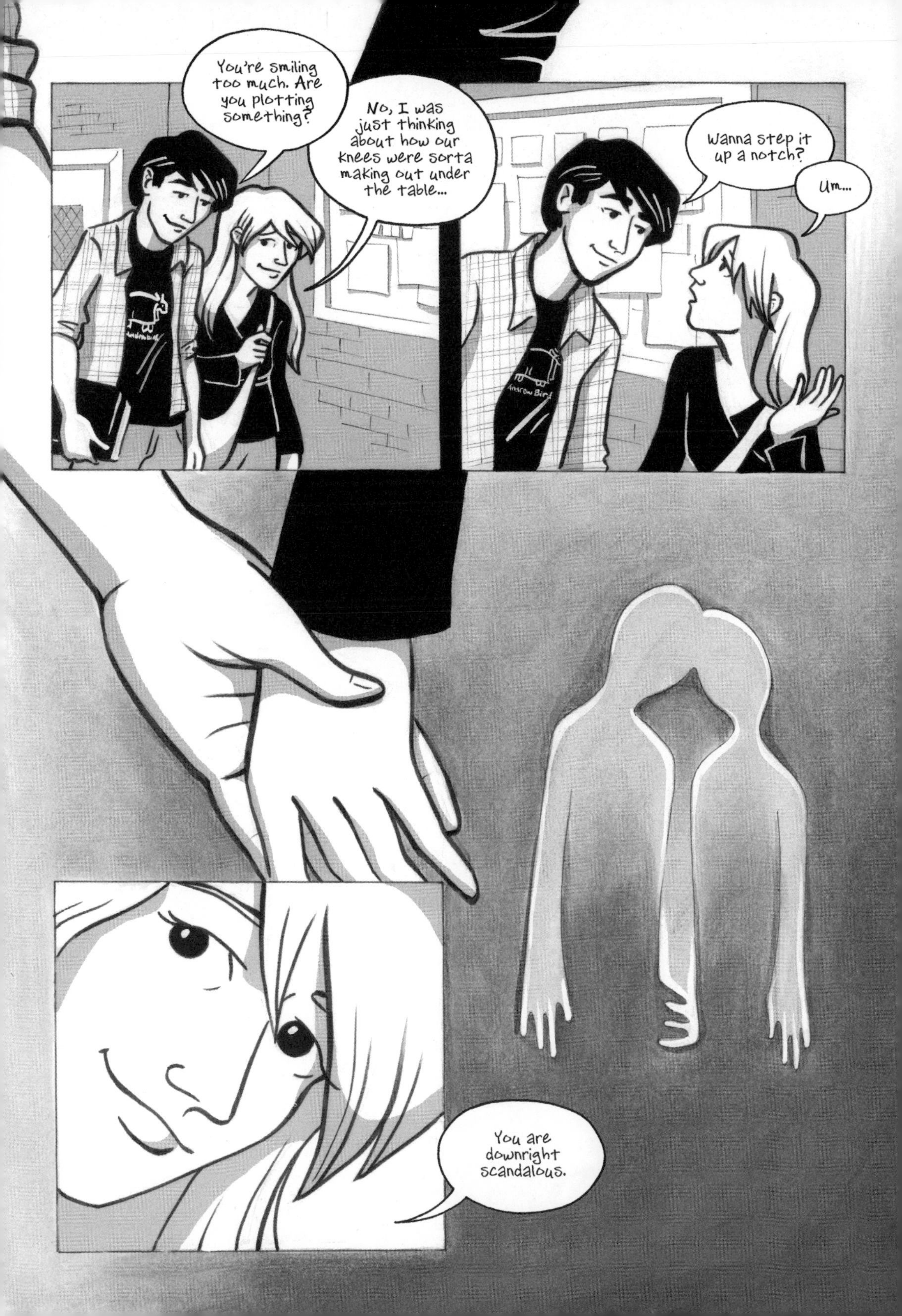
You're smiling too much. Are you plotting something?
No, I was just thinking about how our knees were sorta making out under the table...
Wanna step it up a notch?
Um...
You are downright scandalous.

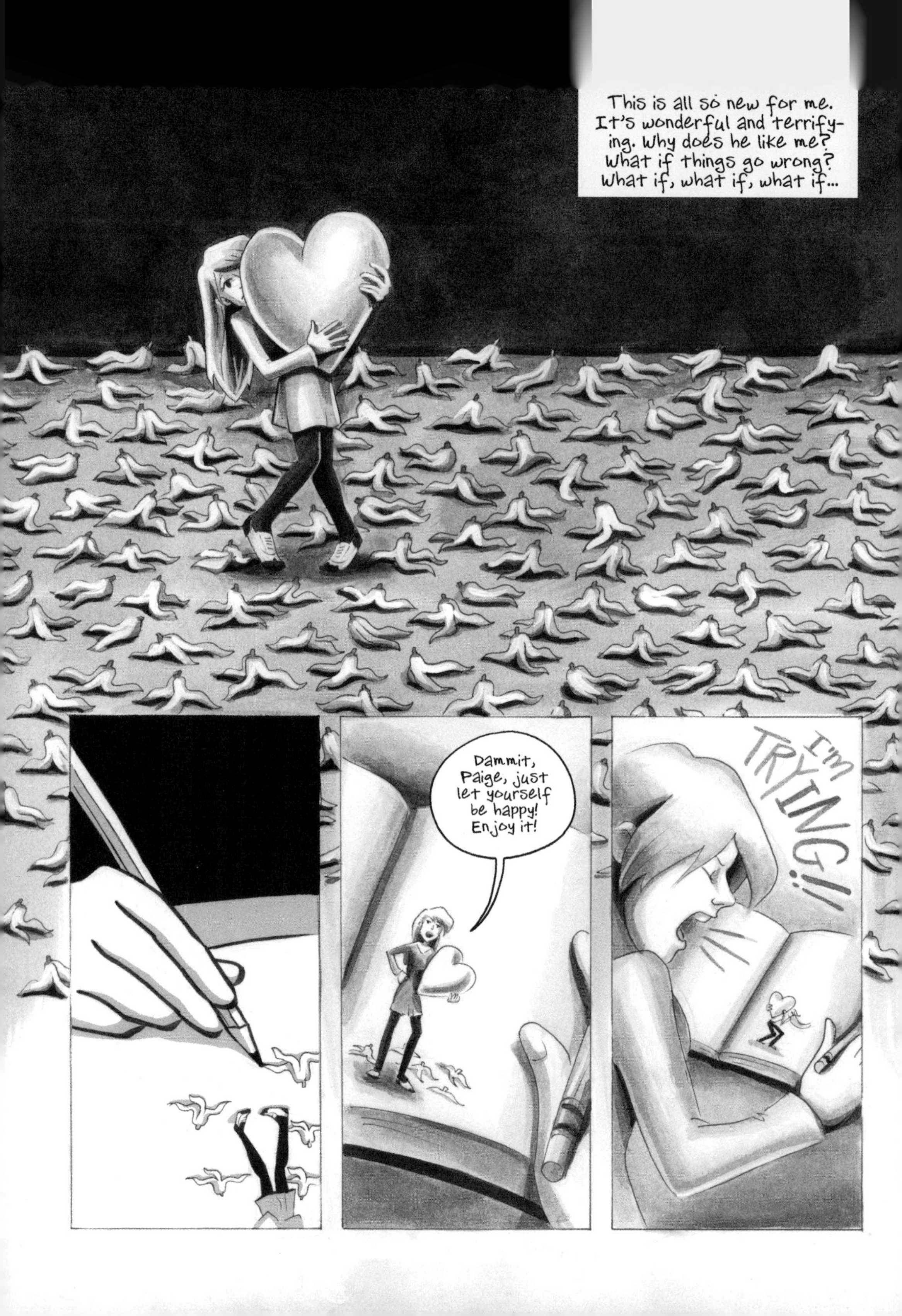
This is all so new for me. It's wonderful and terrifying. Why does he like me? What if things go wrong? What if, what if, what if...
Dammit, Paige, just let yourself be happy! Enjoy it!
I'm TRYING!!

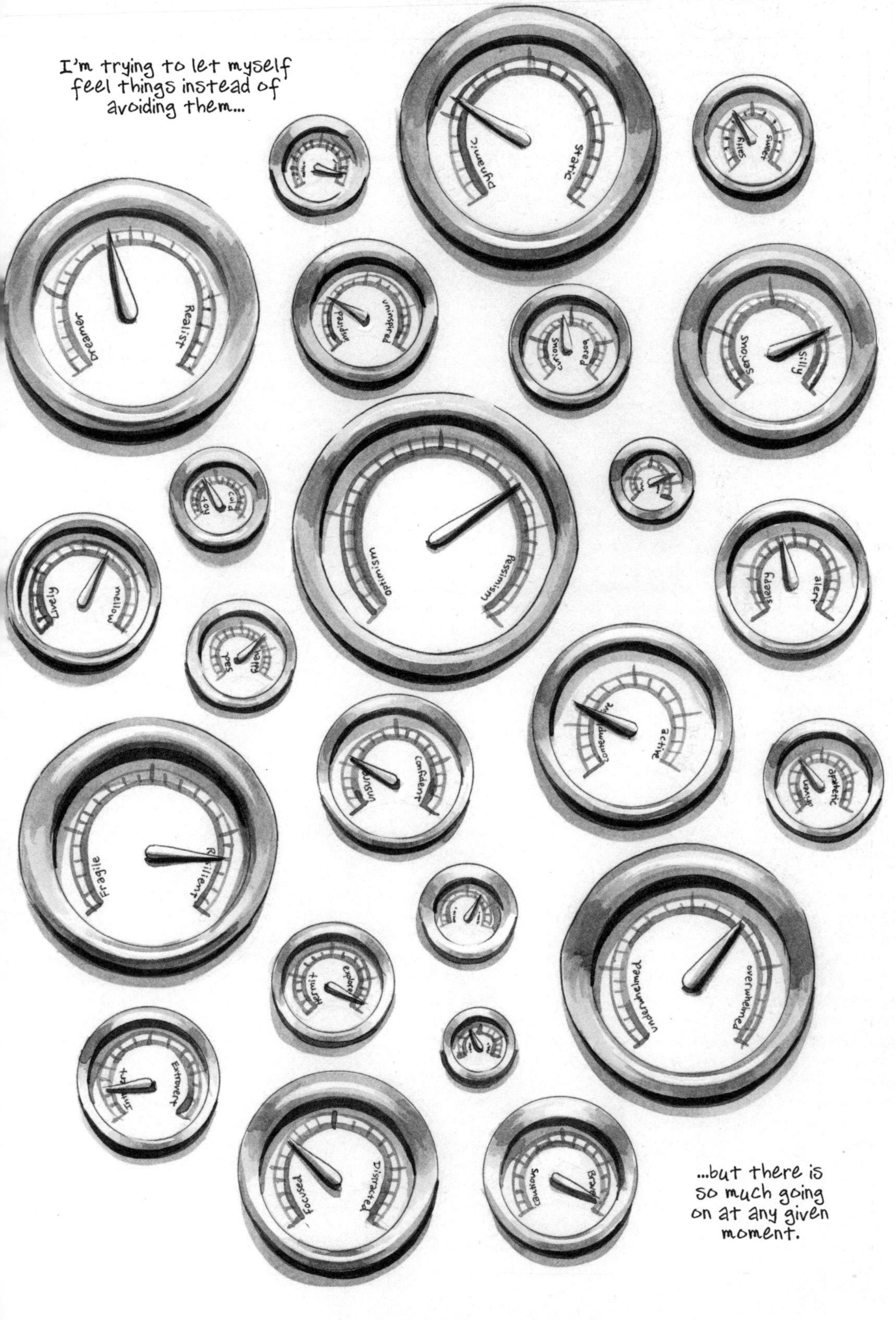

I'm trying to let myself feel things instead of avoiding them...
Dreamer
Realist
Static
Serious
Silly
Pessimism
Lively
mellow
sleepy
alert
Confident
active
apathetic
Fragile
underwhelmed
overwhelmed
Extrovert
Focused
Distracted
...but there is so much going on at any given moment.

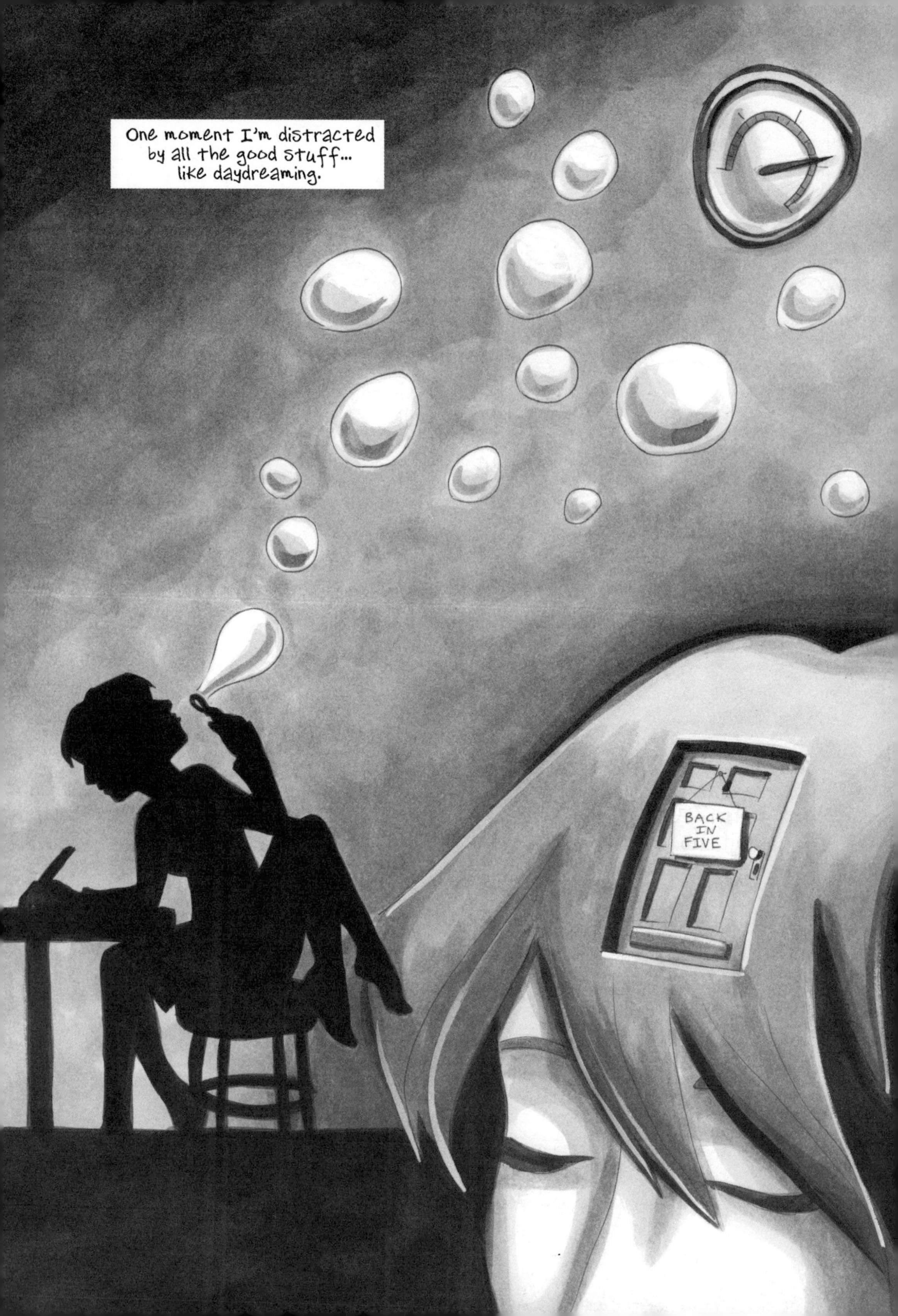
One moment I'm distracted by all the good stuff... like daydreaming.
BACK IN FIVE

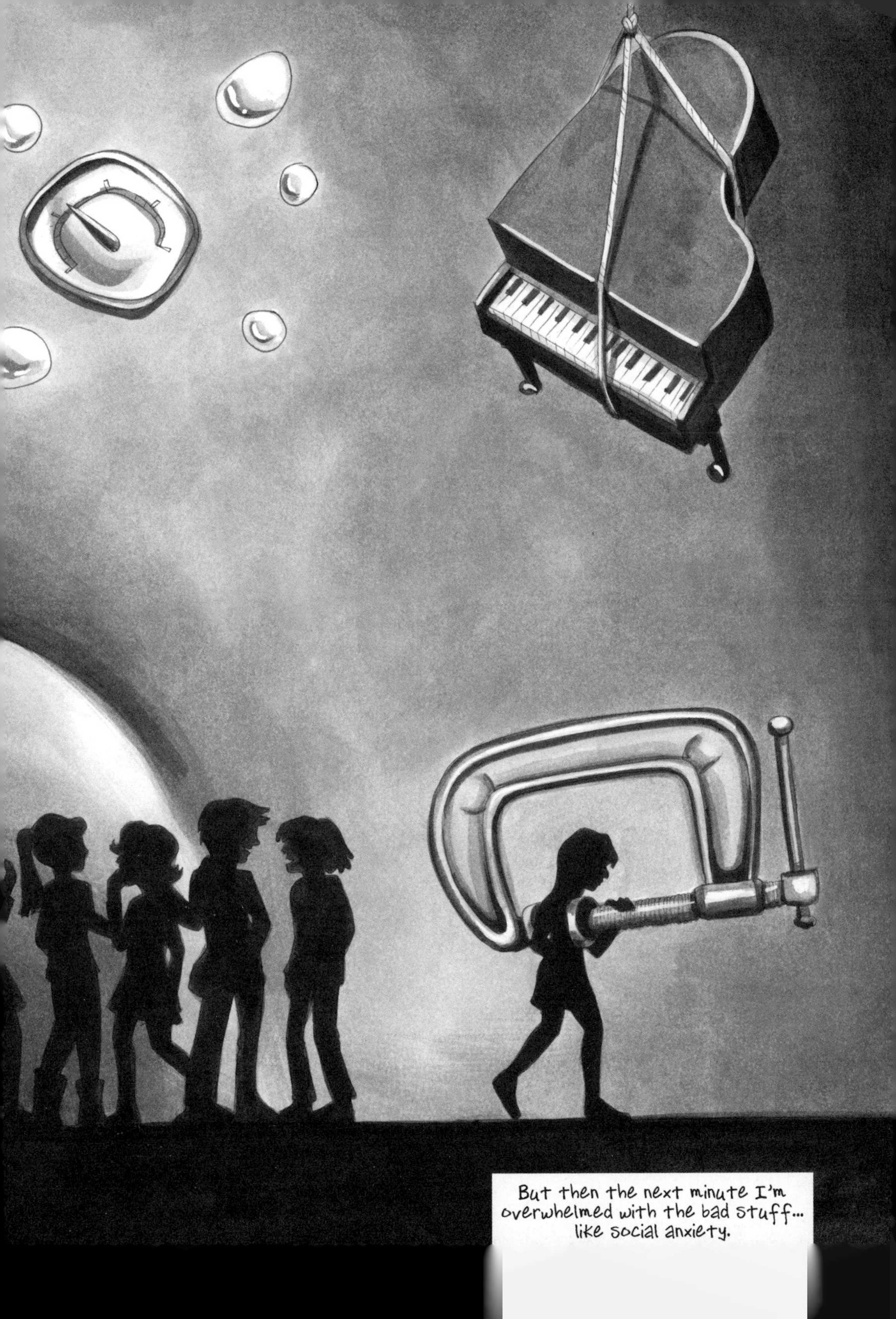
But then the next minute I'm
overwhelmed with the bad stuff...
like social anxiety.

In fourth period we had a sub, so Longo and I made some drawings together. It made me think of Diana, since we used to do the same thing back in Virginia.

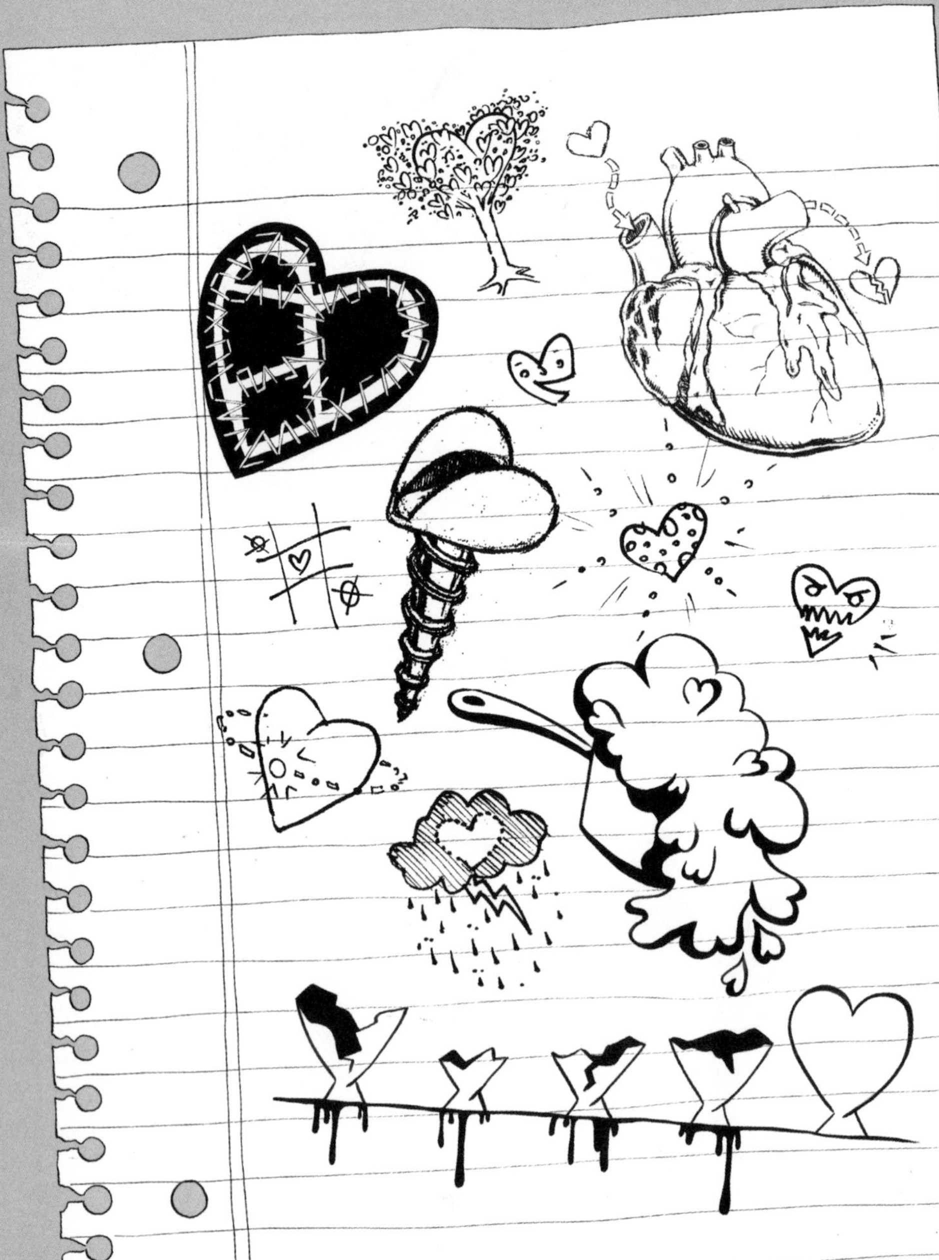

And then we all played a game of Drawing Telephone. How do you play? Well...

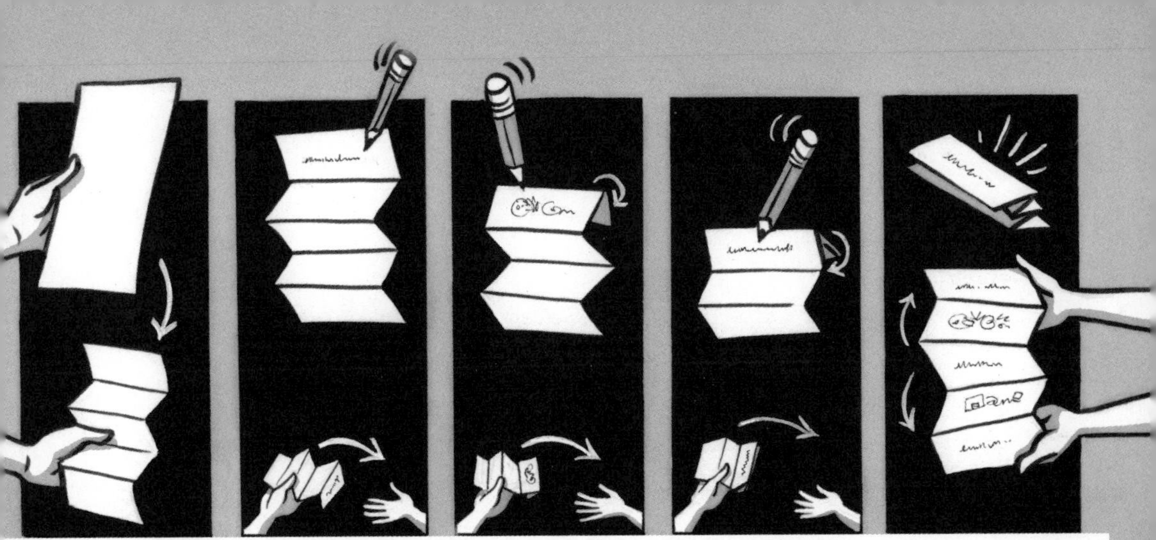

Each person needs pencil and paper. You can use a stack of loose sheets or a single sheet folded up.

Write a sentence. Any sentence! Pass it to the next person.

Next person reads the sentence, folds it back, and in the next section illustrates it.

Pass it. Look at the drawing, fold it back, and write a sentence of what you think it is.

Pass it. Next person illustrates the new sentence. And so on, and so on...

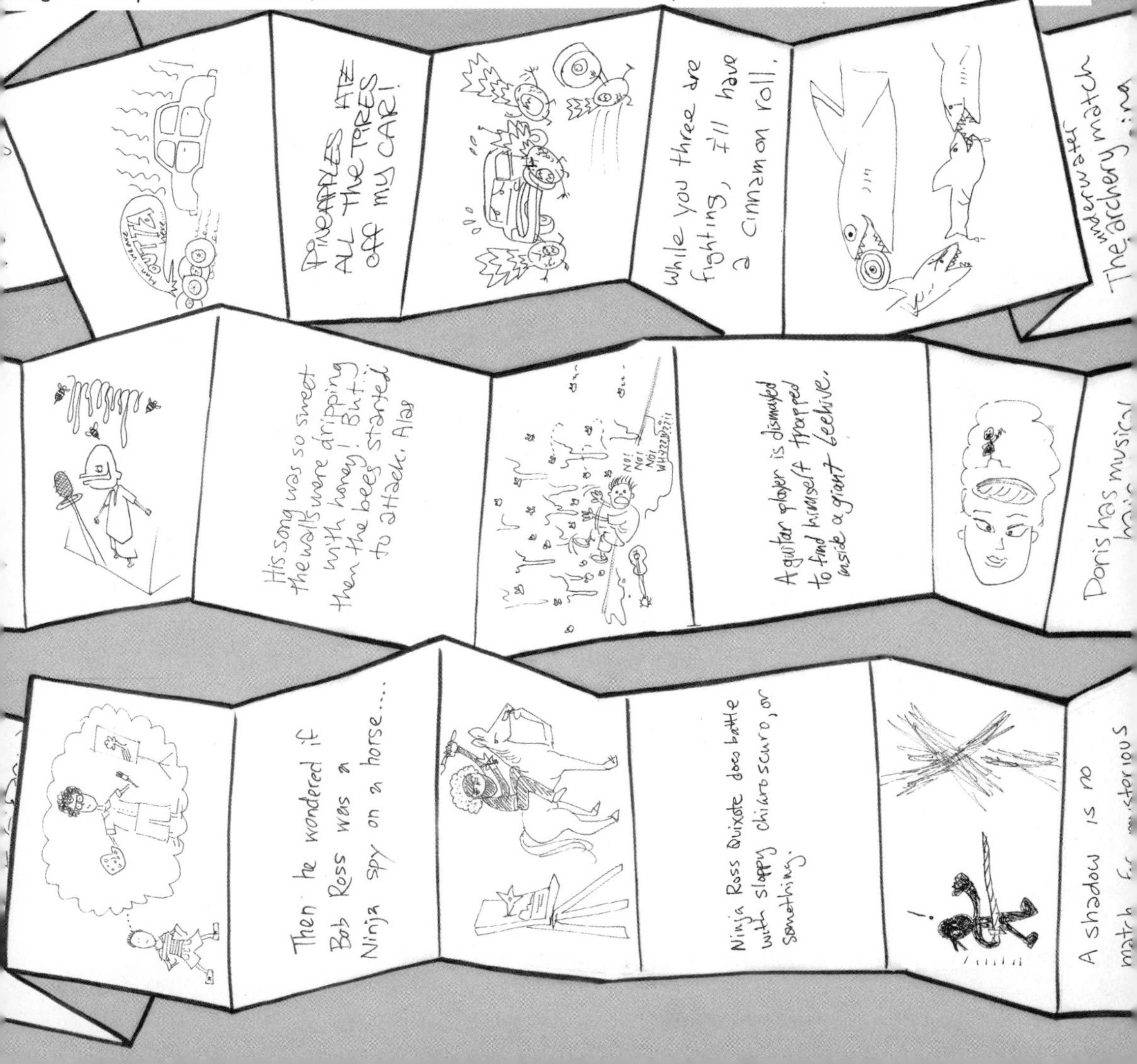
PINEAPPLES ATE ALL THE TIRES off MY CAR!
While you three are fighting, I'll have a cinnamon roll.
The underwater archery match
His song was so sweet the walls were dripping with honey! But then the bees started to attack. Alas
A guitar player is dismayed to find himself trapped inside a giant beehive.
Doris has musical
Then he wondered if Bob Ross was a Ninja spy on a horse....
Ninja Ross Quixote does battle with sloppy chiaroscuro, or something.
A shadow is no

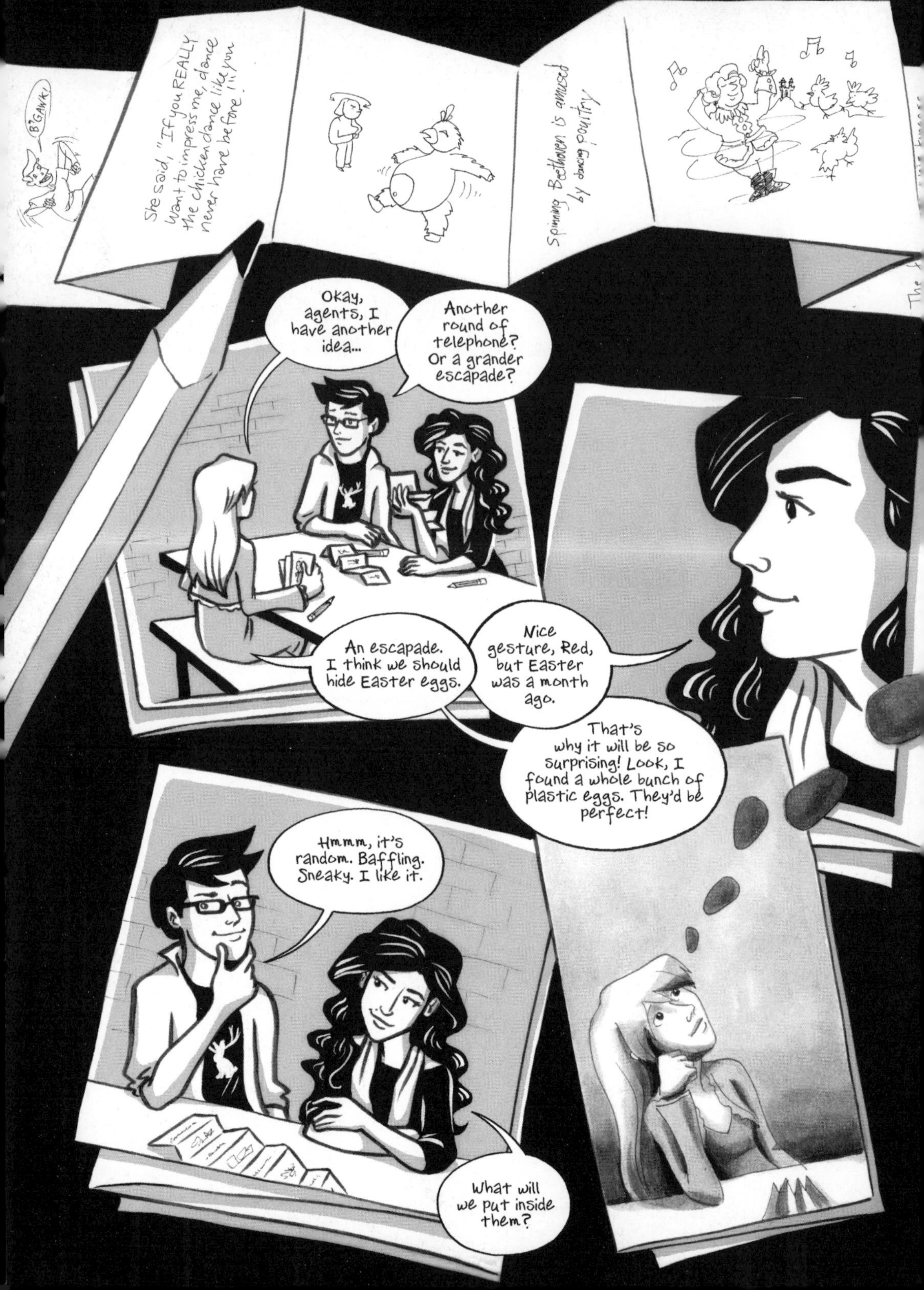
B'GAWK!
She said, "If you REALLY want to impress me, dance the chicken dance like you never have before!"
Spinning Beethoven is amused by dancing poultry
Okay, agents, I have another idea...
Another round of telephone? Or a grander escapade?
An escapade. I think we should hide Easter eggs.
Nice gesture, Red, but Easter was a month ago.
That's why it will be so surprising! Look, I found a whole bunch of plastic eggs. They'd be perfect!
Hmmm, it's random. Baffling. Sneaky. I like it.
What will we put inside them?

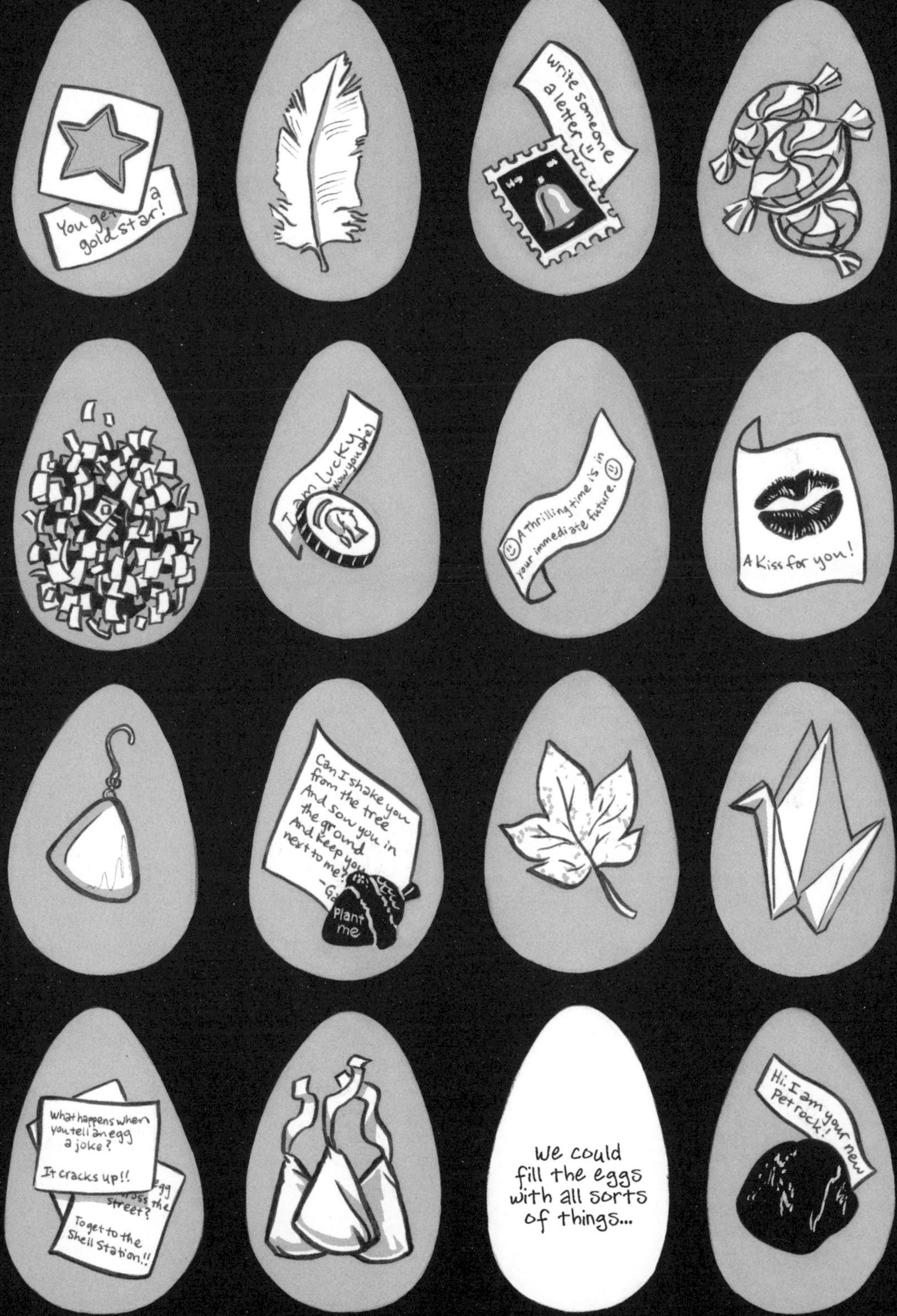

You get a gold star!
write someone a letter :)
I am lucky. (Now you are.)
A thrilling time is in your immediate future. :)
A Kiss for you!
Can I shake you from the tree And sow you in the ground And keep you next to me? —G
Plant me
What happens when you tell an egg a joke? It cracks up!!
egg
ross the street?
To get to the Shell Station!!
We could fill the eggs with all sorts of things...
Hi. I am your new Pet rock!

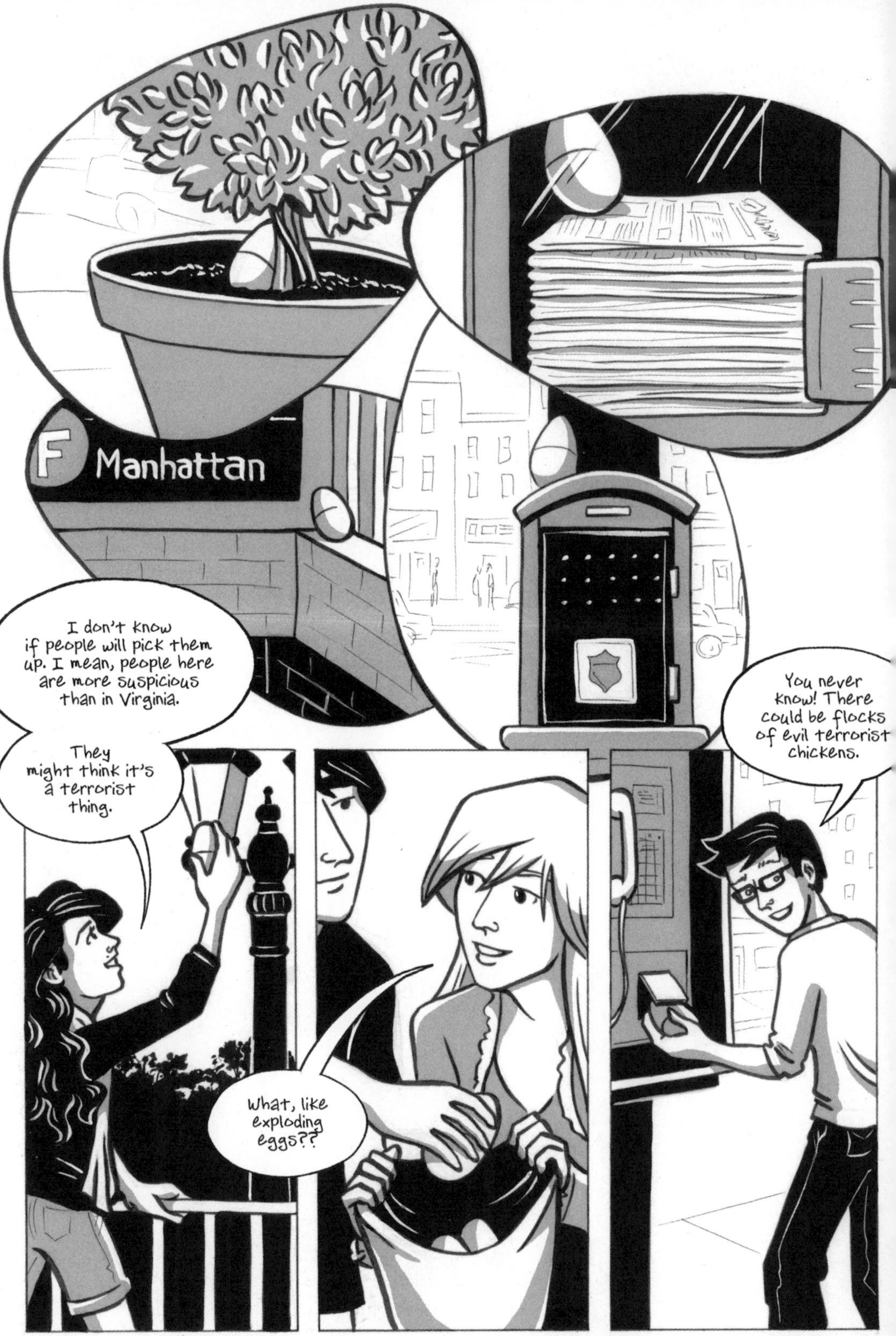
Manhattan
I don't know if people will pick them up. I mean, people here are more suspicious than in Virginia.
They might think it's a terrorist thing.
What, like exploding eggs??
You never know! There could be flocks of evil terrorist chickens.

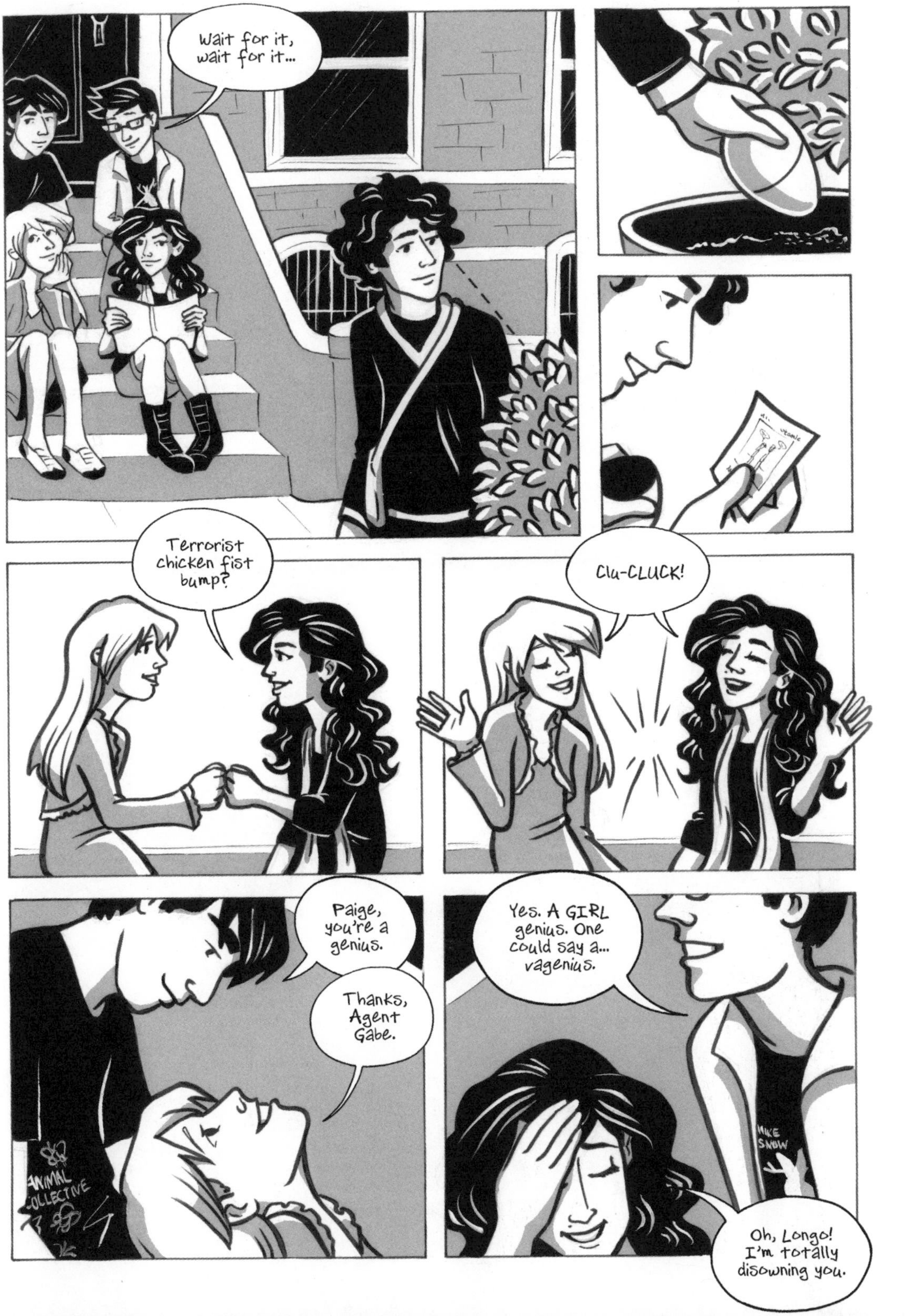
Wait for it, wait for it...
Terrorist chicken fist bump?
Clu-CLUCK!
Paige, you're a genius.
Thanks, Agent Gabe.
ANIMAL COLLECTIVE
Yes. A GIRL genius. One could say a... vagenius.
MIKE SNOW
Oh, Longo! I'm totally disowning you.

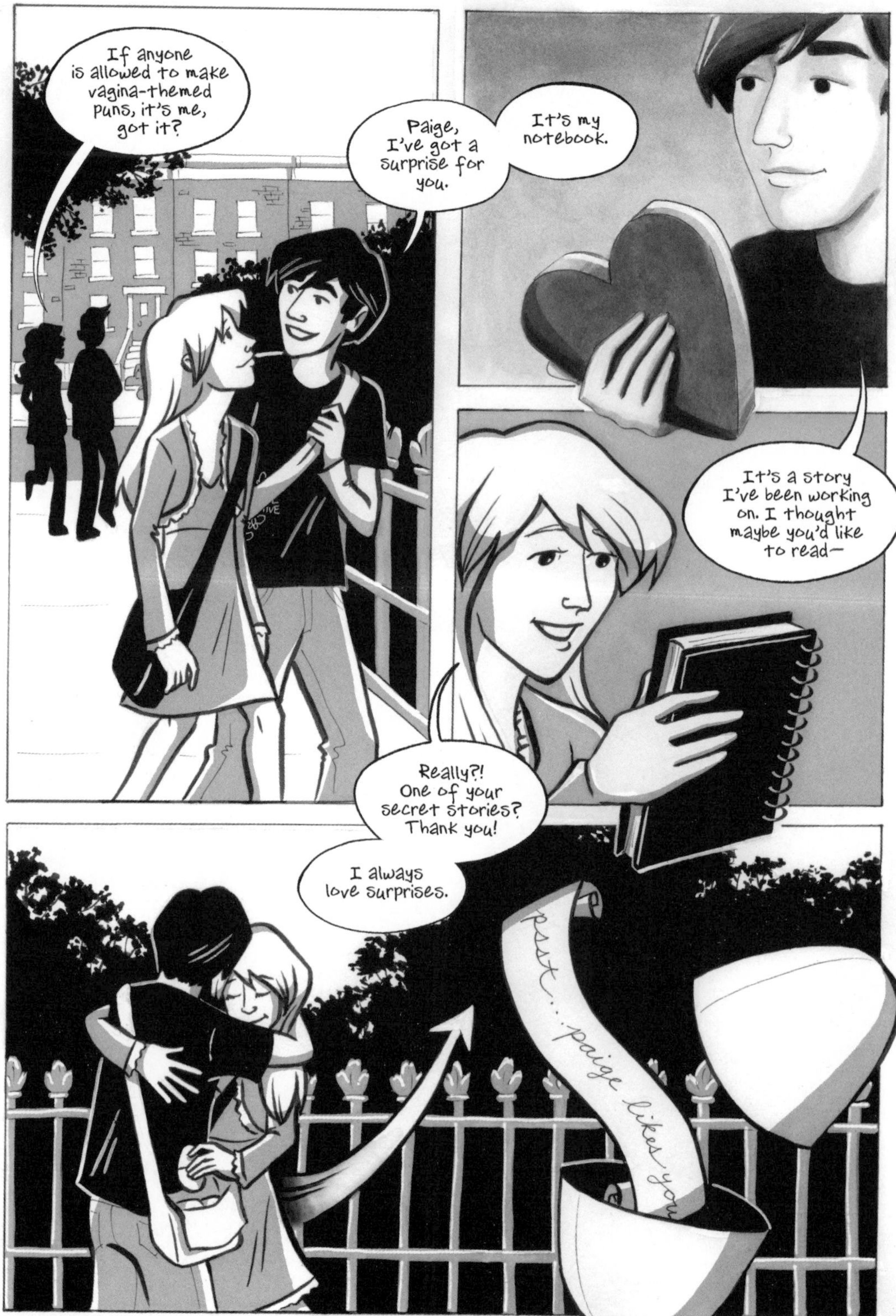
If anyone is allowed to make vagina-themed puns, it's me, got it?
Paige, I've got a surprise for you.
It's my notebook.
It's a story I've been working on. I thought maybe you'd like to read—
Really?! One of your secret stories? Thank you!
I always love surprises.
psst... paige likes you

Reading Gabe's story felt strange, like I was invading his privacy somehow. I decided to copy down part of it here... I hope he doesn't mind.

"...but our story didn't start 'Once upon a time...,'" the boy objected.

"Did, too." The old man sniffed. "But we didn't hear it, because we're lucky enough right now to be the tale, not he who tells it."

"Well, who's telling it?" the boy asked, looking around as though he expected to see a storyteller nearby.

"Maybe you, one day, to another young mind. Maybe another teller of tales readin' this, not knowin' they're in the middle of their own story."

"I still don't get why stories are important," said the boy. "What's wrong with leaving happenings just being stuff that, y'know, happened?"

The old man clicked his tongue and said, "Now that is a right-thinkin' question! I'll tell you why: Tellin' stories makes us impossible."

The boy threw his hands up in the air in exasperation: He'd thought he'd been on the edge of understanding the old man, but now he was once again adrift in seeming contradictions.

"Take Mister Flutterbye, if you need an example," said the old man, extending a finger like a gnarled branch. To the boy's amazement, a butterfly came to rest on the offered perch.

"Mister Flutterbye, to your eyes, is just a bug, ain't he?" The old man didn't wait for confirmation. "But for all you know, he could have a wife and kids back home, an' you pinchin' his wings there could have ended up deprivin' 'em of a husband an' a father, couldn't it? Unlikely, I know, but it all depends on the kind of story. As another for instance, while this little fella here is flappin' those wings of his, he could be causin' a hurricane on the other side of the world."

"Now you really are making things up."

"No I ain't. That's a kind of magic your little friend Tommy could take a lifetime and never understand, too. This world ain't about how big you are, or how little.

"It's about how every little thing touches every other thing in creation. But if you don't like that, how about we look at you?"

"Me?"

"Yup, you. Ain't nothin' in the world more impossible than a little boy."

"What do you mean?" The boy had never thought of himself as...well, as anything more complicated than a little boy.

"Little boys are like doors into the impossible. Like when you're playin' games. When you're playin' a game of make-believe, are you still you? Or are you a spy? Or a cowboy? Or a knight? Who are you when you're playin' those games? And what do you think you're doin' when you play those games? You're tellin' another story."

The old man waved his hand, dismissing the butterfly the way someone else would dismiss a misunderstanding. "It ain't even just when you're playin', either." He pointed his gnarled finger at the boy.

"Every little boy is his mother's little angel, and his father's reflection. And because all little boys are a little bit wild, they all have a bit of the jungle in 'em behind the eyes...every little boy is a tiger. An' every little boy is someone's shadow, and a hundred other things besides, because every little boy—heck, every child—is a door into the impossible."

"And what are you, then? Are you lots of things, too?"

The old man chuckled, and the boy felt a warm glow of pride in his chest; he was only favored with that laugh when he had impressed the old man with his understanding.

"Old men ain't nothin' except old men. Old men is what you kids become when you've stopped being everything else. An' I'll tell you somethin', my boy, bein' an old man is the one thing you don't get to choose..."

I like the idea that people are made up of different things...so I wondered what would make up Gabe.

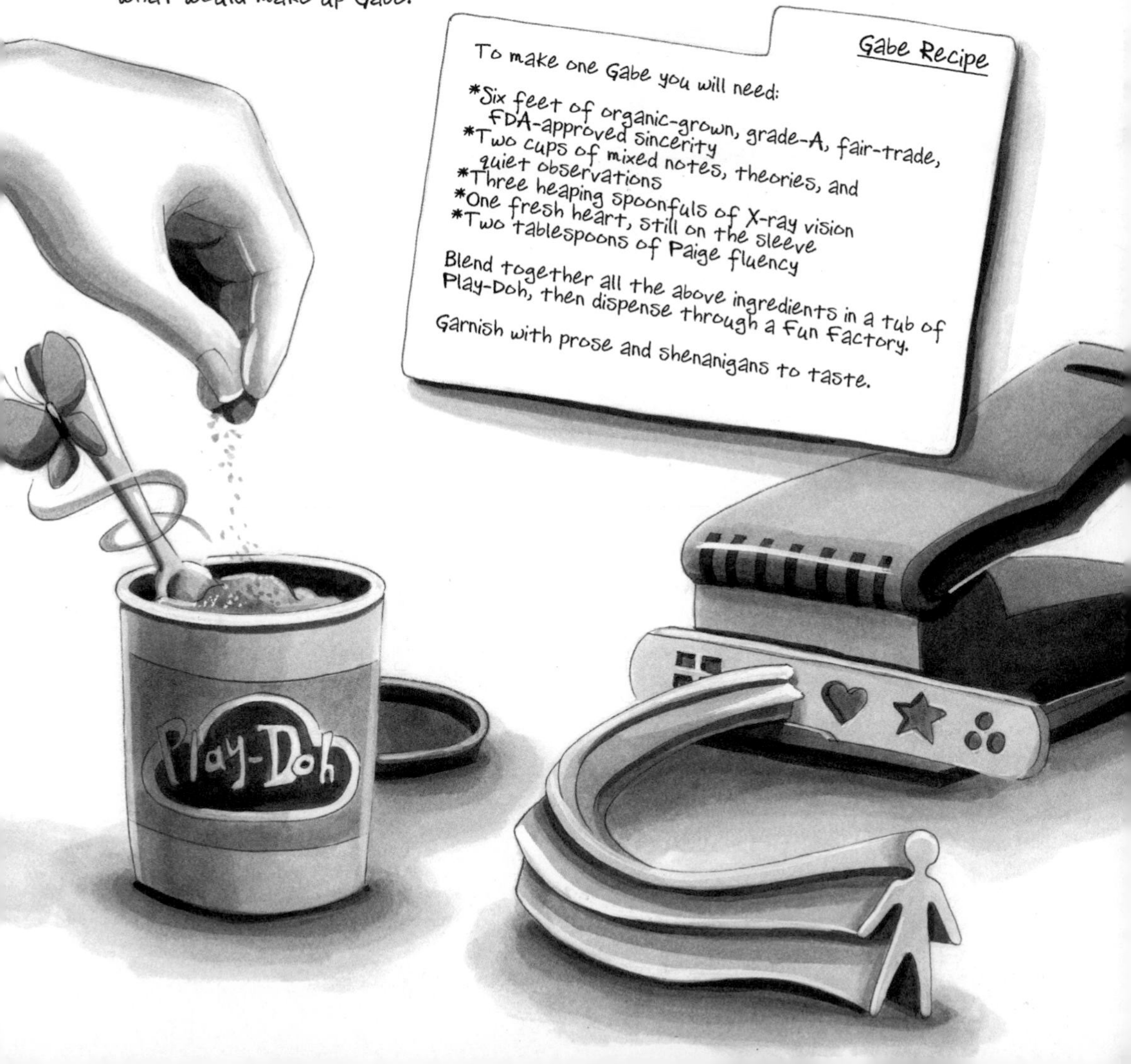

Gabe Recipe
To make one Gabe you will need:
*Six feet of organic-grown, grade-A, fair-trade, FDA-approved sincerity
*Two cups of mixed notes, theories, and quiet observations
*Three heaping spoonfuls of X-ray vision
*One fresh heart, still on the sleeve
*Two tablespoons of Paige fluency
Blend together all the above ingredients in a tub of Play-Doh, then dispense through a Fun Factory.
Garnish with prose and shenanigans to taste.
Play-Doh

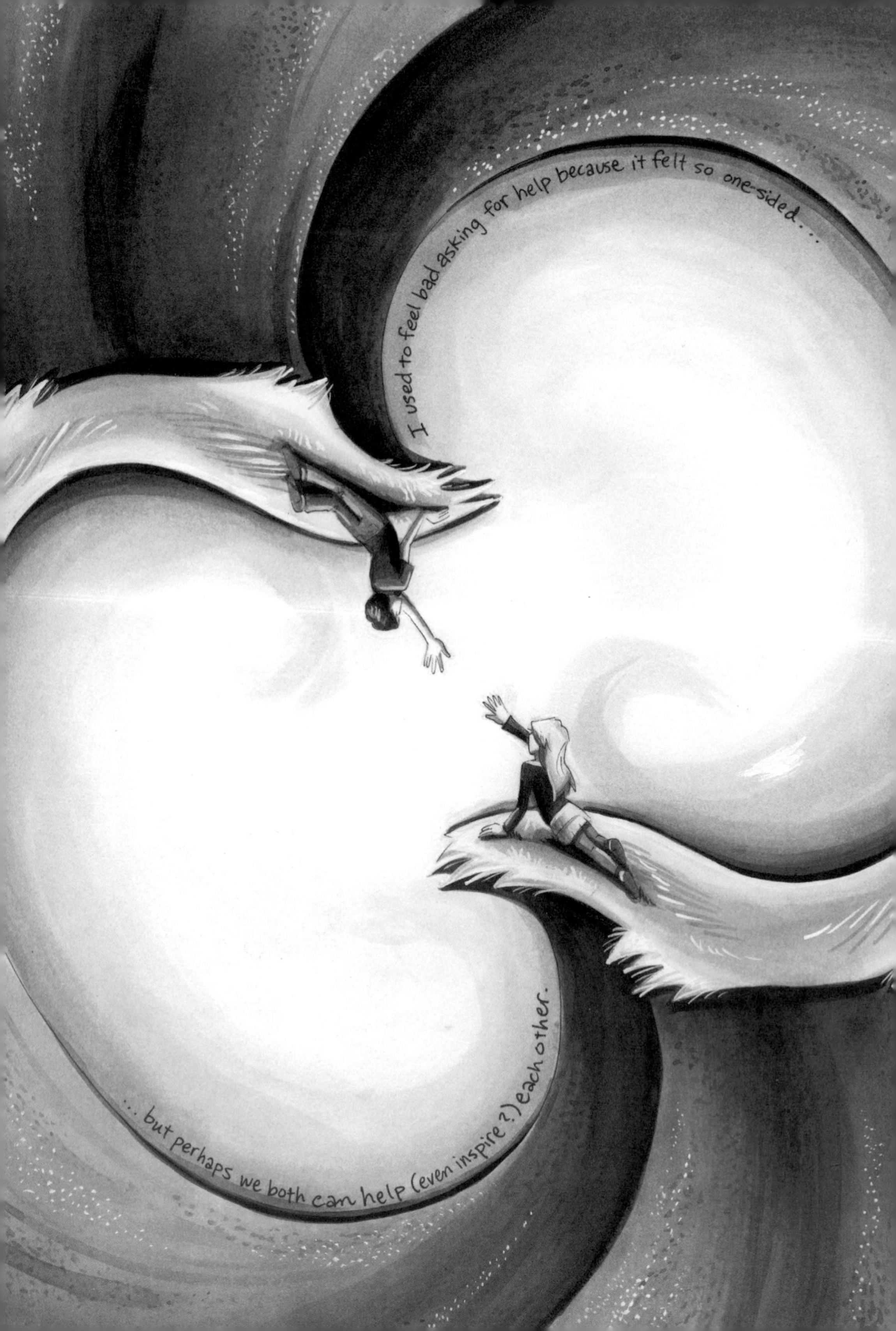
I used to feel bad asking for help because it felt so one-sided...
... but perhaps we both can help (even inspire?) each other.

Rule #8

Stay stimulated
to avoid creative
constipation.

-June-

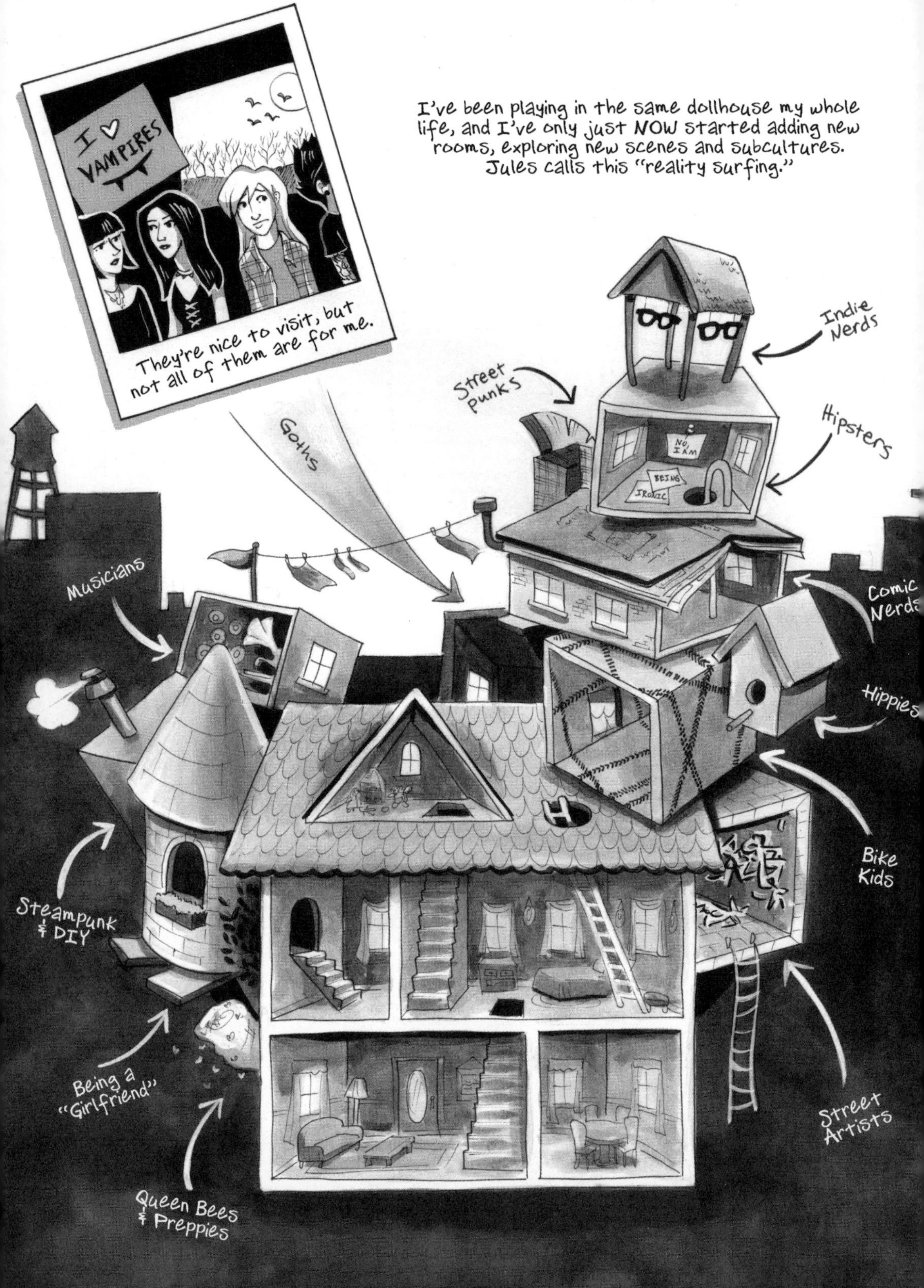
I've been playing in the same dollhouse my whole life, and I've only just NOW started adding new rooms, exploring new scenes and subcultures. Jules calls this "reality surfing."
I ♥ VAMPIRES
They're nice to visit, but not all of them are for me.
Goths
Street punks
Indie Nerds
Hipsters
NO I AM
BEING
IRONIC
Musicians
Comic Nerds
Hippies
Bike Kids
Steampunk & DIY
Being a "Girlfriend"
Queen Bees & Preppies
Street Artists

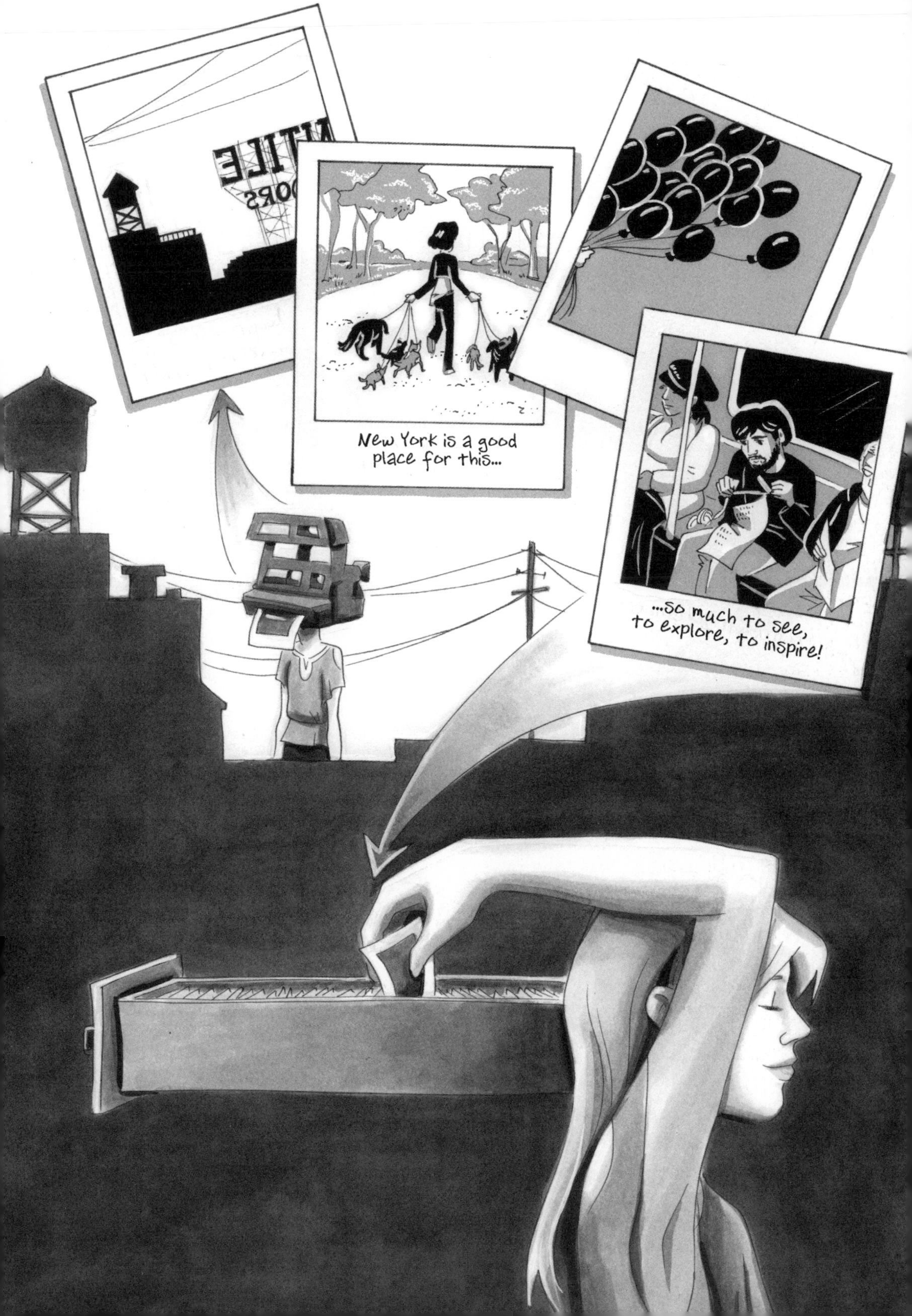
New York is a good place for this...
...so much to see, to explore, to inspire!

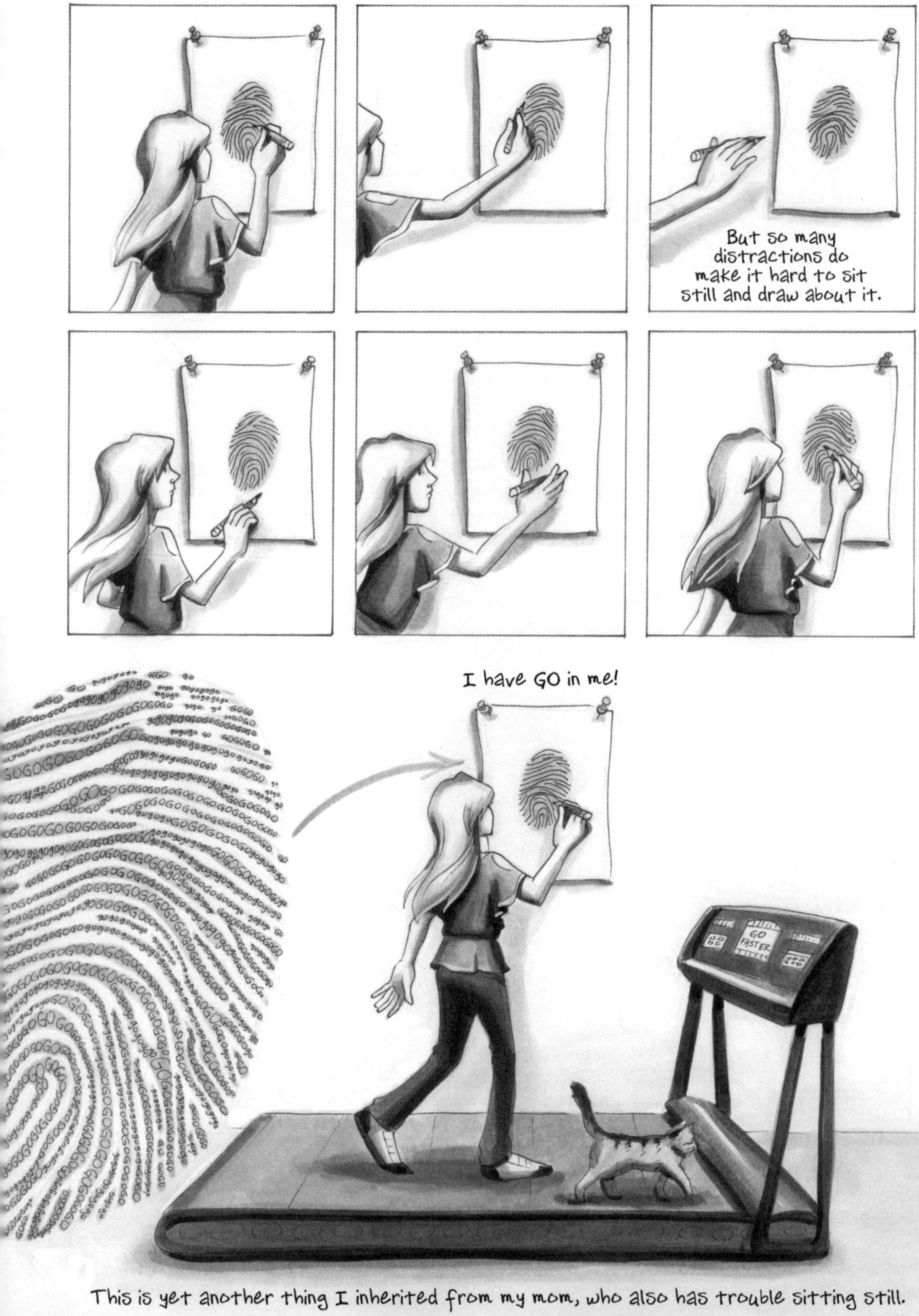
But so many distractions do make it hard to sit still and draw about it.
I have GO in me!
GO FASTER
This is yet another thing I inherited from my mom, who also has trouble sitting still.

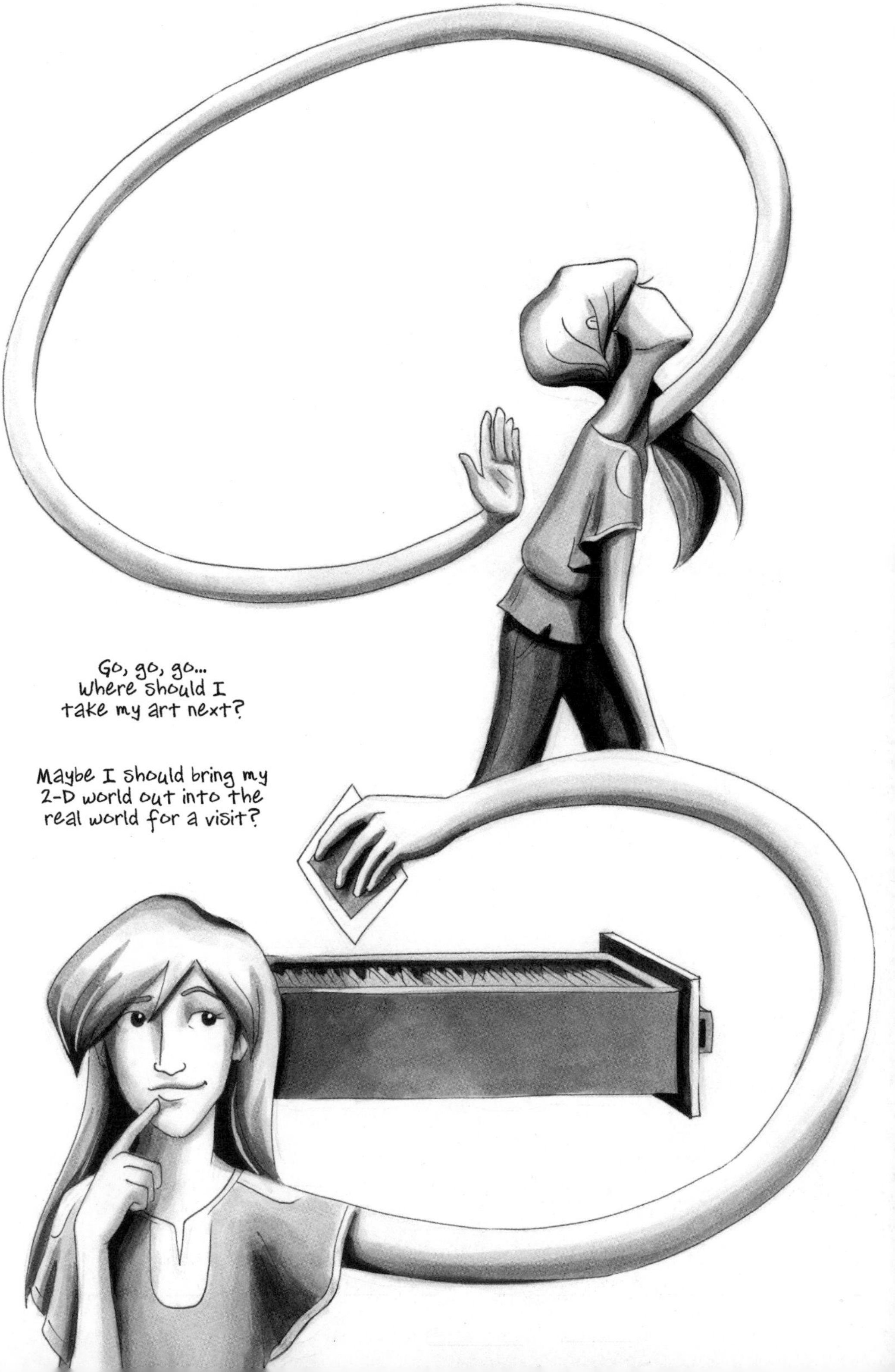
Go, go, go... Where should I take my art next?
Maybe I should bring my 2-D world out into the real world for a visit?

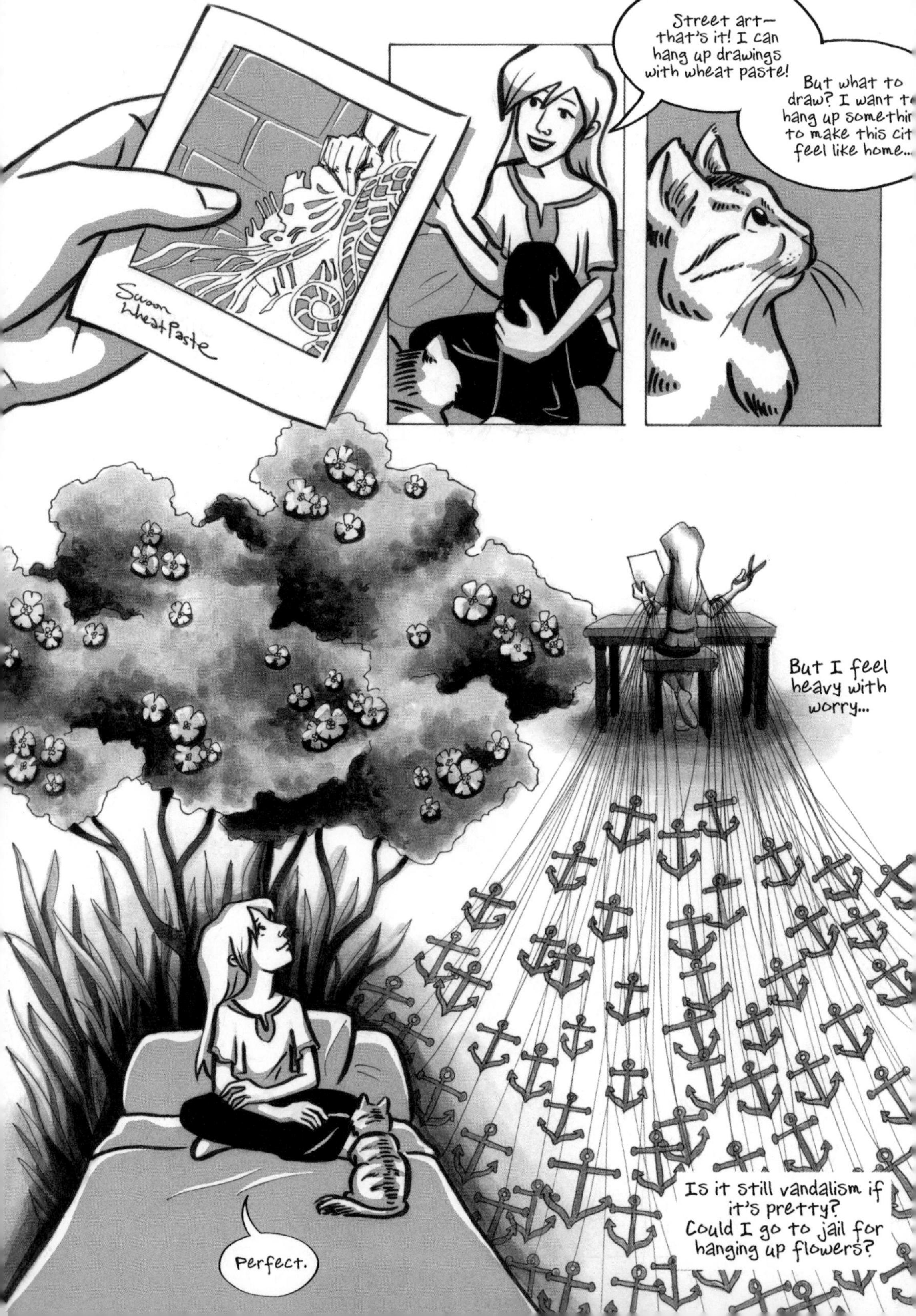
Swoon WheatPaste
Street art—that's it! I can hang up drawings with wheat paste!
But what to draw? I want to hang up something to make this city feel like home...
But I feel heavy with worry...
Is it still vandalism if it's pretty? Could I go to jail for hanging up flowers?
Perfect.

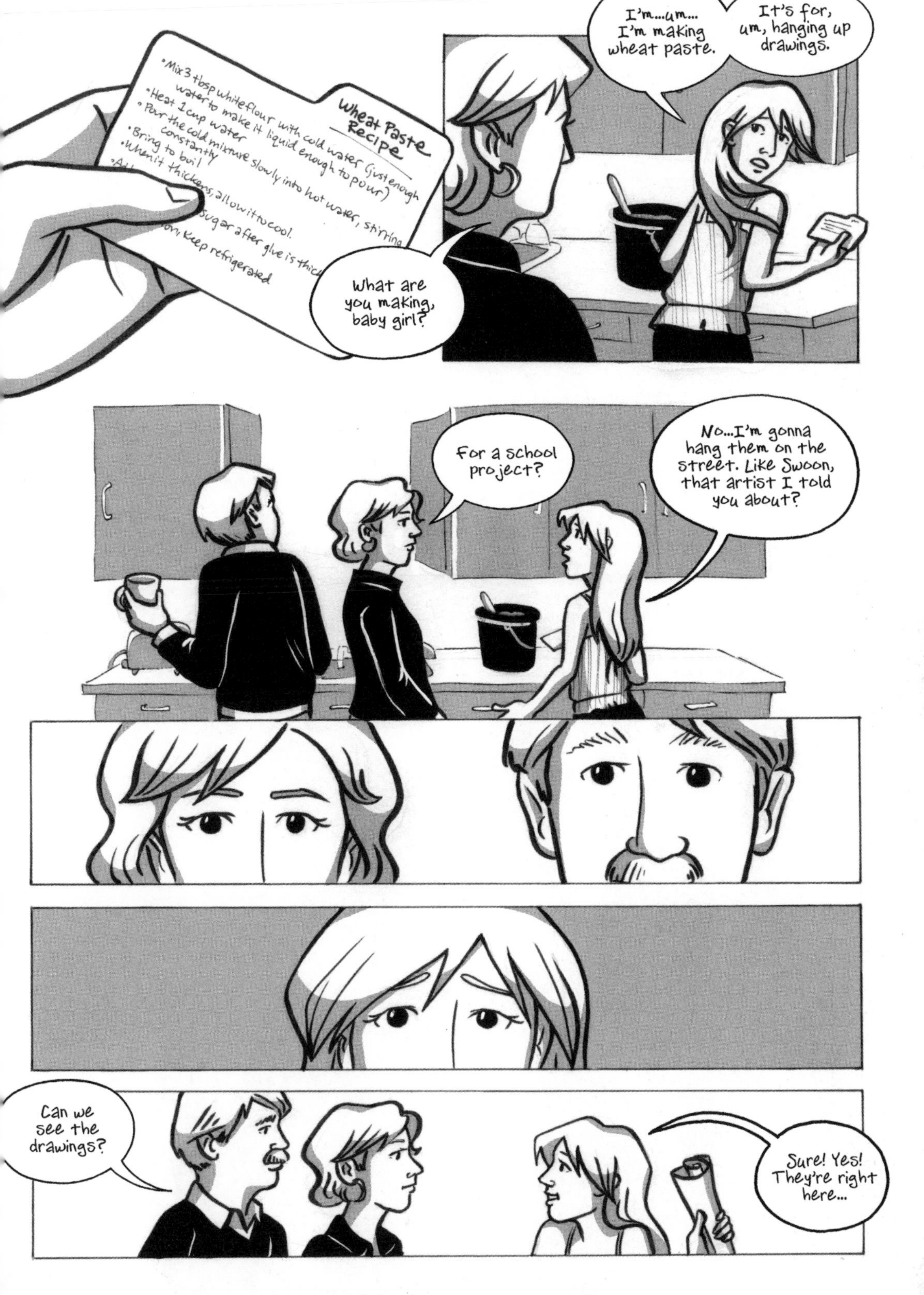
Wheat Paste Recipe
•Mix 3 tbsp white flour with cold water (just enough water to make it liquid enough to pour)
•Heat 1 cup water
•Pour the cold mixture slowly into hot water, stirring constantly
•Bring to boil
•When it thickens, allow it to cool.
Keep refrigerated
What are you making, baby girl?
I'm...um... I'm making wheat paste.
It's for, um, hanging up drawings.
For a school project?
No...I'm gonna hang them on the street. Like Swoon, that artist I told you about?
Can we see the drawings?
Sure! Yes! They're right here...

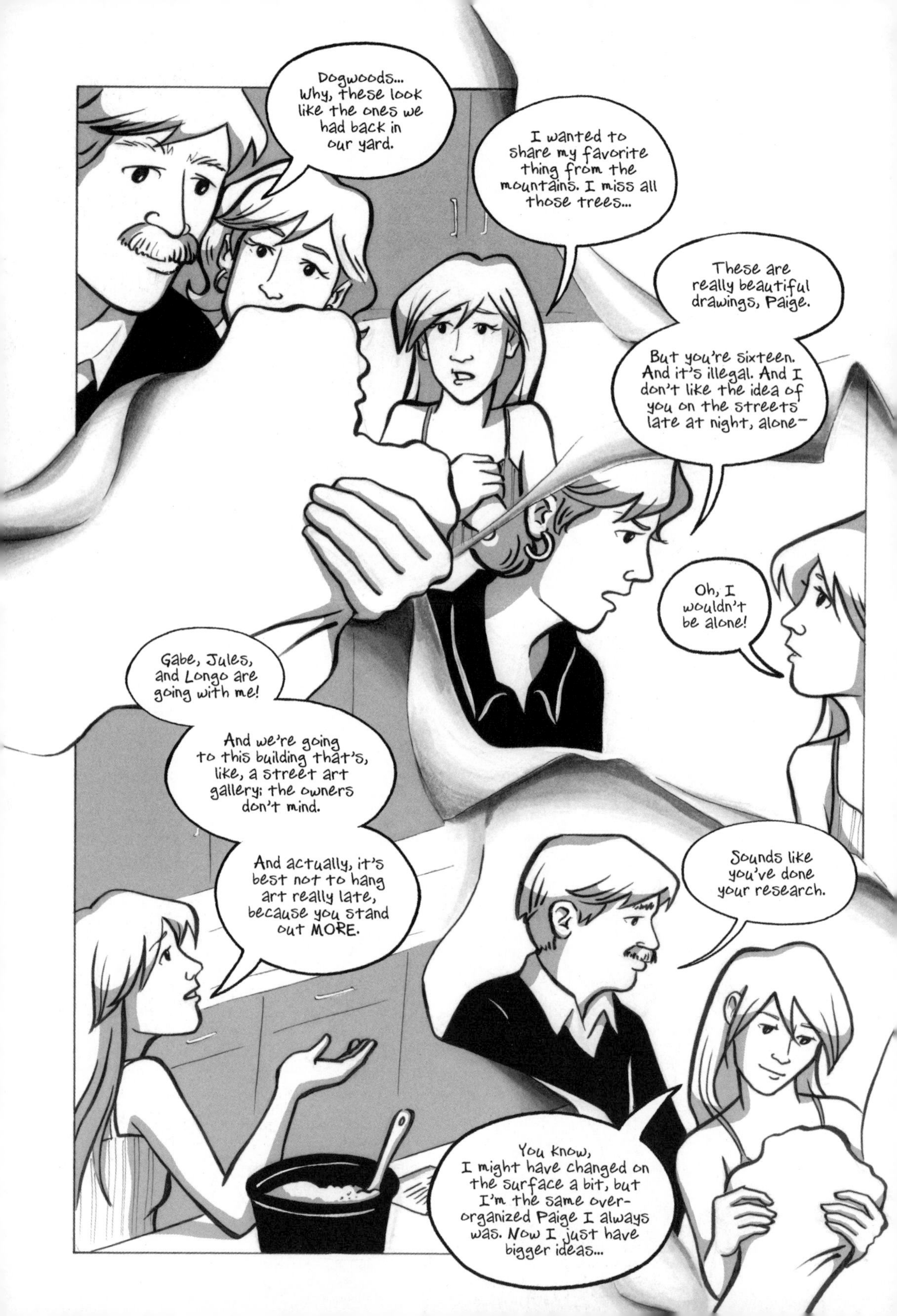
Dogwoods... Why, these look like the ones we had back in our yard.
I wanted to share my favorite thing from the mountains. I miss all those trees...
These are really beautiful drawings, Paige.
But you're sixteen. And it's illegal. And I don't like the idea of you on the streets late at night, alone–
Oh, I wouldn't be alone!
Gabe, Jules, and Longo are going with me!
And we're going to this building that's, like, a street art gallery; the owners don't mind.
And actually, it's best not to hang art really late, because you stand out MORE.
Sounds like you've done your research.
You know, I might have changed on the surface a bit, but I'm the same over-organized Paige I always was. Now I just have bigger ideas...

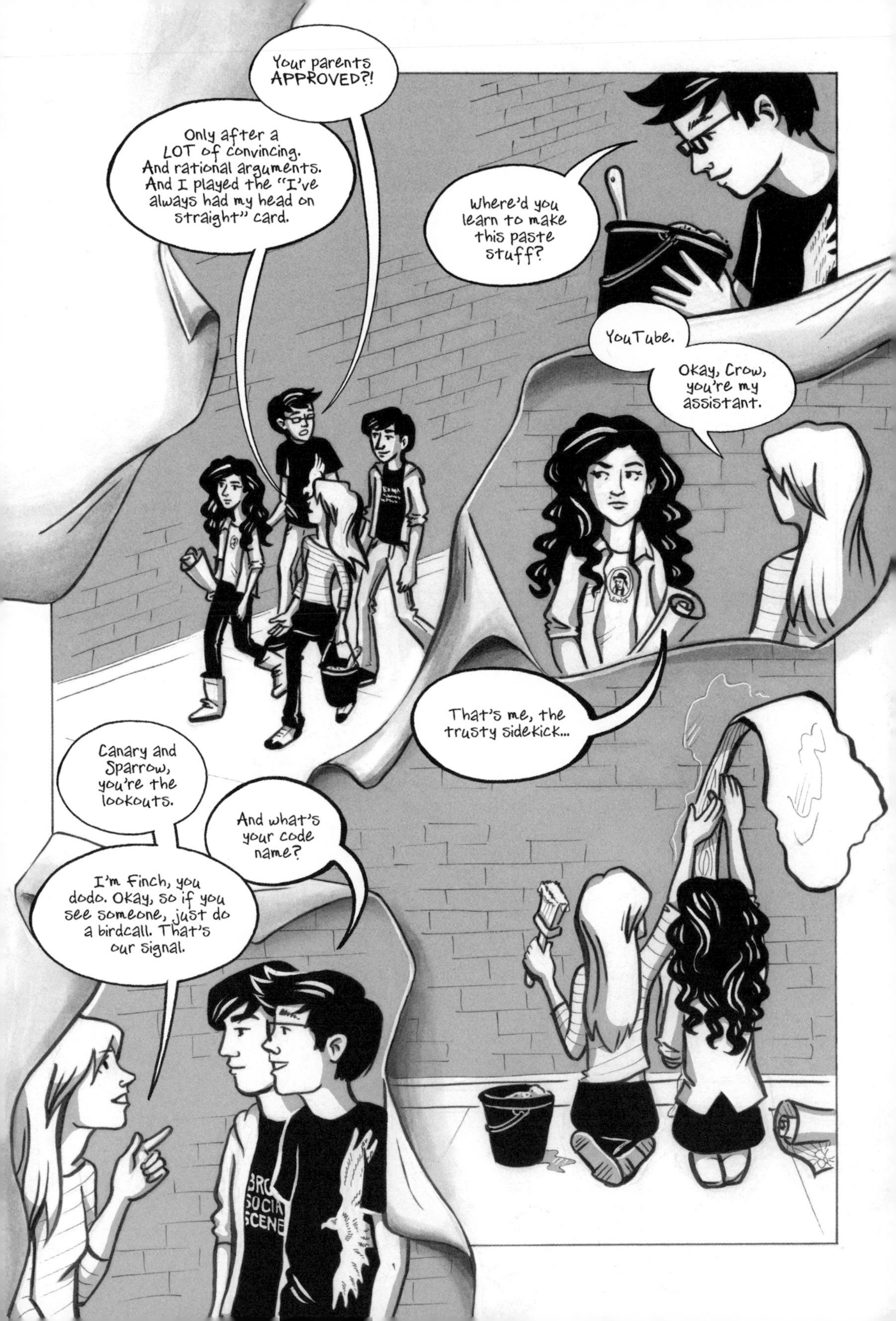

Your parents APPROVED?!
Only after a LOT of convincing. And rational arguments. And I played the "I've always had my head on straight" card.
Where'd you learn to make this paste stuff?
YouTube.
Okay, Crow, you're my assistant.
That's me, the trusty sidekick...
Canary and Sparrow, you're the lookouts.
And what's your code name?
I'm Finch, you dodo. Okay, so if you see someone, just do a birdcall. That's our signal.

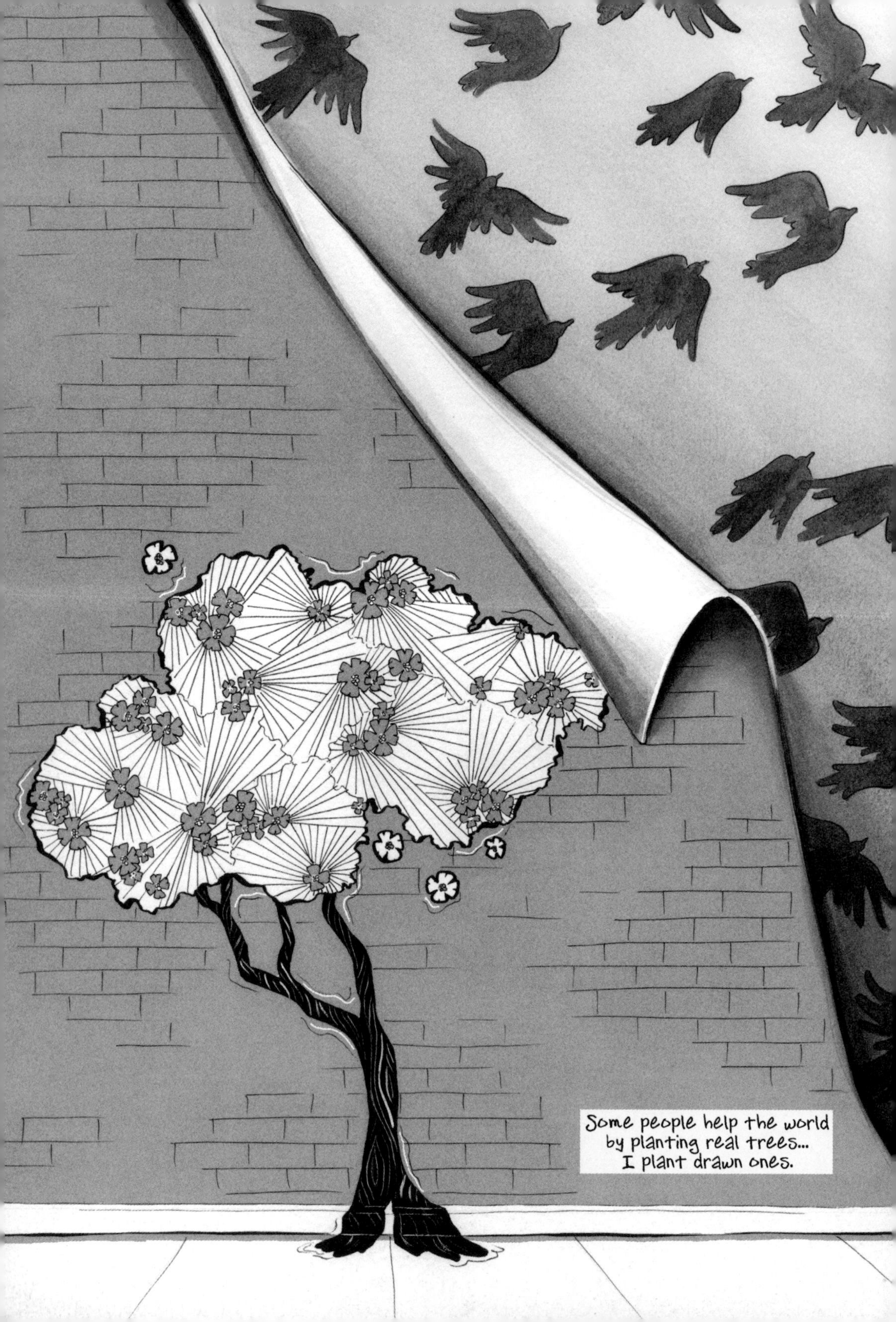
Some people help the world
by planting real trees...
I plant drawn ones.

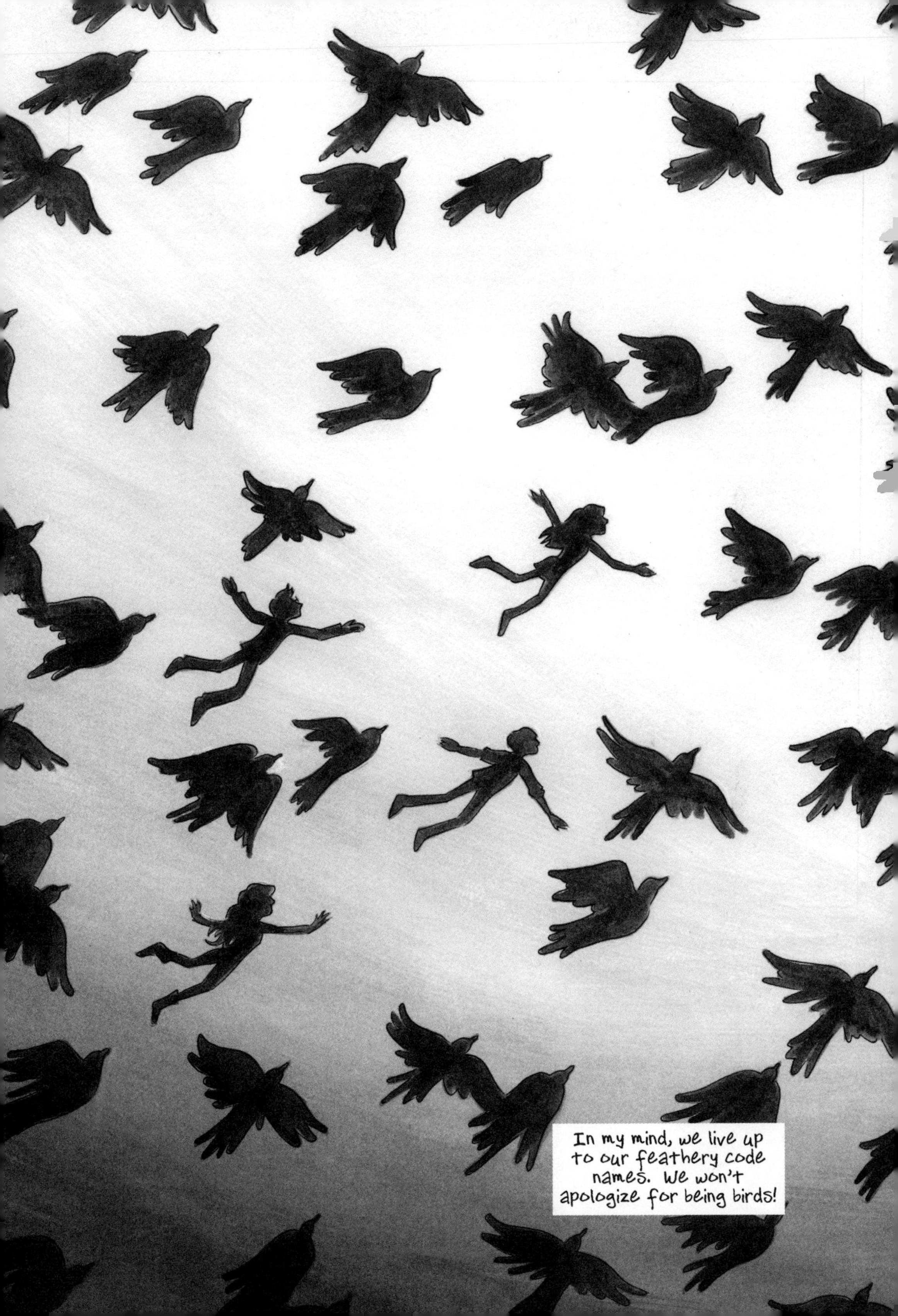
In my mind, we live up to our feathery code names. We won't apologize for being birds!

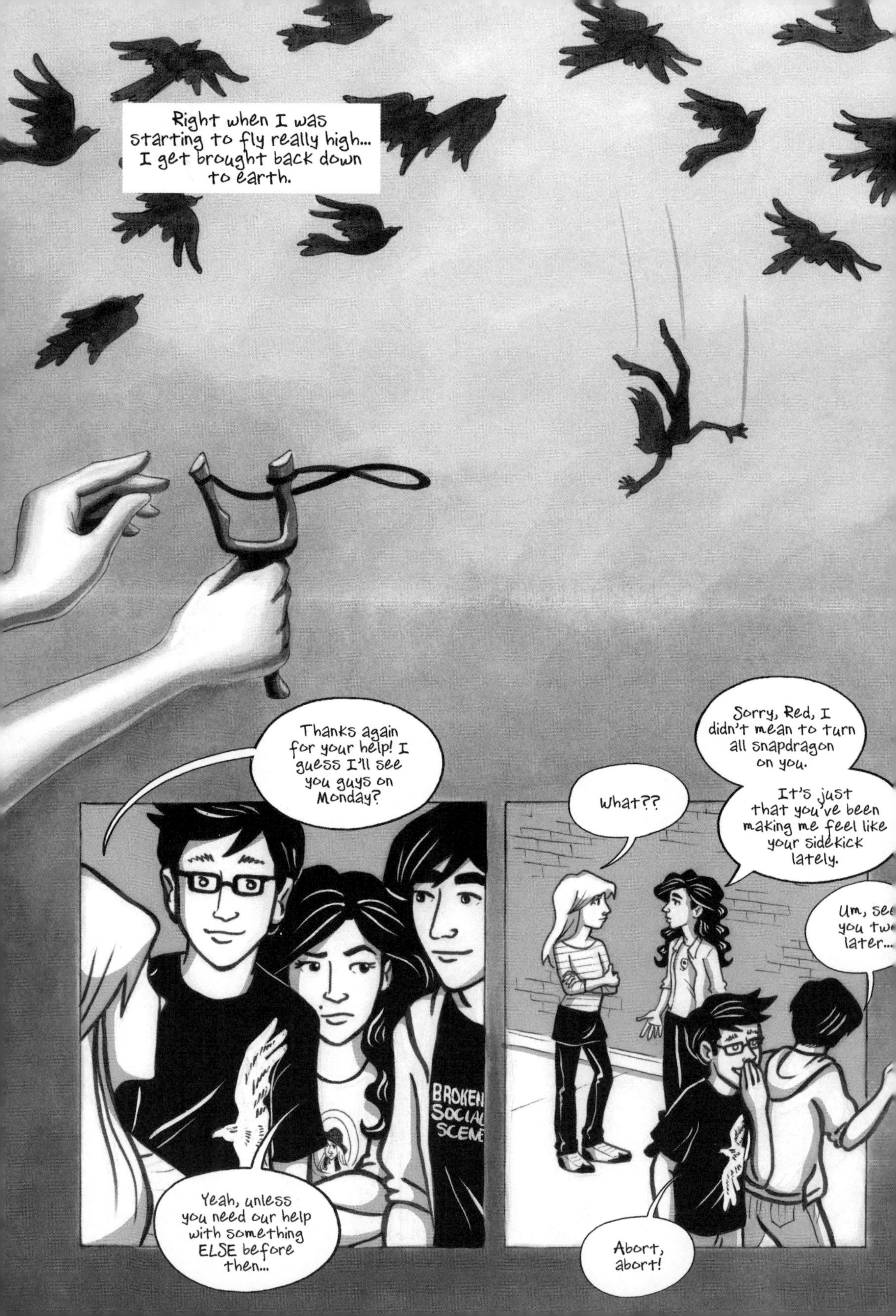
Right when I was starting to fly really high... I get brought back down to earth.
Thanks again for your help! I guess I'll see you guys on Monday?
Yeah, unless you need our help with something ELSE before then...
BROKEN SOCIAL SCENE
Sorry, Red, I didn't mean to turn all snapdragon on you.
What??
It's just that you've been making me feel like your sidekick lately.
Abort, abort!

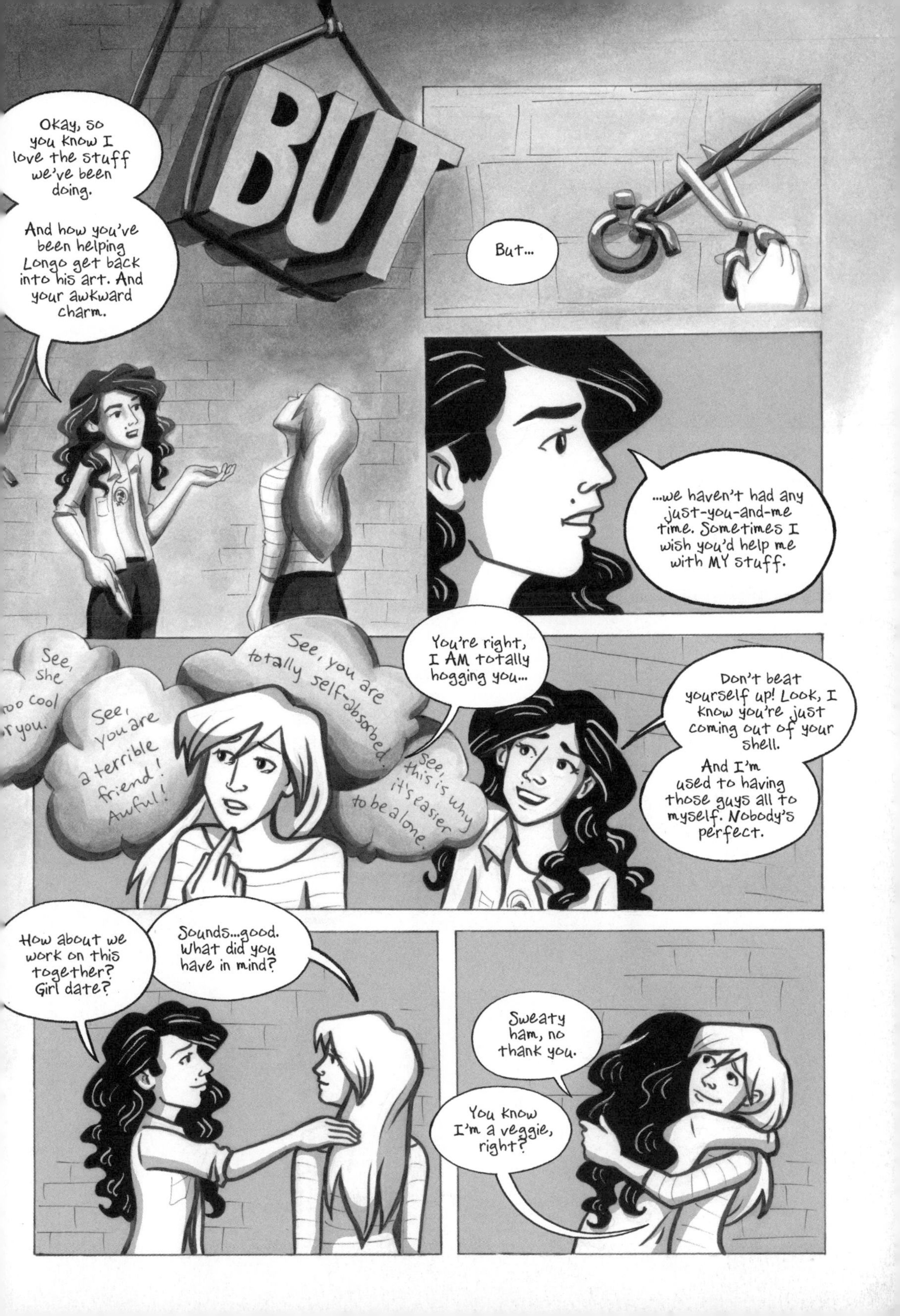
Okay, so you know I love the stuff we've been doing.
And how you've been helping Longo get back into his art. And your awkward charm.
BUT
But...
...we haven't had any just-you-and-me time. Sometimes I wish you'd help me with MY stuff.
See, she
oo cool
r you.
See, you are a terrible friend! Awful!
See, you are totally self-absorbed.
See, this is why it's easier to be alone.
You're right, I AM totally hogging you...
Don't beat yourself up! Look, I know you're just coming out of your shell.
And I'm used to having those guys all to myself. Nobody's perfect.
How about we work on this together? Girl date?
Sounds...good. What did you have in mind?
Sweaty ham, no thank you.
You know I'm a veggie, right?

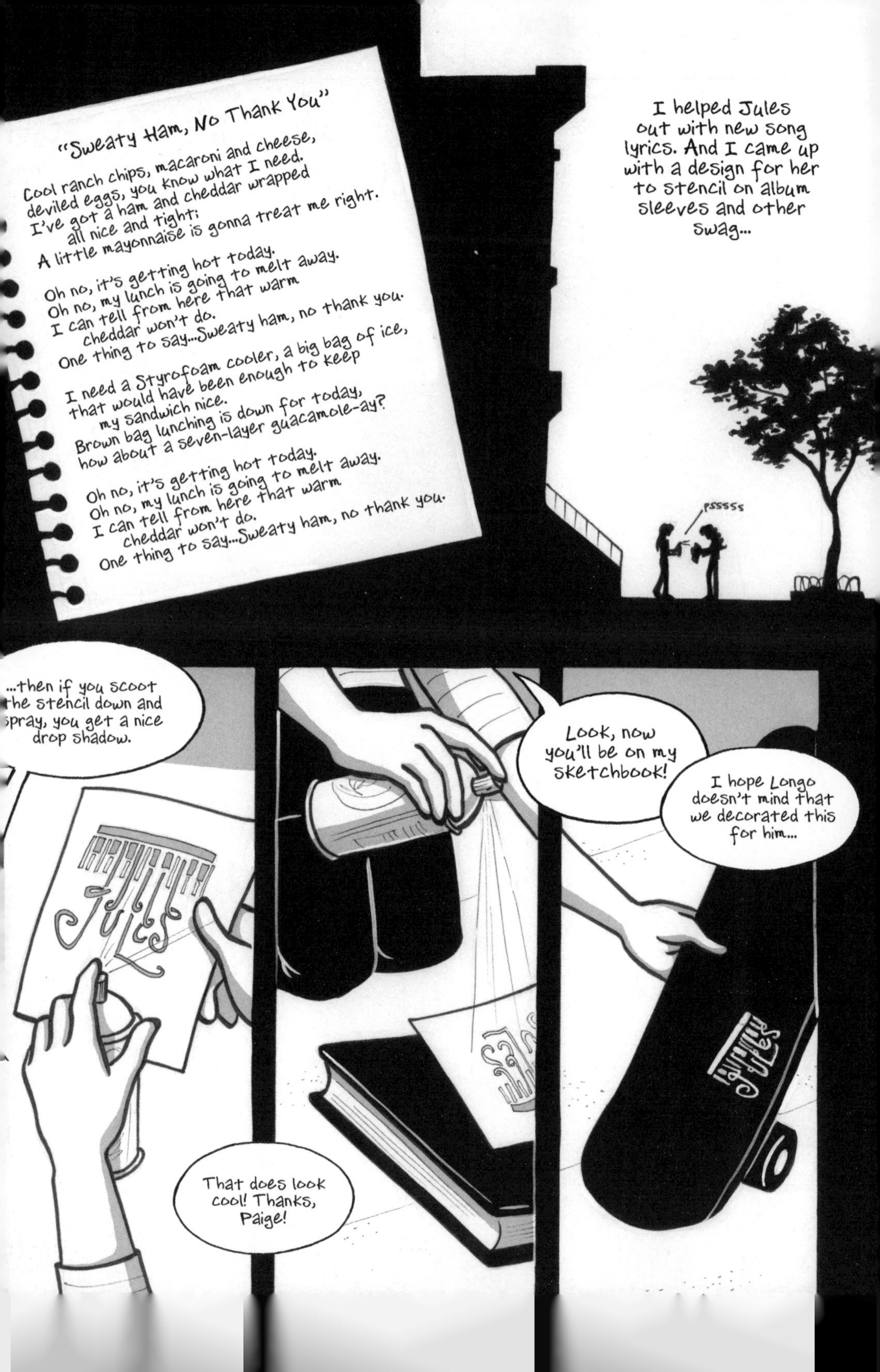
"Sweaty Ham, No Thank You"
Cool ranch chips, macaroni and cheese,
deviled eggs, you know what I need.
I've got a ham and cheddar wrapped
all nice and tight;
A little mayonnaise is gonna treat me right.
Oh no, it's getting hot today.
Oh no, my lunch is going to melt away.
I can tell from here that warm
cheddar won't do.
One thing to say...Sweaty ham, no thank you.
I need a Styrofoam cooler, a big bag of ice,
that would have been enough to keep
my sandwich nice.
Brown bag lunching is down for today,
how about a seven-layer guacamole-ay?
Oh no, it's getting hot today.
Oh no, my lunch is going to melt away.
I can tell from here that warm
cheddar won't do.
One thing to say...Sweaty ham, no thank you.
I helped Jules out with new song lyrics. And I came up with a design for her to stencil on album sleeves and other swag...
PSSSSS
...then if you scoot the stencil down and spray, you get a nice drop shadow.
That does look cool! Thanks, Paige!
Look, now you'll be on my sketchbook!
I hope Longo doesn't mind that we decorated this for him...

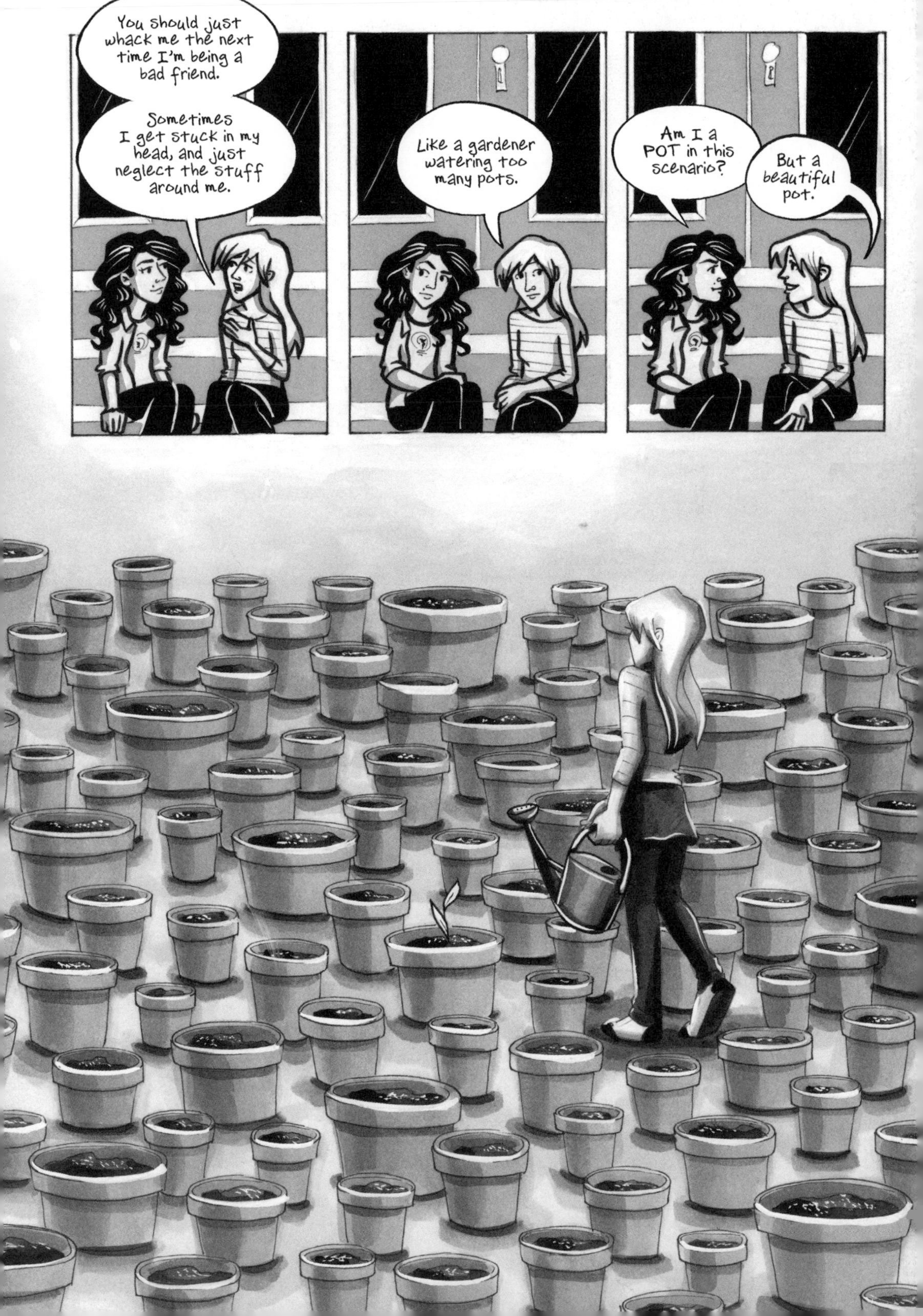
You should just whack me the next time I'm being a bad friend.
Sometimes I get stuck in my head, and just neglect the stuff around me.
Like a gardener watering too many pots.
Am I a POT in this scenario?
But a beautiful pot.

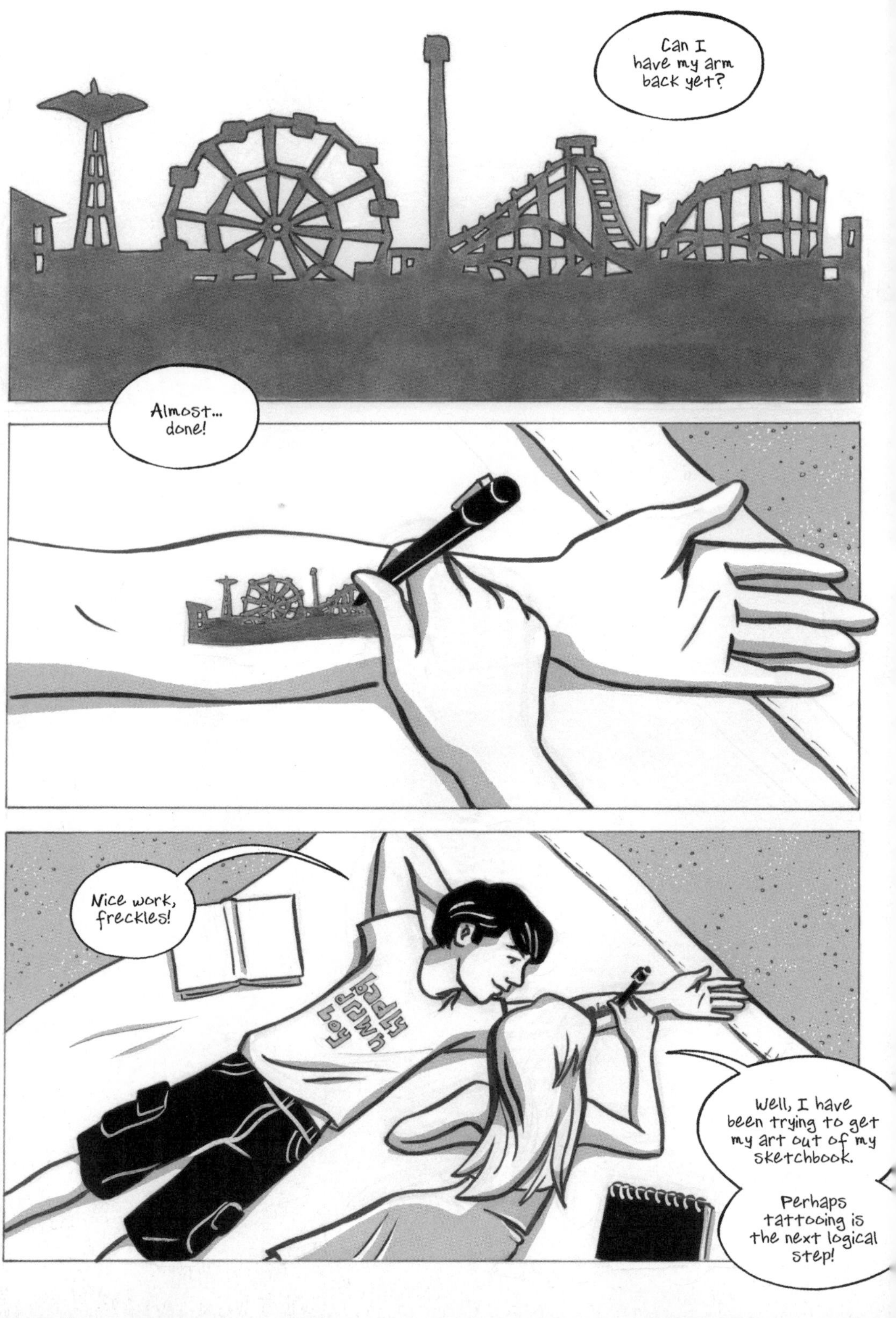
Can I have my arm back yet?
Almost... done!
Nice work, freckles!
Well, I have been trying to get my art out of my sketchbook.
Perhaps tattooing is the next logical step!

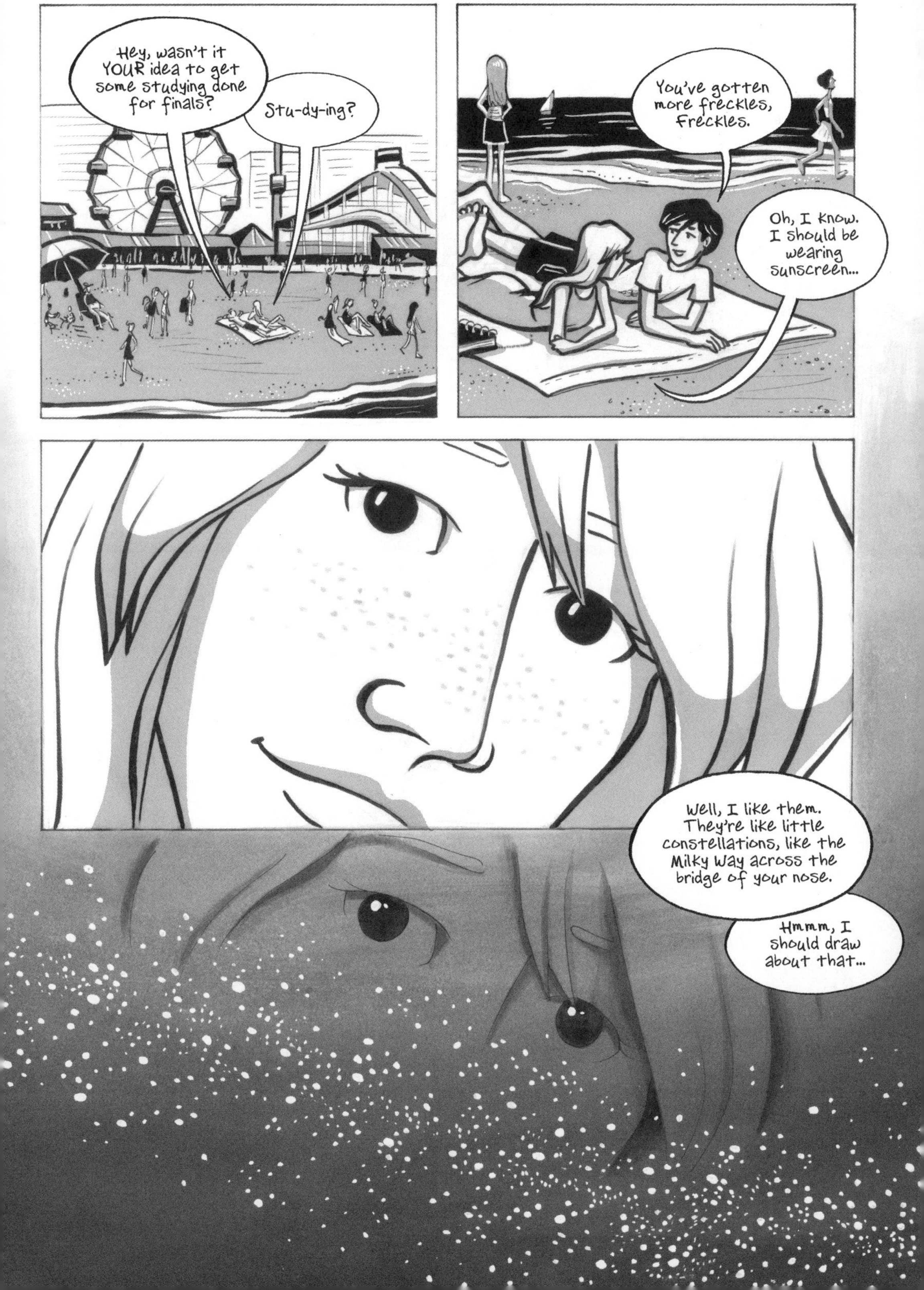
Hey, wasn't it YOUR idea to get some studying done for finals?
Stu-dy-ing?
You've gotten more freckles, Freckles.
Oh, I know. I should be wearing sunscreen...
Well, I like them. They're like little constellations, like the Milky Way across the bridge of your nose.
Hmmm, I should draw about that...

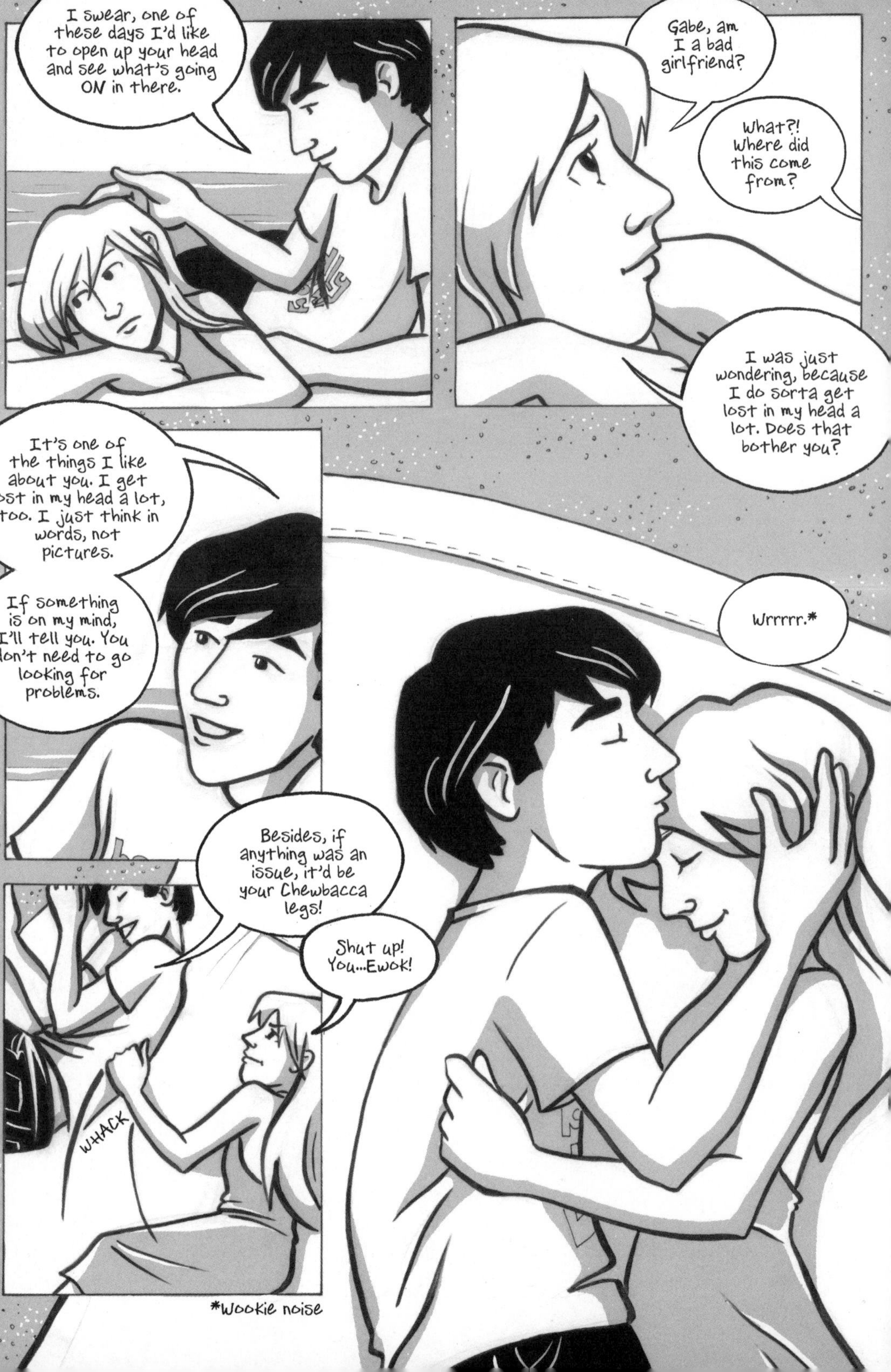
I swear, one of these days I'd like to open up your head and see what's going ON in there.
Gabe, am I a bad girlfriend?
What?! Where did this come from?
I was just wondering, because I do sorta get lost in my head a lot. Does that bother you?
It's one of the things I like about you. I get lost in my head a lot, too. I just think in words, not pictures.
If something is on my mind, I'll tell you. You don't need to go looking for problems.
Besides, if anything was an issue, it'd be your Chewbacca legs!
Shut up! You...Ewok!
WHACK
Wrrrrr.*
*Wookie noise

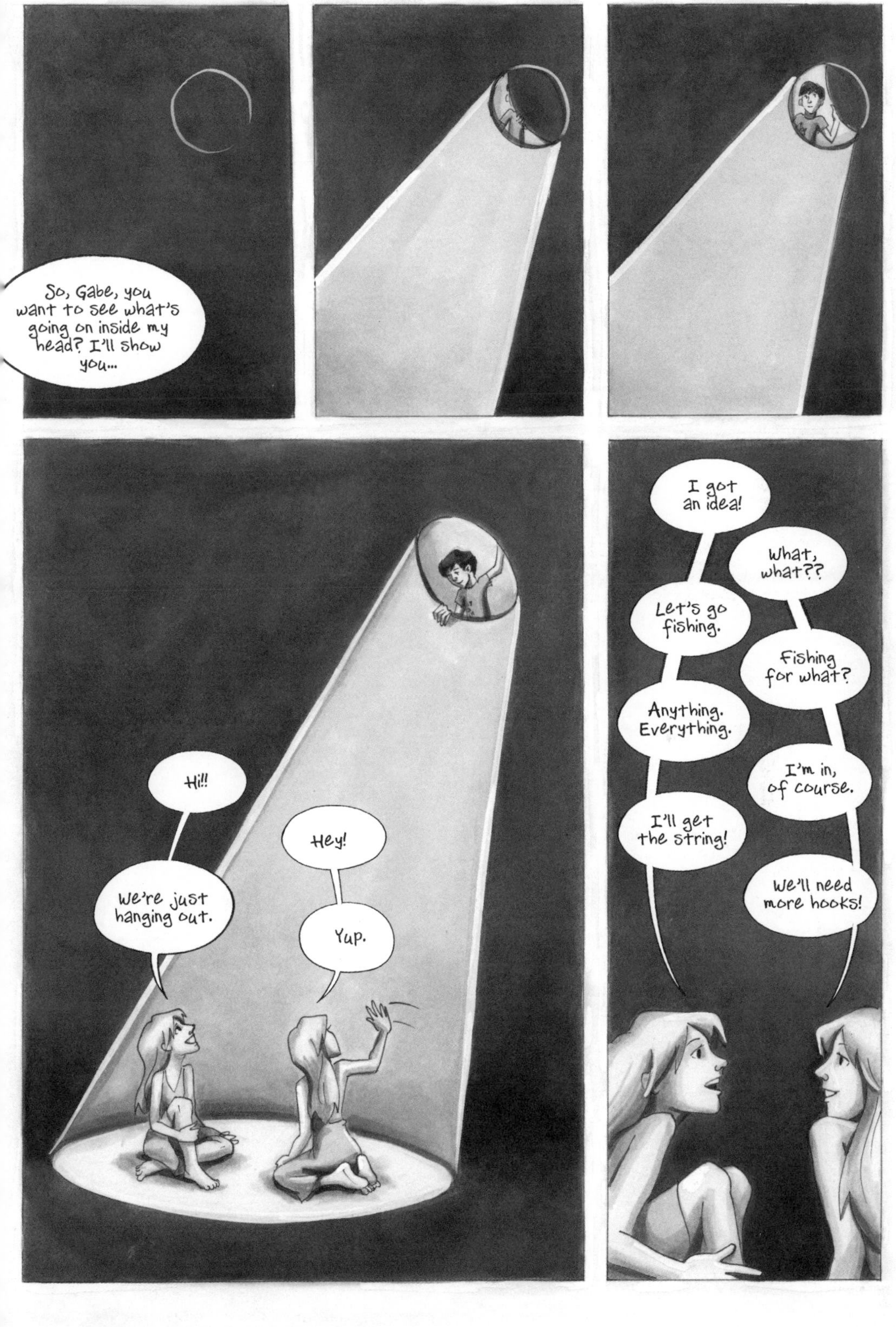
So, Gabe, you want to see what's going on inside my head? I'll show you...
Hi!!
We're just hanging out.
Hey!
Yup.
I got an idea!
What, what??
Let's go fishing.
Fishing for what?
Anything. Everything.
I'm in, of course.
I'll get the string!
We'll need more hooks!

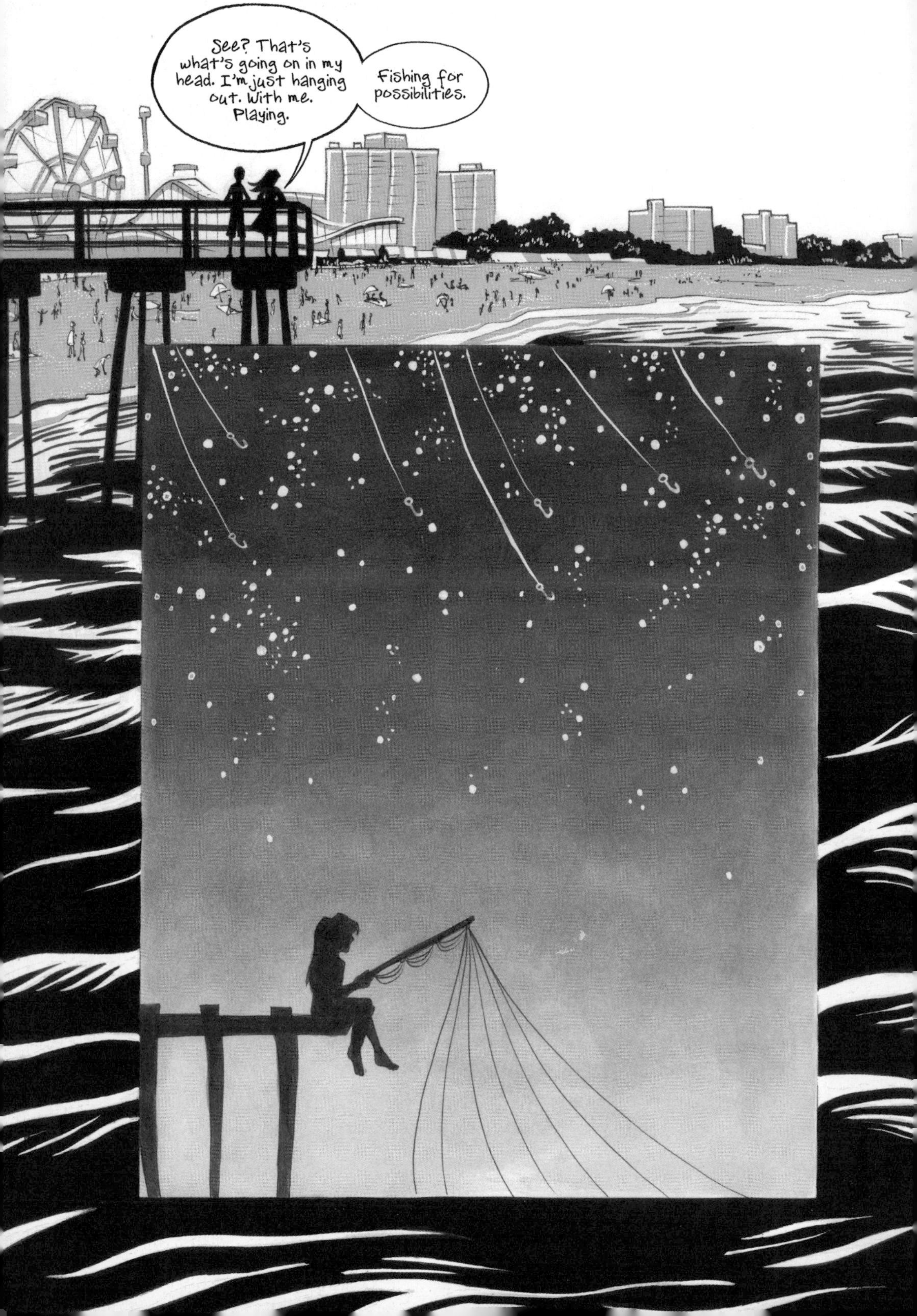
See? That's what's going on in my head. I'm just hanging out. With me. Playing.
Fishing for possibilities.

Rule #9

Trust your gut instinct. Be honest with yourself.

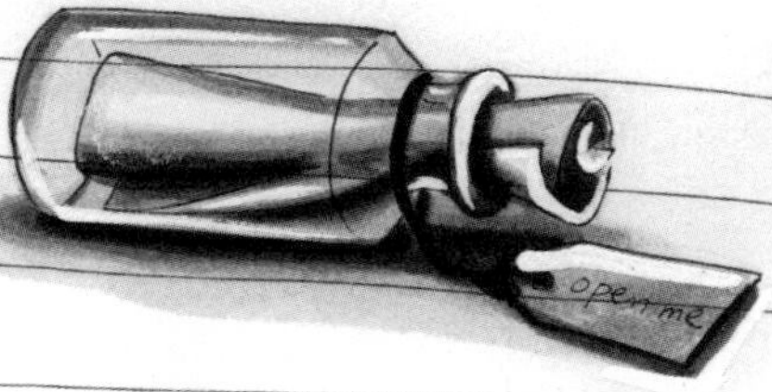
open me

-July-

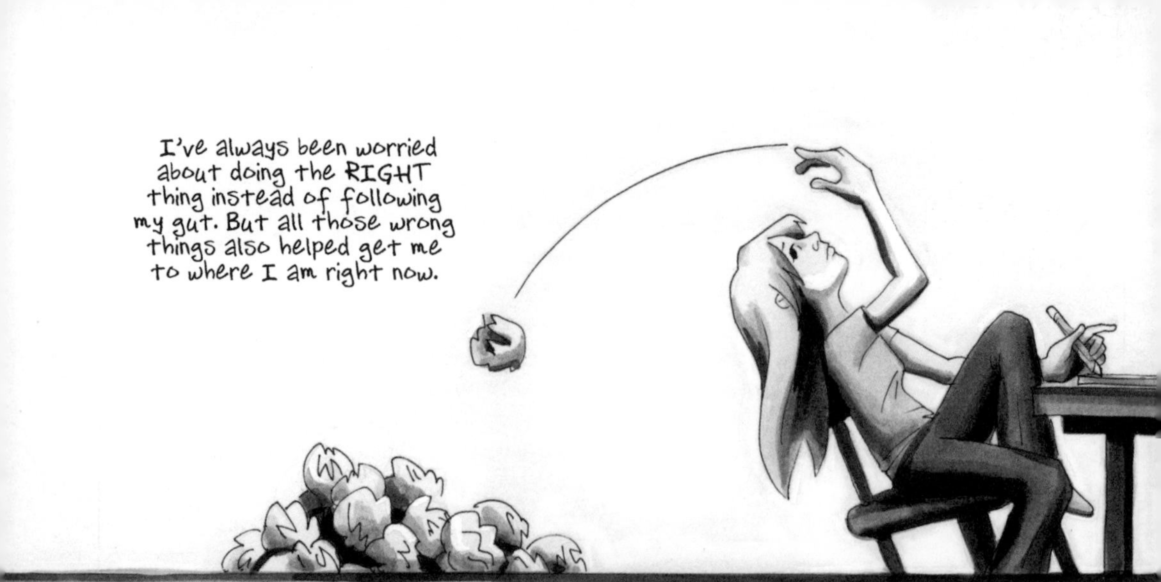
I've always been worried about doing the RIGHT thing instead of following my gut. But all those wrong things also helped get me to where I am right now.

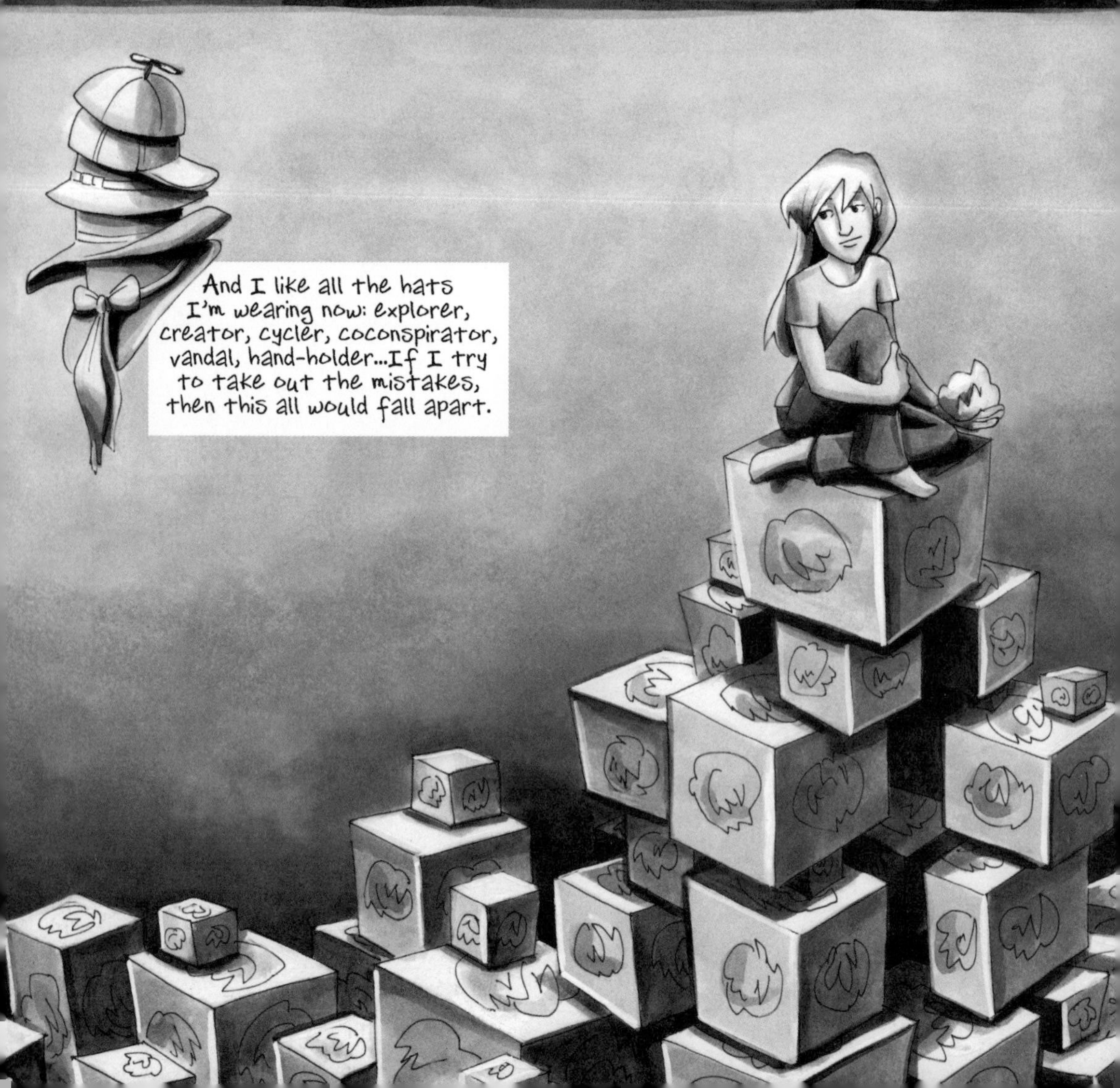
And I like all the hats I'm wearing now: explorer, creator, cycler, coconspirator, vandal, hand-holder...If I try to take out the mistakes, then this all would fall apart.

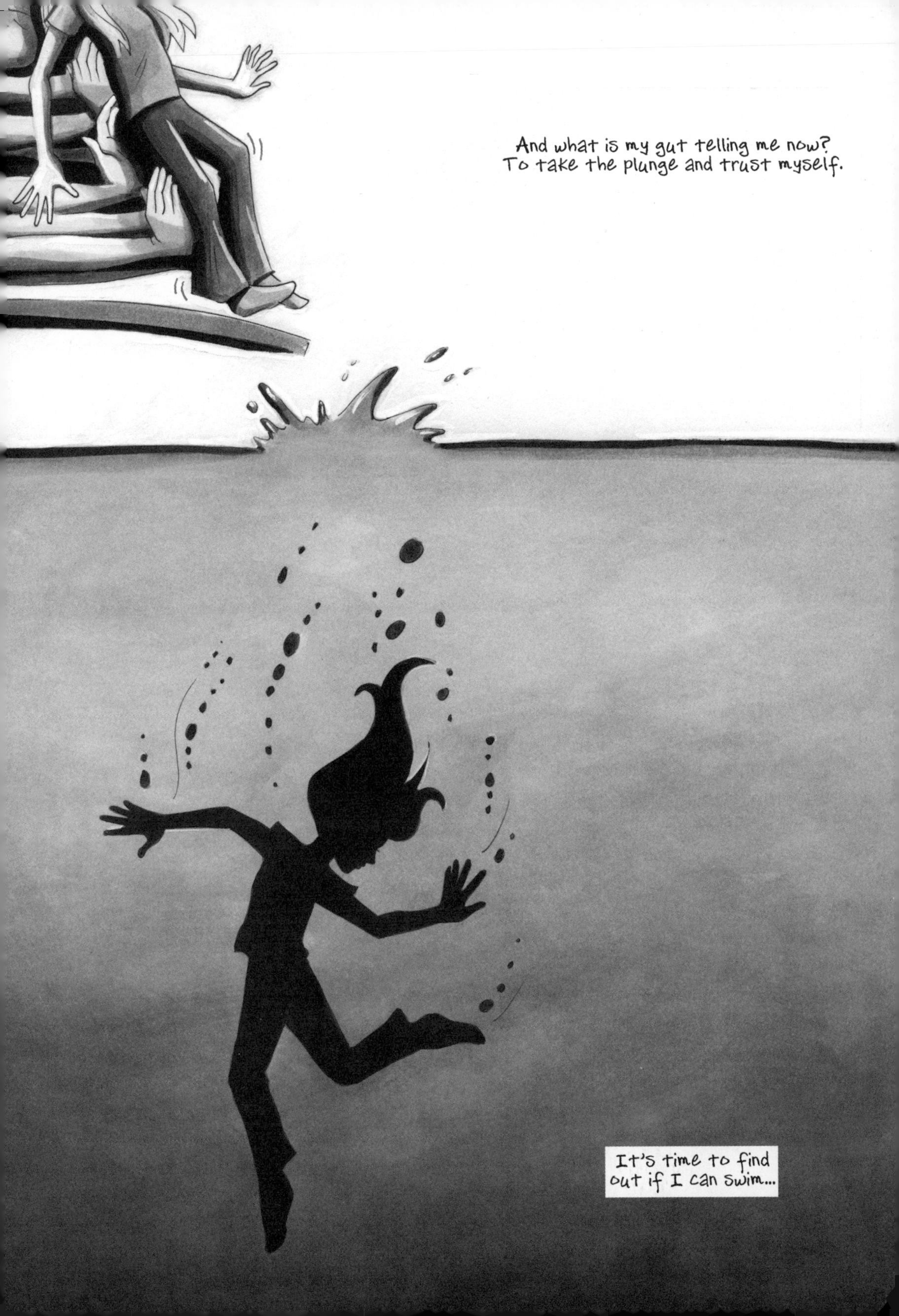
And what is my gut telling me now?
To take the plunge and trust myself.
It's time to find out if I can swim...

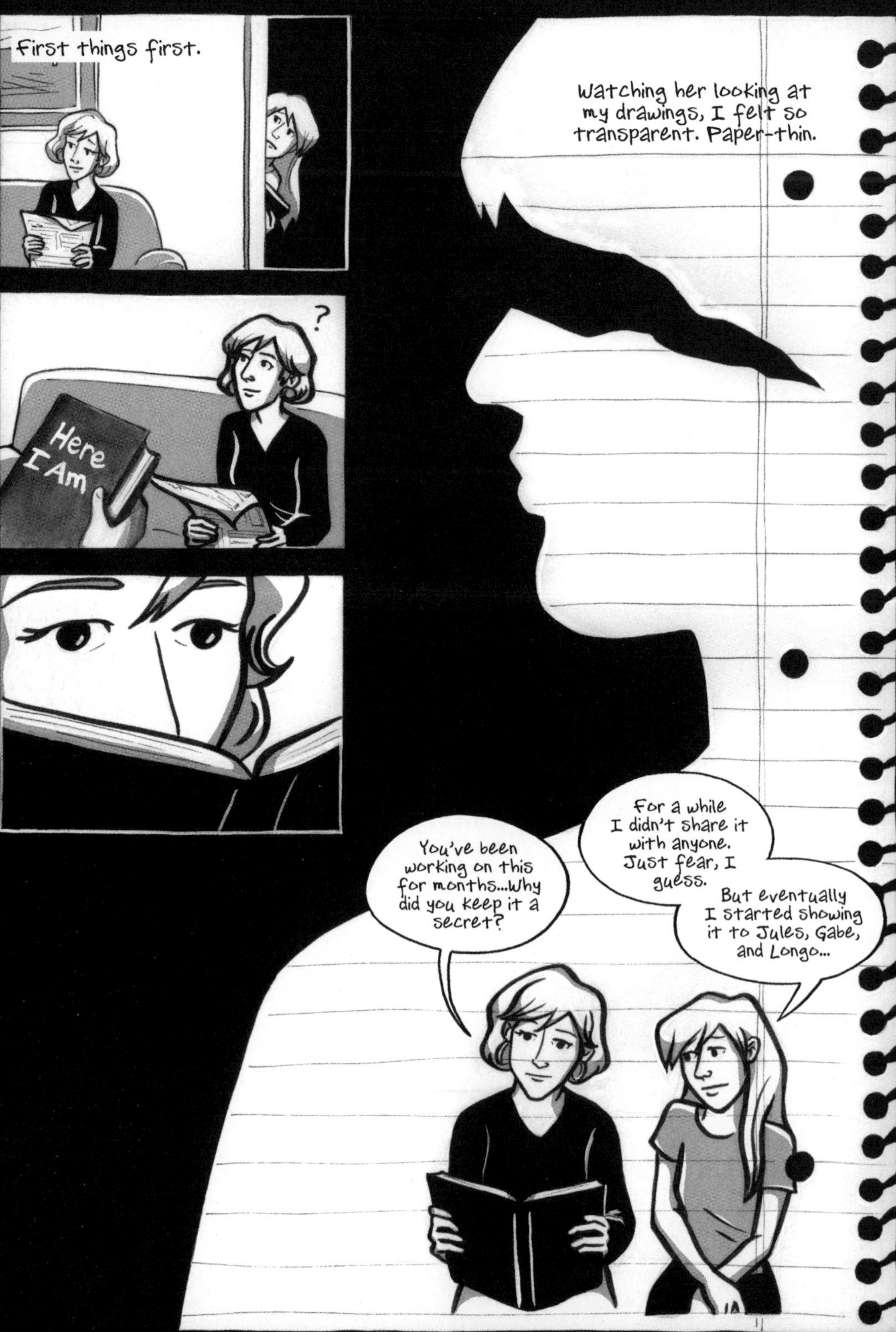
First things first.
Here I Am
?
Watching her looking at my drawings, I felt so transparent. Paper-thin.
You've been working on this for months...Why did you keep it a secret?
For a while I didn't share it with anyone. Just fear, I guess.
But eventually I started showing it to Jules, Gabe, and Longo...

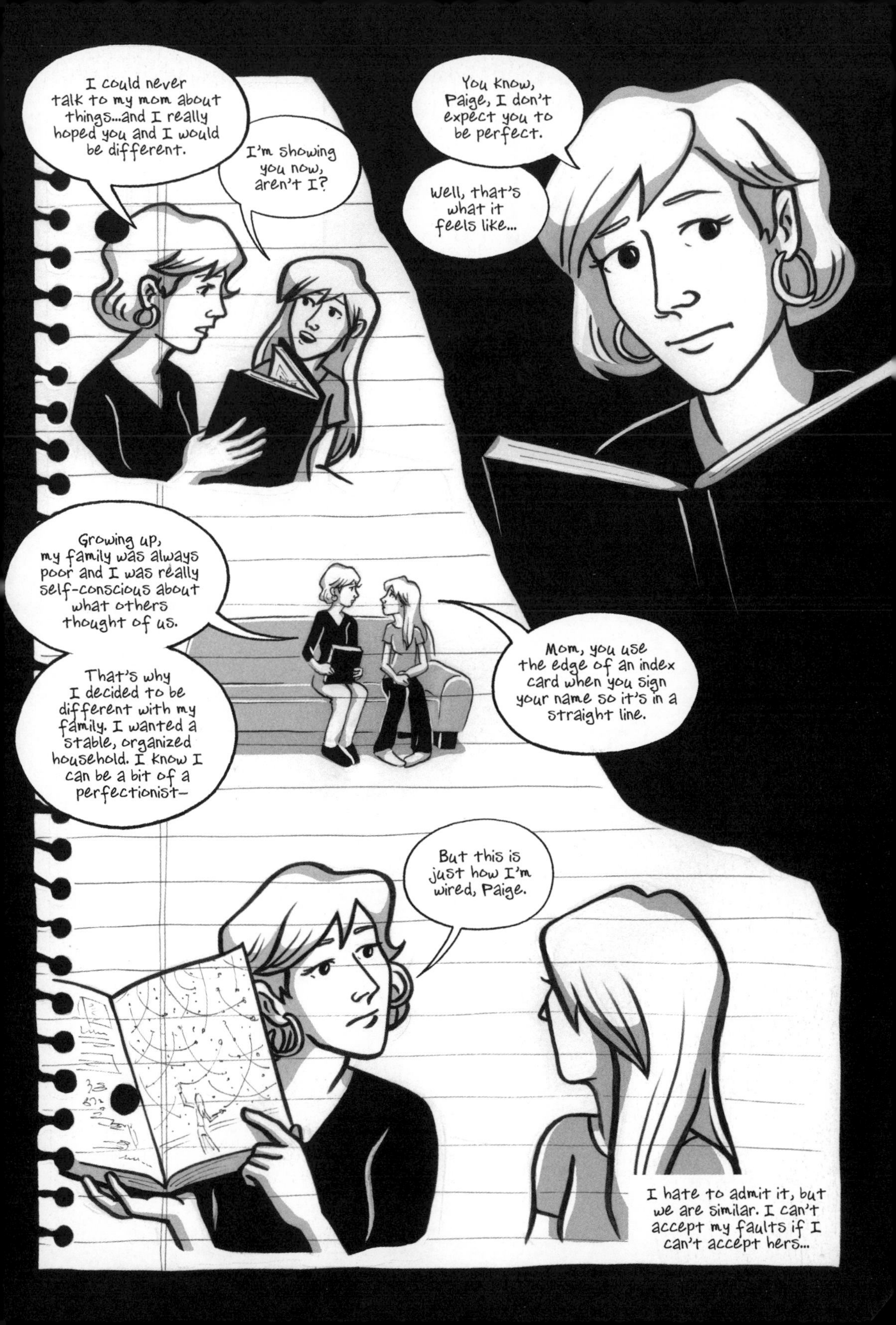

I could never talk to my mom about things...and I really hoped you and I would be different.
I'm showing you now, aren't I?
You know, Paige, I don't expect you to be perfect.
Well, that's what it feels like...
Growing up, my family was always poor and I was really self-conscious about what others thought of us.
That's why I decided to be different with my family. I wanted a stable, organized household. I know I can be a bit of a perfectionist–
Mom, you use the edge of an index card when you sign your name so it's in a straight line.
But this is just how I'm wired, Paige.
I hate to admit it, but we are similar. I can't accept my faults if I can't accept hers...

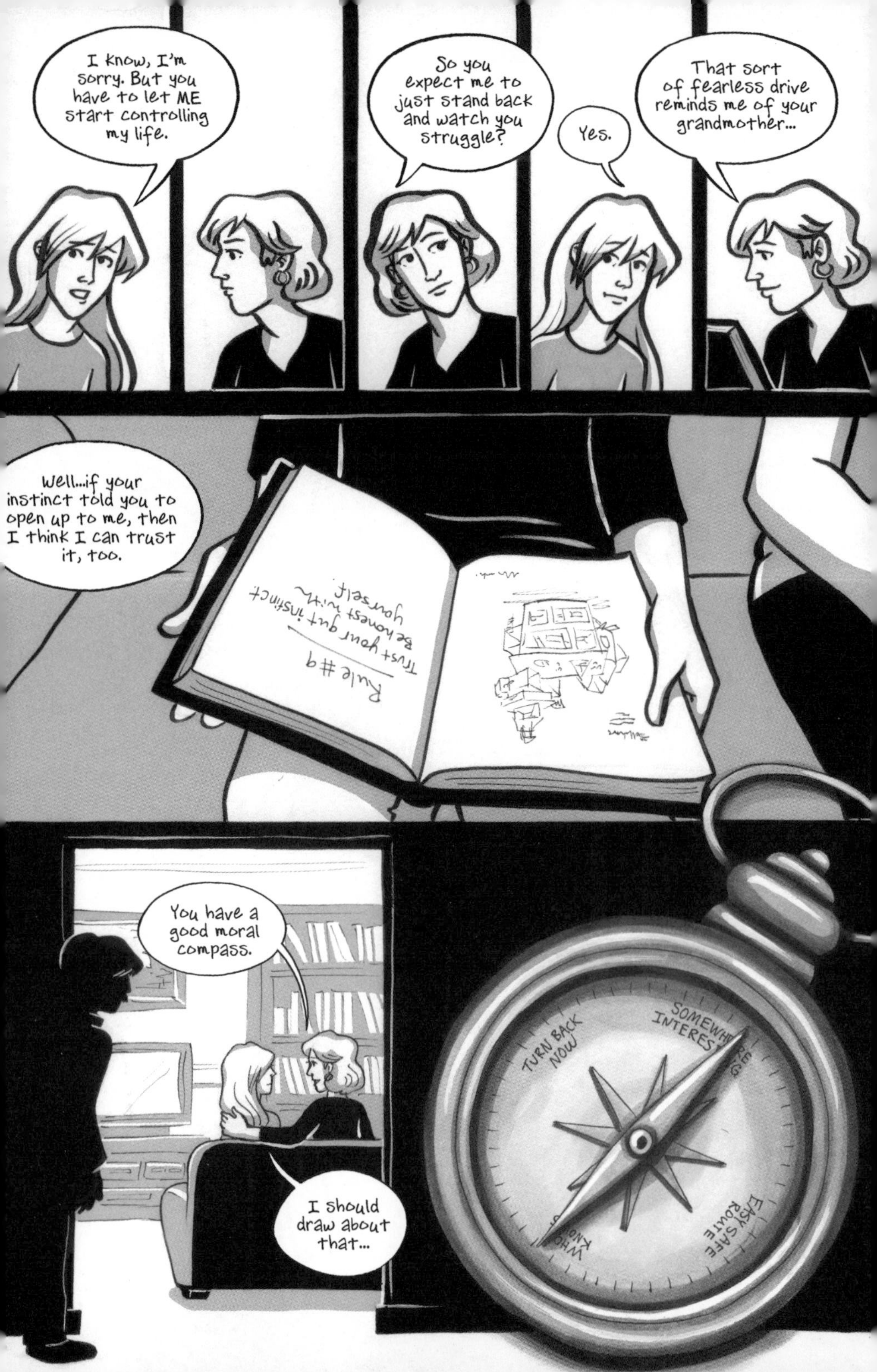
I know, I'm sorry. But you have to let ME start controlling my life.
So you expect me to just stand back and watch you struggle?
Yes.
That sort of fearless drive reminds me of your grandmother...
Well...if your instinct told you to open up to me, then I think I can trust it, too.
Rule #9
Trust your gut instinct.
Be honest with yourself.
You have a good moral compass.
I should draw about that...
TURN BACK NOW
EASY SAFE ROUTE

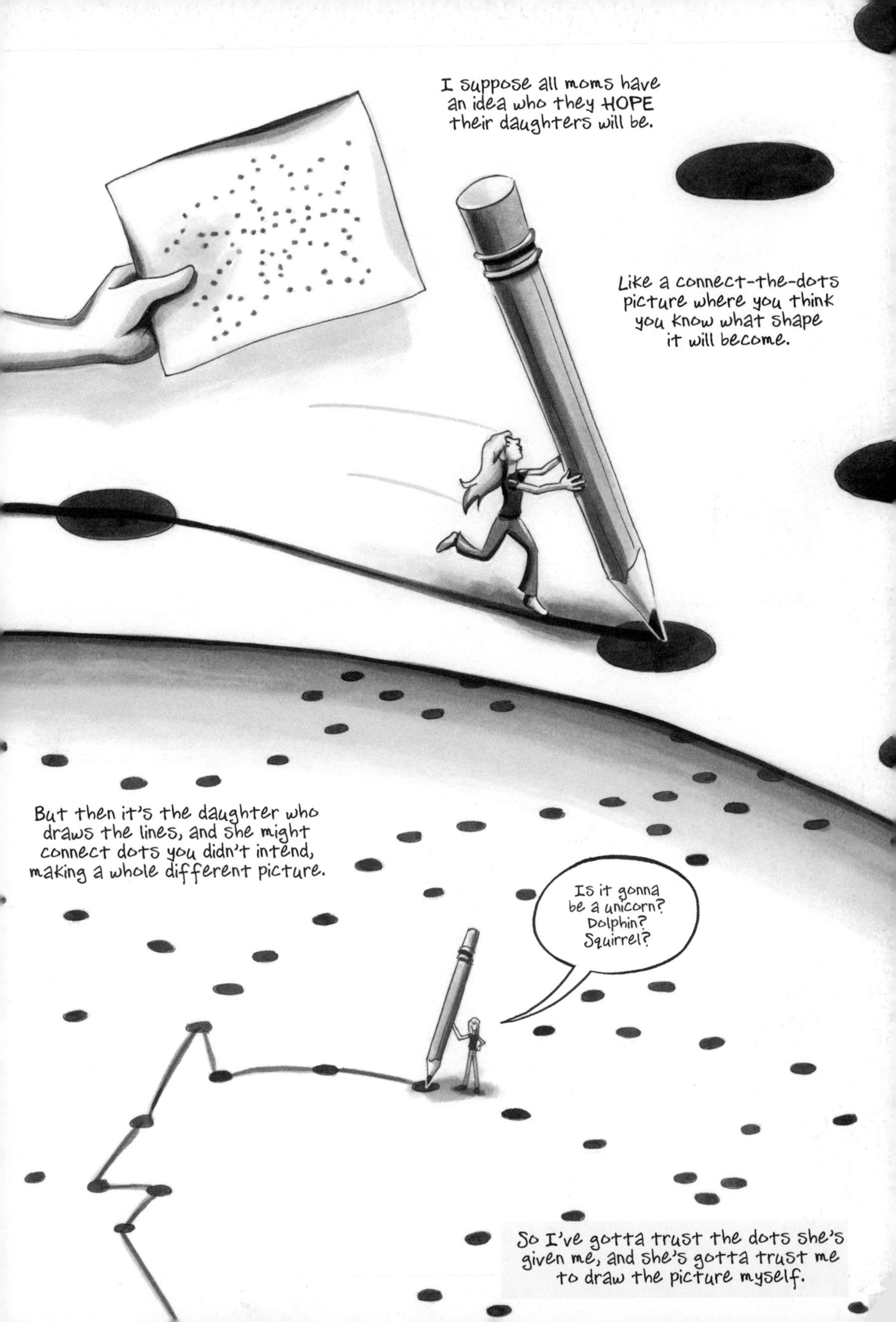
I suppose all moms have an idea who they HOPE their daughters will be.
Like a connect-the-dots picture where you think you know what shape it will become.
But then it's the daughter who draws the lines, and she might connect dots you didn't intend, making a whole different picture.
Is it gonna be a unicorn? Dolphin? Squirrel?
So I've gotta trust the dots she's given me, and she's gotta trust me to draw the picture myself.

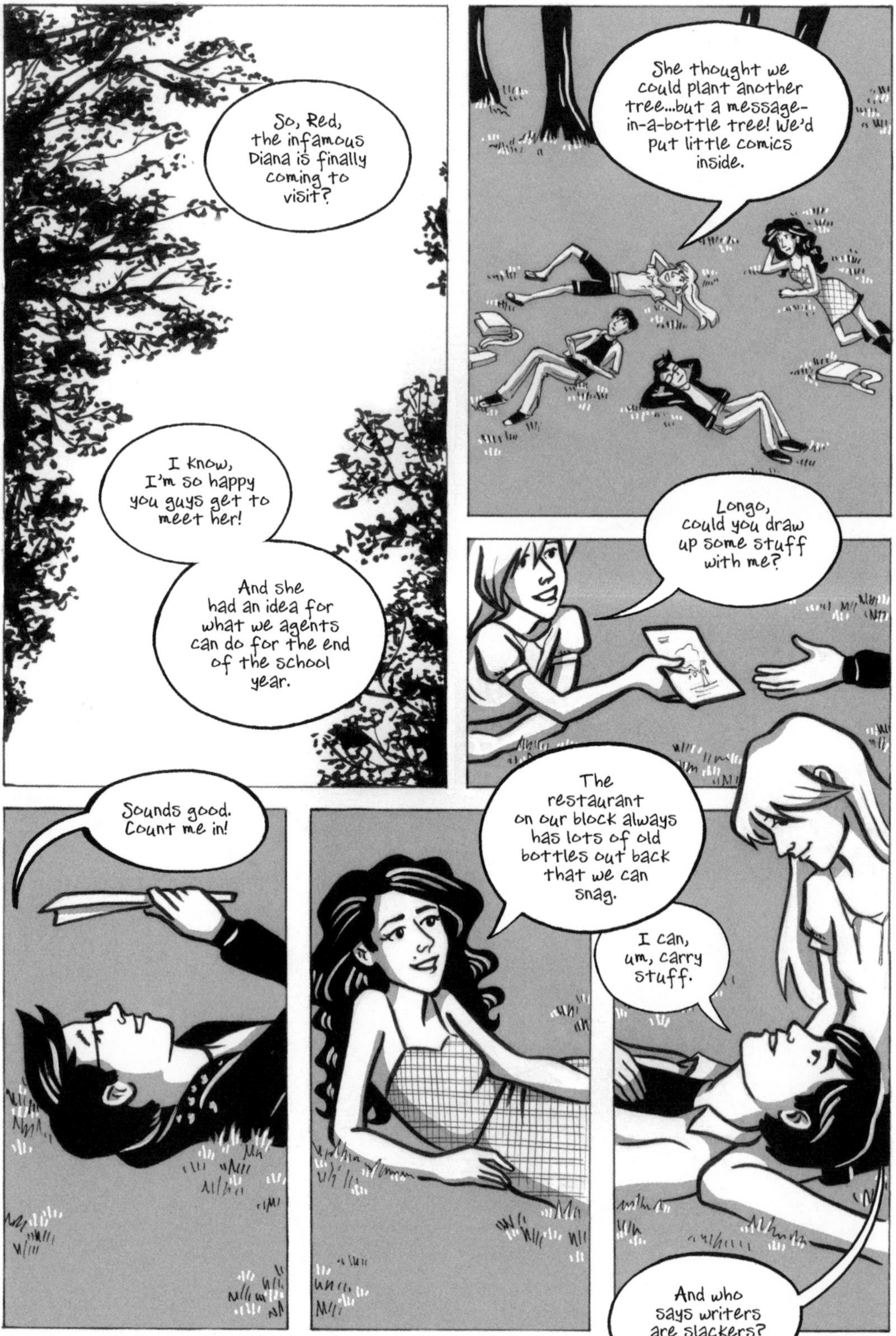
So, Red, the infamous Diana is finally coming to visit?
I know, I'm so happy you guys get to meet her!
And she had an idea for what we agents can do for the end of the school year.
She thought we could plant another tree...but a message-in-a-bottle tree! We'd put little comics inside.
Longo, could you draw up some stuff with me?
Sounds good. Count me in!
The restaurant on our block always has lots of old bottles out back that we can snag.
I can, um, carry stuff.
And who says writers are slackers?

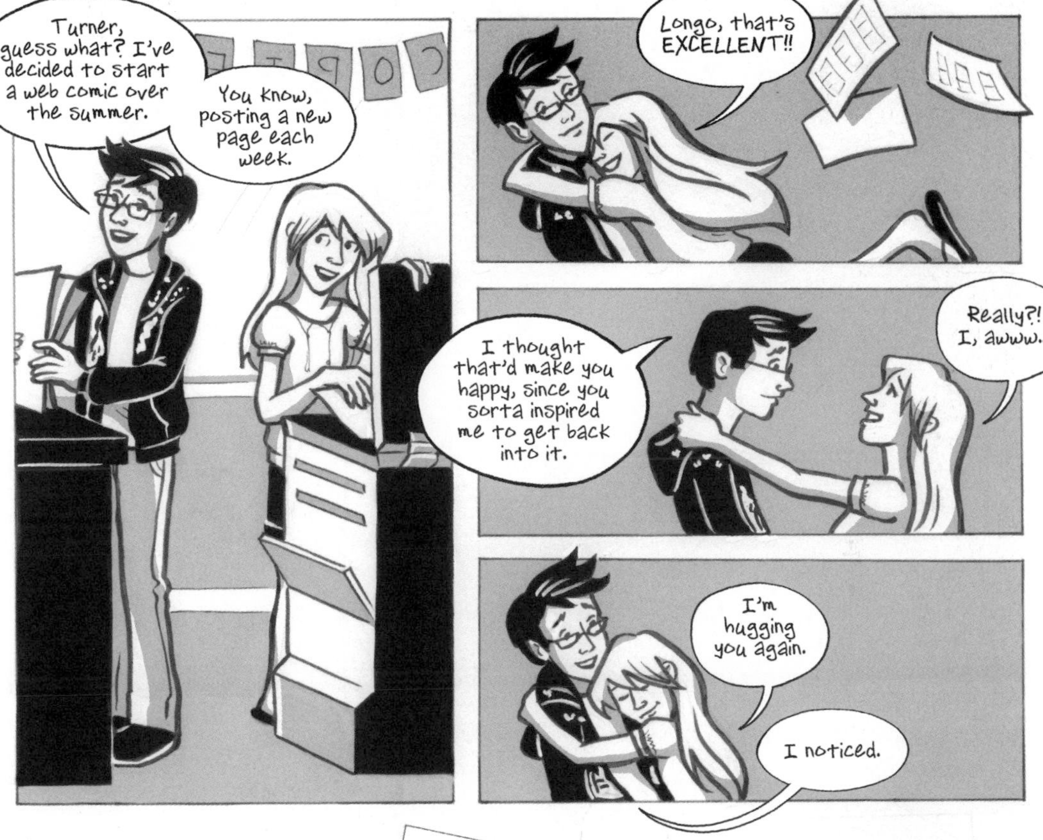
Turner, guess what? I've decided to start a web comic over the summer.
You know, posting a new page each week.
Longo, that's EXCELLENT!!
I thought that'd make you happy, since you sorta inspired me to get back into it.
Really?! I, awww...
I'm hugging you again.
I noticed.

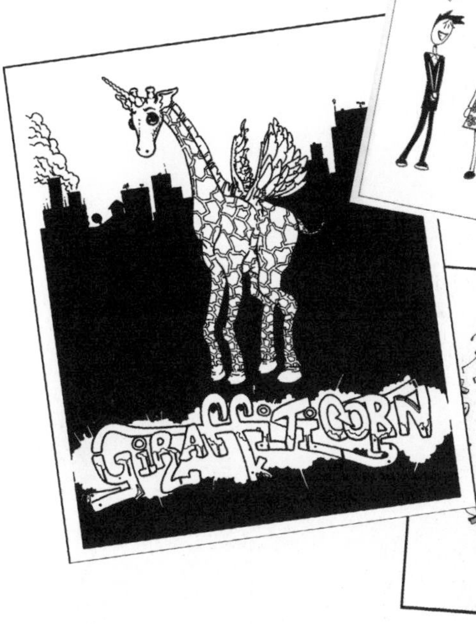

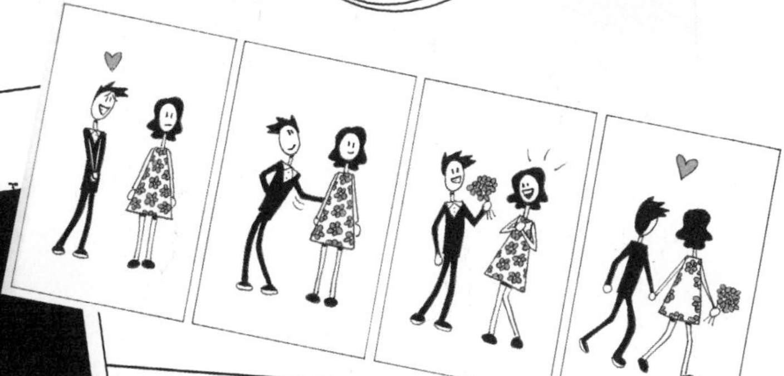

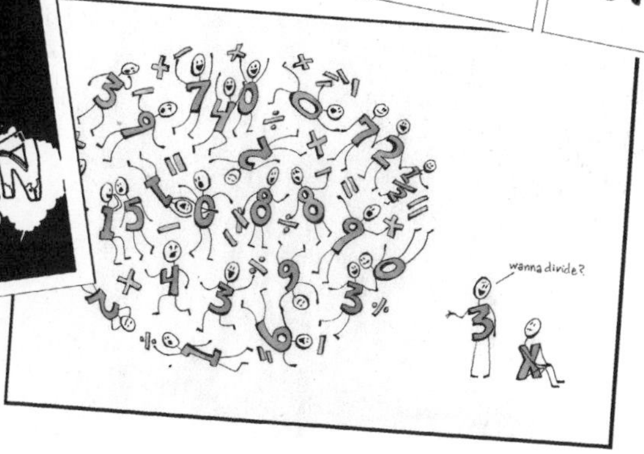
wanna divide?

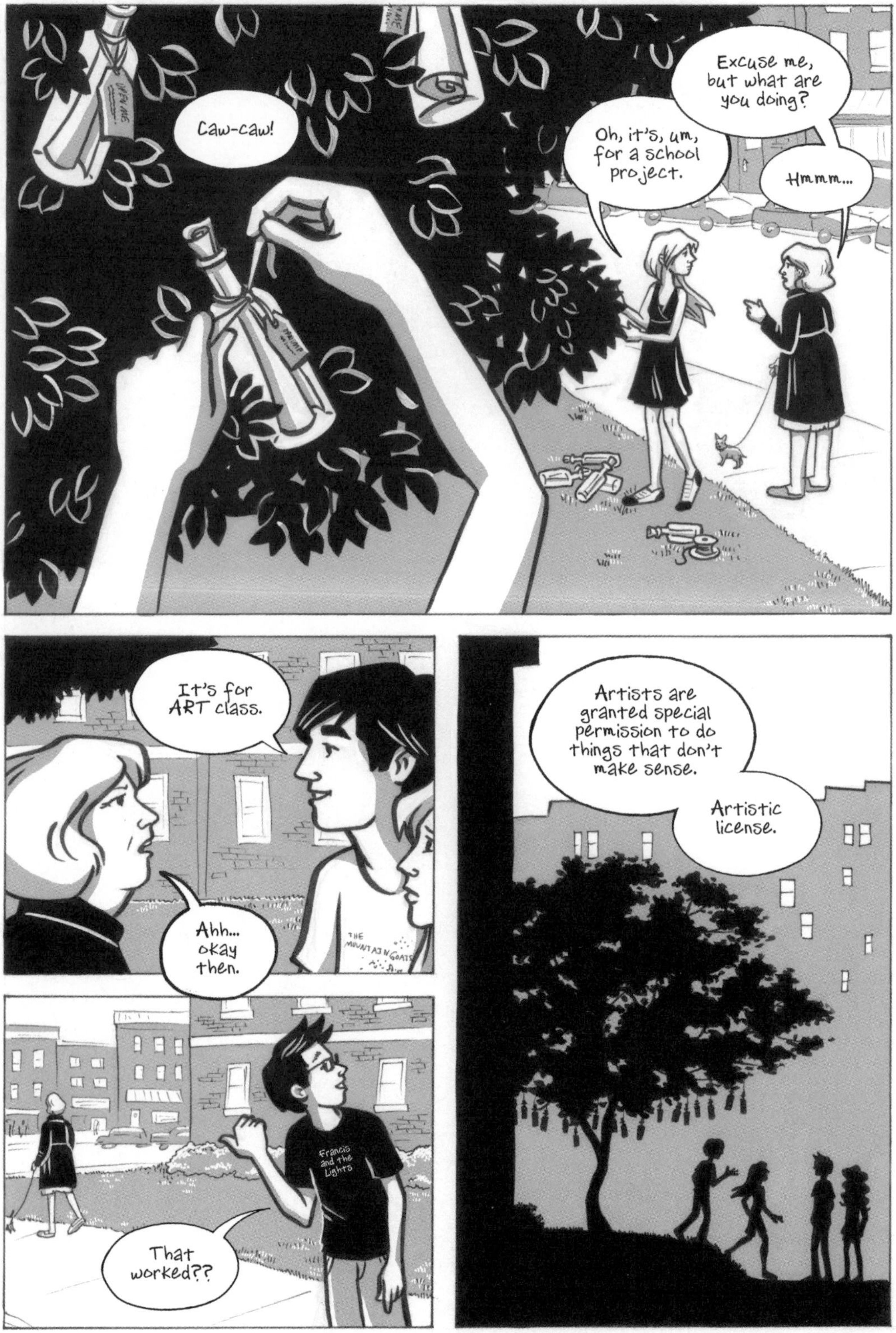
Caw-caw!
Excuse me, but what are you doing?
Oh, it's, um, for a school project.
Hmmm...
It's for ART class.
Ahh... okay then.
That worked??
Artists are granted special permission to do things that don't make sense.
Artistic license.

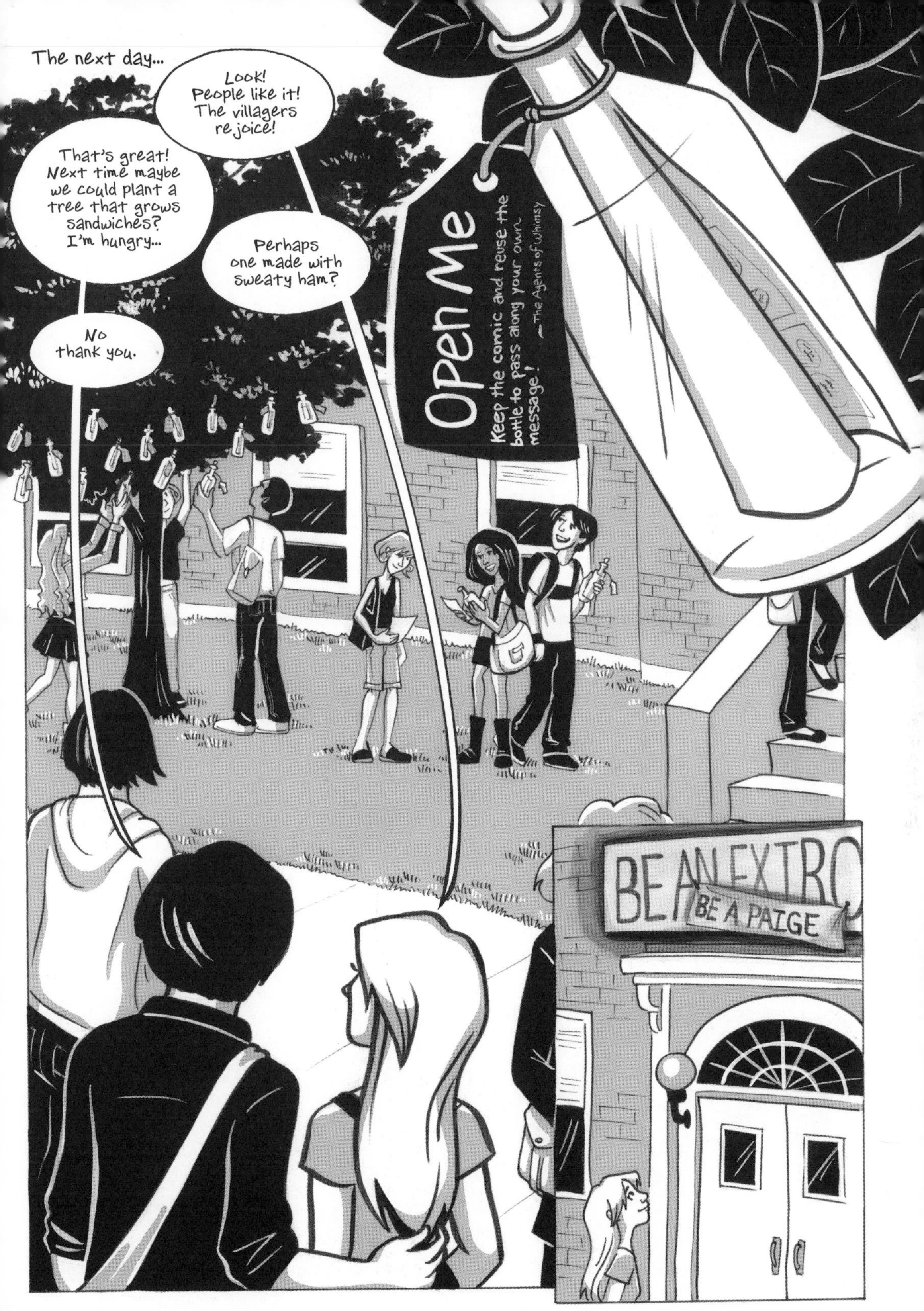

The next day...
Look! People like it! The villagers rejoice!
That's great! Next time maybe we could plant a tree that grows sandwiches? I'm hungry...
Perhaps one made with sweaty ham?
No thank you.
Open Me
Keep the comic and reuse the bottle to pass along your own message!
— The Agents of Whimsy
BE AN EXTRO
BE A PAIGE

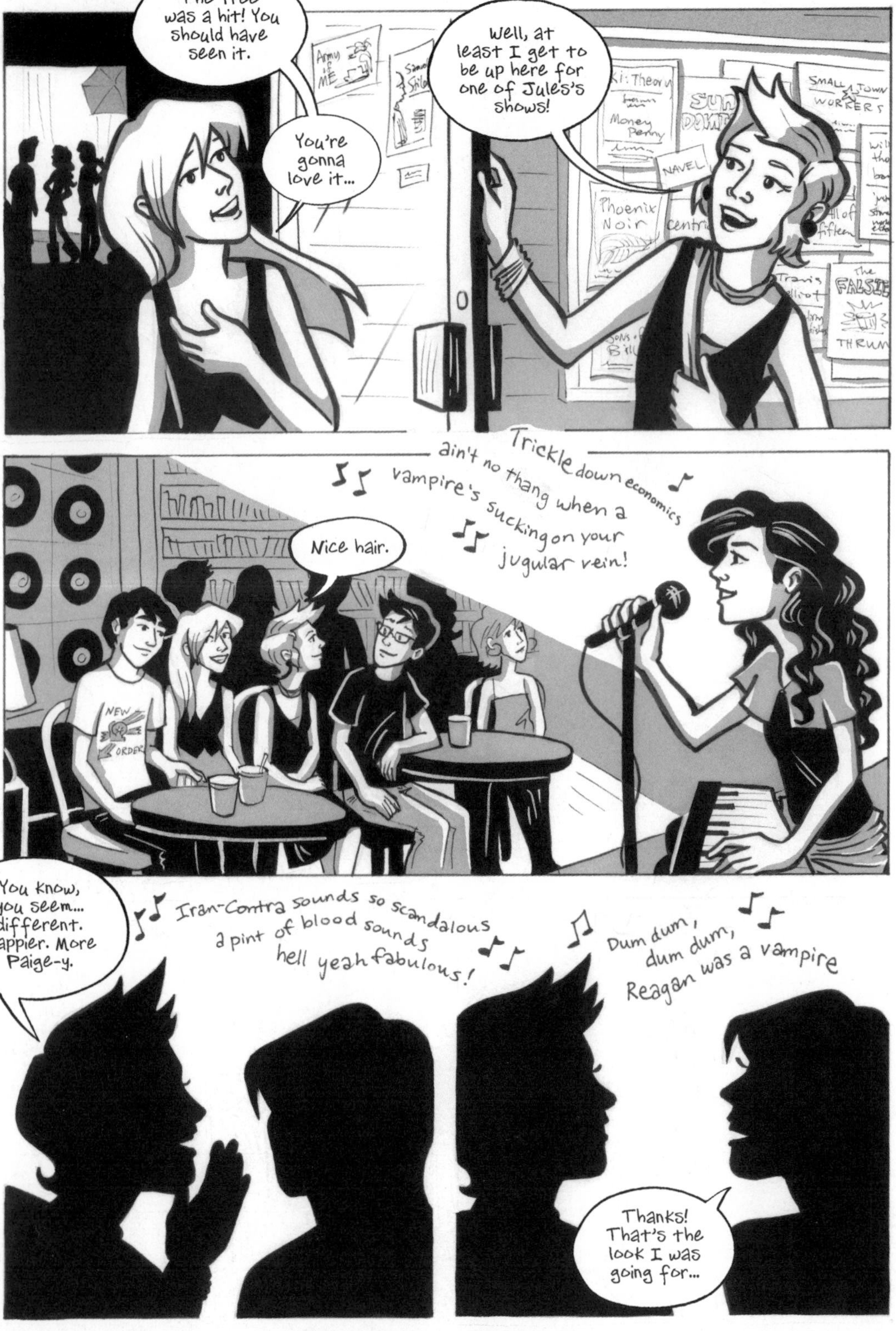
The tree was a hit! You should have seen it.
You're gonna love it...
Well, at least I get to be up here for one of Jules's shows!
Trickle down economics ain't no thang when a vampire's sucking on your jugular vein!
Nice hair.
You know, you seem... different. Happier. More Paige-y.
Iran-Contra sounds so scandalous a pint of blood sounds hell yeah fabulous!
Dum dum, dum dum, Reagan was a vampire
Thanks! That's the look I was going for...

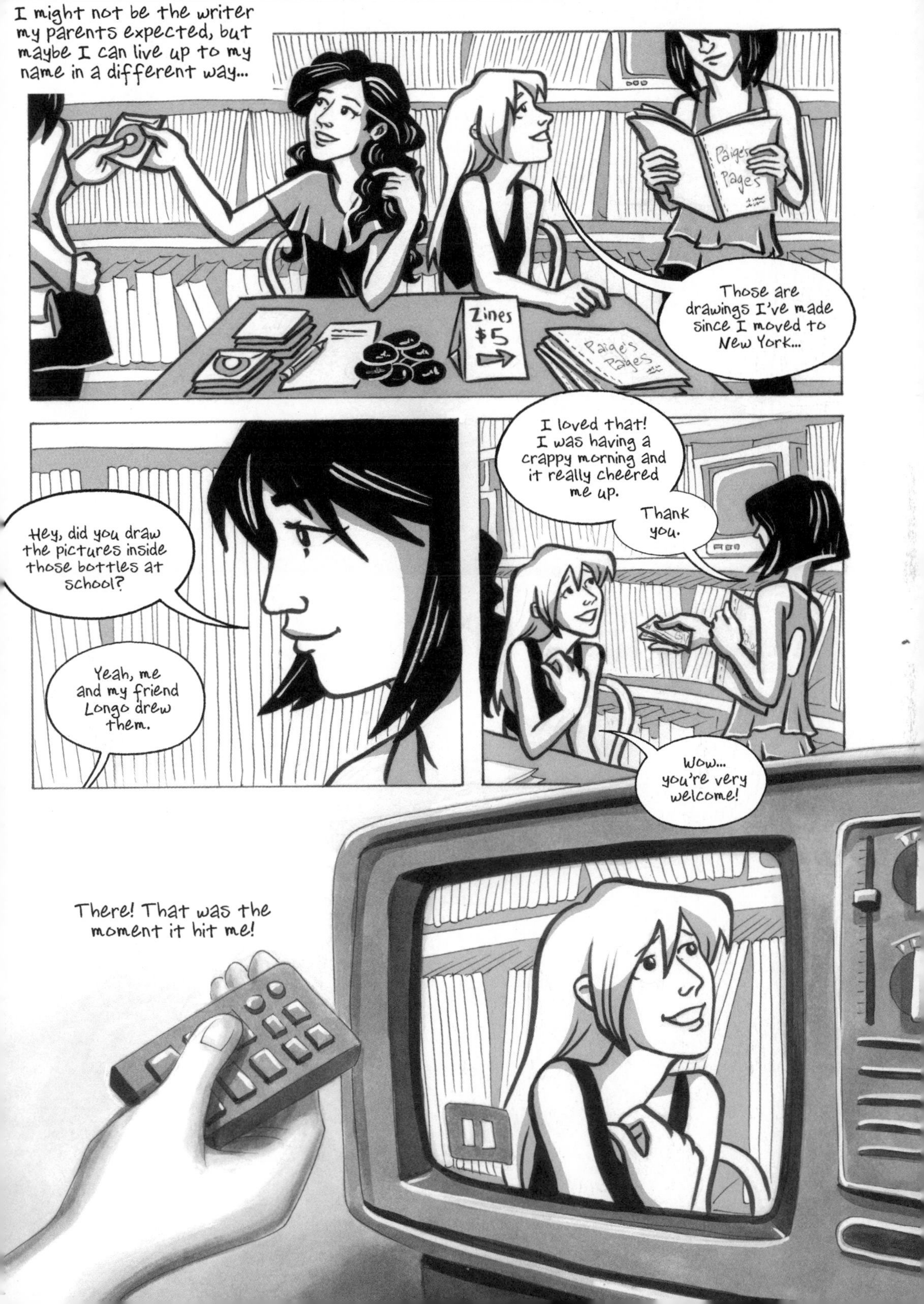
I might not be the writer my parents expected, but maybe I can live up to my name in a different way...
Paige's Pages
Zines $5
Paige's Pages
Those are drawings I've made since I moved to New York...
Hey, did you draw the pictures inside those bottles at school?
Yeah, me and my friend Longo drew them.
I loved that! I was having a crappy morning and it really cheered me up.
Thank you.
Wow... you're very welcome!
There! That was the moment it hit me!

It hit me...
PASSPORT
Land of Make-Believe
CERTIFIED IN CONTEMPLATION
U S
NATIONAL OFFICE OF SOUL-SEARCHING
INTROSPECTOR
...I AM an artist.

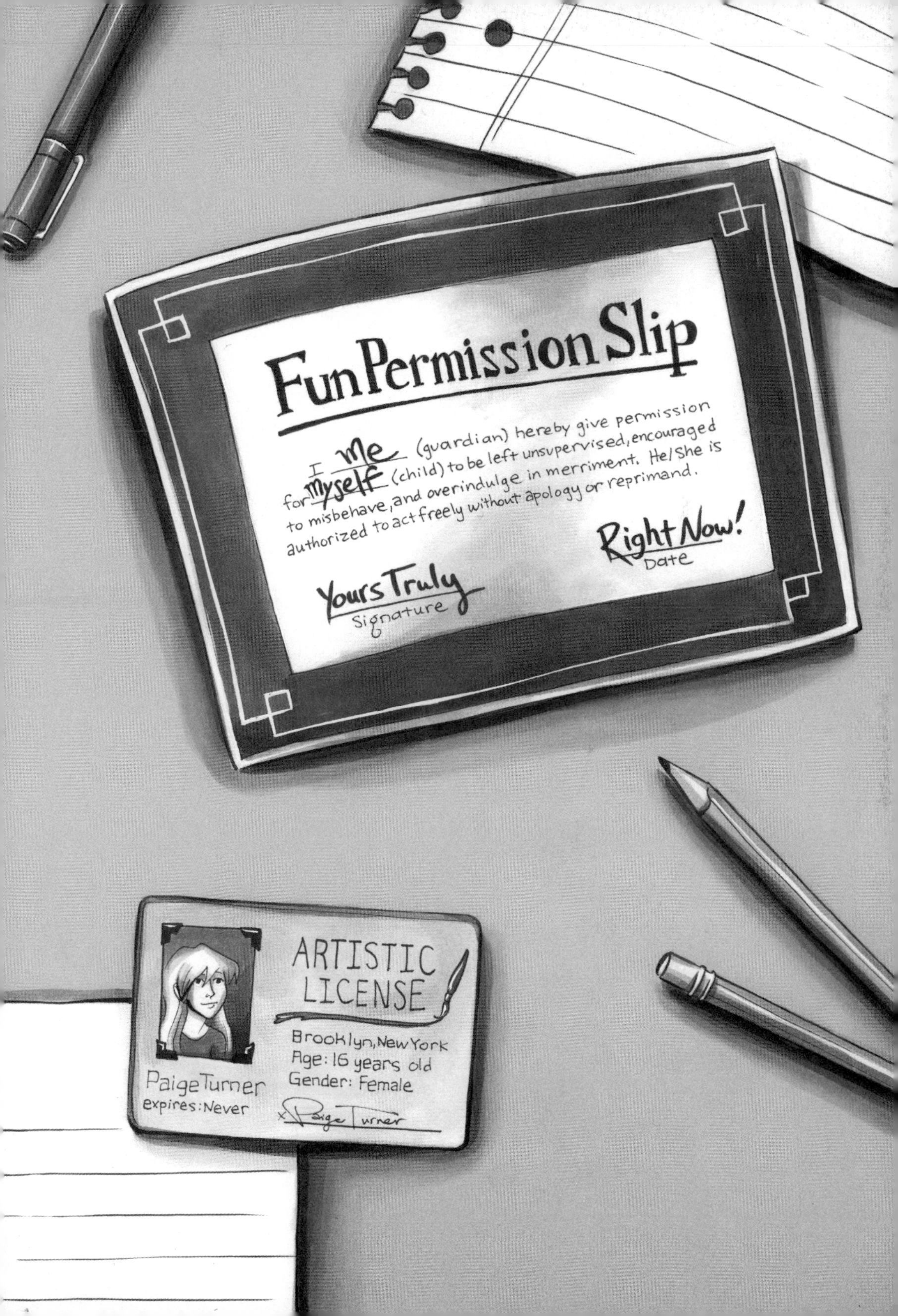
Fun Permission Slip
I me (guardian) hereby give permission for myself (child) to be left unsupervised, encouraged to misbehave, and overindulge in merriment. He/She is authorized to act freely without apology or reprimand.
Right Now!
Date
Yours Truly
Signature
ARTISTIC LICENSE
Brooklyn, New York
Age: 16 years old
Gender: Female
Paige Turner
expires: Never
x Paige Turner

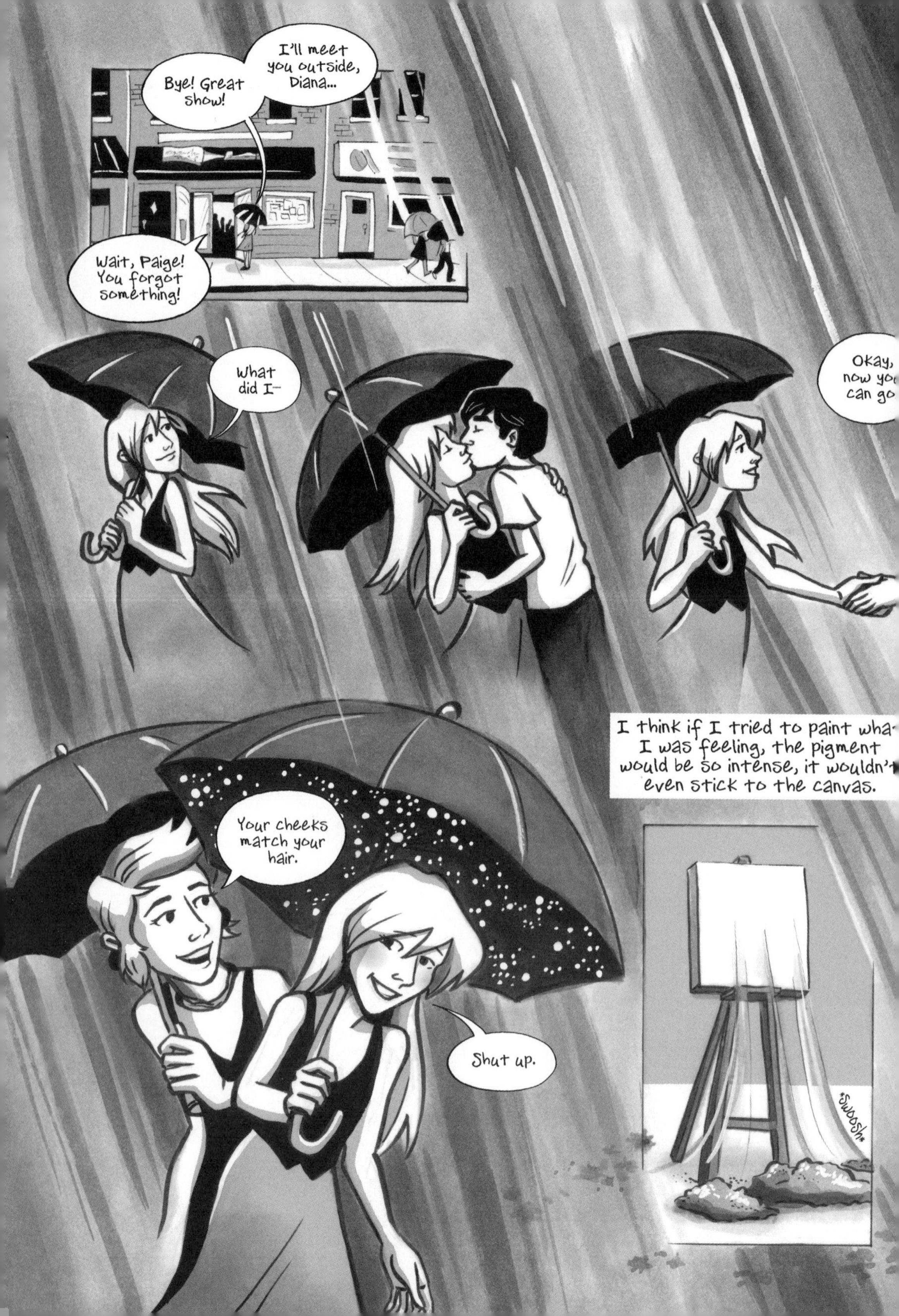
I'll meet you outside, Diana...
Bye! Great show!
Wait, Paige! You forgot something!
What did I–
Okay, now yo can go
I think if I tried to paint wha I was feeling, the pigment would be so intense, it wouldn't even stick to the canvas.
Your cheeks match your hair.
Shut up.
swoosh

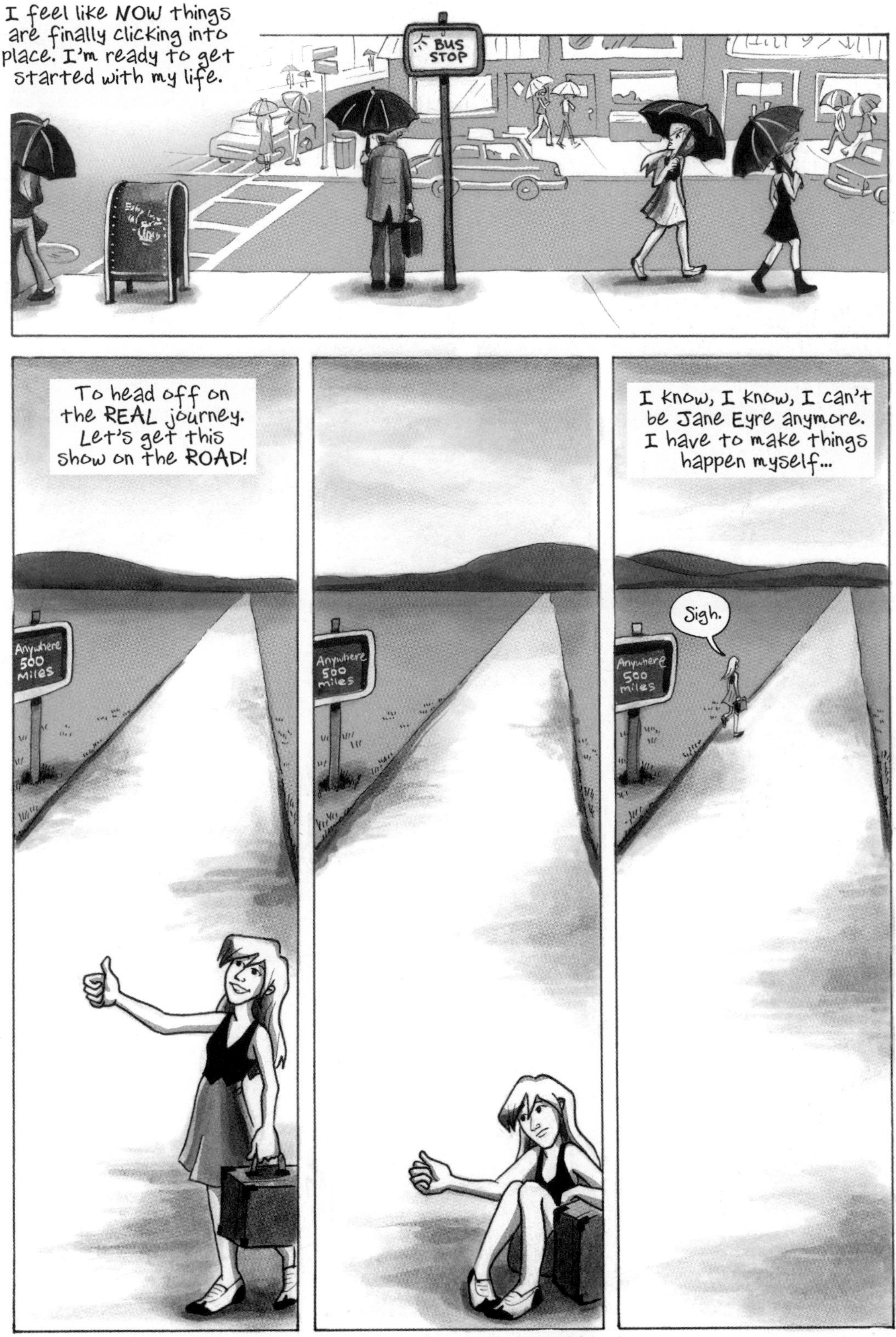
I feel like NOW things are finally clicking into place. I'm ready to get started with my life.
BUS STOP
To head off on the REAL journey. Let's get this show on the ROAD!
Anywhere 500 miles
Anywhere 500 miles
I know, I know, I can't be Jane Eyre anymore. I have to make things happen myself...
Sigh.
Anywhere 500 miles

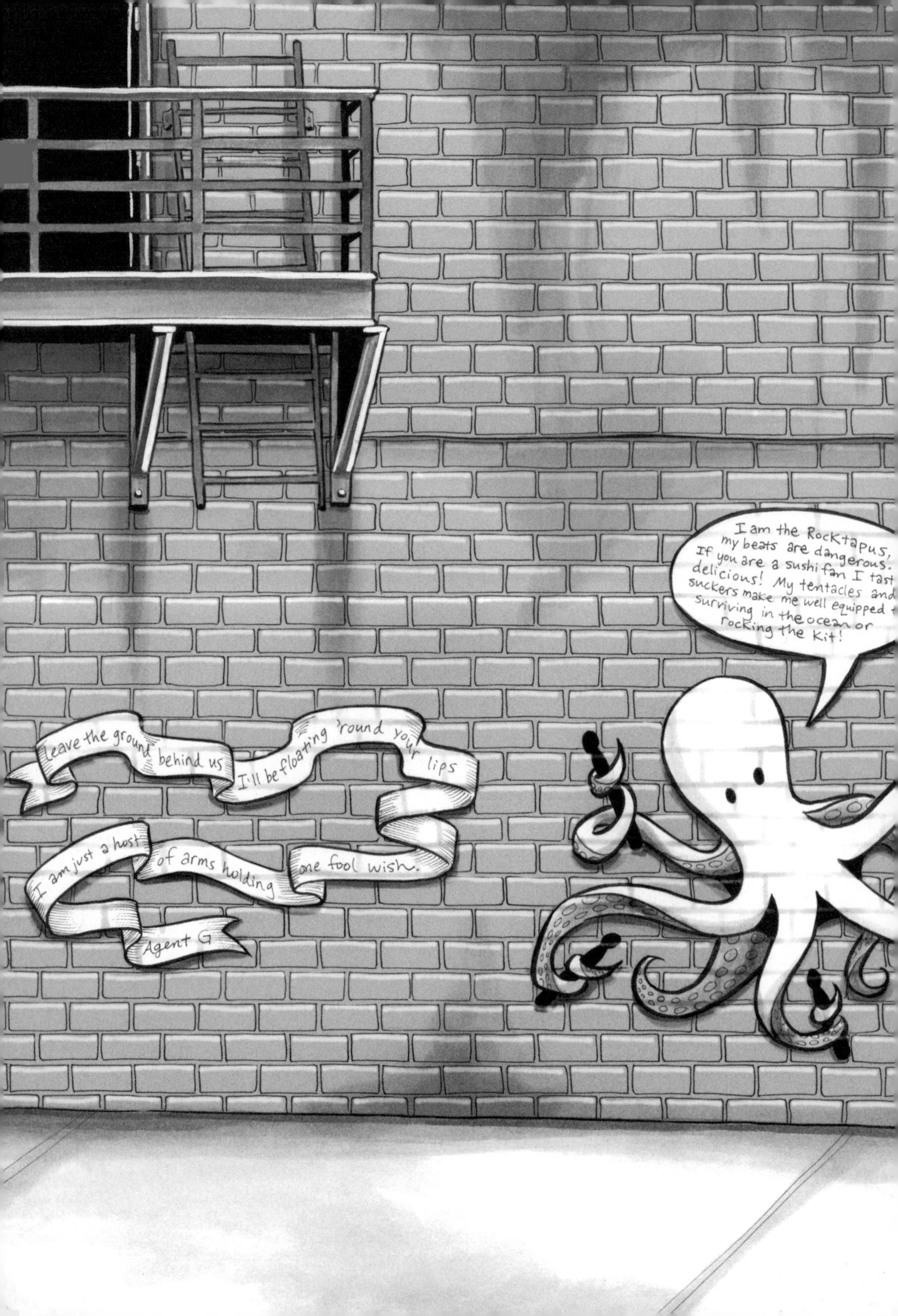
Leave the ground behind us I'll be floating 'round your lips
I am just a host of arms holding one fool wish.
Agent G
I am the Rocktapus, my beats are dangerous! If you are a sushi fan I tast delicious! My tentacles and suckers make me well equipped t surviving in the ocean or rocking the Kit!

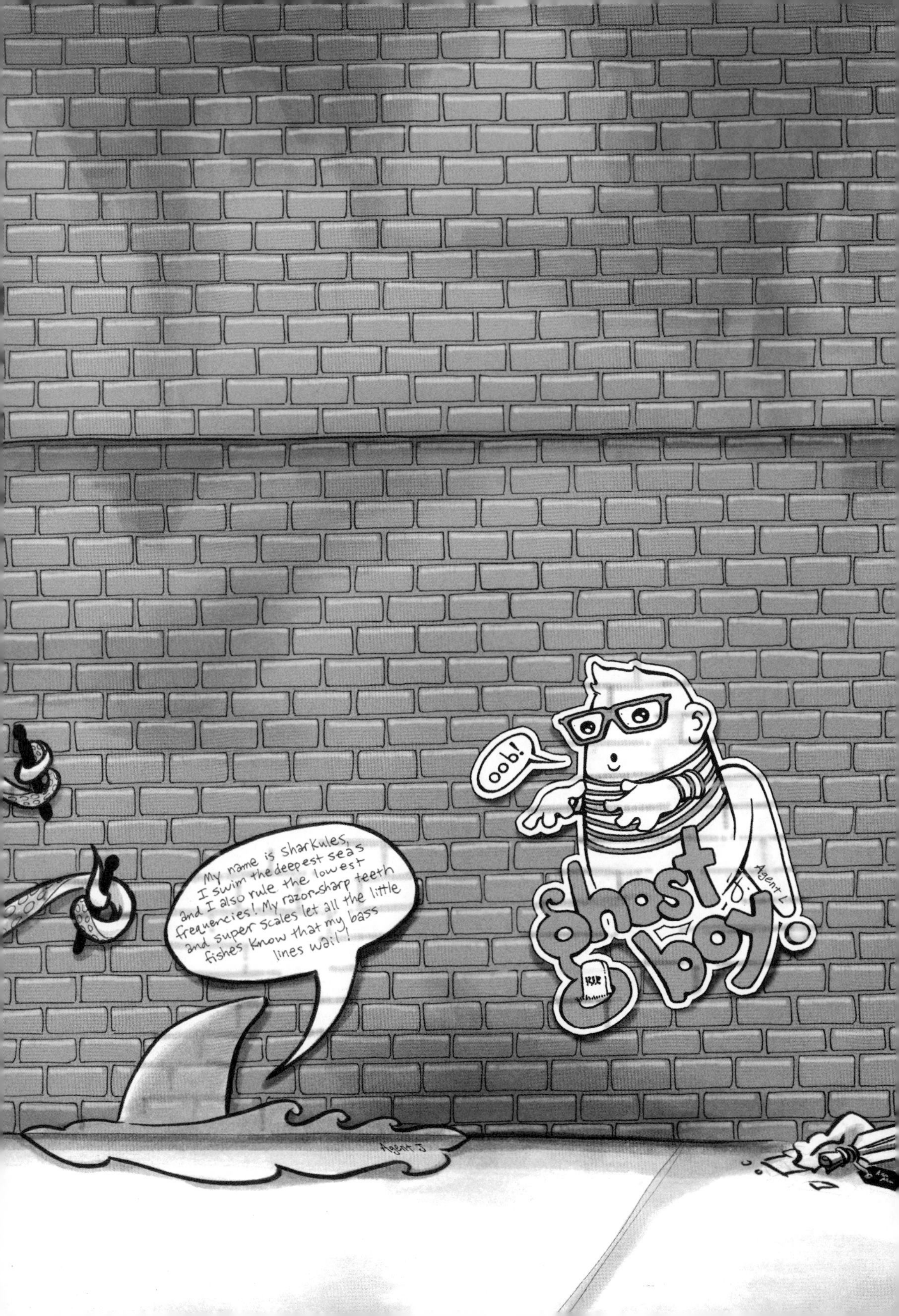
My name is Sharkules, I swim the deepest seas and I also rule the lowest frequencies! My razor-sharp teeth and super scales let all the little fishes know that my bass lines wail!
oob!
ghost boy!
Agent L
Agent J

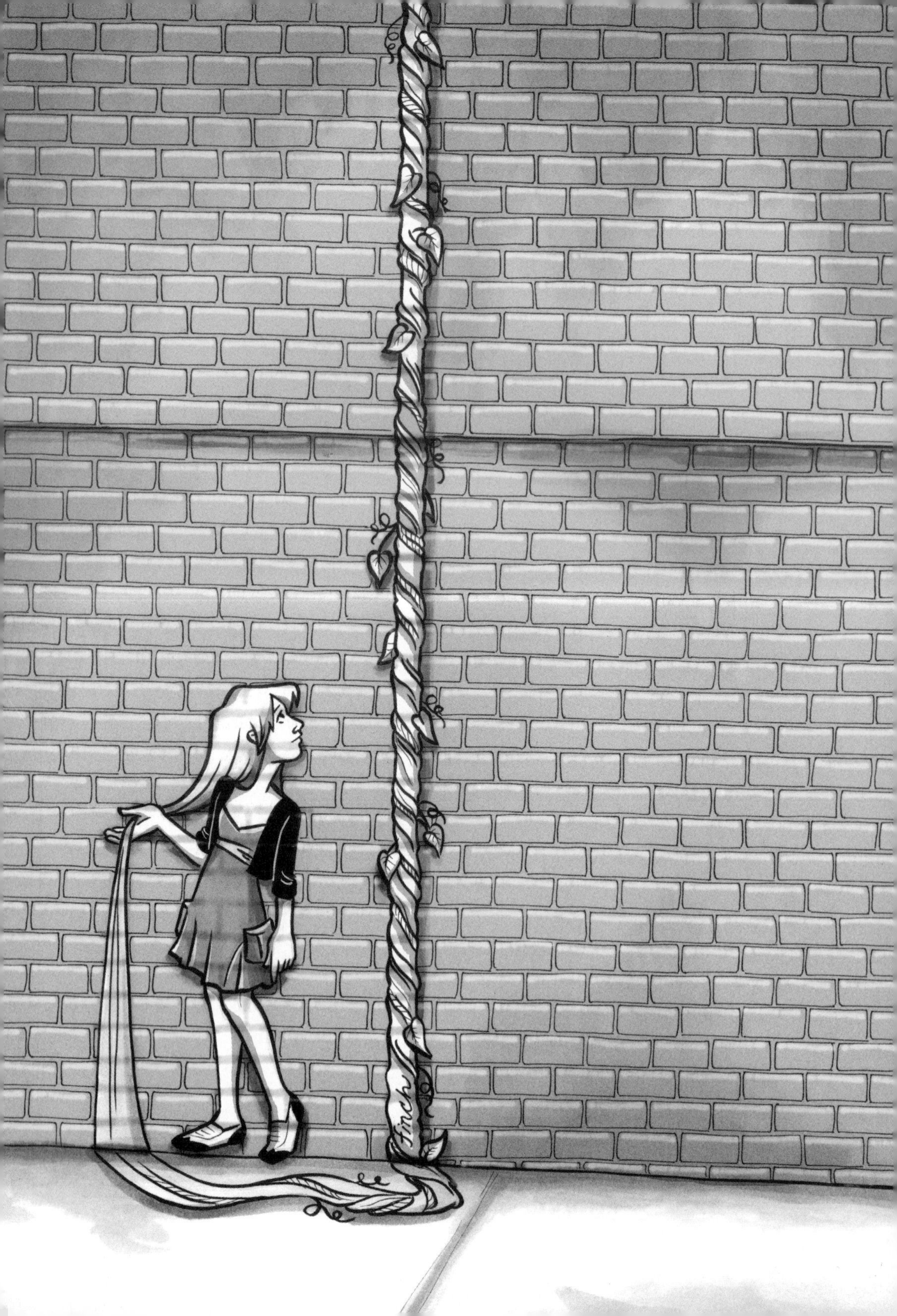
Finch

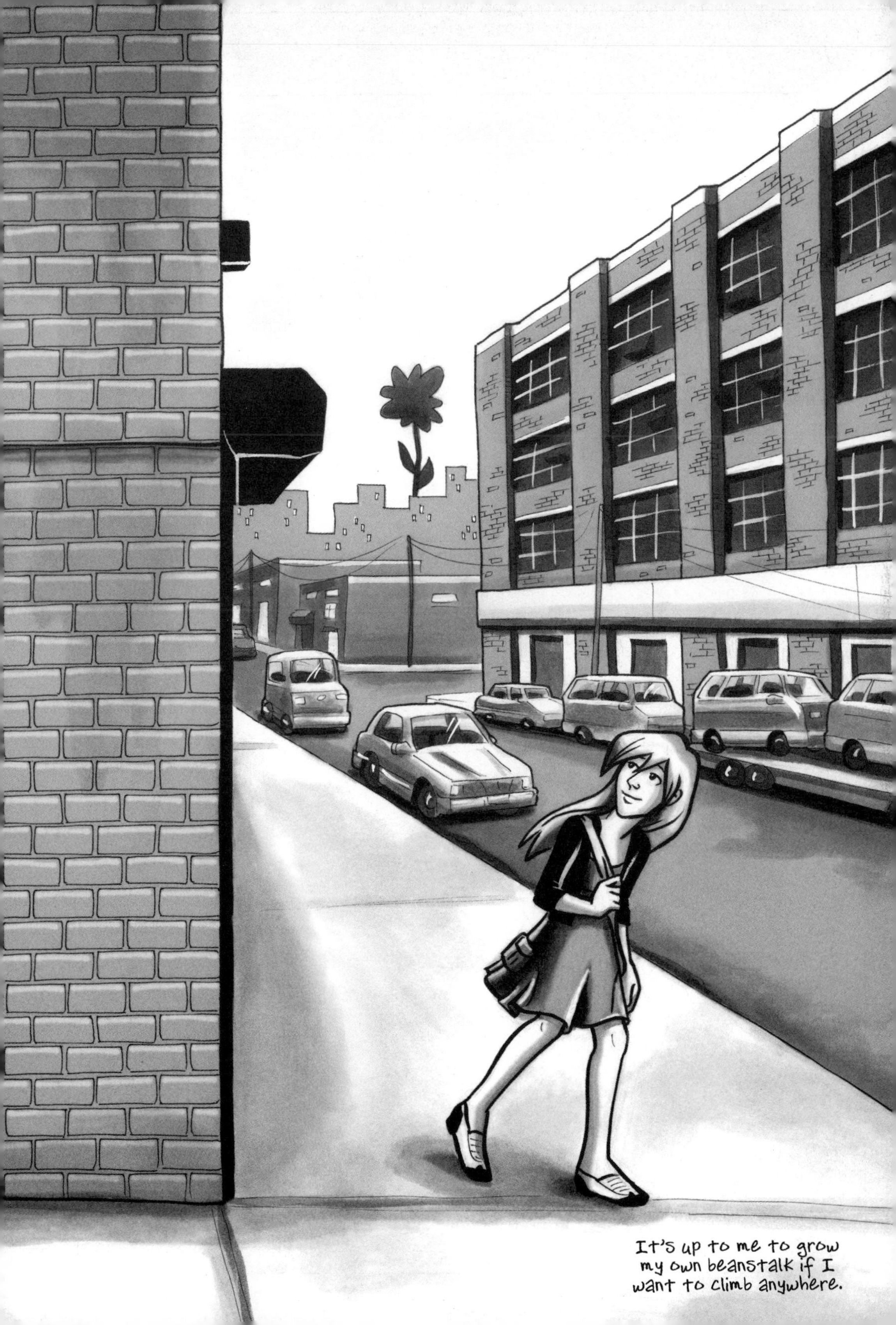
It's up to me to grow my own beanstalk if I want to climb anywhere.

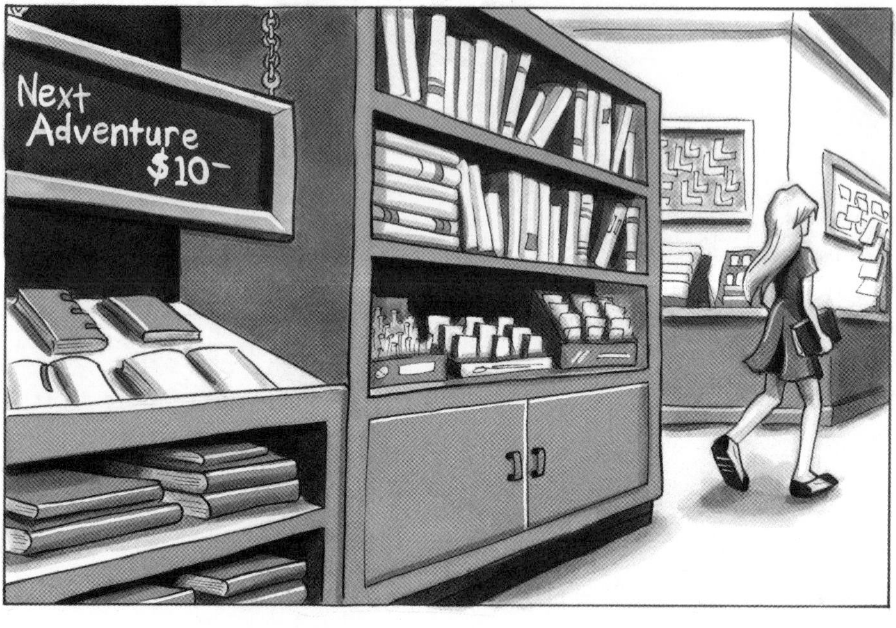
Next
Adventure
$10-

Acknowledgments

Special thanks to: My lovely family for always encouraging me to draw, for your support, and for your trust as my ideas grew perpetually (and foolishly/bravely) bigger. All my Charlottesville and New York friends for knowing when to drag me away from my desk...and for knowing how to inspire me to go back. Jason Longo, Jamie Rodger, Geoff Sprung, and Alex Dezden for contributing your words and drawings on behalf of my characters. Diana Arge, Bishop 203, Matt Mikas, Julie Bissell, and Christian Larson for your game of Drawing Telephone. Maya Rock, Dan Lazar, Maggie Lehrman, Chad W. Beckerman, and the folks at Abrams for taking a chance on me and my difficult-to-categorize artwork.

About the Author

Laura Lee Gulledge, like Paige, grew up in Virginia and moved to New York. Also like Paige, she started sharing her personal drawings online in order to try to better understand herself and her adopted city. She has worked in art education and scenic painting, among other pursuits. This is her first graphic novel. She currently lives in Brooklyn, New York.

ALSO AVAILABLE
BY LAURA LEE GULLEDGE

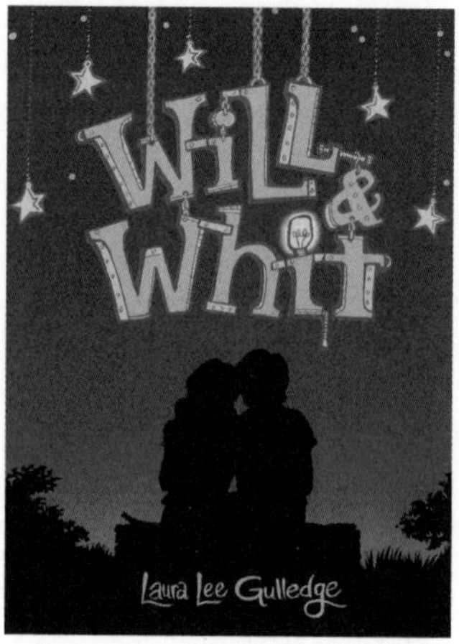
Will & Whit
Laura Lee Gulledge

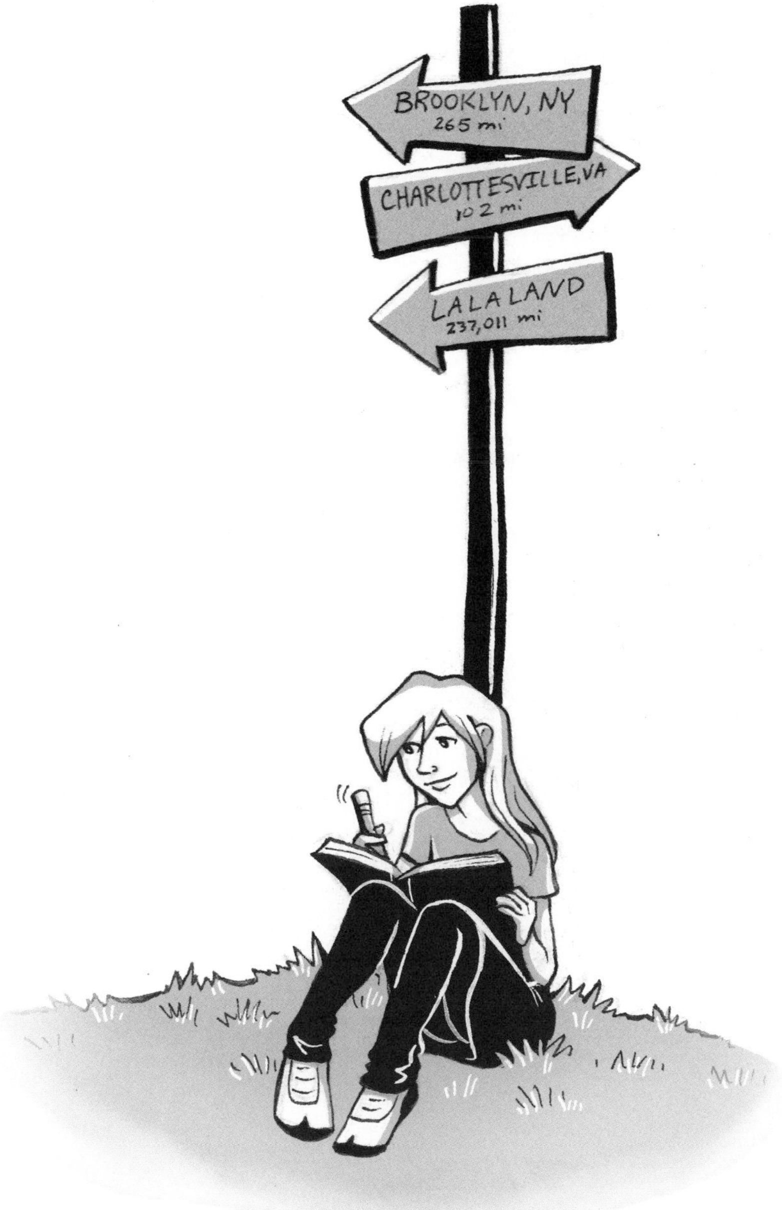
BROOKLYN, NY
265 mi
CHARLOTTESVILLE, VA
102 mi
LALA LAND
237,011 mi

Mix for Paige

Page by Paige Soundtrack

(Selected musicians who were referenced in the book)

Jules's Faves...

"Infinity Guitars" – Sleigh Bells
"Carpetbaggers" – Jenny Lewis
"Easy" – Joanna Newsom
"Better" – Regina Spektor
"Cheated Hearts" – Yeah Yeah Yeahs

Gabe's Faves...

"Hannah" – Freelance Whales
"Scythian Empires" – Andrew Bird
"Anthems for a 17-Year-Old Girl" – Broken Social Scene
"Pavement Tune" – The Frames
"All My Friends" – LCD Soundsystem
"This Year" – The Mountain Goats
"Exo-Politics" – Muse

Longo's Faves...

"Animal" – Miike Snow
"I'll Be Better" – Francis and the Lights

Paige's Faves...

"I and Love and You" – The Avett Brothers
"Ragged Wood" – Fleet Foxes
"Dancing with Myself" – Nouvelle Vague
"The Clockwise Witness" – DeVotchKa
"40 Day Dream" – Edward Sharpe & the Magnetic Zeros
"Gobbledigook" – Sigur Rós

Laura Lee's musician friends
who have inspired and supported her...

"Golden Days" – The Damnwells
"Purple Weather Girl" – Samuel Stiles
"We Will Become Ourselves Reborn" – Ki:Theory
"Up Against Life" – Small Town Workers
"Gravity" – The Dirty Dishes
"Thankless" – All of Fifteen
"Rules of the Game" – Moneypenny
"Going Through Changes" – Army Of Me

Mix for Paige

For my mother, her mother,
and all quiet souls with
loud imaginations
-L.G.

Library of Congress Control Number: 2010930150
Hardcover ISBN: 978-0-8109-9721-9
Paperback ISBN: 978-0-8109-9722-6

Text and Illustrations copyright © 2011 Laura Lee Gulledge
Book design by Laura Lee Gulledge and Chad W. Beckerman

Additional material courtesy of Alex Dezden (pages 120, 137, 182), Jamie Rodger (pages 141-143), Matt Mikas (pages 135-136), Diana Arge (page 135), Julie Bissell (page 135), Bishop 203 (pages 135-136), Jason Longo (pages 118, 134-136, 173, 183), and Geoff Sprung (pages 68-69, 158, 176, 182-183).

Printed and bound in China
10 9 8 7 6

Amulet Books are available at special discounts when purchased in quantity for premiums and promotions as well as fundraising or educational use. Special editions can also be created to specification. For details, contact specialsales@abramsbooks.com or the address below.

ABRAMS
THE ART OF BOOKS SINCE 1949
115 West 18th Street
New York, NY 10011
www.abramsbooks.com